SAWYER

THE BILLIONAIRES OF WHISPERS
BOOK 4

SAMANTHA SKYE

EBOOK ISBN: 978-1-923258-16-7

PAPERBACK ISBN: 978-1-923258-17-4

ALT PAPERBACK ISBN: 978-1-923258-18-1

Cover Design: Angela Haddon

Editor: Nice Girl Naughty Edits

Proofreading: Kimberly Dawn

CONTENT WARNING

As with all my books, Sawyer has a thread of suspense woven throughout. This suspense includes mentions of, and on page descriptions of domestic and family violence.

1

SAWYER SILVERS

I look around this small, pokey office and sigh. I can't believe the things I do.

"It has everything you need," Tanner watches me as I place my briefcase on the office desk that looks like it's stayed in this exact same spot for the past few decades. The thick legal books line the dark timber shelves, and I wonder what a small-town lawyer would ever need them for.

My jet landed in Whispers early this morning. I've already handed over the keys and paperwork to the old florist building to Tanner's son and one of my closest friends, Connor, before meeting Tanner here. I'm now spending more and more time here in this town than I ever thought possible, thanks to the Whitemans. This father-and-son duo run this town, their whiskey distillery the backbone of Whispers.

"Think you could work out of here a few days a week?" Tanner asks, and I whip my head around to look at him. It might be his hometown, a place where he's spent his entire life, but it isn't mine. This is as far removed from my usual life as you can get.

"I'd rather eat cardboard." I'm honest, because Whispers is not part of my life plan. But Tanner and Connor Whiteman and Whiteman's Whiskey certainly are. The two men whom I've worked with for years are now firm friends I would do anything for. Including entertaining the fact that they want me to be the new local lawyer. The whole idea is preposterous.

A town of about two thousand and thirty something, Whispers is quaint, with the population tripling in size on the weekends due to the distillery, spa, and soon-to-be new accommodations down on Distillery Drive. What Tanner and Connor have done for this town is nothing short of amazing. I just prefer to be in Manhattan, with my town car, Michelin star restaurants, and my penthouse in the sky.

"Get a junior in to run it when you aren't here," Tanner adds, knowing that I'm not sold on his idea.

"I don't have time to train anyone." I'm worth fifteen hundred per hour, and there's no way I'm spending my time teaching some country kid the basics of law.

"Make it a secondment from one of your city offices."

I look at him, deadpan, and shake my head. With a main office in New York and a smaller office in LA, I have teams positioned to take on any client at any time of the day. My business over the past few years has skyrocketed. So much so, I now have my own jet, a real estate portfolio, and invest-ments in smaller businesses that bring in a great profit for me each year.

"Yeah, like any city lawyer will want to come out here and do wills and land titles and deeds when there are commer-cial deals for the millions being made in the city." I admire his efforts, but hell, this is crazy. I mean, technology has made it so people can work from anywhere so, it's possible I can run my legal empire from here, especially since the grind of the city that I used to thrive off is now wearing me a little thin. But moving to Whispers is a jump too far.

"You'll need to find a secretary. Jerry's wife handled all his paperwork, so now that he's going, she will too," Tanner tells me, and I roll my eyes.

"Of course she is." I look around, seeing Jerry's half-packed boxes on the floor. He's still in the process of moving, with a few active files he needs to finalize.

"He also sponsors the local kids' baseball team, so you'll need to take that on too."

"Oooh, this just keeps getting better and better." What's the upside for me in all this?

"Being a lawyer in a small town like Whispers is nothing like you've ever experienced."

"How so?"

"Well, you do the law part, but there's also the community part." He's full of pride. His love for this town is almost comical.

"Do I dare ask?" I walk around the office, seeing if I can picture myself here. It's a nice office, with high ceilings and bright light coming in from the large windows. It needs a bit of a refurb, but it's adequate.

"This isn't just a clock-on-and-clock-off, charge-every-one-for-every-minute-of-your-time deal. You work the files, and the cases you acquire, you spend time getting to know the people, learning about their lives, their businesses, offering free advice, opening your fat wallet when someone needs a hand..." He's watching me carefully with every pointed word.

"I get it. I do. But it just isn't me." Can't he see that I'm the furthest from a small-town guy as you can get? I grew up in

New York. The concrete jungle. Multimillion-dollar deals are my life.

"I want all my affairs to be run from this office. Both personally and for the business." He crosses his arms over his chest like a bouncer, playing his final hand, the royal flush he holds hitting me right in the gut.

"What?" I look at him like he's crazy.

"I want all my businesses, the distillery business, the bar, the spa, the new accommodation, Victoria's interiors business, Daisy's new ventures, Marie's place, and the new goat milk soap business to all be run out of this office, here in Whispers. I don't want my business, paperwork, files, accounts, or anything else to leave this office. I want it all to be moved here from New York this week."

I huff a breath at his big reveal. "You've lost your damn mind."

While Tanner isn't my only client, he's one of the biggest, with my brother also taking up a lot of my time. He knows by demanding the Whispers office runs all his affairs, it will keep me here more often than not.

"We've taken care of every single thing you just spouted off just fine from New York, and for years, mind you." There's no reason to move everything from my head office in Manhattan.

"Well, I changed my mind." The asshole has the balls to grin at me.

My head shakes all on its own as I process this. "I manage your entire portfolio, which means I'll need to be here whenever I need to work on something for you," I state, feeling incredulous.

"Exactly. I'm estimating that it'll probably be around three days per week." He doesn't give me an inch. The sly smirk on his face tells me he knows exactly what he's doing.

"You're an asshole. Anyone told you that?" Putting my hands on my hips, I don't know what the fuck I'm going to do.

"Not today, but it's still early." I always knew he had me pegged for running this law office in his small town, but I never gave any indication that I would take the offer. In fact, I made it very clear I wasn't interested. Now he's basically bulldozing me. Although I know he won't have anyone else but me manage his legal affairs. We've worked together for years and have become firm friends, so this is him just trying to prove a point.

"Why?" is all I can ask. I need his reasoning. Need to understand why this is so important to him.

"Because the town needs someone like you, Sawyer. You're the best damn lawyer I know, and I know a few. Whispers needs someone decent, someone they can trust. Someone with connections, knowledge, and experience. There are lots of small businesses here. Lots of large properties and farms. You know as well as I do that the wealthy are starting to move here in droves. New ranches are being built so quickly Griffin and his team might as well be here permanently. He's already talking about building his ranch here and setting up an office where he and Victoria can base themselves. So there's a lot of new money opportunities too, some that may even surpass what you have in the city."

I raise my eyebrow at him. He's right, as per usual. While I might be a city boy through and through, I'm smart enough to know that Whispers is the new hiding place for some of the country's most wealthy. I can already see the dinner party conversations that will happen here soon are bound to birth new businesses and new innovations, and being part of those conversations would be extremely beneficial for me and my law firm.

"Besides, if you live here, you have less flying time to get to your brother."

At that, I roll my eyes but nod, because that's true too. My brother, Sutton, is on the West Coast and is a Hollywood movie star, which has made him a multimillionaire. With new feature films every six months, he's worked himself hard the past few years, received a few award nominations, and has been an A-lister at events, each time with a different leading lady. Managing his business interests is almost as stressful as managing Tanner's.

"He's another asshole," I murmur, and Tanner grins.

"I got you a ranch up on Billionaire Boulevard."

"What?" I'm surprised. Usually, I fly in and out. If I need to stay over, I stay at Marie's Place or his old home at the distillery. Both are beautiful.

"Well, I leased a place from a friend for a month or two. To see if you like it. If you do, you can buy it."

I huff another laugh, knowing this man has had plans in place for me for a long time. He's persistent and clever. I'll give him that.

"You've got it all figured out, don't you?"

"I sure do. Now you need to go and sort out the soap-making paperwork with Victoria's business partner, Annabelle. The two of them are now on the same page with building their little business into something bigger."

"Gertie's Soaps?" I've heard them talk about it before, but thought it was just a hobby for Victoria until now.

"That's it. They've worked their asses off. Turns out, they might have something worth investing in now. Victoria has a vision for growth, and Annabelle needs the cash. So let's get the paperwork sorted for them and see what they can do."

Fucking soapmaking business. Is this what my legal

career has come to? Years at university, long days and late nights in the office, all boiling down to soap.

"Fine. I'll get it organized and go see this Annabelle woman today." There's no point in fighting it; I need to pick my battles with Tanner, and this is not the one. Nothing involving his girlfriend, Victoria, is a battle to pick. I won't be winning.

"Great, while you're gone, I'll get Victoria to look at this office and suggest a redesign. Griffin is in town soon, so he can offer any help we need if you want a full renovation." He smiles, thinking of Victoria, who's now one of the most sought-after interior designers in the country. I look around the small space again, taking in the dust and smell of stale books. Griffin is the country's best builder; the fact that he spends a lot of his time here, too, I'm sure Tanner loves.

"Fine, Tanner. You win. Three days per week here in Whispers, and the rest, I'll be in the city," I relent, already itching to get back to New York. I'm many things, smart, affluent, fueled by caffeine and billion dollar deals, but a country boy isn't in my repertoire. I wouldn't know the first thing about farm life and have no desire to learn it.

"I knew you'd come around," he says with a big shit-eating grin.

It's not ideal, but how hard can it be? I'll just sit behind the desk here and be permanently attached to my phone. I don't need to get to know people. In fact, I can probably accomplish more work here since there are no notable restaurants or bars. I'll work day and night and then get back to the city to live my life. Have the best of both worlds.

It could be just what I need.

2

ANNABELLE DAVIS

I push my hair behind my ear, pausing my work of raking the vegetable patch to look up at my kids. Kevin sprays his little brother, Noah, with the hose as they run around, laughing. The sight brings a warm rush to my chest, and I take a deep breath, feeling blessed.

Bringing my attention back to the garden, I assess my options, knowing the vegetable patch needs redoing with fresh compost and new seeds, something I'll add to my weekend to-do list. I grab a few carrots and some potatoes, before moving across to assess the corn. While ticking off things I need to get done, something else plays on my mind: Gertie's Soaps, the small business I started with my friend, Victoria. For her, it was a hobby, but for me, it was a necessity. A way out of poverty and the only reason I can now provide special things for my kids. Victoria and I have talked about expanding, making it something more, which both excites and scares me. But regardless, it's happening. Things are moving forward, and I have to get prepared.

Hearing my kids' laughter fade, I spot Noah now infatuated with the bucket of water that he splashes in. It's the simple things that keep a three-year-old entertained, and I'm thankful that he isn't running off on us, which is his usual game at the moment.

"Hey, Ma?" Kevin asks tentatively as he approaches me.

"Yes, honey?" I stand up, brushing the dirt from my clothes. My shirt is threadbare, my jeans ripped, but instead of old, they look like the latest fashion trend, meaning I can wear them for a lot longer than I usually would.

"Do you think I can join the baseball team this year?"

He's wanted to play baseball for years. He enjoys catching the ball with his friends at school and is glued to the TV whenever games are on. Kids' sports are expensive, though, and previously, we haven't been able to stretch things that far, but I've been saving all year to make this happen for him. That's the main reason why I want to build Gertie's Soaps. I can see the potential, and it will make a difference to our lives, despite how exhausted I'll be. I already stay up way too late most nights making soaps, since the only time I can allocate is when the kids are asleep. That and the fact that it helps me pass the time until I can barely keep my eyes open. I've been functioning on four hours of sleep a night for almost a year. I know it isn't good for me, but I prefer to handle the development myself. That way I can control the quality of the flowers and aroma oils I harvest and make here at the farm, keeping everything organic.

"You really want to play?" I smile, and he nods quickly.

"Harvey plays, and his dad, Dr. Hamilton, takes him to practice every week. He said they can give me a lift if you're busy here on the farm. I can milk the goats early before school, and I'll make sure I do all my chores..." His words tumble out as he states his case, and my heart sinks a little, sad that he's already worked out logistics in the hope of making things easier for me. I look at my boy and think about everything he's been through and everything he's done for me and his little brother since his dad died. I then look at my hands, seeing chipped nails and scratches from all my hard work, my nightly five-to-nine before getting up the next morning to do my nine-to-five, support teaching at Whispers Elementary. I can't keep going the way I am. It's too much, for both of us.

"We have the money this year, honey. You can play on the team."

He looks dumbfounded for a moment, clearly surprised, thinking my answer would be no, just like every other year. As I smile at him, he lunges at me, his body almost knocking me to the ground. I laugh heartily as I hold him tight, knowing this means a lot to him.

"Thank you, Ma. I promise, I'll try my best every single game."

My eyes blur with tears. Kevin does a lot for me, too much, really. He's only ten and has to shoulder a lot more responsibility than a kid ever should at his age. Playing on the local kids' baseball team will give him the opportunity to be the little boy he's meant to be, not the man of the house he's becoming.

"You just need to promise to have fun." I pull away and look at him, smiling softly when I see him a little glassy-eyed. It's then something catches my eye over his shoulder, and I spot a car making its way up our long gravel driveway.

"Who's that?" Kevin turns, positioning himself in front of me like a shield. My boy is very protective of me, probably because it's just been the two of us looking after everything for so long, little Noah included.

"I have no idea." I watch the vehicle get closer. The truck

isn't familiar, but it's shiny and new and the sun reflecting off it almost blinds me.

"Why don't you grab Noah and go inside to get cleaned up for supper."

He frowns at my suggestion, looking back at the truck and then back at me. We don't often get visitors, so he's wary, but I nod at him, which alleviates his concerns.

"Sure, Ma." He walks to his little brother, grabbing his hand, and I watch the two of them run into the house. As the truck pulls up, I dust my hands off on my already dirty shirt and push my hair back out of my face again. The unruly, long blond locks never staying back in my ponytail all day.

I step forward a few paces and notice a guy step out of his car and stall. He's suited up. Tailored fabric, his shirt white and crisp, his shoes black and high shine. He's also tall, his shoulders broad, hair on the shorter side and styled. I push my own shoulders back and fix my hair again, not used to having well-put-together, attractive men on my property.

"Can I help you?" I hold on to the small garden hoe I've been using in the garden. It isn't much, the man so tall and broad I doubt it will even create a dent, but if I need to use it, I will. When he finally looks at me, I momentarily forget how to breathe. His handsome face sucker punches me. He isn't someone I know because he's the kind of guy a woman remembers. Tall, dark, and handsome, he looks like he can pick you up and throw you over his shoulder, just like you see in the movies.

"Good afternoon. I hope I'm not interrupting." He pronounces his words carefully, sounding uppity and matching his looks. As he slowly walks toward me, the smile on his face is fake as hell, his teeth blindingly white, his skin flawless with a little stubble. He looks like a male model from a magazine or something. He definitely doesn't belong here. I push my hair back again, feeling a little self-conscious and on guard. It's been a long time since a man has taken me by surprise. Even longer since a man has made me feel something inside. My gut is now doing somersaults from nerves, fear or curiosity or interest, which one, I'm not sure.

"Are you lost?" There's no way someone like him is here for someone like me, unless it's something to do with the bank. I panic slightly, wondering if I've accidentally failed to pay someone and if he's a debt collector. Although, if this is how debt collectors look, I may be incentivized to deliberately skip the next electricity bill.

"I'm looking for Annabelle Davis?" I adjust my grip on the hoe with sweaty hands.

"That's me." My eyes flick to the house where Kevin watches from the window, a scowl on his face, ready to pounce. The man pauses a few feet away from me, his face hard set, but he has kind eyes. He's very clean. Almost comically so. I would say he's from the city, all sophisticated and has that air of rich arrogance. I notice the sun shimmering off his watch, a shiny Rolex glistening on his wrist. Yeah, this guy is rich. I imagine him being quite the catch for some young girl in New York, probably a model or socialite. I feel the dirt on my hands and beneath my nails and cringe. Definitely not for a woman like me.

"My name is Sawyer Silvers. I'm the legal representative for Tanner Whiteman at Whiteman's Whiskey. Tanner and Victoria asked me to organize some business paperwork for Gertie's Goat Milk Soaps." I take a big breath before I release it, remembering his name from when Victoria mentioned him during our conversation about growing the business last week. She mentioned at the time that Sawyer, her lawyer, would handle it all. I drop the hoe in relief, the tool thudding on the ground. He looks at it and frowns before his eyes meet mine again.

"Victoria mentioned that you were doing some paperwork for Gertie's. I just wasn't expecting you to come here." A small grin curls my lips at knowing he's friend, not foe. I haven't had much experience with lawyers before, but if Victoria and Tanner trust him, I guess I can too. Truth be told, I don't have much choice. When my husband passed away, so did all our measly family income. No life insurance, a stack of bills that kept getting bigger, and two kids, and I struggled for a long time.

"Yeah, well, that makes two of us." His tone is slightly condescending as he glances around my property. He gazes at my small run-down house and expansive fields, assessing it all. Taking in the rusted shed out back and the over-flowing garden that I need to weed, he looks back at me, and my shoulders stiffen.

I'm used to the townspeople looking at me with their judgy eyes, so I don't shrivel under his gaze. Instead, I meet his gaze head-on. I wasn't always so sure of myself. Years ago, I was a charity case. I had to be. Taking donations from the church just to get by. Now, I've learned how to survive, and I did it all on my own.

"I have some paperwork that requires your signature." He lifts a folder that's in his hand.

"Oh, sure. Ahhhh, we should go inside, then." I remember my manners and turn, walking to the house, and I hear him follow, his shoes crunching on the gravel. I wonder briefly if the flashy black leather can hold up in this dusty, rough environment.

As I step up onto my porch, I cringe once again at

hearing the boards creaking underfoot. Opening the door, I kick off my boots and take a moment to settle my nerves. Nerves at a stranger turning up at my place. Nerves from having a man in my house. It's been a long time since that's happened. Not since my husband's passing has there been a man who wasn't a doctor or a friend in my home. My brain scrambles, trying to remember everything Victoria mentioned. I push my shoulders back to maintain an air of professionalism, even though he's without a doubt one of the most handsome men I've ever met, and I currently look like one of those trolls from that movie my kids love watching so much.

"So, what do I need to do?" As the words leave my mouth, I feel excitement building. Hesitation? Yes. Worry? Yes. Stress? Definitely. But ever since I met Victoria, my life has become more positive. Like there's light at the end of the tunnel. It's a very long tunnel and the light is barely visible, but it's there. We have a good system going. Kevin milks her goats and brings the milk to me. I make the soaps at night, distilling my own oil from the lavender and roses here on my farm on weekends, and each week produce a few boxes of soaps that Victoria picks up, packages, and distributes.

"There are a few contracts. The legacy paperwork, which covers what will happen with the business if one party isn't involved anymore, and there's also the business name and structure, which I believe Victoria and you have already discussed. I also have copies for the trademark applications and copyright notices for your files."

Nodding, I walk farther inside but then look up and come to a halt. I should've thought about this before I invited him in. The kitchen is a complete mess. All my bowls and tools are out, ready for a long night of soapmaking. Laundry dries on a rack in the sun, my simple cotton underwear that I grabbed in the bargain bin last month on a trip to Williamstown on full display. Unread books are piled near my armchair, with my drawing pad and pencils on top. It's the spot I used to always curl up in to read or sketch, but that indulgence isn't something I've had time for lately. Noah and Kevin are standing in the living room, watching Sawyer like he's the devil. Kevin looks to be about a minute away from telling him to leave and Noah's wearing a pinched expression that's supposed to be tough and intimidating, but it's just too darn cute.

"Sorry, I wasn't expecting visitors. Kids, say hello to Mr. Silvers. He's a friend of Tanner's and Victoria's." At that, Kevin's shoulders lower.

When Victoria first moved to town and into Marie's Place years ago, Kevin helped her with her animals. It was a means to an end. I was newly widowed, with no job and barely two dimes to my name, and Kevin rode his rusted bike down to Marie's Place to milk her cow, bringing a bucket of milk back home. He did this so we would have milk for the day and for his brother's nightly bottle, our own cow not always producing enough.

I flick my eyes to my youngest son, seeing Noah's cute scowl morph into a full-blown grin.

"Tanneeerrrrr!!!!" Noah laughs, his giggle enough to have me smiling. He loves Tanner, probably because Tanner always buys him ice cream whenever we happen to see him in town. Which is rare, but obviously impactful to a three-year-old.

"So do I need to sign them now? I can clear a space." Feeling a little overwhelmed, I scoop up the math tests from school that I need to correct tonight, which I had dumped on the dining table when I got home.

"I can leave them here for you to read over in your own

time and then come back to collect them. You seem a bit...
busy."

I stop what I'm doing and look at him. It's obvious he
doesn't think much of my home, but that's exactly what it is,
my home, and regardless of his good looks, I conclude that
this man is a stuck-up city lawyer who probably wouldn't
know a hard day's work if it bit him on the ass. As I move
papers around, his words filter through my mind, and I'm
somewhat confused.

"How can you come back to collect them? Aren't you
from the city?"

"Yes, but Tanner has me working a few days a week from
the law office in town." He doesn't seem enthusiastic by that
prospect, if his tense body language and tightened jaw have
anything to say about it.

It's always the same with these city people. They have
their head shoved so far up their own asses they can't see the
beauty around them. Whispers is the most stunning place
ever and he's acting so put off, like he's landed on Mars.

"Jerry's office?" Everyone knows Jerry is retiring. I've
been wondering what we'll all do without him, assuming
that we'd need to drive to Williamstown to get anything we
need on legal matters.

"With Jerry retiring, Tanner seems to think I can work
here and support the town in his place." It's obvious he'd
rather be anywhere else and that Tanner made him come to
Whispers. But it makes sense. With Jerry gone, we need
someone new, and Tanner is the kind of man to always have
a plan for this town. I know Tanner Whiteman well; the two
of us have something in common with both losing our partners when our kids were young and single parenting
becoming both our journeys in life. Tanner was the first
person to help me when I lost my husband, ensuring that

Kevin was kept busy and providing the odd bag of groceries that we desperately needed at that stage.

"Is Sawyer your real name?" I continue clearing an area on my table, not sure if we need to sit down.

"It is... Why would you ask that?"

I look up at him, seeing a frown of confusion on his face, and I bite my grin back before I shrug my shoulder.

"It's just... a *lawyer* called *Sawyer*? Sounds like an intro to a joke or something." His frown deepens and he pulls the lapels of his jacket, clearly not amused. He's so straitlaced, I wonder what he would do if he accidentally fell into my vegetable patch and got that crisp white shirt of his dirty?

That thought makes me bite the inside of my lip to tame a smile.

3

SAWYER

The smile she's trying to hold back looks both sexy and evil as hell. It's the only brightness in this small, dark, creepy house.

When Tanner told me to drop off these contracts, I assumed it would be a short drive to somewhere close to town. But I was wrong. With nothing but bare fields, trees, and roads that have seen better days, I thought I was lost until I spotted her small weatherboard place from the road. The entire drive was like something out of *The Twilight Zone*. I was waiting for an axe murderer to jump out at me at every corner. Had I known that a beautiful woman like this was waiting, then I may have driven a little quicker, because as rustic as she is, she's stunning. She's not what I expected at all. A petite pocket rocket of a woman, whose eyes are startlingly blue, with messy, long blond hair.

As I look over the house again, my teeth grind as memories swirl. It looks similar to my family home as a kid, taking me back to memories of my life I'd rather forget. Sure, I was in an apartment in Queens, but the toys, clothes, cramped quarters, and clean but cluttered look is somewhat recognizable. The feeling of it all has my spine straightening. I *never* want to go back to those days. At that thought, I glance back at her kids. The older one looks ready to pounce on me and gut me from navel to nose if he gets the opportunity.

She's isolated out here. No nearby neighbors, her house small and run down, with paint peeling on the outside, the grass needing to be mowed. It's a solo dwelling, with a large, rusted shed out back, surrounded by fields of what looks to be lavender and roses, and grassy spaces where some cows and chickens roam.

"So, I can come by maybe next week to collect them. Will that give you enough time to review and sign everything?" I should've just dropped the paperwork off to her outside and got the hell out of here. But I'm inquisitive by nature, the practice of law coming very naturally to me, and there's something about her that's made me want to stick around a little longer.

I'm not sure if it's the way her jeans cover her perky ass or the way she looked holding that garden hoe like it was her only lifeline, ready to do battle with it. She's small, and I'm not sure that garden tool would've done much. But she comes across as tough and probably would've hit me with it before burying my body if she needed to.

"Um, sure, I think a week will be fine..." She sounds unconvincing. My eyes narrow, watching her. Does she need me to sit and explain the contracts to her? Some people can be a little overwhelmed by legal documents.

I wonder how old she is. She's young, much younger than I thought. When Tanner mentioned this new business venture that Victoria is getting off the ground, I assumed her partner was an older woman. But the beauty standing in front of me can't be any older than maybe late twenties, meaning she's at least a decade younger than me. Her youngest boy is small, but her older kid seems well into school age. I try to estimate their ages, wondering how early she started her family.

Having worked in law all my life, my skills for noticing things that other people don't is one of my strengths. My brother and I had a good life as kids, but we struggled, raised by a single mom, with a dad who didn't give a shit and took off when things got too hard. But my mom had enough love for both parenting roles, and we always knew we were her number ones. Now, as I look around, I see no signs of a husband or partner and vaguely remember Tanner telling me that she's a single mom. My chest feels warm at the thought, knowing how hard she must be working out here on her own. My mom scraped together every last dime to support Sutton and me, something we've now both repaid to her tenfold. Retirement in Florida looks good on her.

"I don't want to rush you. It's important that you read and understand everything the contracts entail." I sound like an arrogant asshole. She looks up, her eyes laser focused on me and not in a good way. *Fuck, she even looks beautiful when she's mad.*

As Annabelle goes back to tidying up the papers on the table to make way for my files, her hair sweeps across her cheek briefly. It's something that's happened multiple times since I've been here and my hand itches to grab it. I go to step forward but pause as she swipes it back behind her ear. I have no idea what comes over me, but I swear, if her hair falls in her face one more time, I'm going to have to walk out. The urge I have to brush it from her beautiful face is all encompassing.

"Ummm, Ma," the older kid says in a tone that has my senses on alert, breaking into my inner thoughts.

"What is it, Kevin?" Annabelle walks swiftly to where

he's at by the front window, looking out, obviously aware something isn't right.

"Oh no!" She peeks through the curtain, then she and the boy start running around, grabbing their shoes.

"What's going on?" I sense something amiss as the youngest kid goes to bolt out the door.

"Ahhh, no, you don't!" Annabelle lunges for him and grabs him just in time. Wrapping him up in a hold to her chest, she shakes her head as he giggles.

"Sorry, he's going through a phase of running away lately," she mumbles as he wiggles in her grip.

"Ma!" the older boy says again, louder, jolting her, and she looks back at me.

"Here, can you hold Noah? Noah, go to Sawyer." She thrusts the smaller kid into my arms as she runs to help the older boy outside with something, giving me no time to object.

"Seesaw!" The kid giggles before slamming his hands on my cheeks and squishing my face. They are cold and damp, and he swings his legs around in glee. I have to hold him out from me as he almost kicks me in the balls. Fuck. I don't get paid enough for this shit.

"Wait. I can't..." But Annabelle and Kevin are already running out the back door, so I follow them, still holding this kid out in front of me so he doesn't dirty my suit, glad I go to the gym, because he's a heavy boy and my arms are straining. My mood is now soured even more, knowing I have better things I need to be doing with my time. Like figuring out how I'm going to run my legal empire from this bumfuck, in-the-middle-of-nowhere town.

"Wait!" I call out again as I run down the back porch steps, worried I might actually fall through them, seeing them rotten in places. Noah giggles at me, thinking this is a fun game, his tiny, sticky fingers pulling at my ears. I don't do kids. I don't have them, and I'm not sure I even want them. I don't have nieces or nephews either, so I'm not around them at all, although the way my brother goes through women, it's astounding that he doesn't have multiple love children at this stage. Kids are grimy and loud, and right now, this one's squeezing my ears too fucking hard. Although, he's a bit cute. He has his mother's vibrant blue eyes.

I look back out at Annabelle, seeing her hair flowing wildly in the breeze, her jeans doing everything they should be to her ass, as she and Kevin work together, dragging the biggest cow I've ever seen back into a shed.

"What's going on?" I ask, assessing the risks. Seeing this woman working with the large beast has me on alert. She looks fierce, so striking, yet my protective instincts are pinging at my skin, wanting her to get away from the danger of it, even though it looks as though the cow is more likely to lick her than trample her to death.

"She's in calf. Going a little crazy from being inside so much," Annabelle tells me, although she's concentrating too hard on what she's doing to look at me.

"She's what?" I'm confused, the panic of the situation leaving me, and now wondering if she can hurry up so I can give her this kid back. My arms are aching from how I still hold him at arm's length. Noah, though, is having a great time as he swings his legs around again like he's walking on air.

"Calf!" Kevin yells at me. The look he gives me is one of warning as he gets the cow back into the shed, the door of which looks like it's connected via ropes, the hinges rusted clear off.

My focus snaps when a chicken darts in between my legs

like it's on speed, and I hop around, trying to get away from it. As I do, I lose my grip on Noah, and he wriggles out of my arms, dropping to the ground and landing on his feet perfectly before he starts to run.

"Shit." I give chase, but the young boy is too quick for me.

"Sit. Sit. Sit." Noah yells, trying to pronounce the swear word in between his giggles, and I grit my teeth. Playing tag on a farm was not what I thought my day would entail, even more reason why I shouldn't even be in this fucking town.

I stride forward, trying to grab on to him, not sure what other dangers are lurking and not wanting to be responsible if he breaks a leg. As I stretch to capture him, I slip on something. My designer shoe has no grip, and my feet completely slide out from under me, causing me to fall straight onto my ass, right into what smells like fresh cow shit.

"Fuck!" I shout.

Noah gasps and suddenly stops, looking at me, wide-eyed, face stricken. "You said the naughty word…" he whispers.

"We don't use that language in this house!" Annabelle berates me, and I look up, seeing her march toward me with fire in her eyes. It's a vision that makes me want to do really dirty things to her.

If looks could kill, Annabelle would have me strung up by my thousand-dollar tie. She stands above me, hands on her curvy hips, hair blowing in the breeze, eyes narrowed. I scramble up, just as Kevin locks the cow back in the shed.

"I need to go." My suit is now ruined, my designer shoes completely covered in cow shit, and as I run my hands through my hair without thinking, mud now licks up my cheeks.

I really need to go before I lose my cool. I'm angry and embarrassed and completely out of my comfort zone here on a fucking farm, delivering fucking contracts like some intern.

"Thank you for stopping by. I'll look through the paperwork tonight and let you know if I have any questions," Annabelle says, and I nod. Then, without saying another word, I turn the corner and round the house, spotting a few chickens nearby that look at me like they want to peck my toes, along with rows and rows of thick lavender and roses, both surprisingly fragrant.

Peeling off my jacket, I place it on the seat of my new truck with a huff before I get in and drive straight back to town.

I've been here not even a day, and I already hate it. But when my eyes look to the rearview mirror and I spot Annabelle, hands still on her hips, standing in the same spot, watching me drive away, her image getting smaller and smaller the farther I go, I find that I have to force my eyes back on the road.

As I pull back onto the shithouse road that's full of holes and rocks that flick up onto my new truck, my cell rings, my brother's name flashing.

"What!" I answer, my mood clearly not any better. Probably because I still feel the shit and mud that's coating my suit and skin.

"Whoa, bad day, brother?" the smart-ass asks, and I imagine he's floating around in his pool in LA, without a fucking care in the world.

"You could say that."

"What's got your knickers in a knot?"

I swear if he was here, I'd punch him.

"I'm in the middle of fucking nowhere with cow shit on my suit." Even getting out my frustration, I'm still glancing up at my rearview mirror, searching for the small-town beauty I just met and being immediately disappointed that I can't see her anymore.

"Cows? Have you been eating gummies?"

"Gummies? What the fuck are you talking about?"

"Sawyer, you and cows don't really go together. Where are you? Jersey?"

I roll my eyes. "No, Whispers. Where are you?"

"Home. Just trying to lay low."

I turn the corner onto the main highway again, glad to have smooth asphalt under my tires, even though the stench of shit is starting to fill my truck.

"Lay low? You? Yeah, right."

My brother loves the limelight. Even as a kid, he was always the one showing off in front of everyone. Especially the girls.

"How long are you in Whispers for?" He's never been here, but he knows Connor and is best friends with Hudson, the local doctor.

"Not for long, if I have anything to do with it." I see Distillery Drive up ahead and turn down, needing to speak with Tanner.

"Alright, well, I'll call you later in the week. I might have something for you," he says cryptically, but I don't ask. There's always something going on with him.

"Sure, talk then." I end the call as I pull up to the distillery. As luck would have it, both Connor and Tanner are standing out front, so I jump out and strut straight up to them.

They take one look at me, and their faces morph into shock before they both get matching shit-eating grins.

"What the hell happened to you?" Connor asks, trying not to laugh.

"I ruined my fucking suit, that's what happened."

"You smell like shit," Tanner says.

"That's because it is shit!" I deadpan.

"Annabelle's?" Tanner asks.

"Yes, Annabelle's." Oddly, my temper recedes a little at the mention of her name. Both the Whiteman men murmur and nod.

"You didn't tell me she was a crazy farmer with crazier kids." I don't really mean it, but my aggravation lingers.

"She isn't. She's just got a lot on her plate." Tanner looks at me pointedly.

"Yeah, well, her son looked like he wanted to gut me," I murmur to them, remembering how Kevin's eyes flamed when he was getting the cow back in the shed.

"Kevin? Nah, he's harmless." Connor shrugs and continues to grin.

"I need you to look after her," Tanner says as he watches me carefully, and I frown.

"What do you mean?"

"She'll need help with all the legal things but also the business side. I want Victoria and myself to remain impartial, so I need you to ensure she understands things."

"I'm a lawyer, not a business coach." I scrub my face. I knew I should've gone over the details with her.

"This is what it means to work in a small town, Sawyer. We all rally together and help each other. Not to mention, you'll be paid accordingly. Annabelle has a lot going on and is too proud to ever ask for help. So all I'm asking is if you can make sure that whatever she signs, she knows what it entails. And offer business advice if and when she needs it."

Releasing an impatient breath, I shake my head. "I need a shower."

"Yes, you do." Tanner nods in agreement.

"And a fucking big bottle of whiskey," I say, and they both chuckle.

"Well, you're in the right place." Tanner's grin widens.

"That's debatable." I give them both a death stare.

"Welcome to Whispers!" Connor says jovially as his hands fling out to his sides, and he smiles like he's in a tourism commercial.

My return smile is fake, and they know it. "Fuck you."

They both cackle as I stride back to my truck and drive to my new place on Billionaire Boulevard. A shower's in order, and there are a million things to do, including ordering a new tailor-made designer suit.

Yet the woman with the blond hair isn't very far from my mind for the rest of the afternoon.

4

―――――

ANNABELLE

I settle in at the dining table with my coffee, holding my cell between my shoulder and my ear as I write a few things down while Victoria continues.

"The soaps we make at the moment are amazing, but I think we can expand our distribution."

I take a deep breath and look around my run-down house. The familiar ache in my chest that I'm not good enough pulses through my bones.

When I don't respond, she clarifies, "I mean, we have them for sale through the distillery shop and around town, and they're very popular. But ever since we put them in the new Whiteman's Spa, we've had a lot of interest, and we'll be opening new distribution channels in other spas with the teas and tonics Daisy makes as well, so we could take advantage of those relationships..."

It makes sense, but I'm still hesitant. "If we opened new lines of distribution..."

"Nationwide." She jumps in, her excitement palpable.

I swallow roughly. "National distribution would require

higher quantities, I assume?" I love making soaps, and it relaxes me, but doing more of it on top of my day job as a teacher, as well as looking after two kids and running this small farm all on my own, it's a lot more than I think I can handle.

"Well, we would stick to the three lines we have initially, so no new products, but we would have to increase our stock on those."

I nod, even though she can't see me, trying to get it all straight in my brain. Business and numbers are not my strong suits; I'm more of a creative person. A doer.

"Well, I just planted more lavender in the far field, and the current yield we have is enough to double the production if we require it." I wonder if I can manage cultivating more rosebushes along the driveway and around the house, and how long it'll take me to distill the oil and add it to the soaps.

"Did Sawyer come to see you?" she asks, probably hearing my brain working from wherever she is.

I take a sip of coffee and almost burn my tongue.

"He did. He left some paperwork for me to look at." My eyes search the piles of paperwork on my desk to see if I can spot the small folder, but I can't.

"Well, read through those so we can get all the business paperwork sorted. In the meantime, you continue building the stock, and I'll put feelers out for new distribution channels."

It sounds like a simple thing, but my body feels prickly all over. Is it anxiety, fear, excitement, or a mixture of all three?

"Are you sure you don't want us to hire someone to come out to help you on the farm? I mean, we don't have much money, but we have a little." She knows I'm working myself to the bone. But having someone on my farm, interfering with my crops, isn't something I want.

"No. I can do it." It'll be hard work, but if we can increase our sales, then that means more money in my pocket. And as we continue to talk through our plans, the smile on my face grows, thinking about what could be possible for a small-town girl like me.

It's quiet. I love the peace of the land. The clean country air and the serenity that blankets me whenever I walk through these fields.

"Ma, Noah and I have finished feeding the chickens." My two boys walk up to me where I'm on hands and knees in the dirt, planting more rosebushes. I cultivated these cuttings from the roses I've already planted, knowing the soil and the positioning is just right for this variety. I love this rose because it sports a brilliant red, a double bloom that keeps blooming all summer long. I'm able to get a lot of petals from it for our rose soap collection. It's resilient, hence why it's called the Super Hero Rose. And resilience is what everyone needs. Especially out here. I take a deep breath and let the scent calm me, appreciating the flowers around me. The roses and lavender need less ongoing maintenance than cows and animals do, making this farm something I can build into being somewhat more self-sufficient.

"Thanks, boys. Kevin, can you help me dig these last few holes?"

Kevin moves right away to grab the shovel and starts digging more holes next to me, the two of us working in peace while Noah plays nearby in some dirt.

Being together like this brings me joy. We're close, my

boys and I, but I feel sad that they don't have a father figure or a male role model. Trying to be both parents at times is tough, but I'm doing my best. The expansion of the soap business will help. Although initially it'll be a lot of work, I can see that over time, it'll be the jackpot I need to pull us out of this life we're in and maybe, just maybe, allow me to start saving for college so I can give my boys that opportunity when they're old enough.

At the thought of Gertie's Soaps, I think of Sawyer. The snazzy city lawyer who left here with shit on his suit and smoke coming from his ears. I wouldn't be surprised if I never see him again, though that thought disappoints me for some reason.

As arrogant as he seemed, I felt for him being in a place like this. Farm life isn't everyone's ideal environment, and it clearly isn't his. But I smile, remembering how he held Noah with complete terror in his eyes, yet he did it. His innate care and attention came through, although hidden well behind his suit of armor. And even though he could've asked me to sign the paperwork then and there to get it over with, he didn't. I'm grateful because I have no idea what I'm signing and need time to look through it all carefully and at my own pace.

"How many more we got?" Kevin doesn't stop or slow down, knowing that working on the farm is something we all need to pitch in with.

"Just a few more. We're nearly done." I offer him a smile and get one in return as Noah starts picking some daisies and making a bunch, one I know he'll present to me at the end of our work here. His heart is bigger than the moon, and I know one day he'll make some girl very happy.

As we work quietly, a shiver runs up my spine, the feeling of being watched crawling across my body. I pause what I'm doing and remain still, yet my eyes flit around under my lashes, wondering if anything is amiss.

"Did you lock up the chickens, Kevin?" Maybe the chickens are making a mess on the other side of the house, which is what's making me feel out of sorts.

"Yep. Everything is packed away too." I look around again, not able to put my finger on it, yet feeling a little unsettled, which is new. I grew up on this land. My parents owned it, as did their parents before them. I know every square inch of soil. And I know when something doesn't feel right.

"Is the shed locked up?" Kevin tilts his head as he looks at me curiously.

"Yes, I checked it before we came down here."

I nod and offer him a reassuring smile. He looks a lot like me. Both boys do, and I'm grateful for that. I look a lot like my mom too. The maternal line is strong in my family. Thinking of her makes me a little melancholy, and I stare out at the fields to the left where they had their farming accident, my heart still aching for a different outcome, even a decade later. When my mom and dad both died, it was devastating, but being from the land like this, we know the risks and accept them willingly.

When I don't see or hear anything, I keep working, digging in the soil and planting the roses. Hoping they take and flourish quickly for me.

"Kevin, are you looking forward to your first baseball game?" With the season starting in another week, my Saturdays like this around the yard aren't something that will continue, as we'll have baseball to go to now, my hours for farm work diminishing slightly. But it'll be worth it to see him so happy.

"Harvey and I have been practicing at school. We play Williamstown first, and their pitcher is a pro."

I grin at how excited he is already. "Well, as long as you have a good time, I'm sure it will be—" My words drop as we're all startled by a large bang, and I scramble to my feet and pull both my kids close. I don't think it was a shotgun, but it sounded a lot like it. With my heart racing, I look toward my nearest neighbor. Tim and Tina from the Whispers Toy Store are the closest to me, yet still a mile or so away. I can't see their house at all, but my land meets theirs, and I look to see if they are out and about on this side of their property. Only, it's bare.

Bob from the hardware store owns a lot of property around here as well, where he runs his cattle, his fields butting up to mine on my other side. But again, I don't see him or any of his trucks that sometimes drive over his land when he's fixing his fences and things.

"What was that?" Kevin's head whips around as quickly as mine as Noah starts to whimper, clearly in tune to the emotions that Kevin and I are feeling. Fear. I pull him closer before I spot it. The rusted shed door swung open in the wind, hitting the wall with force.

"Oh. It's just the shed." I try to alleviate their fright, but mine's not totally gone yet.

"The wind must have pushed it open." Kevin's eyebrows pinch. The rusted shed door is now wide open and swings in the breeze. It must've come undone from the rope locks.

"Let me run up and tighten it. You two stay here and finish the holes. I'll be back in a minute."

Halfway up, I look back at my boys, the two of them deep in the dirt, and I grin before I reach the shed. I grab the door and pull it back around, and then the rope to tie the door back in place. I'm surprised it came undone. The rope is new; I just got it two weeks ago, and Kevin said he locked it up.

But as I look more closely at the rope to hook it back around to secure the door, I still.

Because the rope didn't come loose. It was severed. Cut cleanly, something only a sharp knife could manage.

I look up and around, seeing the rest of the farm is as it should be. But that sinking feeling returns. Something just doesn't feel right.

5

―――――

SAWYER

I drink my morning piccolo coffee, my suit pressed to perfection, and sit in my city office, where I should be ready to start my day. Yet it feels different, empty. The large bookcases from Whispers aren't lining my walls, the musty carpet smell vacant.

I was in Whispers for mere days last week, but already, I've packed up and sent a few creature comforts to my new place on Billionaire Boulevard and rescheduled appointments that I had booked over the next month. All due to my new commitments in the small town I know Tanner wants me to call home.

But I've lived in this city my entire life. I'm a New Yorker through and through. The honking horns, the crowds of people, the nightlife, always something to do, all of it's in my blood. But as I sip my coffee, the taste bitter on my tongue, I come to the stark realization that the coffee Rochelle made me at the Delish Diner in Whispers last week was better.

"Sawyer?" I look up to see my assistant, Wendy, at the door. She's been with me for years. Almost at retirement,

Wendy has been the one constant woman in my life, and I'll miss her when she leaves.

"Hey, Wendy. What have we got going on today?" Sitting forward, I'm ready for the daily onslaught to begin. I built my company up from scratch, and now employ over two hundred staff, ranging from attorneys for both corporate and commercial law, to criminal cases, and a small pro bono team, along with a vast administration team to support us all. For Tanner to expect me to leave all this for a life in Whispers is laughable. Although, my firm is a well-oiled machine and I have a great leadership team in place to manage things when I'm away. Which now appears to be often.

"Your nine a.m. had to reschedule to later next week. You have a team meeting at ten, lunch with the head of the Mets at midday, and then this afternoon, you have video inter-views lined up for lawyers out of Williamstown."

As soon as I got to Whispers, one of the first calls I made was to my HR manager to start scouting for potential staff for the Whispers office. While the town is cute, I'm not sure I can commit so much of my time there, regardless of what Tanner wants, so I need some support just in case.

"Thanks, Wendy. Tell HR to provide me with the top two potentials from Williamstown by midweek and align the Mets games with my schedule. If I can make a few games this season, I would like to. My corporate box is gathering dust at this point."

She nods, making a note for herself, before asking, "How's Whispers going?"

"It is what it is. You know Tanner; he loves that town. But it's quiet, not much happening there."

"Sounds like just what you need. Get away from this

hustle and bustle for a while. Give you some space to think, to breathe. You're too stressed here."

"You're the one retiring, not me, Wendy. I've got deals to do, money to make."

She scoffs at me, like only my oldest, most loyal employee can.

"There's more to life than work, Sawyer. Just remember that." She collects some files before turning and walking out the door. My cell rings before I can respond, and she leaves me to it.

"Twice in a week, I'm feeling loved."

My brother snorts a laugh.

"Is that all it takes to feel loved? If so, you're clearly not with the right woman," he jokes, knowing full well I've been single for a while. I played the field in my youth, then had a few years when I worked hard and partied harder before finding a woman I thought might be the one. Turns out, she wasn't. After a failed engagement, I dove back into work and became more successful than I ever thought possible and have been casual with women ever since. My work always comes first.

"You tell me." I know full well, aside from me and Mom, he doesn't call anyone else. The ladies he indulges in are usually for a night or two, never more than that.

"Touché. You back home? Got over your little issue with the cows?"

I lean back, knowing my meeting is canceled so I have time to talk.

"I got a new suit, if that's what you mean." I didn't really need a new one, since I have plenty, but I ordered a full wardrobe to be shipped to Whispers, not wanting to be caught short again.

"Is there much to do in Whispers?" Sutton questions, making me pause.

"Literally nothing, unless you like whiskey, wide-open space, and the quiet of the country." I'm honest with him, before my mind wanders back to the blond farmer I haven't stopped thinking about.

"That sounds good about now. Things are getting a little crazy here, and I had to up my security. Last week, someone got through my gates, and when I got home, they were in my bed."

I sit straighter at that. "What the absolute fuck?" Sutton may be as big and tall as I am, but he's still my little brother. The same one I protected all my life and have no plans of stopping.

"Yeah. Young girl, a little unhinged." He huffs a small laugh, one I know isn't humorous, rather awkward or hesitant.

"What happened?" I want all the details and open my laptop to do a search online for the latest Hollywood gossip. He's often featured, so much so, I pay little attention anymore.

"I had my security team with me, thankfully. They were helping me inside with my bags and things because I had been in Cabo..."

I look at my screen and see photos of him and some model getting handsy on a beach, and I scrub my face.

"We heard a noise, went to investigate, and there was a woman in my bed. Police were called, and security took her away."

"What did Bobby say?" I grit my teeth, hating his agent, Bobby, who, in my opinion, is a thieving asshole. He takes too high of a percentage from my brother at every opportunity. But he spotted Sutton first, and they have a long relationship.

"Told me it was great press and to forget about it. So I hired more security, and now they always walk me inside and do a sweep of the house before they leave."

"Good. Safety first and always, okay?" I tell him like he's ten and walking to school by himself for the first time, instead of being the global movie star he is.

"What've you got lined up next? Do you still promote things on your socials? You know, products and things?" Sutton is always jumping from one movie set to another. Being a workaholic is a trait we both have taken on. The fear of having nothing and the need to make something of ourselves burns deep within us both after being raised scraping by for everything we had.

"Not really, unless it's big. I'm working with a clothing brand at the moment, so I'm sponsored to do a bit for them. Why?"

"A friend of mine has a soap business they're trying to get off the ground. Had some success locally, and now they're wanting to move to a more national distribution. Since they're trying to get some traction, just thinking I'll send you some." I act nonplussed about it, but the opportunity is swelling in my stomach at having my brother play a part in promoting Gertie's Soaps.

"Who is she?" he asks abruptly.

"What?" I pretend I have no idea what he's talking about.

"You've never asked me to promote anything before. Not even your own business. Not even Whiteman's Whiskey, which I'm still hoping to be the face of for some commercials so put a word in. But the last time you asked me for anything, Sawyer, was in eighth grade when you had that crush on

Becca Langer and you wanted me to organize a playdate with her brother so you could walk me over to her place and see her out of school. Which I did by the way. So, who is she?"

"No one," I say quickly, sipping the remainder of my coffee.

"So there is someone," he teases, and I try not to huff.

"No. You're being stupid." Our conversation's turning less professional and more like teenagers squabbling.

"Does it have anything to do with you falling in cow shit the other day? Being at a farm is yet another thing you'd never do, and yet there you were. In Whispers, meeting the townspeople. On their farms!" he says like he has a *gotcha* moment.

"Can I send you some soap or not?" My shoulders feel tight, my brother's teasing grinding my gears, yet I can't help smiling.

"Sure. I'll lather up my naked body in your girlfriend's soap. Want me to take a picture with all the suds on me? Maybe she would like to see it. I work hard on my six-pack; I should show it off..."

My jaw clenches. Clearly, I didn't think this through.

"You're an asshole." He laughs, taking great delight in this conversation.

"Yeah, and you have a crush. About time. It's been years since Mandy, and all those city girls aren't really your style. Maybe this country girl could be just what you need."

I think about his words. Mandy, my former fiancée. The one who left me the minute things got hard.

"It's just soap, Sutton. That's it."

"Fine. You go live on denial island. I'm going for a workout. Gotta have those abs popping when I soap up. See you, bro." He ends the call, not giving me a chance of rebuttal.

As I toss my cell onto my desk, there's a knock at my door.

"Connor's here," Wendy announces, and I stand just as Connor walks in.

"Connor, hey." Blowing out a breath, I try to get my head back in the game as we shake hands.

"Sawyer, I called the local office, and Jerry said you were back in the city. Thought I'd drop by, go over a few things with you before lunch."

It isn't unusual. My door is always open to him, and as we take a seat on my lounge, I wonder what he wants to discuss.

"I didn't know you were in the city this week." He works between Whispers and New York. His girlfriend, Daisy, comes with him for the most part, visiting her family here. The two of them are inseparable.

"Had a few team issues here I needed to fly in and sort out. But I flew in last night and want to be back tonight."

"That quick?"

"You know I hate being away from home, and I sure as hell hate being away from Daisy."

I shake my head. "I don't understand how a man can be so consumed by their woman that he can barely stand being away from her."

"Nothing wrong with going home to a good woman, Sawyer. What's the alternative? Drinks at the Polo Bar? Young girls fluttering their eyelashes at you while also tracking your jet?"

He's right. I've dated for years and nothing serious ever comes of it. Mostly because the women I meet look for my bank balance before they even look at me. So I bury my head in work ninety percent of the time, because my penthouse, although luxurious, can get a bit lonely. I live in one of the world's most populous cities, yet at times feel completely alone.

"When are you flying back?" he asks me.

"Here for a few days, then flying into Whispers on Thursday."

"Great, just in time."

He and Tanner are always doing something, so I wouldn't be surprised if he told me that they're building a theme park next.

"In time? In time for what?" I scrub my face, knowing I'm not going to like his answer.

"Well, you're sponsoring the junior baseball team this year, right? Their first game is on the weekend."

"Yeah, a weekend in Whispers isn't really in the cards for me." I think I'll fly in and out this time. Although, as I hear the muffle car horns and traffic below, I start to think maybe a quiet night or two might be welcome.

"But we all know how much you love baseball. Hell, you own a fucking team, Sawyer." I think about my beloved New York Mets, the team I'm a minority owner of. I've been a fan of baseball since I was a kid, and I still love it to this day.

"Besides, as a sponsor, you have to be there. It's the first game. Can't let the kids down." Connor sits back in his seat with a big shit-eating grin on his face, and I roll my eyes at him.

"That's a low blow," I murmur, not wanting to be the reason kids can't play. As a kid, baseball was my only solace, where I escaped the daily grind and found friends, happiness, and health. "Are you going to be there?"

"Nah, Daisy and I will do our morning yoga and then go down to her new studio and start the fit-out with Victoria. But I'll see you at the bar on Friday night," Connor confirms, plans seemingly already in place. My usual well-planned week is now morphing into something else.

"Fine. What else did you want to discuss?" I ask, and his face turns serious.

"The Grant brothers. I heard they're making moves."

I nod. "Heard that too. I mean, they run a very fucking big empire; their real estate holdings are impressive."

"We're working with Van Cleef, and I love Val and AJ. But if there's an opportunity..." His sentence hangs in the air.

"Van Cleef offers us a pretty good foothold. Plus, we have more meetings we want to line up with them for stocking the whiskey in their hotels."

"Grant Holdings is global. Andre has a corporate box near mine at the games. He's almost permanently here now."

"He's pretty much retired. Tyler is the man we need to talk to."

The Grant family runs hotels and properties across the world, having started in France and worked their way around Europe before hitting the Asia region and now making moves here in the US.

"If we wanted to make a deal, what does that mean for Van Cleef?" he asks me outright.

"We have the usual competitive clauses. But... we could do it. It's a longer-term strategy, so we'll need to build relations, work out exactly what we want from it." It would mean a lot of networking and a lot of contract shuffling, but I know I can do it. "If Whiteman's Whiskey wants to be global, Grant Holdings is the company we need to associate with."

Connor's eyes brighten. "I want to go global."

"My favorite type of deals."

With matching smiles, we start to strategize.

6

———

ANNABELLE

As I walk down the street, I wonder what Fridays feel like for people who can spend the weekend doing whatever they please. There are a few people out and about, having finished work for the week and heading into the diner or Whiteman's Bar for an end-of-week reprieve. Something I never do. It's straight back to the farm for me, as there are animals to feed, vegetables to pick, and dinner to make before a long night ahead of making soaps.

"Hi there, Annabelle." Tina pops out of the toy store she owns with her husband as I walk by. The kids and I always stop and look at their window displays, with me feeling guilty I can never really buy them new toys, and them no doubt wishing that I could.

"Hi, Tina. How's things?"

"You know, same old, same old. How are you doing out on the farm? We haven't seen you in town lately." She has a look of concern on her face. I know what she thinks. I know what all the town thinks. The poor young woman who lives so far out of town, all on her own. The single mom who struggles to manage life since her husband's passing. Steve always used to tell me not to gossip, to not tell anyone anything, and I've kept to myself for years, following his advice.

"It's busy. You know how it is…" I trail off, thinking now's a good time to ask her what's been on my mind for the last few days. "Um, Tina, have you or Tim seen anything strange around your place lately?" I've been anxious and a little on edge after the barn door incident.

"What do you mean?" Her smile slips a bit. "Have you had some trouble?"

"No, no…" I laugh awkwardly, not wanting to worry her. "It's just, I wondered if you've seen any people around or anything like that?" I never wish ill on anyone, but at this moment, I really hope she says yes. At least then I could stop thinking I'm going crazy, thinking I'm hearing or seeing things. If it's just kids hanging around, then at least it would put my mind at ease.

"People? Out on our land? No. Why? What's happened? Have you had a break-in?"

I internally cringe at her questioning, so I laugh again, feeling uneasy.

"Oh, no. But you know, they say to be vigilant. Always new people in town." I'm grinning stupidly now, acting like I'm the head of the neighborhood watch committee or something. God, Steve was right; I shouldn't be talking to outsiders. I should keep things to myself.

"Hmmm… I'll talk to Tim. We'll keep our eyes open." She gives me a nod, and I appreciate it. "Have you heard about the new lawyer in town? I saw him this morning as he got to work. Looks very professional…" She raises her eyebrows, like she's giving me the intel into a man I've already met.

"Yes, we've met... I'm actually on my way to see him now about Gertie's Soaps, so I gotta run." I don't like the fact that the rumor mill in Whispers is already in overdrive about Sawyer's arrival. Although, I should've realized it would be. A new, young, handsome man in town, I can practically see the line of women who'll *accidentally* run into him. I want no part in that. Sure, he's attractive, and I'd be a liar if I said that I hadn't been thinking of him, regardless of how he looked at me and my property like we were contagious.

"Of course. See you around, Annabelle."

With a smile, I wave goodbye and step away, walking down the street a little farther to the small storefront that is our legal office, feeling Tina's eyes on my back the entire way.

I push through the doors to the law office and pause. Things already look different than when I was here last. Jerry's business name has been scraped off the front window, replaced with Silvers Law Firm in a thick all-black font.

"Hey, Annabelle," Jerry greets me, stepping away from a box he is packing at reception.

"Oh, hi, Jerry. Getting things sorted?" Jerry helped me a lot when Steve died. The legal side of things when a spouse passes was too much for me to really understand by myself. He did it all free of charge too, so I have a soft spot for him.

"A few more boxes, and then I'll be done." He sounds a little melancholy, but I know he and his wife are both looking forward to a slower pace of life.

"You'll be missed. Although I hope to still see you around town?"

"I'll be helping out the baseball league this year a little more. Might referee a few games. I heard your young fella is playing this season. It's good to see." His smile is laced with sympathy that I try to brush off.

"He's really looking forward to it."

"Annabelle?" Sawyer comes out from the back, stopping abruptly at seeing me, obviously surprised. As he looks me over, I feel a small flush coloring my cheeks and my breath catches a little. I'd conveniently forgotten exactly how handsome he is. Checking out men is not something I do. For a long time, it was the last thing on my mind. But it's been over three years now since I've been on my own, and when a handsome stranger comes to town, it's a little hard to ignore. Although, he's very clearly out of my league. I'm glad that even though it's been a long day, I look much better than the last time he saw me. My hair is pulled back properly, and with my work clothes on instead of my farming attire, I feel somewhat more put together.

"Hi, Sawyer, I just wanted to drop the paperwork back to you. Save you coming all the way back out to the farm. I know it's a bit of a drive." I can't say I really understood it all, but I did read through most of the papers, albeit close to midnight, my eyes continually closing on me.

"Sure, come on through to my office." He sweeps his arm open, showcasing the hallway, which has been painted stark white. It's refreshed, and although I always liked Jerry's soft blues, this stark white and black branding Sawyer has is nice and contemporary.

"See you on the field soon, Jerry," I whisper to him as I walk past.

"Hopefully a few home runs for Kevin." He gives me a wink, and I smile. I'm wishing for that more than anyone.

As I walk into Sawyer's office, the whole place looks bigger and newer than when I was here last. The blinds have been replaced with something a little more modern. He has a new desk that I'm sure he must polish daily, because it has a high shine to it that my kids would just love to get finger-prints all over. He's gotten rid of the large dark timber book-cases and books that Jerry had here and instead has a dark-brown Chesterfield sofa and armchair, making a small sitting area. It looks very clean. Very him.

"Redecorating?" I try making conversation as I look around his office.

"Victoria's doing it. It was in dire need of an update."

Gee, if he thought Jerry's office needed an upgrade, what the hell does he think of my place?

"I want to apologize for the other day. You caught us at a bad time... With the cow fiasco, and the kids were a little crazy after a big day at school..." I want to at least explain so he thinks my life isn't a total shit show, even though it obvi-ously is.

"No need to apologize. I turned up unannounced, and I didn't want to intrude." He stands near his desk, his eyes piercing and his stance firm. I push down the desire to step forward and ruffle his hair or scrunch his tie, anything to make him look a little more human.

"But your suit?" I cringe, because I've been thinking about it all week. I should've offered to dry clean it or some-thing. But I didn't. I was too frantic after the cow escaped and then hearing him swear in front of the boys... my stress levels peaked. Then he scrambled away so quickly after falling in the cow manure that I didn't get a chance to offer. Not that I could afford to, since dry cleaning a suit like that would cost a pretty penny, I'm sure.

"It's fine, I bought another one," he says so casually it almost stuns me. I'm pretty certain I saw the label on his jacket when he threw it in his truck. I might live in the coun-try, but I know designer labels, and I know that suit probably cost a small fortune. As does the large watch that's on his wrist today. A completely different one from last week yet still blinding in the light.

Spotting a few boxes near his feet, filled with books and files, I ask, "So you're staying, then? For good? Here in Whispers?" He didn't seem to want to when he mentioned it at my place the other day, but by the looks of the redecorating, he certainly is.

"Not if I can help it. I'm not made for country living. Whispers is nice, but I prefer the city."

"It must be nice to have a choice." I wonder what my life would've been like had I left for college instead of marrying my childhood sweetheart. If I'd gotten a proper education while seeing the world instead of falling pregnant as a teen, doing night school, and struggling to pay my bills.

"So you have the paperwork?" He quickly masks his slight look of vulnerability, and I open my tote bag to pull out the file.

"Yes, everything looked fine. I signed them all." I pass the folder over, feeling a little intimidated as he leans on the side of his desk and opens it, flicking through the papers, checking that they're signed. I'm well equipped for most things. I can cook a three-course meal out of basic ingredients, I've taught myself how to sew, I tend to the farm, make soaps, teach kids their reading, writing, and arithmetic, and I'm an expert in making twenty dollars stretch farther than most. But when it comes to legal letters and in-depth details around business and finances, that isn't my forte.

While he looks through the paperwork, I take the time to look at him thoroughly. He's in another suit, and this time, I notice how well he fills it out. Broad shoulders, tall, he still has some stubble, but it's well maintained, as is his hair. He probably gets it cut every week to ensure it's always one hundred percent perfect. I imagine him being the kind of guy who has his own hairdresser, someone who comes to him, while he's taking an important online meeting.

"Ahhh, I think we are missing a page?"

I move my eyes from his body to the folder he has open, and I feel my cheeks flush when I spot my electricity bill front and center.

"Oh, sorry, no idea how that got in there." I quickly swipe the bill from the folder, knowing he couldn't miss the bright-red overdue stamp, so big it's made for the entire world to see. I had misplaced that one and have been looking for it all week. He keeps looking through the papers, not mentioning it, yet I notice his jaw clench, and my cheeks remain heated. Yep, this is me. Hot mess, borderline broke, single mom.

"The last page is missing from the legacy agreement. Did you sign that one?" He looks up at me, his eyes piercing mine, and I freeze like a deer in the headlights. I should know what he's talking about, but I can't find the connection. I play with my hair, an annoying trait I have when I feel nervous or unsure.

"Um, yes, is it not there?" I squint in confusion, my confidence now dissipating. I was sure I had included everything. I trust Victoria and Tanner, so I just signed everything. It may be incredibly stupid of me, but I had no other option. The one time I try to keep things orderly and I fail miserably.

"No, doesn't appear to be," he confirms, and I grit my teeth.

"I can try to get it to you next week?" I offer, mentally calculating what I need to do. I could ask Kevin to cycle down to deliver it, but that boy does too much already. Plus, his first game is tomorrow, and I want him to sit in his excitement and not worry about chores for the weekend.

"I need to get it submitted in a few days... Tell you what, Tanner has talked me into staying here for the weekend. I'll come by your place and grab it."

I was hoping to avoid him being in my space again, given how it turned out last time. But he's offering, and it's only business. He's just collecting a piece of paper. It's not like anyone will see him and the whole town will talk; he'll be at my place no longer than five minutes.

"If you don't mind..."

"Sure, just no more runaway cows..."

Did he just make a joke?

His lips quirk a little, his eyes sparkling a touch, and it looks good on him.

"I can't promise anything," I tell him honestly, one eyebrow raised and a small smile on my lips. He huffs a laugh and nods.

It appears the city lawyer does have a relaxed side, after all. And I like it.

7

———

SAWYER

It's my first Friday night in Whispers, and I have no idea what I'm doing here. I should be in New York. The Polo Bar is my usual haunt, and it's like it's calling to me. Instead, I'm sitting in a booth at Whiteman's Bar, across from its namesake, with fucking country music playing in the background and some of the oldies from town all dancing in a line on the dance floor, kicking up their boots. To say my life is starting to change would be an understatement. At least the whiskey is good.

"How are you settling in?" Tanner asks.

"I'm not," I tell him straight. Although, I suppose it's not the total truth. Rochelle's coffee at the diner is now something I crave, and the fact that it only takes me five minutes or so to get to my office is a great way to start the day. Less stress, less hustle, it feels surprisingly good.

As another plus, the office redecorating is going well and now feels brand new. It's small, but it reminds me of when I started in law. The office I worked in back then was not that dissimilar to Jerry's, and even though I'm busy, it's kinda nice to have an office to myself, instead of my empire in the city, where I'm dragged into meeting after meeting, half of which should be an email instead. Because of this, I'm much more productive. I only attend key meetings online, take all conference calls remotely, and the rate I'm getting through paperwork is almost baffling.

The place Tanner leased for me on Billionaire Boulevard is luxurious and more my speed. Yet out of everything I've learned and experienced since being here, I keep coming back to Annabelle.

I have no idea why I offered to go back to her place to collect the missing paperwork. Obviously, I'm a glutton for punishment. But I've seen her twice now, and both times, I've been stunned by her beauty. Natural, her blue eyes clear, her hair long and sun-kissed, and she doesn't pander to me like the women I meet in the city. In fact, I'm not actually sure she even likes me at all. Tolerating me is probably more likely. Which is fine by me. I don't want to be hanging around Whispers for any longer than I need to. Maybe I need to get back to New York and go out. Find a nice girl for a while. Although that thought is a little harder to get excited about than it once was.

"You agreed to move here." Of course, he's placing the blame for my animosity back onto me.

"No. I agreed to have an office here. I'll hire some local lawyers, and they can run it, and I can do the rest from the city." I take a sip of whiskey, the finest ever made. Connor looks at Tanner, and then they both look back at me.

"There are no local lawyers in Whispers," Connor says, and Tanner smirks. I'm not sure why I'm still talking at this point. It's futile. Tanner has won, but I'm just too stubborn to admit it.

"I'll find someone nearby, then." I'm adamant about

finding someone else, if for no other reason than to assist with the local paper shuffling that's required here.

"Yeah, if I wanted them, I would've gotten them," Tanner reiterates, and I roll my eyes.

"I'm here, aren't I?" I murmur as my eyes flick around the room, and I sit up when I spot a woman with long blond hair. But as she turns, I realize it isn't who I thought it was. I take a sip of the whiskey, the burn pulling my brain out of my stupid thoughts. I have no time or reason to entertain anything with Annabelle, and I'm not sure why I can't stop thinking about her.

"Thanks for staying the weekend too. I think it's important to have the locals see you out and about. They need to know they can trust you, and the best way to do that is to get to know them when you are out of your suit." Tanner watches me carefully as I play with my whiskey glass on the table, wishing the liquor would numb me already, but it's my first one, so there's no chance of that.

"Smile, Sawyer. It's not all bad." Hudson grins from beside me. He's the local doctor, who also moved here not long ago to run the hospital. Although being raised here, he knew what he was getting into. Me, it's been a baptism by fire.

"At least I'm here with you assholes. Oh, by the way, I need some soaps."

"To wash the cow shit away?" Connor chuckles. Another asshole.

"Sutton is going to promote them on his socials. I thought it may increase interest for them, maybe get some sales for the girls."

All three men look at me like I've lost my mind.

"What?" I shrug, taking another sip of my whiskey.

Tanner's expression turns to one of curiosity. "That's a mighty nice thing to do, Sawyer."

"Think Victoria could organize a box for me or something?"

"Probably, but why don't you ask Annabelle? Help build that relationship with her a bit so she can see you as someone she can come to for help," Tanner offers, and I nod.

For some reason, I don't even hesitate. "Sure. Also, Sutton wants to be the face of your whiskey at some point. He keeps badgering me about it."

Connor nods. "Not a bad idea. His latest movie gives James Bond vibes, so it's probably a good fit. I'll talk to Lacy about it. Might be something we can look at for our latest release."

"Have you spoken to Jerry much?" Tanner asks, and I shake my head.

"No. He isn't handing over a lot. Many of his open files he's completing before he goes. Why?" I wonder what Tanner's getting at. Jerry is an older man, well into his sixties, and from all accounts, he's been here in Whispers his whole life. I'm not sure how he did it. Doing wills and deeds for my entire career would drive me insane. I need the big business, the large commercial deals, and a few criminal cases every now and then to keep me engaged. I never want to rest on my laurels. I always want more.

"Just wondering." As he sips his whiskey, I forget about it, assuming he was wondering about a handover so his precious town doesn't suffer with the changes.

"How's Lacy?" I look at Hudson, changing the subject, and his grin is immediate.

"She's going great." His smile widens. They had a bumpy start but both now seem to have a great life together with his little son Harvey. I'm not ready to settle down, but looking at the three very happy men around me, I do start to wonder if I'll ever meet the one. My vision flashes to the blond farmer who was in my office earlier, how good she looked, and I wonder where her kids were.

"How old is Harvey?" I ask him.

"Almost ten now. Grows up too quickly."

"Does he attend school with Annabelle's boy?"

That has Hudson looking at me with a quirked eyebrow.

"Been here a week or so and already know the locals?" Hudson teases.

"I had to drop off some papers to her the other day. Saw her two kids."

"Kevin and Harvey are close. In the same grade at school. Harvey is excited because Kevin is playing baseball for the first time this year. Annabelle no doubt worked her ass off for that to happen."

Now I want to know more. I don't make a habit of checking out my clients, and I certainly maintain professionalism when around them. But Annabelle is a beautiful woman, there's no denying that, and technically, she isn't my client. Tanner is. She's a strong woman, and proud too, by the speed at which she grabbed that overdue electricity notice from the folder today. My back teeth grind, knowing the few hundred dollars to pay it is sitting in my wallet. I would probably spend that on drinks in one night in the city, but for her, it pays her electricity for a month.

"She has a hard time out there on her farm?"

"Single mom, working at the school now, but before that, she was really struggling. I assume she's still playing catch up with bills and things, not to mention trying to get this soap business off the ground with Victoria. No idea how she does it all. I just have Harvey and find it hard to manage everything, but at least I have Mom and Dad here. She lost her parents a while ago, and then when her husband died, it was just her," Hudson informs me, and my gut feels heavy. I think back to my own childhood and remember how tough it was, my mom working multiple jobs just so Sutton and I could get everything we wanted. I have a newfound sense of appreciation for her and admiration for Annabelle and her kids.

"How did he die?"

"Car accident, apparently. It was about three years ago now. Pretty severe, from what I've heard. Gas tank exploded on impact. It was like a war scene, nothing to recover." I swallow roughly. *Shit.*

"Did Sawyer tell you he's going to sponsor the baseball team?" Connor changes the subject, looking at Hudson with a wicked grin, knowing full well I haven't agreed to anything yet.

"Oh great, you're coming tomorrow? Just bring your checkbook, then." Hudson grins at me as Connor snorts in laughter.

"Nah, might sleep in," I joke, really needing another drink already. This baseball game has been mentioned a few times now, and while I don't mind sponsoring kids' baseball, knowing Annabelle and her sons will be there tomorrow has me a little more intrigued.

"You need to come. It's game day for the kids. Down at the fields behind the school. We're playing Williamstown. They'll be hard to beat but it should be fun."

I sigh before looking at the ceiling. How has my life taken a right turn?

"Fine. I'll do it. How much is it and what time?" I feel a small amount of pride at helping the local community building in my chest as all three men start laughing.

"Team naming rights are a cool thousand dollars... Just

give your check to Bob; he manages all that," Hudson tells me, and I'm surprised it's so cheap, but I don't ask questions.

"Who's Bob?" I ask, not wanting to turn up and hand over a check to the wrong person.

"Runs the hardware store in town. He's sitting over there in the blue overalls." Tanner tips his glass to the side, and I look over, seeing an older guy with a glass of whiskey, chatting with others.

"Of course he does..." This small town is starting to sound more like some sort of secret society, where everyone knows everyone.

"Starts at nine," Hudson continues. "I'll be there. Harvey and the kids need to get there about half an hour before game time."

"Don't worry, Rochelle will be open, and the coffee will be hot," Connor offers.

"Another round, gents?" Tanner stands, a small smile of satisfaction on his face.

"Just get the bottle," I murmur, and he laughs.

"Good to have you here, Sawyer."

"Good to be here." It wasn't my plan, and I still prefer the city, but if I'm going to be here on a semipermanent basis, I should at least try to enjoy it.

8

ANNABELLE

When I pull up to the school parking lot, Kevin is out of the car before it even comes to a stop.

"Kevin!" I slam on the brakes but smile when I hear him laugh as he runs down to the field where all his friends are waiting.

"Kev, Kev!" Noah squeals and I turn off the ignition, grab my things, and get him from the car.

"You want to play baseball one day, Noah?" I ask him as he holds my hand and walks next to me, stumbling a little as we head down to the grassy patch where kids and parents all gather.

"Yes. Baseball is my favorite." He grins, his baby teeth on show. He's the cutest little boy, and I pray every night he never has to experience going without like Kevin has. My stomach drops just thinking about it.

"Good morning, Annabelle. Is Kevin all ready for today?" Hudson, our local doctor and the father of Kevin's friend, Harvey, asks.

"He's so excited. I'm not sure he even slept last night." I

grin, trying to stifle the yawn that threatens because I didn't sleep much either.

"Yeah, I think he'll love it. It's all Harvey's been speaking about this week." Hudson and I stand together, watching them all get ready. The kids look comically small for all the equipment.

"Alright, boys. Let's play ball!" I hear Bob yell from the side. He's the general manager of the team, and all the kids scramble as they gather around their coach, another one of the parents, volunteering his time.

"Ahh, about time he showed up," I hear Hudson say, and I follow his gaze, stalling when I see who he's talking about. Sawyer is walking toward us. He isn't in a suit today. Instead, he's wearing jeans and a Henley, with a jacket over the top. Casual, yet still extremely well put together.

"Is he coming to watch Harvey?" I have no idea why he would be here at a Saturday morning kids' baseball game.

"Yeah, he's also sponsoring the team this year, so I made him come."

"Ohhh…" is all I can muster, still in shock at seeing him here. I watch as Sawyer chats to Bob, shaking hands and passing over something that looks like a check. If he's a sponsor, then it's likely he'll come to more games. I'll probably see him most weekends if he decides to support the team with more than just his bank account.

"Seesaw… Seesaw…" Noah says, giggling, jumping up and down, clearly remembering the man who visited us. At the noise, Sawyer looks up, locking eyes with me.

I offer a small smile as I grip on to Noah's hand, keeping him close as the kids get settled on the field and the game begins. I try to watch, but my eyes continue to flick to Sawyer, where he still stands talking with Bob before their conversation ends and he heads our way.

"Morning," Sawyer says casually to both Hudson and me as he stands next to me. Noah gazes up at him like he's a real-life superhero or something. I'm now in the middle of two men who are both probably worth more than most of the town residents put together.

"Seesaw!" Noah says a little louder, and we all laugh.

"Hey, champ." Sawyer puts out his fist, my little son fist-bumping him, and my chest heats. "Nice to see you, Annabelle." His face is a little softer than the other few times we've met. Must be because it's the weekend and he's out of work mode.

"Didn't pick you as someone who would take in kids' sports on a Saturday morning."

He grins at me, and I squeeze Noah's hand to keep me grounded so I don't swoon.

"Yeah, well, Whispers is growing on me a little." His eyes travel down my front and back up again, and my body tingles. *God, is it hot here?*

"It has that effect on people." A tornado could run through the game at the moment and we wouldn't know. Our gazes are locked, our bodies close enough that I can feel his warmth against my own. I have no idea what's going on, but it's like I'm buzzing just from being this close to him.

"Oh, Harvey's up," Hudson says, popping whatever bubble we just found ourselves in, and we all focus. The pitcher is a big kid, and I wonder if he's the correct age for this group.

"Ahhh, what age group is this?" I didn't look at the details; I just signed Kevin up because I knew he wanted to play so badly.

"We only have enough kids to put one team together, so sometimes that means we play older kids. Not always ideal, but at least our kids get to play," Hudson explains, and I frown as I look back to the field.

The pitch is thrown, and it's fast, but Harvey hits it, immediately running to first base, and we all clap.

"That kid looks like he belongs in high school," Sawyer says, and I look up at him, his brow furrowed, not liking this setup any more than I do. As I look back at the game, Kevin's walking up to the plate.

"Oh, Kevin's up next." My heart feels like it's pounding out of my chest as I try to rein in my excitement and pride at seeing him actually playing sports with his friends.

"He looks confident," Sawyer murmurs, and I see him eyeing the pitcher and then Kevin as they get ready to play and my heart races.

"Kev! Kev!" Noah shouts, and when Kevin looks our way, I give him a wave. We're probably embarrassing him, but he smiles, happy just to be on the field.

"Has Kevin played before?" Sawyer asks me, and I shake my head.

"No. I mean, at school and with his friends, yes, and he's always throwing balls at home, but first time on a team." I pray he hits the ball, but I'm unsure given the size of the pitcher if he'll make contact. I swallow past a lump in my throat, not expecting to be this nervous. I'm starting to understand how parents get a little crazy on the sidelines at sports sometimes. I already need to take a deep breath.

"He's fine. He's got this," Sawyer says quietly and stands a little closer. His eyes are warm and watching me like a hawk. He's offering me his silent support, and I feel a little lightheaded. It's not that I don't have men around me; I just don't have them around me like this. And Sawyer makes me nervous, but not in a bad way. In a way I'm just not used to. I give him a small nod, still praying Kevin makes the hit.

"Here we go," Hudson says, and I squeeze Noah's hands tight, holding my breath as I watch.

The pitcher throws the ball, and it's even faster, moving straight past Kevin and hitting the gloves of the backstop with a thud. I blow out my breath as a few parents clap.

"Oh God, I think I'm going to throw up."

Sawyer looks at me, a little panicked, before I smile and he relaxes.

"Breathe and enjoy the moment. No matter the outcome, they'll always remember that you were here, believing in them." Something about his words makes me think he has firsthand experience. His shoulder nudges mine, the movement catching me a little off guard, but I can't help smiling before we both look back in time for the next pitch, which follows the first, straight into the gloves of the backstop.

"You've got this Kevin!" Sawyer claps like many of the other parents around us, and I inhale sharply. Kevin looks around at us in confusion, watching Sawyer, me, and Hudson, and we all clap for him before he nods to me and then turns back to focus. Determination runs through his bones, and I see it set on his little face.

I hold my breath and squeeze Noah's hand so hard I'm surprised he doesn't yelp as the next pitch is thrown, and it connects. Kevin hits it and hits it well. So well, he stands there in shock for a moment.

"Run!" Sawyer shouts his encouragement, and Kevin drops the bat and runs to first base as Harvey sprints to second.

"Keep going!" Hudson calls out, and the two of them keep running as my heart pounds and I feel my eyes water a little.

"Home! Run home!" Sawyer shouts again as all the kids on his team are jumping up and down, the parents all clapping and cheering. Both Harvey and Kevin run straight home and into the arms of their teammates.

"Well, looks like he has some natural talent." Hudson grins at me before he talks to a parent on his other side. I take a deep breath and compose myself, pride, happiness, and gratitude filling me as I watch my son celebrate with his friends.

"See, I told you he had it." I look up at Sawyer and see him smiling too. He's standing so close, I smell his cologne. Masculine, fresh, the kind that makes me a little weak at the knees. God, it's been a long time since I've smelled anything like that.

"Yeah, he did good." I'm filled with relief now that he has the first hit out of the way.

"So did you." He smiles. He looks good with a smile. His teeth are blinding, but he has kind eyes, and the way he looks at me warms me.

"Sorry, it's all a bit new and overwhelming." I try to compose myself as my emotions run rampant at seeing my little boy enjoy the game he's wanted to play for years but never could. Sawyer looks at me in that assessing way he does, although this time, he holds something more akin to admiration in his gaze.

"Don't apologize, Mama," he says, low and deep, and I think I forget to breathe. I bite the inside of my lip, needing to close my mouth so I don't gape at him.

"I used to love it when my mom came to watch me play baseball as a kid."

I tilt my head to look at him. He's opening up, talking more, and I wonder what Rochelle put in his coffee this morning. Maybe Daisy has some type of special tincture that's used at the diner to ensure their customers are always happy or something.

"You used to play?" I ask, not seeing it. I'm assuming he grew up wealthy, probably went to private school, had a chauffeur and all that.

"Played all through school. It was my sport of choice, until I got a bit older and concentrated on my studies for law school."

"Harvard?" I guess, because that's where all the rich kids go, isn't it?

"No. CUNY. Got a scholarship," he says quickly before looking back at the game while I stare at him, open-mouthed. CUNY is a good school, but not where I thought a rich kid like Sawyer would ever go.

"Smart as well as sporty, then?" I say playfully.

He looks back at me with a little grin on his lips. I like this. Talking, getting to know someone new, someone who doesn't look at me with pity.

"What about you? Did you play sports?"

"Not really. I was more into art and literature. I love having my head stuck in a book or sketching something." I grew up here in Whispers, and if you didn't play sports, there wasn't really too much else to do as a kid. Probably why I gravitated to making soap so well.

"Sketching?"

"Yeah. Just objects, plants, the kids..." I shrug. I feel a little embarrassed, no longer having time for hobbies, yet the pencil and small drawing pad sit untouched at home, where I know one day I will get back into it.

"An artistic bookworm, huh?" He's clearly teasing, and it makes me smile.

"Something like that."

Maybe I misjudged him. Maybe he was just stressed this week over the move and the changes to his law firm. I would imagine it would be a pretty big adjustment for him.

"Will you be home later? I might come by and pick up that paperwork."

My smile falters, and I feel heaviness in the pit of my stomach as realization washes over me that he's making small talk because he wants the paperwork. Of course he does. He's a businessman. They call this networking, and I can't believe I thought it was something more. Disappointment fills me, as does the embarrassment at even thinking a man like Sawyer might be interested in me. A single mom, who lives in the middle of nowhere, struggling to make ends meet. *God, I'm so stupid.*

"Yes. That's fine." I continue giving him a smile, one that doesn't quite meet my eyes. Maybe I need to get out more. I've obviously been in my own world for far too long if I can't decipher business talk from personal interest. I can't even read the plays men make anymore. Not that I ever could. I've only ever been with one man, and he's no longer even alive.

Before he can say anything else, some of the women from town come up and start talking, asking Sawyer questions, and he's pulled away. The women crowd around him, some moms I know from school and other women whom I never would've assumed to be at the kids' sporting fields before. They're obviously not here to watch anyone. I take Noah's hand and lead him away from what's clearly a flirt fest with our newest resident.

With Kevin now on the bench, Noah and I hit the playground to burn off some of his energy. Because the new guy in town is not for a girl like me. I need to remember that.

9

———

ANNABELLE

Kevin has been on cloud nine all afternoon. Sawyer left not long after Kevin's home run, then after the game, the team all went for a quick sundae at the diner, care of the lovely Dr. Hamilton. Seeing my son glow with his teammates was the icing on the cake to a terrific morning, one which I hope we can repeat often.

"Did you see that big pitcher, Ma? Did you see how fast he threw the ball at me?" Kevin asks for what feels like the twentieth time today.

I laugh, my grin wide. "I did. You were awesome, honey."

The whole place looks like a tornado has gone through it as he and Noah run around, even though I cleaned it from top to bottom last night. But as I chop the vegetables and get them on to boil, checking the roast chicken in the oven, the smell of my homemade dinner wafts through the air, and I feel very blessed.

"What's he doing here?"

I look up quickly, seeing Kevin peering out the window,

and I move to follow his gaze to the now somewhat familiar shiny black truck. *Sawyer.*

"Sawyer mentioned coming by to grab some paperwork. Be on your best behavior." I look between him and Noah, ensuring they remember their manners. I'm surprised he's here, because even though he mentioned stopping by, I didn't think he'd still come. It's now almost six, the sun is setting, and it's dinnertime for us. I assumed he would've been here earlier, and when he didn't show, I figured he might come by tomorrow.

As his truck pulls up to the house, I wipe my hands on my kitchen towel and glance around. I should scramble to tidy up, but this is my life. This is my reality.

It doesn't help that I'm still a mess from my yard work earlier, wearing my favorite pair of worn-in jeans and t-shirt, my hair in a messy bun, but I've seen him sitting in shit, so we're even. Without another thought about my house or my appearance, I move to open the door.

"Hi," I yell from the open door as he jumps out of the truck. He's still dressed in the same attire from the game earlier, and I'd be lying if I said my breath didn't stall in my chest watching him walking toward me. His Henley top is fitted, showcasing muscles in his arms I didn't realize he had hiding underneath his polished suits. Like this, he could be mistaken for a nice country boy, not the uncrumpled city lawyer he is. But it's his smile that has me grabbing the door so I don't topple. It's bigger than this morning. Like he's actually glad he's here and not frustrated about driving all this way just to pick up paperwork that I forgot to give him.

"Hope I'm not intruding?" Looking right at me, he steps onto the porch.

"No, it's fine. Come in," I offer, opening the door and

letting him follow me inside. "Let me just find that other page of the contract for you."

Moving to the table where I'm sure I left it, I start flipping through the small piles of paperwork and school supplies that I'm sorting this weekend. I tried to look for it earlier and couldn't find it, so I'm not confident it's here. At a guess, I'm assuming Noah has taken it and used it for drawing with crayons, and I'll find it scrunched into a ball in the rubbish, but I'll at least pretend that I'm trying. At that moment, Noah decides he wants me and runs into my leg, cuddling my thigh, leaving me a little restricted before I pick him up, put him on my hip, and continue the search.

"It was a good game today. Nice hitting, Kevin."

My son seems to almost shy away from Sawyer's comment before he speaks. "Thanks," is all he offers. He's a kid of few words when it comes to outsiders. I know it's because of his life these past few years. No time to be a kid with all the responsibilities he's had. He was young when his father passed and hasn't really had a male figure in his life since.

I'm about to add my own glowing thoughts on my son's game, when I hear something boil over on the stove in the kitchen.

"Oh no!" Striding to the kitchen, I would put Noah down, but his tenancy to run around and get into things is not something I need him doing when we have company, hot food on the stove, and missing paperwork.

"Do you need a hand?" Sawyer tentatively steps closer. I'm moving quickly, trying to get things taken care of as best I can with one hand, to no avail.

"Here, can you take Noah?" Without thinking, I offer him my son. Sawyer looks like a deer in headlights but he has little time to think about it before we both get burned, so I thrust Noah into his arms and I step back to the stove, moving quickly to prevent flames and my vegetables from searing.

When the small crisis is over, I look back to where they stand, and I stall. Sawyer is holding Noah out from his body like he has some disease.

He held him like that last time too. I have to hold back a chuckle. "Looks like you've never held a child before…"

"I haven't," he says all too seriously, and my eyebrows rise.

"Really?" I wonder how that's possible. Everyone has held a child at some point, haven't they?

"I have one brother, but we're only a year apart."

"No nieces or nephews?" I'm keen to learn more about the man standing in my kitchen, holding my child, as he slowly brings him to his body, holding him tighter to his chest. Tentatively, like he's getting used to the feel of it, deciding if he likes it or not.

Sawyer huffs a laugh. "No. He's too busy jet-setting around the world."

"Much like you?" I assume that's what someone like Sawyer does. I know he has his own jet. It's parked at the airport, and the town talks.

"What do you mean?" He frowns in confusion as he wrangles Noah, and I bite my lip at how weirdly domesticated it looks.

"Well, you have a jet, don't you? From what I hear, you fly in and out of here most weeks."

"My travel is for work, not pleasure." Again, it's all work from him. I need to remember that.

"Well, you have a way with them," I offer with a shrug, trying to be kind. Because it's true. Noah now has his head down on Sawyer's shoulder, his hands gripping on to his shirt collar. He's clearly comfortable with the businessman.

"Jets?" his brow is pinched, as Noah grabs his ears, and once again, I have to hold back a chuckle from bubbling from my mouth.

"No, kids." I nod to how my tired son rests against him, and Sawyer looks down, taking it in. "You're a natural. Noah doesn't really just go to anyone."

My boy is a bundle of energy, so seeing him like this with a man he barely knows is unusual. But I firmly believe that small kids are pretty good judges of character.

"Hmmm. He's warm," is all Sawyer says, not in a hurry to remove my son from his chest.

Smiling, I hold out my arms. "Here, let me take him. He's already eaten, so I'll put him down, then I'll try to find that contract." I grab Noah from Sawyer, and my boy snuggles into me.

"Make yourself at home. I won't be long."

Kevin is sitting on the sofa, watching TV, ignoring the whole situation as I walk by. Just as I step into the hallway, I notice Sawyer looking around the house. Not snooping but seemingly interested. As predicted, Noah is almost asleep before I even put him in bed, so a quick tuck in and he's in dreamland.

When I get back to the living area, Kevin hasn't moved, and I spot Sawyer looking at some framed photos on the side wall.

"You and the kids look good in these," he says in passing as I once again start looking for the contract, knowing that it's futile.

"Thanks." I smile warmly. I love having a lot of photos around. It makes a house a home, in my opinion.

"I can't help noticing there are none of your husband."

My gaze flicks to his in surprise. I quickly look at Kevin, who's now watching the interaction, and I swallow roughly.

I keep my response simple. "No. There aren't."

I feel his gaze resting on me, waiting for me to say more, but I don't. There's only one photo of my husband in this house, and that's in a box in the cupboard, which I'm keeping just for the kids. There are no others, because I don't want there to be. My eyes return to the piles of papers in front of me, but my mind races.

Before he can ask any more questions, I ask, "Have you eaten?"

"Excuse me?" His head tilts slightly as he turns to face me.

"Eaten. Dinner?" I repeat.

"Oh, no, I haven't eaten yet." He shakes his head.

"Would you like to stay...? For... dinner?" Why I'm asking him for dinner to avoid more conversation about my late husband, who knows? It just came out, and now I can barely put a sentence together.

"I don't want to impose." His eyes flick to the kitchen, and I know how good it smells. I wonder when he last had a home-cooked dinner was, assuming he isn't a cook himself.

"You imposed the minute you drove through my gate." A small, teasing smile dances on my lips as I look at him pointedly.

"Well, since I'm here..." he murmurs, his mouth quirking to the side. Something about the sight has me feeling warm all over.

I really hope this isn't a terrible idea.

10

SAWYER

My mouth's watering, and I'm not sure if it's because of the delicious smells coming from her kitchen or the way she looks at me with that small sassy grin she has or the way her eyes alight when she gets a little cheeky.

All three have my senses on overload. I have no idea what the hell I'm doing. But I like talking to her. I like seeing her do life. I like spending time getting to know her. And I sure as hell like looking at her.

"I've made extra, so there's plenty." She stands at her table, still rummaging through papers that look like they've been sitting there for a while. She's lost the contract. No doubt about it. I notice that she twirls her hair when she's unsure or fibbing about something, which she's doing now. She would be a terrible poker player. I smile, the action happening more today, with her, in Whispers, than it has with any other woman in a long time.

"Great, thank you." I admire her some more as she walks into the kitchen. For a woman of the land, she's graceful, deliberate, sure of herself in a way that isn't obvious. Like a quiet confidence. I'm finding it hard to look away from her, and she lifts her head to look at me quickly, catching me and pausing as our eyes meet.

My mouth curves, and in return, I get a small smile, her cheeks tinting pink before she goes back to what she's doing. I huff a laugh to myself, my chest tingling, feeling like an excited teenager all over again. Peeling my eyes from her, I look at Kevin, who hasn't moved from the sofa where he's watching baseball on TV. I get the feeling he might be obsessed with it. Probably not the time to tell him I am part owner of one of the major league clubs.

Stepping into the kitchen, I ask, "Can I help with anything?"

"Oh, um… sure. Here, can you mix the gravy?"

When I pause, because I've never mixed gravy, she looks up at me. "You know how to mix gravy, right?"

"Pfft, sure." I have no clue. But I step forward, taking the spoon from her, and start to whisk. I don't miss her smile, and it's doing something to my insides. "So law, baseball sponsor, and now professional gravy stirrer. My resume is growing."

"Well, if you do gravy well, you'll be promoted to chicken carver." Chuckling lightly, she slices through the roast chicken with precision.

"Something tells me never to come between you and that knife…" I tease.

"You know what they say…" She toys with me, lips pursed and eyes on mine, and I think my grin is now permanent. I have no idea what I'm doing. I've never cooked with a woman before. Maybe that makes me an asshole, but it's the truth. "A woman with a knife is just like her blade, dangerous if underestimated."

I laugh when she winks, liking her snippets of humor, although I'm sure her words are accurate.

Too busy looking at her, hot gravy spills onto my shirt. "Shit."

"Oh no, let me help." She quickly grabs a damp cloth and steps closer. As she dabs at my chest, cleaning up the gravy, our bodies are almost touching. She registers the closeness at the same time, and her movements stop as she looks up.

"Sorry, I, um..."

"It's okay. I'm the klutz." I put my hand over the top of hers, where it still rests on my chest.

"It shouldn't stain." She sucks a deep breath, her chest pushing out and brushing my own. My lungs fill with her rose scent, the freshness nearly making me stumble.

"I was so focused on you and the knife, I wasn't paying attention."

"Gravy can also be dangerous if underestimated." She rolls her lips so she doesn't laugh at me, and I chuckle, shaking my head as she steps away, my body instantly feeling the loss.

"Kevin, dinner!" Annabelle calls out as she dishes up what looks to be a mini feast. I grab the gravy, my one and only contribution, placing it on the table. "Come. Sit." Her eyes sparkle as she looks at me, and I take a seat where she indicates. She sits at the head of the table and Kevin sits opposite me.

Looking at the meal presented, my stomach rumbles. I shouldn't be hungry; I normally don't eat until late. But seeing the roast chicken, beans, fresh carrots, mashed potatoes, and gravy has my mouth watering all over again. I haven't eaten a home-cooked meal like this in years.

"Kevin, honey. Say grace."

I look up, surprised, as I see Annabelle and Kevin holding hands, and she offers me her other hand. It's small, delicate, and although I know she works with her hands on the farm, her nails are neat, a soft pink polish coating them. As I place her hand in mine, I feel the softness of her skin, my own hand tingling at her touch.

Holding her hand firmly, I watch where we connect for a moment, this whole thing feeling both completely out of place for me, yet one hundred percent comfortable. Her eyes lift and meet mine again, and our fingers intertwine. My shoulders lower instantly, and without thinking, I rub my thumb up to her wrist, caressing her skin slightly. She looks at me, the energy swirling between us almost palpable before I clear my throat and we both look at Kevin.

I can't remember the last time I sat at a dinner table like this, in someone's modest home and said grace. Saying grace was something we did as kids. My mother always ensured that we were thankful for our food, but as we got older, it fell to the wayside. I put my other hand across the table to Kevin, who takes it, and as we all join hands, Annabelle lowers her head and closes her eyes. Her movements are effortless, gratitude for what she has evident. Her hair falls across her face, hiding her from me, but I find that my eyes don't move from her, eager to get any glimpse of her that I can.

Talking with her briefly this morning at the game felt nice. Having never been to a kids' baseball game before, it was something new, but I didn't hate it. It was very much a community event, and like Tanner said, it's a good place to get to know people. To see her watching Kevin play, the emotions so clear on her face, the way she never let go of Noah. I feel like her heart is huge, bringing a sense of warmth and care to those around her.

For a beat, I wonder if I'm losing my mind. Maybe there's something in the water here in Whispers that has me completely forgetting who I am. A city lawyer, who likes fast cars, has expensive tastes, and enjoys beautiful women at my beck and call. A town like Whispers is the last place I ever thought I would be. Yet these past few weeks, my business hasn't suffered; my new little office is quiet, enabling me to be more productive, and my city teams are self-sufficient, used to not always having me around anyway. I'm enjoying this small town more than I ever thought possible, not that I would admit that to Tanner just yet. But it's growing on me, the pace of life here, the possibilities, the stress-free environment that still feels like there's something meaningful happening that I don't want to miss out on. And *her*. Annabelle completely has my attention, especially now, as her hand settles into mine like it was always meant to be there. The weird thing is how comfortable I feel sitting here, at this old timber table, a simple, yet beautiful meal on offer, with a woman who's starting to infiltrate my daily thoughts and her son, who looks at me with a curious eye, like he doesn't trust me, like he doesn't trust anyone.

"Dear Lord, we thank you for this food we are about to receive..." Kevin starts and looks up briefly at me, before his eyes move to where I'm holding his mom's hand, and he frowns. "...and for the company of *Sawyer the Lawyer*." He says it in a smart-ass tone, smirking up at me. "Thank you for helping me get a home run in my first game today and for making me the cool kid for once. Amen."

"You're always the cool kid, Kevin." She squeezes his hand, mine still holding her other.

"You're my ma, you're supposed to say that." He's sweet to her. They grin at each other, the love they have for one another obvious.

"Well, let's eat." Annabelle's voice is upbeat as I let go of her hand and we start to dig in. Taking a bite, I almost groan. It's the kind of homemade dinner that kids love when they get home after a big trip or when they've been away at college for too long. The kind of food that makes you feel like you're eating right, feeding your body and your heart what it needs. You can tell it was made with love.

"So, did you love your first game, Kevin?" I ask, though it's clear he did. I'm just feeling like it's going to take some effort to get him to like me even a little.

"Yeah," is all he offers me, barely looking at me as he shovels food into his mouth.

"He loves baseball, watches it all the time," Annabelle says, giving Kevin a stern look.

"Who's your favorite team?" I know he has one if his TV viewing is anything to go by.

"The Mets."

I smile at that. "They're my favorite too."

Kevin doesn't acknowledge my response, continuing to eat like he hasn't seen food in over a decade.

"Kevin's been working outside with me all afternoon. He's famished," Annabelle tells me, and I start to understand the pressure this young kid must feel. Not from his mother, but from himself. It's something I also endured when I was younger, wanting to be the support my mom needed and putting my own needs aside to help the family more.

"So what did you do today after the game?"

"Well, Hudson paid for the team to celebrate at the diner with a sundae, and then we came home and had work to do around here in the afternoon." There's a little weariness in her eyes.

"Do you have any help?" Surely it isn't just her.

"Oh no, it's just Kevin and me." I take a bite of my chicken, not liking her answer.

"So you do everything around here? You don't have a farmhand or anything?" A farm this size would be a full-time job.

"Yeah, it's just us. It isn't too bad. I prefer it. I like to see what the plants are doing each day, and if I had someone else here, it may interrupt the quality. Everything here is organic. I don't use sprays or fertilizers unless it's organic compost. I wouldn't want to have to worry about anyone following the rules." She takes a drink of water, stopping herself from saying anything else. I'm sure I saw somewhere that their soap is organic, but I had no concept of what that really means from a farming perspective. Clearly there's a higher workload, given the increased quality control. She doesn't take the easy route, that's for sure.

"What do you do when you go away or are sick?"

She looks at me like I have two heads.

"Um… well, I don't go away, and when I'm sick, I just work through it," she says like it's the most normal thing to work yourself to the bone and then keep on working.

"And you work at the school too?"

"Yes, they were so kind in offering me a teaching support position a little while ago. I work in a variety of classrooms and with a variety of subjects. Wherever they need me, really. It's great, because one day I might be assisting in art class, and another, I'm helping kids to read. I like the variety."

"So where do you find the time for soapmaking?" I wonder how she fits it all in.

"At night, mostly. Sometimes on the weekends. It just

depends on what's going on and what the stock levels are like."

I sit back as a renewed sense of admiration fills me. I'm a workaholic. I constantly have my head in my phone or eyes on files. It's obviously something we have in common.

"Enough about me. Tell me, how are you feeling about Whispers now that you have seen our beloved juniors win the baseball game this morning?" She grins, and it's contagious.

"Well, these first few weeks have been... interesting," I tell her honestly.

"I'm surprised you're spending the weekend here. I thought you'd be back in the city already." She laughs, and I join her. She's beautiful every time I see her, but here, at her table, relaxed like this, she's glowing.

"I was planning to be, but Tanner wanted me to spend the weekend here. Get to know the locals, support the kids' baseball team, and let people see me around town."

"Probably a good idea. I mean, if you want people to trust you, they need to see you. That's the thing about small towns, as soon as someone new turns up, they're the latest obsession."

"It's nice to meet new people, like this morning, but I was happy just talking with you."

Our eyes connect, before mine flit lower and settle on her lips. The soft pink is almost taunting me.

"May I be excused?" Kevin pushes out his chair abruptly, the sound bringing Annabelle and me back to the present. His plate might as well be licked clean, his stomach obviously full, and he clearly doesn't want to sit and speak with the adults.

"Sure, honey." Annabelle's voice carries so much affection, it's disarming. Kevin quickly goes back to the TV, switching the game on and becoming engrossed immediately.

"Sorry, we don't usually have people over for dinner. He's probably a bit unsure of things."

I shake my head and wave it off. "It's fine. Not much stands between me and baseball either."

"Oh, well, you're welcome to sit with Kevin and watch the game," she offers, like she's prohibiting me from doing what I really want to do. But what I really want to do is sit and talk with her.

"I'm fine right here. I'll choose you over baseball any day of the week." And it's the truth. I don't even know what I'm doing, other than realizing how good it feels to talk with someone, enjoy a nice meal, a quiet home, and a bit of flirting. Away from the crowded bars in the city, the loud music, and hustle and bustle of people at the clubs I used to go to. I'm not lying, I would choose her and this over that, no question.

Her gaze is full of trepidation, her cheeks turning a cute shade of pink, before she asks, "So, you have a brother?"

I nod. "I do. He lives in LA."

"I've never been, but the weather looks great there. Do you get to see him much?" Her blue eyes twinkle a little in the overhead lights, her shoulders relaxed.

"Not really. We try. Maybe a few times a year. He works in the movie business, so he's always traveling."

Those pretty eyes widen. "Oh, wow. I guess you do need to live in LA for a job like that."

"His name is Sutton. Sutton Silvers." I wait to see the look of recognition. Sutton has been a movie star for a few years now, so people screaming his name and asking for autographs is constant whenever I'm with him. I'm not sure how he copes with it all. It's one of the most common questions I get when I'm dating in the city. The women I meet generally already know who I am and who my brother is.

"That's a nice name." It hits me that she has no idea who he is.

"He's pretty well known…" I still get nothing from her, other than slight confusion in her gaze. "He has a big social media following actually, and I said I might send him some of your soaps, you know, so he can promote them to his followers, maybe give Gertie's a bit of promotion?"

I see her head working at that, her eyebrows lifting. "Um… okay. Wow. I mean, any support would be great. We're trying to expand our distribution, as you know, but Victoria handles all that. I just make them." She acts like what she does is no big deal, when it's actually the biggest part of any business.

"Don't do that."

"Do what?"

"Diminish yourself. You're talented. You work hard. There would be no Gertie's without you. There would be none of this without you." I gesture to the food and the house. My mom used to do that. Still does sometimes. She carried the weight of everything but never wanted kudos. Annabelle needs to know that she's amazing.

"I guess I just see it as a little hobby. I want it to grow, of course. I enjoy making the soaps and it's nice to work with Victoria and Tanner. But I don't always understand the business side of things, so I guess I just keep my influence small…"

"I'm here now. I'll help you with anything I can. I'll explain the contracts if you need me to. I'll send the soap to my brother. Who knows, the girls might love seeing his naked body lathered in soap so much, they'll buy you out." My joke brings another smile to her face.

I admire her, a woman who's clearly a hard worker and fantastic mom, a woman who's not swayed by big names or money, a woman who underestimates her skills and her place in the world. She's a complete contrast to anyone I've ever met before. In New York, everyone is out for something.

"Tanner mentioned that you might have a box of soaps here I could send him?"

"Probably something I should've offered to you on your last visit after the cow manure..." She looks both like she's about to laugh and cringe, and I chuckle.

"Not sure one box would've been enough." My smile is wide with the memory of that day, and her laugh finally escapes. I watch, mesmerized, as her face lights up, her smile widening and her head falling back, and I'm glad I'm sitting down because she's so stunning I'd otherwise be knocked on my ass.

Gathering myself before she notices my staring, I ask, "Have you always lived out here?" I now want to know everything about her.

She stands, starting to clear the table of our dishes, and I follow her lead to help. I notice that besides from the TV, it's eerily quiet. No streetlights on, no cars driving past. Aside from the occasional bellow of an animal, it's silent.

"All my life. This farm belonged to my parents and my grandparents before them."

"So it's a generational thing?" I'm intrigued, her being all the way out here now making more sense. The history of the place is something that captures my interest. Family is important to her. If I didn't pick up that fact by the way she's close with her boys, I see it coming through now.

"Yes, although, I farm it a little differently than they did.

My parents and grandparents mainly had cattle and other animals. I'm trying to cultivate the land and the rich soil to produce the best lavender and roses I can. Obviously, I still have some cows and chickens..." she looks at me with that cheeky smile, clearly alluding to the cow shit again, "...but they are more for consumption than profit."

She lives off the land, I can see that. Her vegetable patch is huge, probably the size of a backyard swimming pool. I know Kevin milks cows, since that's how Tanner knows him so well. No doubt the chickens outside provide the eggs, so she would be reasonably self-reliant out here. An easy environment to become isolated, if you're not careful. Seeing her resilience and entrepreneurial spirit coming out, I'm starting to learn that this woman has many layers, and each one I peel back intrigues me more than the last.

We stand in the kitchen, and I look around, not seeing a dishwasher in sight. In fact, she doesn't have a lot of modern appliances. The TV looks decades' old, the sofas and rugs tattered and worn, no microwave or toaster. It needs a renovation, and while I can't see the rest of the house beyond the living room, the outside is enough to tell me that it would probably blow over in a small breeze. I watch her concentrating on what she's doing at the sink, and she bites her lower lip as she scrubs a dish. I need to swallow the growl that feels like it might escape, suddenly wanting to be the one biting that lip.

"How do you do it?" I ask her quietly, and her head swivels to look at me.

"What do you mean?" Her eyes search mine, and I swallow.

"How do you do it all?" We're standing close, our voices low. Kevin's totally engrossed in the TV, the commentary loud throughout the house. I look down at her, her soft pink lips parted slightly, her blue gaze looking me square in my eye. I'm barely breathing as my gaze darts between her eyes and her lips. My body wants to lean in, just for a little taste.

"Because I have to," she whispers, and as we look at each other, her hair falls, a strand coming across her cheek, and with her hands wet in the sink, I don't hesitate before I lift my hand, bringing it to her face. But before I can push her hair behind her ear, she flinches, and I still.

"Shit, I'm sorry," I say immediately. "What was that?" My heart is racing, my body unmoving.

"Nothing." She forces a smile on her face, huffing a weird laugh that's not humorous but awkward. My blood starts to boil at what her reaction could mean.

"Annabelle. Who..." I lower my hand, not touching her. It's clear someone has touched her, and it wasn't in the same way I want to.

"Yes! Home run!" Kevin yells, and Annabelle jumps like she's been burned, then moves away, breaking the moment. I run my fingers through my hair and blow out a breath, not liking this at all.

"You know, let me just see if I can find that paperwork and grab that box of soap. I don't want you driving home too late in the dark." She dries her hands on the kitchen cloth and moves past me, not looking my way, and I feel on edge. I'm not stupid. There's only one reason a woman flinches like she just did, and I'm feeling very fucking protective of her about now.

"Annabelle..." I step toward her slowly, taking a breath to calm myself, not sure what to say with Kevin in earshot.

"It has to be here somewhere." Her voice sounds nervous, her movements a little jerky and shaky. I step up beside her, giving Kevin my back, offering her some privacy from him for this conversation.

"I would never hurt you," I grit out softly, hoping she can hear my sincerity.

She looks up at me, those large blue eyes of hers filled with so many emotions.

"I know. I'm sorry…" She shakes her head, releasing a heavy breath.

I frown. "You have nothing to be sorry for. I want you to know that I'd never lay a hand on a woman, and I'm sorry if that's something you've had experience with." I breathe through my nose, because my teeth are clenched so tightly, I'm bound to break a tooth.

"Thank you, Sawyer. But I'm fine. Really." Her hand finds mine. It's a small move, but I grab on to her small palm and squeeze it, then I lift my other hand and slowly bring it to her cheek, brushing the hair from her face like I tried to before. She lets me this time, my touch so light I can barely feel her face.

I knew Annabelle was special from the moment I first laid eyes on her, ready to end my life with a garden hoe and scalding me for my language. But it's becoming increasingly clear to me that this woman, while young, has had a lot of life experience and much of it's not so positive.

My city charms aren't going to work on her like they usually do with women in the city. It shouldn't be surprising; she's nothing like them, and in the best way possible.

"Let me just look in this pile." A small smile dances on her lips as she breaks the tension, and I drop my hand from her face and let go of her other hand as she gets busy, looking among some more paperwork that's scattered on the table.

I look out the small window that's above her kitchen sink, seeing it's pitch-black already, even though it can't be much past seven. There are no lights, the cloud cover tonight hiding the moon so that doesn't even create a glow on the land. Anyone or anything could be out there, and you wouldn't even know it.

"I can just print a new one for you to sign," I tell her, following her into the living space.

"I'm sure it's here somewhere, but that might be for the best." She runs her hands down the front of her thighs before she plays with her hair again. We both know she's lost it.

"Oh, here. For your brother." She sidesteps and grabs a small box of soaps from a shelf, sitting among papers and crayons and a myriad of other things. The whole setup should give me anxiety. Nothing is in place, most things in disarray, yet I feel more at home here with her than I have in a long time.

"Thanks for dinner," I say as we both head toward her front door.

"Of course. Thanks for the company." Her cheeks pinken, and I bite the inside of mine. She's cute when she's nervous. I quickly look over at Kevin who hasn't moved.

"Bye, Kevin."

I get a grunt in return, his eyes not moving from the TV.

Once we walk out the door, Annabelle stands on the porch as I walk down the steps and look around. The darkness almost shrouds me, and a chill runs up my back. Aside from the lights of the house creating a glow around Annabelle, it's darker than I'm used to experiencing in the city. I listen for any sounds, but there are none. Her neighbors are so far away, they wouldn't even hear her scream.

"Are you sure you're alright out here?" I turn to look at her, not really wanting to leave her.

"We're fine." She swallows and plays with her hair again. My little liar.

"Have you got your phone?" I walk back to the porch, taking the steps two at a time before I'm right back in front of her.

"Ahh... sure?" She looks confused as she pulls it from her back pocket.

"Unlock it." It's more like a demand, so I clarify. "Just in case you need anything or just if you want to talk."

Quirking her eyebrow, she unlocks it and hands it to me. I put in my number before handing it back.

"You going to rush back from the city to little ole me?" she jokes, and I grit my teeth, not liking the fact that I wouldn't be here, even if she did call.

"My jet's pretty fast; you would be amazed at how quickly I could be here."

"A real-life Superman, then."

My smile doesn't meet my eyes, because I don't like leaving her out here alone. She looks up at me, and I lean down, my body moving before I really think about it. I press a tender kiss on her cheek, so close to her lips, all she would need to do is turn her face and her lips would be on mine.

I hear her sharp intake of air, but I pull back just as quickly, seeing the flush to her cheeks as she smiles. Biting my bottom lip, I step away from her, walking backward to my truck.

"Thanks again for dinner, Annabelle." I can't remember the last time I had a good time on a date and was so hesitant to leave.

"You're welcome, Sawyer." Her voice is so soft, I almost dash back to her and take her lips with mine. Instead, I grit my teeth and force my feet to move away from her. And as I jump in the truck and drive away, my stomach feels heavy. I tell myself it's because she's out here alone and it isn't safe. But the truth is, even if she lived on the busiest street in New

York, I still wouldn't want to leave her. My eyes flick to the rearview mirror as I make my way down her driveway, seeing her silhouette on the porch, watching me the entire way. This is the second time I'm seeing her this way, and I like it a little less every time.

11

ANNABELLE

"Boys! We need to go!" The school rush of the morning is usually fraught with speed, due to the few farm chores we need to complete before we even start getting ready for school. But we all slept in a little more than usual, the busy weekend obviously catching up with us.

"Coming! Have you seen my shoes?" I hear Kevin yell from down the hall as I dig into my bag to find my keys and open the front door.

It's a beautiful day. The sun is shining, and I've been feeling good ever since Sawyer stopped by and had dinner with us. He's the first man I've taken any romantic interest in, in a long time, and I'm still not sure that's smart. My initial thoughts on him have tempered, and while he's still immaculately dressed without a hair out of place, we found some common ground.

I tried to keep things professional, keep things friendly. I mean, it was dinner, but I assume it's okay to have dinner with a client. But then, when we were in my kitchen and he pushed back my hair, I was almost scared to breathe. When

I flinched, his gaze of surprise turned angry pretty quickly. I know he wouldn't hurt me; I feel it deep in my bones that he's a good guy. But old habits are hard to break, and the last time a man touched me, he almost broke my jaw.

I haven't had a man touch me as gently as Sawyer did, ever. Steve was somewhat charming when we first fell in love, but we were both teenagers, our movements clumsier. I can't even remember the last time I orgasmed. I touch my cheek now, still feeling Sawyer's soft touch, my skin tingling at the memory, wondering what it would be like to kiss him.

"They're here at the door!" I yell back to Kevin as I dash outside to start the car. I think about when Sawyer left the other night, watching his truck slowly drive away, his tail-lights getting smaller and smaller until I couldn't see them anymore and the darkness consumed me once again, making me feel alone. Stupid, really. I hardly know the guy, and I've lived here alone most of my adult life. But there's something about him that puts me at ease. For a country girl like me, a lawyer from the city should be the last person who makes me feel safe, yet he does.

As I get to the car, I go to open the door to throw my bag in but pull up short. The world around me tilts a little, and I wonder if I'm seeing things.

"We're coming," I hear Kevin say from near the front door, Noah giggling right next to him, but I don't look up. Instead, I look at my front tire, the one that has a big slash across it, and my nerves spike.

"Ummmm... We have a flat. Let me just... Um..." My pulse races, and I try to keep it together, but panic, fear, and disbelief all rush through me. The same feelings that my husband used to evoke when he'd come home late at night, after having too many drinks at Whiteman's Bar with his buddies. Knowing what would happen when he walked in the door is exactly how I feel right now. I look up and around, trying to see something, someone, anything. But as usual, there's nothing and no one. Everything else is as it should be. There are no tire marks in my driveway, no damage anywhere else.

"Oh. Wow," Kevin says, coming to stand next to me.

"It's fine. Let me get the jack, and I'll change it real quick."

I should probably call the sheriff, but there's no evidence of anything. I already know how to change a tire, so he could offer me little else. He'll probably just think I'm going mad. Maybe blame the kids for playing around or something. But there's no doubt that my tire is slashed. Had it blown, we would've heard it, and even if we didn't, there would be pieces of rubber nearby. No, this is a clean cut, the rubber sliced by something that was clearly very sharp.

I move on autopilot as I grab the jack and tools I need from the trunk and get to work. The nice clothes I put on this morning, feeling good about myself after Sawyer's visit, are instantly dirty from where I kneel, bringing me right back to reality. Ensuring that my daydreaming about a handsome man in a suit remains just that. Reaffirming that he isn't part of my reality.

Gosh, if Sawyer could see me now, I'm sure he would run. I can't even stay clean for more than five minutes. But his words come flooding back to me. To not diminish myself and my achievements. To be honest, I do it so often it's almost a natural response. I don't even think about it. But all day yesterday, I reflected on my life and how much I do and how much I've accomplished.

I think about calling Sawyer. Maybe he'll know what to do. A flat tire, I can change, but a slashed tire means someone was here. On my property. While I was sleeping. A shiver runs through me, and I wipe my brow as the morning sun beats down, my arms already tired as I pull off the slashed tire and put the new one on. I've never had anyone to call before. But he's likely already back in New York, doing real legal work, not that of a crazy single mom who's probably just seeing things. Besides, he didn't mention how long he was staying this week, and he's a busy guy. If he's already flown back to the city, then who knows when he will be back in Whispers.

Noah starts playing around, his legs jittery from waiting too long, and the fright and agitation start to consume me more.

"Noah!" I yell, so much it startles me. I never yell at my kids, and it shows by the looks on their faces.

"Sorry." I take a breath. "Please just hold Kevin's hand and stay close, okay?" I tell him, and both boys do what I ask, watching me carefully as I quickly take another look around, feeling unsafe in my own home.

"You okay, Ma?" Kevin asks quietly.

"Yeah, of course. Nothing to worry about. We'll just be a little late for school." Knowing that by the time we get going and drop Noah off to his sitter and then get to school, we'll miss the first period.

"It's okay." Kevin's hand rests on my shoulder, and I close my eyes. I try to calm my breathing, my emotions getting the better of me. My son is giving me the little strength I need to keep going today. I squeeze my eyes shut as disappointment fills my bones. I started today on cloud nine. Now the tire has dragged me right back to the ongoing feeling of never being able to get myself out of this situation.

"You're not just saying that because you have a math test first period, are you?" I tease, trying to lighten the mood.

"Well..." He tries to hide his smile.

I grin, glad he isn't feeling scared like me. Kevin isn't stupid. He may be young, but he's seen and experienced blown tires and flats before. He knows by looking at this that it isn't normal.

"How did that happen, Ma?" he asks, confirming my thoughts.

"I probably just ran over a nail." I grab at my loose strands of hair, pushing them back.

"But it's cut, Ma."

I shrug it off. "Then I ran over a sharp object."

"Maybe the ghosts did it?" he mutters, and I look up at him sharply.

"The what?"

"I feel like sometimes I see him..." There's a flicker of terror in his eyes as he says it.

"See who, honey?" I wonder what he's seen; maybe it could explain some things.

"Dad."

I go rigid, my heart nearly stopping. Kevin was young when his father died, but he has seen photos of him. While I don't want to have Steve's eyes following me all around the house, I do think it's important for his son to remember him.

"I dream about him too sometimes, honey." I rub his arm, making sure he feels safe, even though I'm lying through my teeth. He fills my nightmares, never my dreams.

"No. Not in my dreams."

"What do you mean?" My brow furrows, wondering what he's getting at.

"I mean, sometimes when I'm out in the fields, checking the cows or the lavender after school, I see him."

Maybe I'm working him too hard. He's clearly seeing things. Just like me, it seems.

"Your father died in that car crash, honey. The car was

burned. I know you miss him. But he isn't here." I swallow roughly as Kevin nods.

"I know."

"But if it happens again, make sure you tell me. We don't want anyone on our land. No trespassers, remember?"

"Sure, Ma." I get back to work, finishing up with the tire, then rustling the kids into the car and driving to school. All the while my mind spinning about how to pay for a new tire and what the hell it is my son is seeing.

Knowing that he never lies.

12

SAWYER

The crisp morning air hits me as I jump from my truck and head into my new office. I have a spring in my step that's not usually present on a Monday morning. Taking a deep breath in, I feel like I could take on anyone and anything.

The weekend in Whispers wasn't as bad as I was expecting. Between the baseball game and dinner with Annabelle, Saturday was busy, and then on Sunday, I buried myself in work.

Opening the office, I wonder what time the town wakes up. It's only just eight, but in the city, I would've been at work for an hour at least already. I look out the front window, seeing Rochelle at the diner, and I walk to my desk, already dreaming of her coffee.

Looking around, with the new paint job now complete, it's starting to feel like mine. Jerry has taken most things or condensed them into the small office down the hall, which is where he'll work from to close his remaining cases. The furniture's now all replaced, my branding on the window, and I can't help but smile. It feels kind of nice.

As did Saturday night with Annabelle. I've been thinking about her all weekend, wondering if I should send her flowers as a thank-you for dinner. That would be my usual thing to do, since flowers are my go-to. But to send them to a woman who has fields of them seems a bit thoughtless.

I run my hand through my hair, feeling so sure about her it's startling. I need to be in New York, I need to focus on work, I shouldn't even be entertaining the fact that there's a woman here who has completely knocked me off my feet. But I am.

I'm also acutely aware that she's not like anyone I've met or dated before. She isn't going to be impressed by my bank account or my law success. I can't just roll up with a bunch of flowers and impress her with my nice car. No, Annabelle is a woman of substance, and I have no idea how I can put my best foot forward with her. Hell, she might even chop it off with her hoe if I step a foot wrong. That thought makes me smile.

I put my briefcase on my desk and walk back outside, beelining for the diner, expecting it to be empty, but it's a hive of activity.

"Good morning, Sawyer. Good to see you," Rochelle greets me with a big smile that I find myself reflecting.

"Morning, Rochelle. Got the coffee on?" I look around at who's here. I see Bob, the baseball manager and hardware store owner, talking to a guy I haven't met yet but who's wearing a taxi uniform. He gives me a wave, and I offer one back. This should feel weird. I normally don't have time to talk with my barista in the city; hell, I barely get my own coffee, that job reserved for Wendy. But I find the more time I spend here in Whispers, the more I'm at ease. I've worked my ass off for years to get where I am, and as I think about it,

I know I lost my way a little. The Sawyer I am now is not the Sawyer I grew up being, and spending time in this quiet small town is making me realize that even more.

"Sure is. Let me grab you a cup."

"To go, thanks," I add quickly, and she nods to me. I spot a young boy sitting at the end of the counter, having a small breakfast, probably close to Kevin's age. He's talking with the young woman who works at the diner. They're clearly related; they look alike, but she seems awfully young to be a mother. Glancing at her name badge, I see her name is Nikki, and I wonder if Kevin and the young boy are friends.

"Counselor," a man says next to me, and I look at him. In uniform, the local sheriff is a man I haven't met yet but probably someone I should get to know.

"Morning." I extend my hand. "Sawyer Silvers."

"Tony." He smiles, and I could make some quip about a policeman in a diner, but I refrain.

"Jerry tells me you're settling in?"

"Getting there. Starting to meet people, learn about the town."

"Well..." He stands, his breakfast clearly all eaten. "Don't hesitate to stop by the station. I'd be happy to give you an overview of the legal issues we face. We're a small town, but don't let that fool you. We may not be New York, but we have our own kind of crazy out here." With a nod, he puts on his hat.

"Sure thing." I make a mental note to stop by to see him at some stage. While I don't suspect my work in Whispers will be focused on criminal cases, I'm familiar with some of the issues, given my history of working with Tanner, Connor, and Hudson. So I understand better than he thinks about the crazy that can be found in a small town.

As I wait for my coffee, I feel my cell vibrate, and I grab it from my pocket. Seeing my brother's name on the screen, I frown. I've heard from him more this past week than I have all month.

"Sutton?"

"Hey." He sounds weary. Rochelle comes back with my coffee, and I drop some cash on the counter for her before giving her a small smile and fleeing out the door.

"Why are you up so early?" I walk back across the street, that same pep in my step.

"Some asshole sent an overnight courier to my place, and they were buzzing the gate this morning."

I roll my lips to keep from laughing. "I thought you'd be up early, working on your tan or your six-pack," I tease him, not feeling bad at all about having the box of soaps shipped to him overnight.

"She must be pretty special if you're giving me a fucking box of rose-scented soaps. I'm going to smell like a fucking florist."

I can hear him making a coffee, his machine whirling in the background.

"At least I got them to you in time for your morning shower." I ignore his comment as I walk into my office, then to my desk and fire up my laptop.

"Yeah, well, my co-star might like them, so I'll get her to soap up in a minute too," he says, implying that she slept over.

"Just tell her to tag Gertie's," I add, feeling like I'm doing something good. Helping a small business get a leg up, helping Annabelle.

"Now you're her marketing guy? Damn," he teases me right back, and I scrub a hand down my face.

"I don't think she likes me very much."

"So she's smart too, then."

"Ha. Ha. Asshole."

"I need to go. The shower and soap are waiting. You owe me."

"Fine. Talk later." We hang up, and I grin, knowing that the orders for soap are going to increase and hopefully put Gertie's on the map a little more for Annabelle and Victoria.

Before I dive into my emails, I call Hudson.

"Sawyer?" Hudson says, and I sit forward, his tone sounding panicked. I wonder if I'm the only one fucking relaxed today. My mind briefly flicks to Annabelle once again.

"Bad time?" I hear voices around him, making me think he's in the middle of something.

"I have no idea how Annabelle does it." Now he has my interest.

"Does what?" I try to connect the dots.

"Teach these fucking kids," he hisses to me quietly. "They're out of control." It's then I hear kids giggling in the background, noise from yelling and laughing coming through the phone, and I smirk.

"Why? What's happening?" I lean back in my chair, enjoying hearing our usual unflappable doctor sounding completely stressed.

"She's late. She's supposed to manage the class today, and she isn't here yet, so me and a few other parents are trying to get them all into the classroom. It's like herding cattle." I laugh at the image, knowing that Annabelle would have those kids following her every word; she has that way about her.

"Where is she?"

"Car trouble."

I frown. I saw her car on Saturday. It isn't new, but it looked in good condition.

"Is she alright?"

"Yeah, flat tire or something. I think she'll be here soon." I don't hear as much noise now, assuming he has walked somewhere quiet.

"So I just spoke to Sutton."

"Oh yeah, how is that lucky bastard?"

"He said to say hello."

"Hopefully. we get to see him soon. Ahhhh. She's here now. You know, I've never been more relieved to see someone as I am Annabelle right now."

"Yeah, she has that effect on people," I mumble, not really thinking.

"Does she now?" Hudson asks curiously, and I pause.

"Well, so I've heard." I try to cover up my loose tongue.

"Hmmmm. I gotta run, so you're off the hook. Talk later." Hudson ends the call, and I throw my cell on my desk and rub my eyes.

I try to go through emails and reply to a few before I let my thoughts get away from me. I hardly know Annabelle, and I sure as hell shouldn't be starting anything with a woman with two kids, on a farm on the outskirts of a town I have no permanent ties to. But here I am, unable to focus, as she's at the center of my mind.

While a flat tire is usually a quick fix, now that I think about it, her tires were all looking a little bald. Knowing she'll be stressed about it and worried about how to pay for it, a thought comes to mind, and I call Tanner. Because looking after the townspeople is what he wants me to do, so I might as well start today.

13

ANNABELLE

It's been a long day, and after I dismiss the kids, I grab my things and walk to my car. As I do, I catch a glimpse of myself in the window reflection of the school door and cringe. God, I look a wreck. Usually managing the kids and working at the school is great and I love it. But after the issue with the tire and rushing around, being late to school, I've felt frantic all day.

With Kevin playing baseball with Harvey after school, I just need to pick up Noah on my way home. Not that he'll want to come. Debbie, the lovely lady who watches him for me during the day while I work in exchange for soaps and eggs, makes delicious cookies and cupcakes for him and he never wants to leave.

As I walk to my car, I pull up short. It looks different. Frowning, I run my eyes over it and look at the tire that I changed this morning, seeing it gone. The old yellow metal rim is no longer there, and in its place is a brand-new one. In fact, the entire car has four brand-new tires. I walk toward my car slowly, my mind whirling, my eyes wide, trying to figure out what's happened. Did someone mistake my car for someone else's? Putting my bags down, I peer into my car, thinking maybe I'm the one who's mistaken, but I spot the box of tissues on the seat, the ones I used to rub the dirt and grease off my fingers this morning, and Noah's racing car in the back.

"Heard you had a hectic morning," a voice says from behind me, and I scream. Jumping as I turn around, my body clearly still in fear mode from this morning, my back flattens against my car and I look at him, wide-eyed.

"Shit, you okay? I didn't mean to startle you." Sawyer strides toward me, his hands falling to my waist. He holds me tight as his eyes canvass my body, and my breath catches in my throat. "I'm sorry. I thought you heard me walking up." His words rush out, his face laced with concern.

I'm not sure if it's the adrenaline moving through my body or the way his thumbs are rubbing my waist tenderly, but I shiver as I take in a deep breath, willing my eyes not to water. Things are just getting too much for me today. Clearing my throat, I try to pull myself together.

"Sorry." I wish this insane fear that I've seemed to develop would leave me so that I could at least act normal.

"I shouldn't sneak up on you. I should've known better."

I grab my hair, twirling it a little with my finger, the move centering me.

"I'm okay, just a little startled." I fake a wide grin, giggling awkwardly. "I didn't hear you coming." At least that part is the truth. I was so bamboozled by my car, I didn't hear anyone next to me. It's probably extremely stupid of me. I need to keep my wits about me at all times.

"You sure?" His frown deepens as he steps closer, his eyes on mine. I plant my feet on the ground. All it would take is another small step forward, and I would be in his arms, burying my head in his chest, and that can't happen because I would break. But I would be a liar if I said I didn't want to.

"I'm sure." I bring my hands to rest on his forearms, him still holding on to me. This is nice, I can do this. Have him in my space, not feel scared by having a man's hands on my body. I've never felt this comfortable before, and with a complete stranger at that. It should feel weird, my body should tense at being this close to him, but I almost melt every time he touches me. I find myself blushing each time I catch him looking my way.

I hear the school door open with more staff filing out. They look toward us, some of the ladies grinning before walking away.

"I heard what happened this morning." Still looking at me, he lifts his hand and pushes my hair off my face, not dissimilar to how he did at my place on Saturday night. But this time, I don't flinch. I lean into his touch.

Only, then his words hit me, and panic flares. How would he know about the slashed tire? Only Kevin and I know what happened. It dawns on me just as quickly that he's talking about my flat tire, not my slashed one, and I offer him a small smile in the hopes it communicates that I'm fine. But I can tell by the way he's looking at me he doesn't believe me. He's very perceptive. I wonder if that's a natural ability of lawyers. They see through people's bullshit easily.

"Oh yeah, I just had a flat. But I... um..." I swivel around in his arms, looking at my car again. "But I..." As I walk to the back of my car, looking at the tires and then back to him, his arms drop from my waist. "I'm just not..." I can't understand how I have all new tires now.

"I had your tires changed," he answers my confusion, and my head whips up to look at him.

"You what?"

"I heard you had a flat this morning, and I remembered seeing your tires were a little bald on the weekend. So given that I knew you needed one new one and all the driving you do from home to town each day, I just had a guy come from Williamstown and change all of them. Thanks for leaving your keys in the car, by the way. Very helpful." He acts like it's no big deal as he pulls my car keys from his pocket and offers them to me.

I blink a couple of times, my head scrambled. I was so rushed this morning, I even left my keys in the ignition.

"But I can't afford new tires." I feel slightly embarrassed, but he needs to know. This is me. Frantic, always something going on, can't afford four brand-new and what looks like top-of-the-line tires. Hell, I wouldn't be able to afford the cheapest tires right now; that horrible yellow rim spare was going to stay on for a few months, at least.

"That's fine because I paid for them." He clearly sees nothing wrong with this at all.

"But I can't pay you back." I suddenly feel short of breath. There's at least a thousand dollars' worth of tires on my car. Sure, I agree I needed it, but I was saving to have them done, and I should have the money together before next winter.

His eyebrows pinch. "I don't want you to pay me back."

"But you can't do that," I say, shaking my head, not knowing what to do.

"I can. I did." There's that arrogance of his. Sneaking right into his tone and the nonchalant shrug.

"I'm not a charity case," I grit out, and I see the flash of understanding wash across his face, my own face flushed with shame. God, I wish this parking lot would open up and pull me under.

He takes a step toward me, and I watch him, willing myself not to cry, but my eyes sting anyway. No one has ever done anything like this for me before. Sure, I had help from the local church when things were really bad. Tanner and a few others around town sometimes delivered groceries and things, knowing me and the kids were roughing it, and he always gave more pocket money to Kevin whenever he milked their goats or cows. But this is too much.

"Breathe, Annabelle. Just breathe." He lifts his hand slowly and cups my jaw, his calming voice unexpected but having the desired effect as I slow my breathing.

"You know, I thought about sending you some flowers, maybe a box of chocolates to say thank you for dinner. There are these nice chocolates from the city... I thought about flying them in for you." His thumb brushes against my jaw, and I swallow against the movement. It's so soft I almost cry. *Flying in chocolates, who does that?* "But then, I thought about how you are surrounded by big, beautiful roses and lavender at home, so flowers and chocolates may not hit the mark with you."

I bite my lip, unsure where he's going with this. "You don't have to buy me anything."

"I'm trying to sweep you off your feet a little here, Annabelle..." he murmurs with a little smirk as his other hand reaches for mine. My heart rate escalates at his admission, and I take in a shaky breath, feeling unsure yet somewhat happy that the connection I feel between us isn't one-sided.

"It was just roast chicken." I know he probably eats at the fanciest restaurants and has had the most amazing meals.

"It wasn't the chicken, although that was delicious. It was you. So when I heard that you had a flat tire, I wanted to do something to say thank you for having me in your home and welcoming me to your dinner table."

I can barely breathe. "Sawyer, I… It's too much…" I start to shake my head. Declining help is my usual response whenever it's offered.

"Tires are on and there are no takebacks." His hand holds mine tight, entwining our fingers, and I let him, knowing I probably shouldn't. I'm a single mom, living on the outskirts of Whispers, but it has been a long time since a man touched me, and I really, really like it.

I take a moment to look him over. He's wearing his signature black suit and a crisp white shirt, but his expression is different. Not as hard-set as it was when I first met him a few weeks ago. His eyes sparkle with kindness, like the shield he wore has completely dissolved.

"Thank you. For the tires…" I know the words are not enough, but I'm unsure what else to say. My heart races as his thumb strums patterns onto my palm. His continual soothing touch completely puts me at ease.

"You are very welcome." He smiles as he lowers his hand from my jaw.

"So you're in town for the week?" I thought he would already be back in the city after being here for the weekend.

"Flying out tonight, and I'll be back on Wednesday."

"The work never stops, I guess." He works just as hard as I do, just in a luxurious office, not on a dusty farm with ghosts.

"Why didn't you call me?"

I think back to this morning and how I almost did. I swallow past the lump in my throat before I answer.

"I'm no damsel, Sawyer." Regardless of what he thinks of me, I can take care of myself. "Maybe you don't come across strong women in the city, but out here, we're bred a little differently. I don't need a man to hold my hand or keep me safe at night."

"I'm not trying to insult you. I know you work hard and are capable. I just want you to know there are people who will help you if you are willing to accept that help."

I huff a laugh at the ridiculousness of this conversation. "People?" Having people help me is mortifying. I'm still mentally trying to figure out how I can save enough money to pay him back for these tires.

"Me."

The sincerity in his tone, the way he's looking at me, emotions start to build all over again.

"You don't even really know me." I breathe out the words. I don't trust easily. My gut is telling me that this guy is someone I can trust, yet my head is forcing that option away. The internal struggle going on inside of me is terrifying and exhausting. I try to think about what he's saying, what he means. I haven't had to navigate men or dating. It's hard to know if he's flirting or being serious.

"I know enough to want to know more." I squeeze my eyes shut, and he squeezes my hand again. I can't break down in front of him. I pull in a breath, open my eyes, and smile.

"Then you will know that I will pay you back every penny these tires cost," I tell him adamantly, and he grins like I humor him.

"And you will soon learn that I won't accept it," he banters back. Seems like this is an argument that neither of us will win.

"I need to go get Noah. I'm cooking stew on Wednesday night if you want to come for dinner when you come back..." I hold my breath as I offer him another meal. Another date of sorts. I tell myself it's to start paying him back for the tires, but that's another lie. I like having him around.

"I'll be there at six." There's no hesitation. His grin is wide as he steps forward, putting his lips to my forehead, leaving no question that he feels for me in a way beyond the professional. I hold my breath, as his kiss is so gentle I can barely feel it, before he steps back. Our hands still hold each other and reach out between us until we reluctantly let go, and he walks back down the street to his office, and I get in my car.

I let go of the breath I didn't know I was holding and say a quick prayer to heaven to give me the strength I need to enjoy spending time with a man like Sawyer. Hoping the fear I have from my past doesn't hold me back from something that could be amazing.

14

ANNABELLE

I sit at the table at Marie's Place while Victoria makes us a coffee, ready for our weekly catch-up. My cell vibrates just as I grab it. When I see a text from Sawyer, I smile.

> How are those tires doing?

> All still on. They make the car go faster. I'm like a Formula One driver. I get to school a whole twenty seconds earlier now. How's the city?

I send the message before I stress a little that he may not like my humor. But I watch with bated breath as the bubbles dance with his reply.

> It's fine. I've been working on the files for Gertie's. I have some ideas I want to talk to you about.

> And I also look forward to seeing you.

I smile. I haven't talked to a man like this before. I don't want to sound too eager, but I really want to see him too.

> I'm looking forward to seeing you too. Six on Wednesday?

> Six on Wednesday. Can't wait.

"Here, one coffee for you and tea for me." Victoria slides the steaming cup across the table.

"Thanks, it's been a day." I put my cell back into my bag, trying to contain my grin, the texting with Sawyer just now making me feel young and carefree, even though I'm far from it.

"I have no idea how you wrangle fifteen kids in a class-room." She shakes her head at me, and I chuckle.

"The kids were very rowdy today because we did pottery. Actually, I'm pretty sure I still have clay stuck in my hair somewhere." I touch my hair and feel the small piece that I'll have to wash out tonight. Victoria and I meet at least every month or so to talk business and chitchat, although we talk often. Late-night phone calls are our main method of communication, given how busy we both are.

"So catch me up. What's been happening?"

We're settled in, my boys both happy outside, milking the cow and playing with the goats she has here.

"Well, the lavender yield is still looking good, and I've actually tried something a little different."

"Love it. What?" Her excitement over building busi-nesses and trying new things is palpable.

"You can get different types of lavender, and for the most part, all varieties grow best in summer, but I've found some that bloom early summer and some that bloom later summer into early fall, meaning that the growth will be available a little longer, allowing me to pick and dry the flowers more consistently, and we'll have fresh blooms for more of the year." I smile, proud of myself and how much I'm learning about flora.

"That's brilliant. You know, if they're different varieties, we could expand and offer different lines of soap."

My brow furrows as I think about it. "Like English Lavender for early summer, and then French Lavender for late summer into fall?"

"It gives us the opportunity to provide new and different products without the need for us to invest in new scents, different plants, or additional materials. We keep everything the same, just offer two types of lavender and, therefore, two different types of soaps."

I love that idea.

"I mean, they'll smell similar. But maybe we can add in some lavender seeds in one, so that will give a soft exfoliant effect."

Victoria sits up and claps in excitement at my idea.

"Oh, I love it! Brilliant." She taps a few notes out on her laptop. "I will work on some fresh packaging, make sure it looks different on the shelf."

Her cell chimes, and her eyes widen. "Oh... Ooooooh."

"Everything okay?" I sip my coffee, the caffeine hitting my body right where I need it.

"Have you heard of Sutton Silver? The movie star? He's Sawyer's brother," she says, and I shake my head, taken aback by that information.

"Sawyer's brother is a movie star?" He mentioned he lived in LA and worked in the business, but I have no idea about movie stars, my head too buried in survival to be looking at anything like that. I can't even remember the last time I went to the movies or even watched one. Kevin is always taking over the TV to watch baseball.

"Movie star? He asked for a box of soaps to give to his brother, but..."

"Sutton is big-time. One of the most high-profile stars in the world right now. And he just put us on the map." Biting her lip, she moves her cell to my face, and my eyebrows hit my hairline.

"Whoa!" I take in the glistening abs before me.

I feel bad for a moment that I didn't know about Sawyer's brother, and I hope I didn't offend him. But I have no idea about any of that kind of thing. Most people scroll social media at night, in their downtime. But I have no downtime. I make soaps or have a myriad of other things to do once the kids are in bed, and by the time my head hits the pillow, I'm so exhausted, I'm out.

"Ooohhh my gosh, look. His latest co-star put an image up too, which is a little more on brand for us." Victoria shows me another image on her phone, this one of our products on full display in a gorgeous bathroom, near a vase of lavender.

"Wow, what a bathroom." I take in the double sinks and granite countertops, the kind of bathroom I envy. My small bathroom at home is the same as it was when I was a kid, making it decades old by now.

"Our followers are growing," she nearly squeals.

I can't help but get caught up in her excitement. I pull out my own cell again. I have social media and full access to our channel, but I rarely look at it. I bring it up now, refreshing every few moments, seeing our followers rise.

"This is amazing." I look at the image of Sawyer's brother again and bite my cheek, wondering what Sawyer will think, and I can't help but laugh.

"Sawyer is going to hate that image," I say, and Victoria looks at me with a quirked eyebrow.

"Probably. Although, he loves his brother. They're super close." With her curiosity shining through, I already know what she's about to say before she says it. "So you and Sawyer have been spending some time together, hmm?"

I roll my lips. "A little."

"That makes sense."

"What does?" I ask, taking a sip of my coffee.

"Why he hasn't hightailed it back to the city, like we all thought he would."

"But he is back in the city?" I question her tentatively, trying to put the dots together, and she gives me a smile.

"He is today, but not permanently. He loves the city and definitely isn't a country boy at all. I mean, Tanner has been trying to get him to move here for years, but he never truly thought he could get him over the line. So it's clear that something else, or should I say, *someone else* has caught his interest," she teases, and I feel my cheeks blushing.

"Oh, I just had him over for dinner. It was nothing..." I try to deny it's anything, but she calls me out.

"So he came for dinner?" she murmurs.

"I had plenty... sooo I offered for him to join us. That's all." I almost stumble over my words, slightly embarrassed. I'm still trying to sort out exactly what's going on between us, so I don't think it's time to gush about him just yet.

"Of course... I heard he was also at the baseball game to watch the kids?" she asks, and I still.

I clear my throat. "Yes, he was there."

"You have him over at your place for dinner, spending time with him at the baseball game... It sounds like you are getting along well."

"Just getting to know each other a little." I take comfort

in that statement. We had one meal, a bit of flirting. But he did get me a set of all new tires and is coming for dinner once he's back.

"Well, if he's flying back and forth to the city each week, then he's clearly keen to get to know you. The Sawyer I know, he likes his city comforts too much to ever spend too much time here in Whispers." She sits back with a satisfactory smile on her face.

"He said he wants to sweep me off my feet." I can't help but share that tidbit, and she smiles like the cat that got the cream.

"Good. Make him work for it." She winks at me, and I suddenly feel giddy.

"So Sawyer grew up in New York?" I ask, wondering what she knows.

"Yes, born and bred there, raised by a single mom. Tanner tells me that it was tough when they were kids, only finding success in their twenties. I think that's why Tanner loves him so much. He came from nothing and made something of himself. He has good morals." Victoria starts tapping on her laptop, looking at something.

I swallow as I take in the information. He was raised by a single mom? He hasn't mentioned that. I start to feel a little odd, given that I'm a single mom of two boys as well. Does he feel sorry for me? Does he feel some weird connection to me because of his own upbringing? Self-doubt starts to creep in, because I was already struggling to understand why a man such as Sawyer is interested in a woman like me when he could have anyone in the city. I know all those women in the city are glamorous, beautiful, smart. Yet as I lift my phone and look at my text messages, I see the one where he mentioned he was looking forward to seeing me, and my heart still skips a beat.

"Oh, wow." Victoria breaks into my thoughts.

"What?" I look over at her and see a wide grin.

"Our sales. They're going through the roof!" I look at her screen and see in real time, orders coming through for the soaps, and my eyebrows rise.

"Thank God we've got good stock levels stored at the distillery warehouse. I'll be packing these all night!" She laughs, and I join her, both of us dancing in our seats.

Sawyer didn't have to do that. Just like he didn't have to fix my car, and he didn't have to deliver the contracts to my door. I just hope he's doing everything for the right reasons. As much as I'm looking forward to seeing him again and cooking for him, I want him to look forward to it because he has feelings for me, not because he's trying to save me from a life he's already endured.

15

SAWYER

As I drive from the airport and snake my way around the roads, an odd feeling of contentment lowers my shoulders. I feel like I'm home. Like I can breathe for the first time in days. Which is odd, because I left New York this afternoon and just landed in Whispers. The one place I swore I'd never settle, yet the one place that's feeling more and more like it's where I'm meant to be.

As I edge closer to Annabelle's house, an excitement twirls in my stomach that hasn't been there in a very long time. She has me off my game. I'm usually so much smoother with women. I give flowers, chocolates, and pick them up for dates, sweeping them off their feet at the top restaurants in the city with the best bottles of wine. Getting her four brand-new tires was obviously too much for her, but I was at a loss at what to get her to show my affection. When it comes to Annabelle, I'm some idiot who falls in cow manure, says or does the wrong thing, and can't even flirt properly over text.

I pull into Annabelle's gravel driveway and slowly make my way up to her place. The late afternoon sun is hitting the lavender, making the entire field look vibrant purple. It's beautiful. She mentioned having great soil, and it's clear by the large bushes that she's right.

Spotting Kevin outside, I turn off my truck and jump out. "Hey, Kevin." I walk up to him, pocketing my hands. I'm in my usual suit, not really farm attire as per usual, and I watch Kevin, with a baseball and a glove on, throwing the ball into a small stack of hay bales, before running and grabbing it, and then heading back to the same spot and throwing again.

"Hey." He pays me little attention. By the look of concentration and the sweat on his brow, I'm assuming he's been out here for a while.

"Are you practicing your pitching?" I squint at him, watching his throw. He has a good arm on him. Strong, fast, and accurate. The ball hits the same marker on the bales each and every time.

"Yeah." His vocabulary is clearly not in working order today either.

"Do you have a spare glove? I can throw with you." It's been a while since I threw a ball, but it's something I enjoy doing. I look at his glove. It's old, falling apart, and the ball doesn't look much better.

"No, just got this one." He continues throwing the ball. Not even looking my way. At least he offers me more words this time.

"Looks like you need a new glove. It seems like an old one."

"Was my dad's." I swallow. *Fuck.*

"Oh, a bit of family history, then," I offer with a small smile. I wonder how he's coping without his father. I know too well how hard it can be when you're young and don't have that father figure in your life, someone you desperately need.

"It's a piece of shit, just like he was." For the first time this conversation, he looks right at me. His eyes flame.

My jaw clenches as I take in his words and see the hurt and anger in his gaze. I never really knew my father, but it seems like Kevin remembers his all too well. That feeling I had when I last saw Annabelle, the way she flinched when I touched her cheek, these little snippets of her story are now starting to add up, and the picture I'm getting is not a good one.

"Kevin! Oh Sawyer, you're here." Annabelle's voice breaks through our moment like sweet honey, and Kevin's face immediately softens. "Sorry, I was just out the back; I didn't hear you come up."

She walks down the porch steps toward us. The small breeze blows through her pretty blond hair, her eyes sparkling like she's happy to see me. With her wide smile aimed my way, I release the breath I was holding, my body relaxing instantly.

"I was just chatting with Kevin; he's got a good throw on him. Looks to be pitcher material."

Kevin looks at me like he's confused that I would offer him a compliment.

"He should be. He's out here often enough." Annabelle gives him a wink, and he chuckles.

"Go clean up for dinner, honey."

Kevin nods and runs inside.

"How have you been?" I step closer to her, grabbing her hand, needing her in my space.

"Fine. No more flat tires." She bites her lip to contain her grin, and I huff a small laugh. She seems good today. Not as frantic, her skin is glowing, her eyes bright. She's looking like just me being here is all she needs, making me feel genuinely wanted just for being myself.

I wonder briefly if this could be life. Coming home to a beautiful woman and kids after a long day of work. I never imagined my life being like this. My city upbringing provides an alternative fantasy, but now the universe is painting an entirely different picture, and I'm liking it.

"I forgot to mention, my brother posted something online about the soaps," I tell her, scrubbing the back of my head, a little sheepish. My brother is a moron, and I'm going to kill him. I said as much today in the text message I sent him when I got the notification from his social media post.

In between meetings, I saw the image pop up on my screen. Him in all his naked glory. His wet body and six-pack on full display in the shower, water running down his abs, holding a Gertie's soap bar to cover his dick.

The caption. *Get dirty with Gertie.*

She hums, nodding. "I met up with Victoria this afternoon to talk about the business, and we both saw it. Our orders have increased online, and she's had a few new inquiries from some retailers. Looks like your plan worked. Thank you. I really, really appreciate it." Her smile has me smiling, even though I'm still annoyed with my brother.

"Yeah, well, I'm not entirely sure about the photo he put up," I mumble, wondering what she thought of it. Sutton works hard on his physique, as do I. I'm glad the house I'm leasing on Billionaire Boulevard has a fully equipped gym because Whispers doesn't have one.

"Hmmmm, I saw it, and I didn't really think about my soaps covering a man's appendage when I made them..." Her cheeks tint pink, but her grin remains. Now that she mentioned it, I don't really like the fact that something Annabelle made with her hands is so close to my brother's dick either. I should've thought about that before I sent them to him.

I huff a laugh. "Yeah, the ladies love him." Now that she knows who he is, she'll probably fangirl like the rest of my dates usually do. I swallow, having never felt this vulnerable before, jealous of my own brother. Fuck, this woman is under my skin.

"Couldn't pay me to be fawning over a celebrity. Give me a lawyer in a suit any day of the week."

Relief fills me instantly. "Are you flirting with me?" I ask her cheekily, and she looks at me with a playful glint in her eyes.

"Am I doing it right?" She squints, like she's not sure what my response will be, and I laugh as I grab her hand and pull her to me.

"It's working on me..." I tell her, kissing her forehead, and we walk inside.

This night is already feeling just right.

Coming to Annabelle's for dinner, I've discovered, is like going to watch a Broadway show. There are usually three acts.

To start the night, Noah joined us for dinner, and Annabelle gave him the task of saying grace. His wide grin should've given it away, but having gone on and on about how much he loved his day, he concluded his fifteen-minute spiel, asking God for more of Debbie's cupcakes, which made Kevin snigger, the first real smile I've seen from him.

Act two consisted of watching her walk around the house and her property, ensuring all doors and windows were locked, while the boys got ready for bed. I took that time to race to my truck and grab the paperwork I needed to go through with her, as well as check my phone a dozen times, all in order to tamp down my concern for a young woman living out here all on her own.

Now, in act three, the boys are in bed and the house is deathly quiet, except for the low hum of the TV as we sit near each other on the sofa. I reprinted the contract Annabelle misplaced, and now it looks like a rainbow shit all over it because I have sticky notes on almost every page, highlighting the key things I want to explain to her in more detail, knowing that she might need an extra hand in understanding some of the terminology.

"So, this goes through what will happen with the Gertie's if one or both of you are unable to work in the business anymore," I tell Annabelle, liking sitting close and having her interested in what I'm saying.

"Oh, okay." She reads through it. My lips thin as I watch her, because she clearly didn't read through it properly the first time, and if she did, I'm positive that she didn't understand it.

"In the case where one of you passes away or can no longer work in the business, this outlines that the other party will buy out the other fifty percent ownership and hold one hundred percent of the business," I explain to her, and her brow furrows.

"But if Victoria passes, there's no way I could buy her out." She looks up at me, concerned.

"If that happens, there are a few ways to go about it. One way is to get a business loan and borrow the money." Now her expression morphs, like I just asked her to kill a cat.

"I don't think I would get a loan." I'm not entirely sure of her situation, but it's becoming clear she doesn't have much in the bank.

"The other option would be to sell the business to

someone else, either finding a new fifty percent partner or selling a hundred percent of the business to them."

Her shoulders slump, not liking that prospect either.

"It's a very unlikely scenario, but one that you do need to consider when entering a business arrangement such as this. It's always good to have plans for when things go bad so that you're a little more prepared," I explain, and she puts the paperwork down, leaning back on the sofa.

"Nothing really prepares you for death." She swallows roughly.

"It can be a hard time." Turning my body to her, I give her my full attention.

"When my parents died, there were so many things that had to happen. Not only in trying to process the grief, but also trying to figure out what to do with all their things and make sure their wishes are adhered to."

"How old were you when your parents died?"

"Eighteen. I was pregnant with Kevin at the time. I was made to be an adult before I was ready. Steve, the boy's father, and I were childhood sweethearts, and we both decided to stay in Whispers to start a family. In hindsight, that probably wasn't the smartest decision, but I was young and thought I was in love, and as an only child, I knew that the farm would become mine one day, so why not start working on it as soon as I could..."

My breathing becomes shallow, knowing this woman has had a tough life for most of it.

"My parents died the day before Kevin entered the world. Kevin was my father's name."

I rub my chest, a deep pain blooming behind my rib cage. I can't imagine losing my mom, especially not right before bringing a child into the world.

"After my parents were gone and this farm was mine,

Steve took over. He controlled everything and ran it into the ground. A financially successful farm became almost ruined in a short amount of time. It was hard for me to do anything, having a new baby to care for and pushing through sleepless nights. I was a zombie for almost twelve months. Now that he's gone and it's firmly in my hands, I'm doing everything I can to build it back up again."

There's determination in her eyes, and I think back to what Kevin mentioned about his father earlier.

"I obviously didn't know your parents, but I think they would be pretty proud of you and the kids. Proud of what you've done here so far and of how you're raising the boys."

She looks up at me before asking tentatively, "Victoria told me that you were raised by a single mom?"

I nod. "I was. Never really knew my dad. My mom now lives down in Florida."

"Is that why you're here, Sawyer?" I can tell she's holding her breath, and I frown.

"What do you mean?"

"Are you here to try to save me or something? Are you here because you feel sorry for me?"

My head nearly rears back, but I keep it together and look her in the eye. *Is that what she thinks?*

"I think we both know a woman like you doesn't need saving. I think you're pretty amazing, Annabelle. I admire you. I enjoy spending time with you. I think you're one of the most beautiful women I've ever met, both inside and out," I tell her, becoming more in awe of her each time I see her. I feel different around her. Not myself, but in a good way. It feels easy, natural, a genuine connection.

Taking it really slow, I reach out my hand. She doesn't flinch this time but watches me carefully. The gravity of the situation sits heavy in my gut, the feeling of trust that she's giving me unmatched to anything I've felt before. I tenderly touch her cheek, pushing her hair back from her face. I hear her suck in a breath, her lips parting a little.

I've never moved this slow with a woman before, but I touch her cheek so softly, like she is made of glass and might break. As I lean forward a little, our eyes search each other's.

"Sawyer..." She says my name so quietly I can barely hear her.

"Yeah, Annabelle?" I whisper, our noses nearly touching as I breathe her in.

Vulnerability shines in her eyes. "It's been a long time since a man kissed me."

"I would like to rectify that situation." I remain still, not moving until she tells me to, my heart thumping out of my chest as I brush my fingertips along her jawline.

"I'd like that too," she says sweetly, and I look down at her lips, spotting her pulse racing in her neck just before I take her lips with mine.

I go slow, my lips brushing hers before she meets me halfway with a little more pressure. Moving my hand from her cheek, I cup her jaw, my other hand lifting to her other side. As her mouth opens with a barely audible moan, I kiss her more thoroughly. Like it's a green light for us both, her hands run up my arms and grip on to my shirt, and my tongue flicks against hers. The weight of her head sits in my hands as our tongues tangle and the kiss becomes more heated. When I groan against her lips, I know it's time to rein myself in.

Even though I want so much more with her, I pull back a little but keep her close, the two of us panting. I watch her, seeing a mix of emotions on her face. My heart races, anxious for her to say something, hoping that wasn't too much. Not wanting to push her too hard, too quick, wanting to do the right thing. City me would have her in the bedroom tonight, but I'm learning country me is a totally different person.

"That was worth the wait." A smile brightens her face, and I blow out a breath. She laughs breathily, her head falling to my shoulder, her cheeks red. I laugh with her as I bring my hands to her waist and pull her tight to me, knowing that I'm falling a little more for the woman who has completely taken over my thoughts. And I don't know what the hell I'm going to do about it.

16

ANNABELLE

I fold the clothes, my nightly chores feeling less and less like a burden these days. I bite my lip, trying to tame the smile that threatens to cramp my face every time I think about how I kissed Sawyer last night. How his hands felt, how he asked permission, waited for me to give it, and then touched my lips with his in a way that was so soft, yet so committed, it left me feeling utterly giddy.

The heat and passion I feel when in his arms is unprecedented. I thought I was in love with my husband, at least initially. But in hindsight, it was merely a schoolgirl crush that led to a teen pregnancy and then being widowed in my late twenties.

No, the feelings I get with Sawyer are much more than that. So much more that they can't be compared. My body almost aches for him, my mind a whirl when I think about him. I've been scared of getting close to another man. Some scars are still present on my body from the last person I thought I loved. But the more I get to know Sawyer, the more I trust him. He doesn't have a short temper, doesn't think my kids are annoying or in the way. He's warm, intelligent, charming, thoughtful. All the things Steve wasn't.

"Kevin, five more minutes, and it's bedtime," I tell my son, who's glued to the TV, with Thursday night baseball on.

"I just want to watch Jefferson pitch."

I smile, having no idea who he's talking about. Not for the first time, I think about how he and Noah feel with Sawyer coming around. It's new, different, not just for me, but also for my boys. And while I feel excited at the prospect of meeting a man who has already admitted he wants to sweep me off my feet, I need to ensure my kids are happy. They are my number one priority.

"I'm going out to check that everything is locked up, and when I get back, it's bedtime, okay?" I say as I step around the table and head to the door.

"But I locked up everything already." He looks at me over his shoulder, and I give him a small smile in return.

"I know. It just doesn't hurt to triple-check." I swallow down the fear that's building now that it's gone dark, not wanting to tell him that something feels off around here lately and that I don't even trust myself to know what I've locked up and what I haven't. Pushing open the door, I turn on the porch light. It's small, but at least it's something.

In reality, I should have the whole place bathed in floodlights. That's what other farms have. But installing large light poles and buying the bright outdoor lights is a cost I just can't cover at the moment. Yet another thing on my future to-do list.

I stand on the porch and look out at the black night. I've always loved the quiet, but as a small breeze skirts over my arms, an involuntary shiver moves through me. Looking to where Sawyer's truck is parked whenever he visits, I'm already starting to notice the absence of it. Probably because

I don't get many visitors, but I already can't wait to see him again.

I step down from the porch and start walking across the yard, completely lost in thoughts of him, of our kiss, the touches we share, and I swallow roughly as I think about where it's leading. I've only ever slept with my late husband, and I already know a man like Sawyer would be well experienced. One look at him tells me that. He probably has women fawning all over him in the city, and I don't think I even have a matching set of underwear. I push my hair back, the unruly mess a constant in my life, and take a breath, pushing away the feelings of not being good enough, knowing that I'm doing the best I can with what I've got.

Sounds of the TV become fainter the closer I get to the shed. The eerie feeling that I've felt these past few weeks creeps around me, like a blanket shrouding my shoulders, making my skin prickle with goosebumps. All thoughts of Sawyer and my sex life dissipate as I look at the shed, stepping closer and closer, all the while darkness envelops me, the isolation almost suffocating as I clench my hands at my sides.

"Come on, Annabelle. You're tougher than this." Stepping up to the shed door, I unlock it and move through. I look over at the one cow we have in here, seeing her all safe and happy for the night, and I'm about to turn to walk back out when I hear a noise outside the door.

I freeze, calling out, "Kevin?"

No one answers. My hands start to shake as I tentatively take a step back.

"Kevin?" I yell a little louder as my heart thumps, my wide eyes darting everywhere. But in the darkness, mere shapes and shadows are all I can see.

My footsteps across the floorboards sound daunting as I

make it to the door and start to push it open so I can step out. "Kevin?" I ask again, quieter this time, unsure now. Maybe I was just hearing things. But as I take one more hesitant step forward, the shed door comes whipping into me, pushing me back with force.

I scream as the door hits my forehead with a rough smack, and I lose my footing, falling to the floor and landing on my ass.

Shaking off the thudding in my head, I look up and see no one. I scramble to the side of the shed where I know my garden tools are. With trembling hands, I reach out, grabbing the hoe.

"Who's there?" I pull myself up to stand, breathing rapidly as I start to panic. "Answer me!"

"Ma?" I hear Kevin, and I rush to the door, pushing it open without another thought for my own safety, scared that something will happen to him. "You alright?"

He's up near the house, and I stride toward him as my head flicks around in every direction, looking around wildly, the hoe in my hands held up, ready to use.

"Kevin. Be careful."

I look at the shed, around the door, then around the corner, but see no one, nothing. I look out the black expanse of my farm, not able to see a thing, the cloud cover blanketing the moon's usual glow.

"Ma, you're bleeding. What happened?" That jolts my focus, and I lift my hand to my head, feeling it wet.

"I, um..." I start to say, my voice breaking. "I... just... um..." I stumble, trying to pull my thoughts together before I close my eyes and take a breath. My head's now throbbing, the shock of it all wearing off, and the pain of where I landed on my ass also pulsating.

"I just tripped," I settle now really wondering if I'm going crazy. Scuffing my feet on the floor, I feel for any loose board or tripping hazard that could tell me that was a possibility. But I already know it isn't. That door swung back and hit me, and without a breath of wind felt, I know someone must have pushed it. "I just tripped on the hoe and scared myself. I must not have put it away properly earlier."

Kevin looks at me like he doesn't believe me. I get busy locking up the shed, checking the lock three times before I grab Kevin's hand, and we stride back to the house, the blood on my forehead now dripping down my cheek.

"It looks bad, Ma." His voice is shaky, concern evident in his eyes as he looks at my head.

"It's fine. I'm fine, Kev." I don't want him to worry as I get us inside quickly and lock the door behind us. Again, checking it a few times to ensure it's latched properly before I pull a chair in front of it for extra protection.

As I turn to walk to the kitchen to get a clean cloth for my head, I feel a little woozy and grab on to the table when my vision blurs.

"Ma!" Kevin comes to my side and grabs my elbow, and I blink a few times until I see more clearly again.

"I might just take a seat. Rest a little. Can you get me a glass of water, honey?" I ask him as I walk slowly to the armchair, my eyesight fading again as I take a seat. My son rushes to the kitchen for the water, bringing it back to me right away.

I take it, my hand shaking so much the water almost spills.

"I'll just check on Noah."

I nod. He's such a good boy. I have no idea what I'd do without him.

17

———

SAWYER

"Here, gents." Connor brings a tray of whiskey glasses to the table.

"Thank you." Hudson grabs a glass, his one and only tonight, which he'll drink along with a large bottle of water.

"Appreciate it." I need at least a few of these to drown out that blaring country music on the large jukebox at the end of the bar. Thursday night drinks look a lot different now than they used to.

Tanner and Connor each grab one, and the four of us sit there, relaxing.

"Soooooo, Annabelle?" Connor looks at me with a shit-eating grin on his face, and I bite my lip so I don't do the same.

"What about her?" I act nonchalant, taking a sip of my whiskey. I can hardly wrap my thoughts around it all, so I'm sure as hell not going to start gushing about her to these guys.

"What's going on? What did I miss?" Hudson looks at us all, confusion written all over his face.

"Sawyer here has been spending time with Annabelle..." Tanner looks at me like he's waiting for me to fuck up. I swallow but meet his gaze.

"Really?" Hudson asks me.

"Just dinner, getting to know her a little bit." I prefer to keep my cards close to my chest, yet in a town like this, that's impossible. But Annabelle is a private person too. And I respect that. My thoughts about her consume me most days. I haven't felt like this about a woman in forever, and that scares me a little. Leaves me feeling a little vulnerable, like my chest is wide open for her.

"A nice woman, pretty quiet, keeps to herself," Hudson adds. "I had a feeling you might be interested in her."

"She's great. She's smart, good work ethic, a great mom, beautiful, independent, an amazing cook, easy to talk to, fucking beautiful..."

"You said that already," Connor jumps in, chuckling as he cuts off my rambling.

"Who would've thought our city boy here might actually come to like Whispers," Hudson teases.

"It's growing on me." As I take another sip of whiskey, Tanner's gaze is still on me. I can already hear his warning before he speaks.

"Just..." Tanner starts to say, and I interrupt.

"I know. Go slow. Take care of her. I know, trust me. I'm not a total asshole. She's been through a lot and I'm not about to add to her troubles." This feeling is entirely new. I have no idea how to go slow. I've never had to work hard for a woman before and never had the desire to before now. But as I sit here in Whiteman's Bar, my tie loose, my collar open, my usual pristine suit no longer feeling necessary, my want for her continues to grow.

He nods, then says, "That remains to be seen," making

Connor and Hudson laugh. Before I can say anything more, my cell vibrates in my jacket, and I pull it out, seeing Annabelle's name, a grin coming to my face immediately.

"Hey, Annabelle."

All three men look at me intently, trying to get the inside scoop.

"You need to come here." But it's Kevin's panicked voice on the line.

"Kevin?" I frown, sitting forward as my concern rises. "Everything okay?"

"Ma hurt herself. You need to come," he says, and I'm already standing.

"Hurt herself? I'm coming. I'll be there as soon as I can." He doesn't say anything else, just hangs up, and a rush of nerves moves through me.

"What's going on?" Tanner asks, the three of them already on their feet.

"That was Kevin, said Annabelle has hurt herself."

"Let's go." Hudson strides out the door without another word, clearly in doctor mode, and we're quick to follow.

"SHE NEEDS to move closer to town," Tanner mumbles as we turn up her long driveway. It's pitch-black out here. Even the moon offers little solace.

"It took us fifteen minutes to get here. Way too long in an emergency, if you ask me." I spot Connor and Hudson in front of us, pulling up to the house. "She's in the middle of nowhere. With no neighbors nearby, a single mom with two kids..." I trail off, getting worked up just thinking about it.

"Well, would you look at that. You do care about this town and its people," Tanner says sarcastically as we jump out of my truck and walk up the door that Kevin now has open for us.

"What happened?" Hudson, doctor bag in hand, walks straight to Annabelle, who's sitting in her armchair, Noah on her lap.

"We're fine. Sorry, Kevin panicked."

Kevin stares at me, a serious look on his face. I don't like it. I don't like it at all. Noah is wiggling around on Annabelle's lap, and I see her wince a little.

"She went outside to lock up. I heard a noise and her yelling and found her with her head cut and bleeding," Kevin says, and Annabelle doesn't meet anyone's eyes. Something feels off. Like they're not saying something.

"It was just the animals." Annabelle flicks her gaze to Kevin. One thing about working in law for so long and growing up how I did, I know when someone is lying.

"You said you tripped over the hoe?" Kevin calls her out.

"Yes, I did. After the animals made a noise." She recovers badly, and my nostrils flare as I clench my jaw tight.

"I noticed the gate out front is damaged?" Connor asks her, and I look at him. I hadn't noticed anything, but to be fair, I have no idea how a gate on a farm is supposed to look. I lift my gaze and glance around the house. Everything else seems in order, her usual chaotic self on display with things everywhere, but otherwise, nothing seems amiss.

"Bears or coyotes, probably." She holds a towel to her head. Her hand finds her hair, her fingers twirling it in her grip as another lie falls from her lips. My shoulders tighten even more.

"Looked like the lock was cut with bolt cutters," Tanner says, and I have no idea how they noticed all that when it's so dark outside. She needs more lights around the house, around her shed. Shit, even all the way up her driveway.

"It was rusty." She has an answer for everything, apparently.

"Connor and I will go take a look around, just in case. Check the animals." Tanner and his son share a look, their commanding presence felt around the room before they walk past me and straight out the door.

"Alright, I might as well take a look at your head while I'm here." Hudson steps toward her with his doctor bag. Annabelle turns, her eyes settling on me, and I keep her gaze until Noah wiggles again and I spot another wince she tries to hold back.

"Let me take him." My feet move before my mind actually thinks about what I'm doing.

"It's fine." She's stubborn, even now.

"I've got him." I don't listen to her as I scoop up Noah, who proceeds to slap both my cheeks and giggle.

"You know that stings, right?" I tell him, this time holding him closer to my body.

"Like a beeeeeee," he says, and I chuckle.

"Okay, well, it's a good size gash on your forehead there." Hudson pulls my attention to Annabelle, and I see a large wound across her forehead. I grit my teeth harder, not liking seeing her hurt.

"I just tripped. I'm sure it will heal fine," she says, as Hudson wipes away a little of the blood.

"I'm sure it will too. We've got to have you all ready for the season. Kevin, are you excited to be on the team this year?" Hudson's bedside manner is admirable, and Annabelle's face lights up in pride as she watches Kevin chat with Hudson about the upcoming baseball game this weekend.

"Buzz, buzz, buzz..." Noah's hands smooth over my stubble, and I look back at him.

"You think I'm a bee? Or are you a bee, hmm?"

Noah smiles at me, breaking down a little more of my city armor. He's a cute kid.

"Well, outside is all fine, but you'll need a new lock. The other one was broken," Tanner says as he and Connor come back inside and both pause mid-stride when they see me holding Noah.

"Ahhhhhh. Are you feeling alright?" Connor's smirk rises, looking between me and Noah, who's now squishing my nose and flapping my tie, continuing his buzzing sounds, totally oblivious to anyone else around him. If this had happened months ago, I would be aghast. This is a thousand-dollar tie and Noah is playing with it like it's his new toy. And as he grabs it and pulls it to his face, using it like a comfort blanket, I find myself pulling it from my neck and giving it to him. His small hand grabs it, then he rests his head on my shoulder with the tie now firmly in his grasp.

"Do. Not. Say. A thing," I grit out to the guys, who both look at me with equal parts confusion and understanding.

"Okay, a few butterfly strips will hopefully do the job. But I prefer to stitch, just to make sure..." Hudson says.

"No. I'm fine, really. Just a small head bump," Annabelle says, and Hudson sighs, clearly preferring the other option.

"Ma, Ma, Ma!" Noah reaches for her now that Hudson is finished and packing up, so I put Noah down and let him run to her. I can't help the small smile on my lips when he climbs up onto her lap carefully before snuggling into her, my tie still in his grip.

"I'm sorry to drag you all out here. Thanks for coming. I appreciate it." She puts Noah on the chair and stands. I'm sure I'm not the only one who thinks she looks pale.

"Kevin, keep your mom hydrated with some water and make sure she gets plenty of rest. Come and see me tomorrow if the butterfly strips don't hold, and we'll put a few little stitches in it just to keep it closed. But I think you'll be all fine after a good night's sleep." Hudson's words are soothing but don't appease me at all.

"Thanks, Hudson." Annabelle's smile is small, her exhaustion obvious.

"You tell us if you need anything," Tanner says to her as he scruffs Kevin's hair.

"Sure," Annabelle says, lying again as she walks the four of us to her door.

I look at Tanner. "Think you can get a ride home with Hudson? I might hang around for a bit."

He nods. "Probably a good idea." The look he gives me is not one that fills me with confidence.

As the other three men start walking out, I remain, looking around the room.

"You staying?" Kevin comes to stand by my side. I look down at him, brow pinched.

"Thinking about it."

"I'd like that," he says quietly, and I see it then. A little fear in his eyes.

"Thanks for calling me."

"She didn't want me to. But I was worried."

I nod, gripping his shoulder lightly. "You did the right thing. Call me anytime."

"Boys, I think that's enough activity for one night." Annabelle turns from the door, and I watch as both boys go to her and hug her tight, then Kevin takes Noah's hand and walks him down the hall, to where I assume their bedrooms are.

Once they're gone, the two of us stand, looking at each other.

"You want to tell me what really happened tonight?" I

feel tension in my shoulders as she gives me that fake smile that she offered me when we first met.

"I just tripped." She shakes her head like it's no big deal as she starts acting busy, packing up things around the house that don't need to be touched.

"Annabelle, I think you and I both know that's not what happened." I step toward her, and she stops what she's doing and looks at me.

Taking a big breath, she blows it out. "Fine. I'm going crazy. I hear things, see things. Things that don't make sense. I think I've actually lost my mind."

That has my concern rising all over again. "What things?"

She looks weary, but she softens a little. Opening up to me a touch.

"Just things. Things around the farm." She rubs her eyes, not offering me much more. I drop it for now.

"I'll stay tonight. I'm sleeping on the sofa." There's no way I'm leaving her tonight.

Shaking her head, she huffs a laugh. "I'm pretty sure that sofa will leave you with a bad back."

"Then I'll sleep on the floor."

She looks at me as though I'm crazy. "I'm fine, Sawyer. Thanks for coming, but you don't need to worry about me." Her small smile does absolutely nothing to appease me. My gut churns, feeling like something is amiss.

"I want to help you, Annabelle." I need her to understand that I'm not just someone from town here to help. I want to be here for her. To support her.

"I don't need help," she grits out, her independence and pride too much.

"That's what friends do."

"Is that what we are? Friends?" I see it then. Something in her eyes.

"Yeah, I'd like to think so. I'd also like to think we could be more, because the more I get to know you, the more I want to."

"Are you trying to rescue me again, Sawyer?" she asks sarcastically, and I grin.

"I think we both know you're the kind of woman who rescues herself. But you might be surprised with what I can do. Who knows, maybe you'll be rescuing me?" As I walk toward her slowly, her shoulders seem to lower.

"Do you have a Superman cape under that suit you wear?" She looks me up and down, and a small smile dances on my lips at seeing her a bit more relaxed.

"Oh, believe me, Lois Lane, I'm no hero."

"Hmm. I think you are. At least you were tonight," she whispers. "Thank you for coming." Feeling her tough walls breaking down, I grab her hand, squeezing it in mine, before I pull her to me gently, and she comes willingly. She melts against me as I hug her to me tight. Her arms wrap around me, hanging on like I'm her lifeline as she buries her head in my chest. My heart swells, and I kiss the top of her head. She feels good in my arms, delicate, the contrast between her fiercely independent personality and her small, soft body now obvious.

Her hands smooth up my chest, and she remains close as she pushes her head back to look at me, her chin resting on my pec. As she does, her hair falls back, tickling my fingers, and I splay my hands wide, wanting to touch as much of her as I can. I've had many women. Held them, kissed them, enjoyed amazing sex with them. But this is the first time I've never wanted to let one go.

"You don't need to thank me," I say softly. She swallows,

the movement taking my eyes from her as I trail her neck and lift my hand, skimming it up her side to cup her jaw.

"Maybe not with words…" And then she lifts onto her tiptoes and presses her lips to mine. My mind zaps with energy, knowing she initiated this kiss and wants me as much as I want her. As I skirt my tongue across her luscious lips, she opens for me. We've kissed, we've become closer and closer every time we're together, but right now, my body feels like I'm on fire from having her mouth on mine. I pull her closer to me, my hand on her lower back, pressing her body flush to me. As I do, she releases a little moan that shoots right to my balls, my skin tingling beneath the light touch of her hands as she wraps them around my neck and pulls me down for a more thorough kiss that has me moaning right back.

Our height difference is noticeable, so I drop my hand, grab her ass, and lift her up, her legs wrapping around my waist immediately. I don't know if it's because tonight has been a little frantic, whether it's the fact that I've got her ass in my hands, or if it's because she came on to me tonight, but I'm so fucking hard for her, it should be embarrassing. This feels so damn good. As her body molds to mine, our lips mesh together, my tongue exploring, wanting more of her, and she holds on to me for dear life.

I step forward a few paces to the wall, pressing her back against it, relishing her gasp that turns into a moan at our closeness. My hands palm her perky ass, and I groan into her mouth, feeling like I'm in heaven.

Pulling back a little, I look at her, my eyes immediately catching on the gash on her forehead, and I internally curse. She's injured, and I'm fucking groping her. I swallow, trying to catch my breath as she watches me, her own breaths quickened.

"Wow..." she says on an exhale as she looks at me, and I can't help but grin. There's a fire inside of us that's simmering, building. When she adjusts herself a little, her hips grinding into mine, I clench my jaw as she feels all of me, hard and ready, and her legs wrap around me tighter.

"Hmmm, I probably shouldn't be manhandling you. I should be putting you to bed with pain relief. But it appears that you are my kryptonite, Lois..." Even though she chuckles at that, I feel conflicted. City me probably wouldn't care. City me would strip her bare, fuck her right here against the wall, on the dining table, anywhere I could. But Whispers me knows better. I lean in and kiss her quickly on the lips again, not wanting to stop, but knowing I should.

"You can't sleep on the floor tonight, Sawyer... But you can sleep in my bed." Her eyes are full of anticipation before I nod, my heart pounding harder. Even though she's inviting me to be closer to her, I know with her injury and her history that we need to go slow. This is her trusting me to keep her safe, not just physically, but emotionally. I can't remember the last bed I slept in with a woman where sex didn't happen, and it's going to be hard having her right next to me and not touching her in the way I so desperately want to.

But ever since I've come to spend more time here in Whispers, I'm seeing that there's a first time for everything. Tonight is no exception.

18

———

ANNABELLE

As I stand in my bathroom, getting ready for bed, I look at myself in the mirror, staring at my reflection.

Who am I? I was literally dry humping my lawyer against the wall in my kitchen. I almost groan now thinking about it. The warm, throbbing feeling is still present down below. It's not something I've ever done or ever thought I would do. Make out with a man like that. And that's exactly what he is, *all man*, if the bulge I felt when I wrapped my legs around him was any indication.

But it wasn't just a make-out session, it was much more than that. The feelings that are building for this man are undeniable.

I want to giggle and swoon in excitement, but it isn't just about me. I have two boys, both of whom are asleep in this very house. So even though my body is humming for Sawyer like it hasn't hummed for years, tonight needs to be calm, because my life is very different now. Not to mention, there's something going on here at the property, and I have no idea what it is.

Am I going crazy? Did I hear something? Do my eyes show signs of some kind of neurological condition that maybe makes me think things are happening around me that really aren't. Sighing, I look at the gash on my head and use a cool cloth to wipe the dry blood off my cheeks and around it carefully, hissing when it stings.

"You alright?" I look in the mirror, seeing Sawyer in the reflection behind me, leaning against the doorframe, watching me.

"Yeah, it just stings a little."

"Let me." Coming to my side, he grabs the cloth from my hand.

"I'm okay," I tell him but let him take the cloth from me anyway.

"I know," is all he says, a sweet look in his eyes.

I swallow as he tenderly brushes his fingers across my skin, my face soothing immediately. I close my eyes, reveling in his touch, the way he holds me like I will break. As hard as it is for me to give myself over, that's exactly what I do in this moment as I let him take care of me.

Looking down, I take in his new look. With his suitcase still in his truck from his trip here, he has a t-shirt and sweatpants on hand, and he's already changed for bed. Out of his suit, wearing casual clothes like this, makes him a hundred times more approachable, more real.

"I still can't believe Kevin called you."

"I'm glad he did." He continues to clean my skin.

"He never uses my phone for anything. I guess he doesn't have anyone to call." Although my son is quiet around Sawyer, he clearly trusts him enough to call if needed. That brings warmth to my chest, realizing that this could be Kevin accepting Sawyer, or at least starting to.

"That boy would do anything for you, including calling

me, a man who he seems to only grunt at for the most part," he says with a soft smile.

"I think he likes you."

"Hmmm. I've never had to prove my worth to kids as well as their mom before, but it's a challenge I'm going to take on." His honesty hits me right in the chest, and I swallow hard.

I lift my hands and hold on to his torso, feeling his solid frame underneath, as he continues to run the cool cloth gently on my face. His muscles clench a little at my touch, and I'm surprised by how firm he is. In a t-shirt, his arms are showcased more, his biceps a clear indicator that he works out. Probably at a gym or something since he works at a desk all day. My mind wanders to what might be underneath his t-shirt, that thought making me shiver, anticipation right on the cusp.

"Are you cold?" He moves the cloth, putting it under water to rinse. Once he squeezes out the water, he looks back at me, one finger under my chin and lifting my head to meet his eyes, before he puts the cool cloth back on my forehead.

"I'm fine." I stand in front of him in my shorts and singlet. My sleepwear is just as casual as his, although I bet a lot cheaper and a lot older.

"You will have a nice little bruise here for a few days." He growls a little. I know he isn't happy, and the fact that he's here, doing this, staying the night, shows me that he cares. I'm not sure many other men would do this. In fact, I'm almost positive they wouldn't. My fear has almost all left me now that he's staying. Having another adult in the house, a man, provides me a little relief, allowing me to lower my guard.

"At least it isn't a black eye or something."

"Still beautiful to me." Lowering the cloth from my head, his eyes take in every feature of my face.

"Thank you for staying." I feel a little vulnerable as his hand comes to my cheek, his fingers skirting over my skin before his thumb brushes across my bottom lip. He leans down, his eyes firmly on mine before he places his lips on mine.

"Ma!" I hear a groggy voice and quickly pull back from Sawyer.

"Noah, honey, are you alright?" I look to the doorway, seeing that he has red eyes from crying.

"I saw monsters again and my monster spray is empty," he cries, and I leave the small cocoon I was in with Sawyer to walk over and scoop him up.

"Monster spray?" Sawyer asks from over my shoulder, where I feel him standing at my back, just as quick to get to Noah as I was. His hands rest on my waist, and I lean back a little, feeling my back hit his solid chest and my body eases. He's here. He's supporting me.

"It's a special spray we use to keep the bedtime monsters away."

"Where do you get it from? Do you want me to go buy some?" He's seemingly ready to do anything I need, and I roll my lips to hold back a grin.

"Ma makes it for me," Noah says between sniffles as he leans away from me and puts his arms out to Sawyer. I feel my heart skip a beat.

"You want to come to me, buddy?" Sawyer seems surprised if his wide eyes are any tell.

"Yeah," Noah hiccups, and I look at Sawyer in question.

"I got him. You go make your monster spray." He takes Noah from my arms and pulls him to his torso. Sawyer's large arms embrace my son, and I can't move as I watch the two of them, Sawyer immediately grabbing a tissue and wiping my son's face with the same soft touch I just experienced.

"Should we go to your room and wait for your ma?" Sawyer asks Noah, but looks up, asking me the silent question. I nod as Noah hiccups a yes. I walk to the kitchen to quickly fill up an empty spray bottle with water, adding some blue glitter from my small craft box and mixing the concoction until it's ready to fight the monsters.

Walking back down the hallway to Noah's room, I pause at the door. Sawyer's sitting by Noah's bed, my son tucked in tight and cozy, and reading him a book. I swallow past the lump in my throat as my heart lurches in my chest.

"Here we are." I step into the room, holding out the water bottle. Noah instantly sits up and grabs it.

"Where did you see the monsters, buddy?" Sawyer asks him, putting the book down.

"Over there." Noah points toward the window, and I frown. I move over and triple-check it's locked before I pull the curtains firmly closed.

"There, all locked and tight. No monsters in here tonight."

"But what if they come back? What if the sprayer doesn't work?" Noah asks with teary eyes.

"They won't come back. But in case they do, do you want to test the spray on me?" Sawyer asks, and my eyebrows rise.

"But what if it hurts you?" Noah asks, his little eyebrows pinching together.

"The monster spray only works on monsters, darling. It won't hurt Sawyer," I add, coming to his side and kissing him on the forehead.

"Here, have a practice." Sawyer stands close by and puts

out his arms. I internally cringe that his crisp white t-shirt is about to be covered in blue glitter, but he asked for it.

Noah lifts the spray bottle and pulls the trigger a few times, squirting Sawyer right in the chest.

"Good shot. See, I told you, it's in perfect working order. Your ma wouldn't have it any other way." Sawyer grins at him, and I smile. With Noah now seemingly happy, he snuggles into bed, the water bottle firmly in his grasp.

"Good night, honey." I give his head another kiss and step away.

"Good night, Ma. Good night, Seesaw." He's already half asleep, his words mumbled.

"Good night, buddy." Sawyer takes my hand and leads me out and down the hall to my room.

"I'm sorry about your shirt. I can wash it now, if you like." I'm ready to fix it, even though it's late and I'm exhausted.

"Get into bed, Annabelle," he says firmly.

"But I don't want it to stain or ruin your top..." I add, wondering how bad it will be by morning.

"You're practically asleep standing up. You've had a hell of a night. Don't worry about my top. Get into bed." I move around to my side of the bed and slip in. At the same time, he grabs the shirt at the back of his neck and pulls it from his frame.

I gulp. I saw his brother's body on my cell phone, which surprised me. But now that I'm seeing the same defined muscles and the contouring of Sawyer's body in real life... I can't move my eyes.

"This alright? I don't want to wear wet clothes to bed." He remains standing, looking at me. I like that he asks me. He doesn't take it for granted that he can move around my space without my approval.

I pull the covers up to my chin. "Uh-huh." I nod, somewhat dazed, wondering if he can see drool on my chin from looking at his beautiful bare chest. The small smirk he gives me tells me that he does. He slides into the bed beside me, and my heart races like I've run a marathon. I haven't had a man in this bed in a very long time. Closing my eyes, I take a calming breath.

"Come here, my little warrior." He reaches for me, his large, strong hands finding my waist, and he pulls me across the bed and into his warm embrace. With my back now firmly against his bare chest, he hugs me to him, and I ease into it, feeling safe, secure, and content for the first time in forever.

"Warrior?" I grin, even though he can't see me.

"Hmmm, stubborn for sure, prideful, resilient, determined, courageous... beautiful..." he trails off, and I bite my bottom lip, scared my grin will split my face apart. I've never been complimented like this before. The attention he's bestowing on me is entirely new. He leans over and pecks a kiss on my bare shoulder. At that light touch, I close my eyes, my body feeling a sprinkling of warmth all over.

"You smell so good," he murmurs against my skin as his hands massage my waist, which sends an electric rush through my body, turning me on so quickly it's embarrassing.

"I forgot what it's like to be touched by a man..." I whisper mindlessly. My mouth dries, thinking about Sawyer's hands exploring me. Wanting it more than anything.

"Do you want me to touch you?" His words caress my neck, where he continues to pepper my skin with kisses. Both kids are now fast asleep down the hall, and even though the house is quiet, I know they'll be out for a while. We won't wake them.

"Yes…" I'm almost scared to ask, my heart still racing as my skin prickles under his touch.

His kisses on my neck become a little deeper as his hands start to roam. My body moves in response, back arching a little, my head and shoulders next to his as I push my hips back and grind into him.

I feel him again. Big, hard, ready. I have no idea what I'm doing, really, but my body appears to have a life of its own. I might as well be a cat the way I'm rubbing up against him.

"You keep grinding on me like that, and I'll need to get rid of my sweatpants too," he murmurs as one of his hands smooths up my torso, grabbing on to my breast and pulling a moan from my throat. I place my hand on top, silently asking for more. My breathing has increased, my skin hot and tingling as his hands roam my curves.

"That wouldn't be so bad." I'm already panting at the thought of it, trying to stay as quiet as possible. Sawyer growls then, his other hand lowering, slipping under my sleep shorts and finding my bare center. As he slides his fingers across my sensitive skin, I lift my other hand, cupping the back of his head and pulling him to my neck.

This feels so good. His solid body behind me, protecting me and pleasuring me. I feel equal parts safe and sexy as hell. It's almost like he's playing me like an instrument, and I've never felt more wanted.

"Sawyer," I whimper as he slides a finger inside of me, and I jolt a little in his arms. It feels so good. His touch is one of wanting, yet softer than I've ever experienced.

"Fuck, you're wet," he groans under his breath, like he's trying his best to be quiet too. His hips grind into my ass, his lips never leaving my skin, now biting and sucking on that sensitive spot where my neck meets my shoulder. I push my head back a little more as his fingers circle my clit, working in a rhythm that my mind can no longer make sense of because my feelings are becoming overwhelming.

I haven't had this before. Sex with my late husband was brutal, hurtful, rough, and many times without consent. He was clumsy, only thinking of himself and his own needs, with me acting as a mere doll underneath him that he positioned in any way he damn well wanted.

But now, even though Sawyer is all over me, he's taking care of me. He's making me bloom inside. I feel alive and desired and deserving. His hold on me is firm, yet it doesn't hurt, and it isn't prohibiting me. His kisses on my skin, the way his other hand molds to me, it's like he's worshipping me. Not just using me for his own sexual relief, which is what my entire previous sex life was about.

"Oh God, Sawyer," I say through a soft moan. Biting my bottom lip to hold back the sounds trying to escape, my hips move against his hand, the pain in my head now long forgotten as my body thrums for release.

"That's it. God, you're so fucking sexy..." His tone is low, almost feral, his dick so hard and pressing into my back. He quickens his pace, his fingers tools of magic as he rubs my clit, and I feel my body right on the edge. It's like I'm vibrating and about to combust.

"I'm going to... Oh my God... Sawyer..." I almost hiccup, feeling out of this world, like I'm on drugs or something. My orgasm is one that's built up over years, the sensations so strong, I start rocking my entire body on his hand.

He lifts his other hand from my breast and runs it up to my neck, holding my jaw firmly and moving my lips to meet his with a moan.

His kiss is brutal, our breathing labored, my body now shaking.

"Let go for me, Mama. Come for me," he growls.

A loud moan nearly bursts from me, but Sawyer is quick, moving his hand to cover my mouth as I chant his name, my body shuddering as his movements intensify. I come so hard, it's almost embarrassing, my body completely letting go for the first time in a very long time.

As the tension releases, Sawyer removes his hand from my mouth, kissing me again as I relax back into him. His hands move back to my waist, his mouth back to peppering my shoulders. I feel him still rock-hard, and I go to move, wanting to reciprocate.

"Stay where you are and go to sleep, Annabelle. That was hot as hell, and I want to do that again in the morning, so I can see your face clearly when I make you come. But right now, you need your rest, and I want to fall asleep with you in my arms."

I swallow roughly, wondering if there's a sign-up sheet for that morning activity, because it can't come fast enough.

I hum a laugh, and I feel his lips as he grins against my skin, both of us getting more comfortable as I cuddle into him. I've never felt this safe in my entire life. With my body and mind now calm, within moments, I'm out.

Having the best sleep of my entire life, all wrapped up in his arms.

19

SAWYER

I wake with the sun on my face and immediately know I'm not in my bed. The sheets feel different, the light too bright, and as I open my eyes, I understand why.

"What the fuck." I sit up, a little groggy and discombobulated. Annabelle is still beside me, sound asleep, and I admire her for a moment. Her face is relaxed, her beautiful long hair sweeping over the pillow. She's even beautiful when she sleeps. The way she came last night, the way her body molded to mine, the way she grinded her ass into my raging hard dick had me feeling so many things. Even now, thinking about it, my cock is rock-solid. In bed, with me, her body moved in a way that was all woman. I felt every dip and curve, and now my feelings for her have grown even more. I bet she looks fucking amazing naked.

I spot the gash on her forehead and frown. It doesn't look much better, but at least the butterfly closures held overnight, meaning she doesn't need stitches. I reach out for her, my hand gliding across her waist, over her curves, her soft skin feeling like heaven.

"Hey..." she says sleepily, grabbing my attention as she

rolls over. Her singlet pulls a little, giving me a view of her chest that teases me. I spot a few red love marks on her neck and bite on my back molars, knowing I was the person to put those there.

"Morning, Mama." My voice sounds like gravel.

"You're still here?" She smiles, but my brow furrows.

"Where did you think I'd be?" I wonder what time the boys will wake and whether I can have her again beforehand.

"I thought you might've snuck out in the night or early this morning."

I lie back down next to her, the two of us now face-to-face, our noses a mere inch apart.

"I'm not sneaking out of here. I like waking up with you." My hand rests on the dip in her waist. I move my fingers a little, her top lifting a bit, and touch her bare skin. I'm itching to take her lips in a searing kiss, to feel more of her like last night.

"Mmmm... kids in the room when you wake is probably not your ideal scenario?"

I freeze my movements. My eyes flick to the floor on her side, and I see a bundle in front of her. Noah, still holding his monster spray. He must've crept in during the night. Then my eyes sweep down next to him, where I spot Kevin. Lying with his brother, the two of them are still asleep, covered in blankets.

Fuck. No morning glory for either of us today.

I run my hand through my hair. "That's not something I've had to navigate before."

"It doesn't happen often. But they're kids." Shrugging on her side, she watches me carefully.

"It just gives a new meaning to the word edging..." I tease her, and as she smiles up at me, I lean over and take her lips with mine. The kiss is short and not scorching like I want it to be, but her hand lifts, cupping my jaw, and I pull her closer, enjoying the feel of her in my arms.

"Are you a breakfast guy?" she asks as I pull back, and I grin.

"Sometimes. Other times, I rush to the office and live off coffee for the day."

"What are you today?"

The answer is, I have no idea. I'm usually well attuned to my schedule. I'm up early to work out, and I hit the ground running on emails and ensure I clock in for all my meetings. I probably have a million things to do, but having no idea what time it is, and with my cell phone still in my suit jacket hanging on her bedroom door, I find that I couldn't care less. Today, my mind is blank. For the life of me, I can't think of anything but her.

"Breakfast sounds pretty good right about now." I rub her nose with mine, and she hums, the sound warming my chest.

"Pancakes okay with you?" she asks quietly, our lips moving against each other, albeit incredibly slowly.

"Anything you make, I will love," I whisper into another kiss. My workday's starting in an entirely new way. Who knew a Broadway show over breakfast would be much more entertaining.

I'm on my second coffee for the day, and the fact that the diner is close by is either a really good or a really bad thing. My waistline is no doubt going to grow from Rochelle's food, as well as Annabelle's.

I've spent most of the day in meetings, filed a few key contracts, and I'm feeling relatively stress free.

"You have a minute?" Jerry walks into my office, and I smile.

"Sure, let's take a seat." I gesture to my Chesterfield lounge. The small space is completely different to my city office, yet one that's strangely comforting.

"How are you feeling?" I know that retirement is different for everyone. When my mom decided to retire, she was scared. Having worked all her life at low-paying jobs, she didn't have much money of her own. But Sutton and I got her set up, paid into her retirement fund, and she's now having the time of her life. Wendy, my assistant, is itching to start her twilight years. The all-expenses-paid cruise I purchased for her and her husband will no doubt see them off in luxury.

"I'm feeling ready. But the question is, are you?" Jerry looks at me inquisitively. Of course I'm ready. Whispers is child's play compared to the city.

"I'm sure I'll be fine, Jerry." I smirk. Cocky perhaps, but I know what I'm doing.

"You know I used to work in the city."

"You did?" I didn't know this piece of information. I assumed he worked here his entire life.

"Have you heard of Walker and Co.?" Walker and Co. is one of my competitors. They aren't as big now, but back in the day, they were the law firm everyone wanted to work for. They were who I modeled my own firm after.

"Yes..." My head tilts, wondering where he's going with this.

"Well, I started Walker and Co. when I was in my mid-twenties, not long after I finished law school."

"You started Walker and Co.?" I clarify, because none of

it makes sense. But as I look at him, his appearance seems somewhat familiar, knowing I've probably seen his photo somewhere along the line, perhaps when I was researching internships in college.

"I did. Built it up over a decade or so, before I came to Whispers." He grins at the memory.

"What made you come to Whispers? You were at the top of your game. Your law firm was worth millions. Still is," I ask, bewildered.

"Love," he says, and my questioning thoughts pause.

"Love?"

"Met my girl Bernie here when I was passing through one day. My jet had to land to refuel, some issue we had when flying from the West Coast back to the East. Ended up staying a night, met Bernie at the diner. Had dinner and never left. We just celebrated our fortieth wedding anniversary last month."

I'm a little baffled. "But Walker and Co. was one of the bigger players. You would've been a multimillionaire."

"Still am. Sold at the height. I got my millions, invested them well, and moved here to the love of my life. I've worked in this office ever since." He huffs another laugh as he looks around, taking in the walls, like he's saying a silent goodbye.

I shake my head, trying to process this. "But... that doesn't make any sense..."

"Well, work back then isn't what it is now. You kids run meetings online, any time of the day or night. Back in my day, it was all face-to-face, in an office. I had to make a choice. Work or Bernie."

"But you built an empire. Then you just left it all and came to Whispers?"

"Yeah. You know what they say, love makes you do crazy things."

"Didn't you miss it? The hustle, the thrill of the chase, the deals, the negotiation?" I grew my career on big deals, on million-dollar contracts. I've negotiated some large transactions, helped many of my clients with significant business growth, Tanner and Connor one such example.

"None of it really means much. More about your own ego than anything else. Besides, my Bernie has given me lots to negotiate, lots of thrills, and lots of good times over the years. I wouldn't change it for the world."

Nodding, I find myself smiling, one person on my mind as I ask, "How did you know?"

"Know what?"

"That Bernie was worth it." I swallow, knowing he knows. Hell, the whole town practically knows about Annabelle and me if the look Rochelle was giving me in the diner earlier today was anything to go by.

"I knew the minute I laid eyes on her."

I feel a jolt of realization zap me to my core. I can still remember exactly what Annabelle was wearing the first time I saw her, including her scowl when I cursed in front of the kids.

"But how were you satisfied from a work perspective?" What he's talking about is somewhat admirable, but my work fuels me. It's been my driving force for years. The one constant, the one thing I can control and build, making me a billionaire in my own right.

"Whispers may be a small, sleepy town, but even in your sleep, you still have nightmares. Don't underestimate the problems that will arise for you here. Sure, they may not be every week, or maybe they will be, but you'll have a good workload, one that keeps you busy and pushes you to your limits at times. But you'll also have a good work/life balance and get to go home to a warm hug, a hot, home-cooked meal, and the love of a good woman. That's something I never found in the city, and I don't imagine it's any easier to find there now." It feels like he's a parent, inadvertently offering me advice.

I'm familiar with some criminal cases here in Whispers over the years. Hell, just the issues my friends have had with their partners is enough to keep me busy for months. I look at my calendar, knowing I have a few locals booked in for meetings over the course of the next few weeks. At the time, I assumed it would be simple paper shuffling, a few signatures, and a low level of work required, but I'm starting to see that it may be more than that.

"Alright, well, I need to go. Will I see you at the game tomorrow?" He stands like he didn't just drop a bomb on me, and I walk toward him, putting out my hand to shake his.

"I think so." Weekends in Whispers are something I was adamant I wouldn't do, yet now I don't want to miss the game or miss spending more time with Annabelle and the kids.

"Good. It's nice to have a new face to support the teams. Good luck here, Sawyer," he says as we shake.

I grin. "Enjoy retirement, Jerry."

"I plan to." He grabs his bag and walks out, this law office and its clients now all mine.

As I watch him go, I look out across the street. People are walking around, women stopping to chat, a couple of older guys carrying some furniture into a building, and I see Jerry heading straight across to the diner, which seems to be the place to be during the day.

Maybe Jerry's right. I know Whispers is where billionaires come to hide, and maybe this little town has more to offer me in business than I originally gave it credit for. I think about his words, about him and his wife, and then I think about Annabelle. I have meetings scheduled with my team and a to-do list to check off, but knowing she's now home from work and the boys are not with her at the moment, I grab my jacket and head out the door.

20

───────

ANNABELLE

With Noah still with Debbie baking cookies and Kevin at baseball training with Harvey, I have a few hours at home on my own before I need to collect them both. So that means my hands are in the dirt, trying to sort out the vegetable patch I've been meaning to get to for weeks.

Summer's coming, and things are looking good. The peas have started to slow, so I have cut them back. The broccoli and cauliflower have completely stopped, which both my boys will be happy about. So I clear them out and then plant some cucumbers and tomatoes, already salivating at the fresh summer salads I can make. I wipe my brow and cringe a little, forgetting for a moment about the slash on my forehead. My eyes canvass the farm quickly, as they have all day. I no longer feel safe here, especially on my own. But it's quiet now, so I just get on with things. I have no other choice.

Just as I finish, I hear a vehicle approach, and my heart jumps as fear takes hold, but I relax the minute I notice it's

Sawyer. I smile. He stayed last night. For the first time in years, I had a man in my house. In my bed. The way his hands caressed my body still makes me throb down below. Even now, as I watch him drive up to the house, my skin prickles. I never realized what I'd been missing all these years of having my mind focused on the boys and our livelihood. Entertaining a man was not a priority and not something I was looking for.

I wasn't expecting him back so early. We didn't talk this morning about what it all means, but I hoped he would come back. I hoped my feelings weren't one-sided. I enjoy spending time with him, and the way he made me feel last night, I want to repeat over and over. It's been a long time since I felt like a wanted woman. A woman that a man wanted to touch, that a man wanted to kiss. I wasn't a mom, I wasn't a teacher, I wasn't a hardworking, struggling parent. I was just me, and he wanted me, and it felt good.

"Hey." Tilting my head in question, I stand as he hops out of his truck, the shiny polish reflecting the bright sun, his suit wrinkle free, his shoes high shine. I brush my dirty hands over my thighs, trying to look at least half as decent as he does, but it's futile. "You're back early."

He smiles, his eyes locked on mine. "Missed you."

I think my knees give way. This is what every girl dreams of. This is the moment in all the movies I watched as a teenager, the ones where I dreamed that someone would sweep me off my feet. Both literally and figuratively.

"Me too." My heart is beating out of my chest for a whole different reason now, my fear long forgotten. I've been thinking about him all day.

"I also forgot something."

I frown, pretty sure he took his briefcase and all his

things this morning, not remembering seeing anything else of his left behind.

"Oh? What was it?"

He stalks toward me, steel determination on his face and a sneaking glint in his eye.

"This," is all he says once he's in front of me, his hands cupping my face before he slams his lips into mine so fiercely it almost knocks me from my feet.

But I don't fall. He drops one arm and wraps it around my waist tight, my chest flush against his as his fingers run up to my scalp and thread into my hair. His lips are demanding, and after a split-second of surprise and awe, mine follow suit.

"Sawyer?" My body melts like butter in his hold as I lift my hands and run them up his arms. Feeling safe and wanted in his embrace, I kiss him back just as feverishly.

"You're all I can think about," he says, and I moan in agreement.

"The feeling of you..." he continues as I try to get a hold of myself, my body now feeling out of control with desire.

"The smell of you..." His lips take what he needs, and I'm nearly breathless.

"The way your body moves against mine. Your beautiful little moans..."

I moan again in response, one he swallows with another consuming kiss.

"I haven't stopped thinking about you either." I dig my fingers in his hair, pulling his head closer, not getting enough of him. "The kids aren't home..."

Instantly, he leans down and grabs the back of my thighs, scooping me up, and I wrap my legs around him.

"Tell me you want to go to your room."

I know he would stop if I wanted to, but I don't. I very much want to keep going.

"Yes. Please."

That's all it takes before he strides to the house, carrying me like I weigh nothing, our lips not leaving each other's. I'm glad no one is around, because we probably look ridiculous, him all high polish, me like I crawled out of a cave, yet our bodies fit so well together. We mesh just right.

He climbs up the porch stairs, pushing through the front door, leaning me against the wall, the same place we started last night.

"Are you sure? I don't want..."

Before he finishes, I'm pulling off my extra layer of a sweater, and his words trail away. "I'm sure," I tell him, and the look in his eyes has my stomach flipping.

"I want to taste every inch of this beautiful body." He brushes each word into my skin, his lips dragging along my shoulder and down to my chest, where my tank top still covers my body. Pressed against the wall, my head falls back, opening myself up to him. His hand roams, cupping my breast, molding it in his palm before he trails it down my torso, opening my jeans.

"Yessss," I pant, whimpering when he grazes the waist of my underwear teasingly. I've never wanted a man to touch me as much as I want Sawyer to right now.

"Your little whimpers are going to be my undoing," he lifts me from the wall, walking me to the dining table, the one half covered in paperwork and kids' crafts, all now swept to the side as he sits me on the edge.

"I've ruined your suit... again..." I push his jacket from his shoulders, seeing the dirt that was on me now covering his white shirt.

"Better take it off, then." He makes quick work of it,

unbuttoning then removing his shirt, and I swallow. I saw him half-naked last night, so his bare chest isn't a surprise, but it's just as breathtaking in the daylight, even more so, as I can fully see every chiseled muscle on his chest, all the way down to the six-pack that ends with that little V-shape men get. My mouth waters at the sight.

"Your turn." He waits, his breathing labored, and I grab the hem of my top and lift it off my frame. My long hair falls around me, now only in my bra and jeans.

"So fucking beautiful," he groans like it pains him, lifting his hand as his fingers softly run down my bra strap, all the way until he dips them inside my cup.

I look him in the eye as I move my hand around my back and unclasp my bra, slight nervousness sprinkling down my chest. I haven't been naked in front of a man in a very long time. Even with Steve, it wasn't like this. He never admired me, never looked at me the way Sawyer is. Pulling the bra down my arms, I drop it on the floor.

"Fuck me..." His lips come back to mine with a needy groan. His hands are on me, molding my breasts, feeling my curves. My whole body heats, shaking with lust. Last night, I had my first orgasm given to me by a man in years. And right now, I really want to have another one.

"More... I want more..." I whisper as my hands move to his waist, and I grab his belt, undoing it, then I open his suit pants.

"Lie back."

I ease myself back, the table feeling a little unstable underneath me as his hand runs down my bare body, between my breasts until he hits my jeans, which are still undone. Grabbing them at my waist, he pulls them down my legs and off my body, and I'm left in nothing but my plain white cotton underwear. No lace in my life; this is as sexy as I get. I start to feel mortified and move my hands to cover myself.

"Don't move," he grits out, then he lowers onto the chair, positioning himself at the table, right between my legs.

"Sawyer?" I'm unsure until I feel his kisses on the inside of my thigh, and it dawns on me exactly what is going to happen.

"Relax, Mama," he murmurs, probably having felt me stiffen. His hands smooth up my legs, before they land on the inside of my knees and he pushes my legs farther apart.

Nerves take over me as I stammer, "I've never... I mean, I haven't."

"You've never had a man go down on you?" I swallow, my heart ready to pound right out of my chest.

"No." Shaking my head, I wince as I look down at him. From where he's still placing light kisses on my inner thighs, his eyes find mine.

"If you want me to stop, I will, but I really want to taste you right now... I want to make you come on my tongue." He doesn't move, waiting for permission. My thighs quiver as I nod eagerly.

"Yes..." I'm too scared to speak too loudly in case I start begging.

Moving closer to my center, his finger traces over the cotton fabric that still separates us. My body almost liquifies as I lean back, my head hitting the table, my legs spread with Sawyer between them.

"Oh shit..." I whisper to myself in anticipation and disbelief, but I feel Sawyer's grin on my skin, knowing he heard me.

"Fuck, you have a pretty pussy." My cheeks heat instantly as he pulls my underwear to the side. Before any other words can be spoken, his tongue swipes through me, making me gasp. I hold my breath as he circles around my clit, my arousal now heightened even more. My legs widen automatically, letting him in closer, and his two hands push my thighs farther apart.

"That's it," he encourages me, and I start moaning like it's my job.

"Oh my God," I pant, the sensations overwhelming. His hold on me is tight, his tongue working magic, and then he sucks on my clit, and my back arches completely off the table.

"Sawyer!" I gasp as my hands fling to his head and fist his hair, but he hasn't finished. He keeps sucking and lapping at me, and my body starts trembling. This is new, the blissful feeling wrapping around my body, and I think I'm having an out-of-body experience. I'll wake up from this dream any minute, I'm sure of it.

I'm chanting words that I can't even comprehend as he eats me like I'm his last meal. I had no idea it was this good. I had no idea what I've missed out on. I'm so glad I don't have neighbors nearby, because they would hear everything.

"You gonna come for me, Mama?" He speaks against my clit, sucking, then licking, the rhythm making my eyes cross. I bite my bottom lip as my whole body tenses, and with one last tease of his tongue swirling around and around, I detonate.

"Sawyer!" I scream, shaking uncontrollably as I grip his hair tight. He sucks on my clit harder as I convulse under him, and when he growls into me, the vibrations can be felt right down to my toes.

Slumping back onto the table, I try to catch my breath as Sawyer goes back to peppering soft kisses to my thighs before he looks up at me. The blush to my cheeks is as instant as my wide grin as he licks his lips.

"Mmm. Probably my favorite meal I've had at this table so far," he murmurs with a wicked gleam in his eyes. I can't stop the giggle that bubbles past my lips, because I know I will never be able to look at this dining table the same way ever again.

21

SAWYER

I look down at her, her beautiful naked body on full display as I pull the underwear from her hips, throwing them on the floor to meet the rest of her clothes.

She's breathtaking. Smiling brightly, her eyes glistening, her body perfect and all mine.

"This seems unequal." She sits up, the dining table squeaking as she moves. Her long, messy hair falls behind her, her face now inches away from me. I briefly look at the gash on her forehead, and I grind my teeth. I still need to get to the bottom of what happened because I need her safe. I thought about grabbing her and the boys and taking them to my place, but I know she would never come. She would never want to leave the farm here, even for a little while.

"What does?"

Her hands come to the waist of my suit pants, and my eyes immediately hook back on hers.

"I'm the only one naked..." she says sweetly, trailing off. I'm hard as a fucking rock, but I wait, letting her feel comfortable, not wanting to make a wrong move.

When I came here, I had to calm myself a dozen times in the car. I wanted to grab her and take her straight to bed. I wanted to rip the clothes from her body and have her in every position I know how. I wanted her hard and fast before I rocked into her slow and needy. But I have to be mindful; I don't want to misstep or do something that may trigger a bad memory for her. I still don't know anything about her past, but it's clear she's a survivor.

"You can fix that." I move my hand up to cup her jaw, and she promptly pushes my pants down my legs. As I run my thumb across her cheek, I kick off my shoes, my eyes never leaving hers.

"Nearly done," she says seductively, a look on her face that makes me think she wants the same thing as I do. Her fingers grab the waist of my underwear, and she pulls them down without an ounce of hesitation.

Her eyes widen a little at the sight of me, and I smirk as I palm myself, feeling my cock full, hot, and heavy in my hand.

"You okay?" I wonder what she's thinking as I run my thumb across her cheek to her bottom lip, pulling it from her teeth as she looks back up at me.

She swallows audibly. "It's been a long time."

"We don't need to do anything you..."

"I want this. I want you. And I don't want you to go easy."

I raise my eyebrows at that, a little surprised.

"Are you sure?" I'm right on the edge, wanting to scoop her up and have her in every way.

"I've never had a man give me pleasure before, Sawyer," she whispers, and I can feel the desire in her gaze as she stares up at me. My dick jerks in my hand just from looking at her. "I want you to treat me like you want me."

I chuckle darkly. "Oooh, make no mistake, Mama, I want

you," I growl, and her hand joins mine on my cock, the air around us growing thicker with tension by the second.

"Then prove it." She smirks slightly, like she's laying down a challenge, one I'm all too prepared to meet.

I lean over, grabbing a condom from my wallet as she continues to palm me. I grit my teeth, because her hand on my body is almost too much.

"You want me to show you how much I want you?" As I sheathe myself, she leans back on the table, watching me, biting her bottom lip, the independent vixen she is now on full display. I watch the table sway a little and wonder briefly if it will hold us.

"Fuck me like you mean it." That's all the approval I need before I'm on her.

Grabbing her around the knees, I pull her to the very edge of the table. It rocks a little as she sits up and her hands reach out, looping around my neck, my own moving to her bare, beautiful ass. I squeeze her muscle, moving her so her glistening pussy is right where I need her to be, then enter her in one swift movement.

Her body stiffens with a sharp intake of breath before she moans, relaxing around me.

"You don't think I want you, Annabelle?" I grit out as I start to thrust.

"Sawyer," she pants, her hands tightening around my neck.

"You don't think I would want a sexy, smart, fucking breathtakingly beautiful woman like you?" I say again, huffing and groaning, thrusting into her, deeper and deeper with every movement.

"Oh... my... God." Her body jolting with every thrust, the table rocks underneath us as she whimpers for me.

"You're so fucking sexy, it's sinful. I just had a taste of

you, and I already want more." I feel my balls drawing up to my body, my heart racing, putting all my thoughts and feelings about her into my movements. She feels good, too damn good. Her enticing rose scent sweeps over me as she reacts to me in a way that has all my senses on high alert. I'm rock-hard with her pussy clenching around me, and I think I might pass out.

"Sawyer, you feel so... so good." Her voice becomes high-pitched when I hit that spot inside her that has her eyes rolling back, making my stomach tighten, my orgasm building.

"I've never craved a woman as much as I crave you," I tell her honestly, my hands digging into her flesh so hard, I know I'll leave bruises. I thrust into her hard, over and over, sweet and soft not on the menu today. Our desire for each other is too much, and she asked for this, so I'm nothing if not a man of my word.

"Sawyer! Yes... riiiight there..." She bites her bottom lip as I grind myself against her G-spot before thrusting nice and hard. I grin, feeling how she's getting close.

"Your pussy is perfect, clenching on me, telling me you want more..." I look down at where we're joined, seeing how we fit just right.

She moans long and loud, her nails digging into me. "Don't stop, please, please, please..."

Fuck, she's amazing. The table is getting punished, but I care little for it. I just want to make her come.

"You like this? You like me fucking you on your table, Mama?"

"Yes, yes..." she pants, her moans increasing as she thrusts herself against me.

"You like me taking you the minute we walked in the

door, not able to wait until I had a taste, had you a screaming mess on my tongue."

"Sawyer..." She says my name almost in warning, and my jaw tics, feeling pushed to the brink, my release so close. Her head is thrown back, her breasts jiggling right near my face, and it's a sight I won't soon forget. She's fucking magnificent.

"You like me fucking you like I want you. You better know now how much I fucking want this, Annabelle. I want you so fucking badly... Want you to come with me inside you," I grit out, and she lets go with a scream, her head flinging up to lock her eyes on mine.

My thrusts quicken even more at the intensity of her orgasm, fucking her harder as I let go with her.

"Fuccckkkkk," I groan, feeling feral, pounding into her like she's my lifeline before we both slow and come back down to earth. She leans her head forward, resting on my bare chest, our bodies coated in a light sheen of sweat, naked, right here on the dining table.

"I didn't even get you into the bedroom... that's how much I want you, Annabelle," I murmur as I run my hand up and down her bare back, kissing her shoulder. I feel alive. The most alive I have in years. My body is humming, my mind is clear, and it's like I'm finally exactly where I need to be.

"I want you too." She pulls back, looking at me. We stare at each other for a moment, and I swallow, my feelings for her growing to a place I wasn't sure I would ever experience in my lifetime. I lean over, taking her lips with mine, my kiss featherlight and in complete contrast to how I just treated her. The only thing that stops our kiss is when we hear a crack, our eyes widening.

"Oh shit..." she says, just as my hands scoop her up, and

the table falls from under her, the legs giving way and breaking completely.

"We'll be needing a new table, then..." I grin, and she huffs a laugh as I walk her down the hall to clean up so we can fix the mess before the boys come home.

22

ANNABELLE

The sun is lowering as I wipe sweat from my brow.

"What if I pushed it and you pulled it?" Kevin suggests, the two of us trying to lift a large oak barrel that Tanner gave us about a year ago.

"It's too big. It's too big to roll, too big for me to lift. It's just too big." I sigh, my hands finding my hips. We are both tired after a big day at school, and since Noah is still with Debbie for a few more hours, Kevin and I are getting some things done around here. But moving this barrel has taken up most of our time, and we have only managed to get it a few feet across the barn floor.

I admire the new nook I'm putting together to store all my soapmaking utensils. It looks good with my homemade shelves and a small old cupboard I found. My idea was to have this barrel at the side to use as a high-top table, giving me some extra bench space. That idea is feeling less and less genius, though, as the afternoon wears on.

"Why don't you go inside, wash up, and start your homework. I'll just fix up out here and see if I make the space work without it."

Kevin looks at the nook, to the barrel, and then back to me.

"Okay..." He sounds unsure, but he knows it's futile. I watch him go inside, the door closing behind him before I look back at the barrel.

"You are not getting the better of me today." I roll my shoulders and get back to the task at hand. Grinding my teeth, I push it, feeling it roll a little but not much. Tanner warned me that this was a bigger barrel than usual, which is why I wanted it. Seeing it sitting out back of his distillery one day when I was there to see Victoria, I knew immediately how good it would look in my barn and have only now taken the time to try to move it.

That task appears to be easier said than done. But I'm not really concentrating. My mind keeps going back to Sawyer. Because of him, we have a brand-new dining table and chairs, which he had flown in from the city within a few hours of us breaking it. I have no idea how he did it, but I guess as a man with means, he can get things quickly and easily. While I offered to pay, he declined, a move I'm not overly comfortable with; however, the fact that he half broke it helped me to reconcile the purchase. It's now been a couple of weeks since that day. He's working more and more from Whispers, his travel time away becoming less and less. He's here almost every night, helping with the boys, spending quiet nights with me. My bed hasn't broken yet, but it will. With all the activity that we're doing, it's only a matter of time.

My cheeks heat as I think about how good we are together. My lack of a sex life has now well and truly been eliminated, the two of us unable to keep our hands off each other some days. We have sex just like in the movies. The kind of sex that we both want so much, we can't even make it to the bedroom. The kind of sex where I feel wanted, desired, craved by a man who could literally be on the cover of those fancy men's magazines.

"Come on…" I grit out, trying to focus on the barrel as I put my whole body into it, pushing as hard as I can. I can lift it a little, I'm not totally inept, but being small-bodied, I have no weight behind me.

"What the hell do you think you're doing?"

I jump a little before I look up and see Sawyer standing at the barn door, looking as polished as ever in his suit, with his hands on his hips. My lips twitch, his presence making me smile. I have developed serious feelings for this man, and that's impossible to deny.

"Hey." I stand up, blowing out a breath as I push the hair from my face.

"Please tell me you are not trying to move that by yourself." Even with all the time he's been spending at my place, this is the first time he's been inside the barn.

"Well…" I shrug, because he caught me in the act, and I can't lie to him. Moving closer, his hand skirts around my waist and his lips meet mine too briefly.

"Where do you need it?" He steps back and removes his jacket, folding it over his arm before placing it over the rack of garden supplies.

"No! You'll get dirty…" I tell him, but he pulls his tie from around his neck and opens the top buttons of his shirt, lifting his eyebrows in my direction.

"Where do you want it, Annabelle?" His voice is a little deeper, the sound tracking from my nipples straight down to my core. *God, this man.*

"I was thinking over there." I point listlessly, my eyes now only on him as he rolls up his sleeves, his polished veneer now ruffled and sexy as hell. Men in suits are hot, men in suits that are undone I now realize is a new level of hotness unlocked.

"Here…" Leaning forward, he wipes his thumb over my lower lip. "You're drooling." His grin is wicked before he grips my chin, bringing my lips to his and kissing me hard. I lift onto my tiptoes as his hands land on my ass, and he squeezes my curves tightly in his palm. I melt like butter, leaning into him, his arms holding me so tight it feels like there's nowhere else I'm meant to be.

"Missed you," he murmurs against my lips, and my chest warms even more.

"Mmmm, me too." And then I'm kissing him again.

"At least you kiss better than you give directions." He chuckles as he pulls back slightly. "Now, try again… Tell me where you want it."

Rolling my lips, I point to where I'm trying to move the barrel. "Over in the corner… on the left."

I squeal as he slaps my ass before stepping back from me, and I need to hang on to the shed wall where I'm standing so I don't topple. I swear this man is a continual surprise, and I can't get enough.

"Right, got it." He squats to pick up the barrel and my eyes widen. I thought he would just roll it, push it along the floor, but he picks it up like it's as light as a feather and walks it over to exactly where I need it, putting it down carefully before standing back up.

In awe, I step over, my mouth now watering. I knew he was strong, but he isn't really a man-of-the-land kind of guy. But seeing him just now getting his hands dirty, helping me, does something to my insides.

"Right here okay?" He dusts off his hands.

"Uh-huh." My eyes roam over him, nearly speechless.

"You're doing it again…" he warns, watching me.

"Doing what?" I'm not really paying attention to our conversation, my eyes glued to his white shirt that's now dirty, the way his forearms are showing from his rolled-up sleeves, and the tease of his bare chest from where his shirt is open at his collar.

"Drooling... But I'm not complaining." He's smirking when my eyes make their way up to his face.

"You need to take off your shirt, it's dirty..." My hands hit his chest, and I start opening the buttons in a hurry.

"Are you trying to get me naked in the barn, Mama?" His hand comes to my waist, gripping me there, and I have to hold back a moan from how aroused that simple touch makes me. Opening the last button, I push the shirt from his shoulders, Sawyer's chiseled body now right in front of me.

"God, yes..." I lean in and kiss him, and his grip on me tightens. Pulling me close, our lips fight for dominance, my body thrumming for him, never having felt this needy for a man before.

You would think we haven't seen each other for weeks, not just mere hours it's been since this morning when he woke up in my bed. I lower myself down his body, leaving trails of kisses along his chest, my hands touching him all over, feeling every ridge, every muscle. I move them to his belt, making quick work of it before I open his pants and fall to my knees on the floor at his feet.

"God, this is like every fucking wet dream I've had coming to life," I hear him murmur as his hand dives into my hair. Tugging his underwear down, my thighs clench at seeing him hard for me already. I should pause; I should hesitate. But I know we won't be interrupted, with Kevin firmly inside and no one else here.

My need for him is too much, and I take him in, hungry

to please him, my mouth teasing his tip a little before licking along his length.

He hisses. "Fuck, baby... this was not what I was expecting when I walked in here..."

"Well, I need to thank you somehow..." I say playfully, my eyes on his as I take him back into my mouth, my tongue sliding down his length again before I suck on his tip.

"I will move any damn barrel you have... any day of the week, if this is the thanks I get. Fuck, this feels good. You're so good to me." When he groans, I take him deeper.

Leaning back on my heels, I take a breath, palming him with my hand as I grin.

"There are some things on the farm I need help with..."

"Name it. I'll do it," he says eagerly, and I giggle.

"Hmmm... you will ruin your suit, though..." I say as I feel him thicken even more in my grip.

"You will ruin me the way you are teasing me right now. Let me feel your throat, Mama... Take me deeper..." I follow his instructions and do as he asks, taking him deeper, all the way to the back of my throat, sucking on him thoroughly as desire courses through my own body.

I quicken my pace as I rock my hips, needing some friction, needing something. His fist tightens in my hair, the sting on my scalp welcome as he pulls my head back into his hands so I'm looking up at him again.

"Fuck, I'm going to come, baby... I'm going to come so fucking hard down your pretty little throat." He grunts, his thighs tensing, and I whimper around him, swirling my tongue and sucking him in the way I've learned he loves. With one more husky, rumbling groan, he comes with jerking hips, his orgasm coating my throat.

Swallowing him down, I pull off with a pop, sitting back on my heels, and catching my breath.

"Best Friday night I've had for a while," he says, breathing heavily, and I grin as I move my thighs together, still feeling needy.

"Me too," I admit, loving that our time together has been this good, and knowing that I'm falling a little more every day for the man I can't stop thinking about.

"Come here." He grabs me under the arms and hoists me onto the barrel he just moved.

"Sawyer!" I squeal, laughing at the unexpected manhandling.

"Let's test this barrel, see if it can hold you when you come on my tongue." He opens my jeans when I moan my yes, and I lean back as he strips them from my legs, then devours me with his mouth, my burning need for him satisfied. For now.

23

SAWYER

I watch Kevin pitch for what feels like the hundredth time, the ball hitting the hay bale hard. After working from the office this morning, I came back here to spend the afternoon with Annabelle and the boys.

It's something I never really did in the city. I never left the office early. If anything, I worked late almost every night. But out here, I don't want to be stuck in the office when I know I could be doing this. To the surprise of everyone, including myself, I'm now here in Whispers most days. My travels back to the city are reserved for quick trips to attend key meetings or to troubleshoot emergency issues that arise.

Every day keeps getting better than the last. Time with Annabelle is amazing. The conversations we have, hanging out here at the farm, our mind-blowing sex, all of it makes me happier than I've ever been. Now, while Annabelle's inside with Noah, preparing dinner, I thought I would try to spend some time with Kevin. If I want to be with Annabelle, I need to forge connections with her kids. Noah is easy, the kid loves me. But Kevin, he's a completely different can of worms. One I've been attempting to open little by little.

"Good shot. Why don't you try repositioning your hands like this? It will help if you ever want to throw a curveball." I grab the ball and show him the grip to take, and he concentrates on exactly that. I ordered him a new mitt and a few new balls. I got myself one too, and Noah, so that we can all play here on the farm. It was an easy thing for me to do, but when I gave them to him, he looked like I gave him the moon and all the stars. My heart actually hurt at how grateful he was. It brought us a little closer, I think.

"Okay." He steps back, moving the ball in his grip and then throwing it. "Missed," he mutters, frowning at his attempt.

"Not bad for your first try, and it's a new ball. Go again." I throw it back at him, realizing he's his own worst critic.

He positions himself and gives it another go. This one lands similar to the first.

"Missed again," he grumbles, kicking at the dirt.

"Keep trying, you'll get it," I encourage him.

"Noah! No!" I hear Annabelle scream from the house, and Kevin and I look up, seeing Noah running away at speed, straight down the hill.

"Noah!" Annabelle admonishes him as she rushes to follow him outside.

"Ahh, what's going on?" I ask as Kevin and I stand next to each other, watching his little brother evade his mom's grasp.

"He's chasing the chickens," Kevin says, starting to give chase.

"I'll go," I tell him, giving him a break, letting him stay and play while I help. Kevin looks at me with raised eyebrows.

"You practice; I'll go get your brother," I assure him, jogging off in the direction of the ruckus, but not before I see a small smile on Kevin's face, one which holds what looks to be gratitude.

"Everything okay?" I ask Annabelle as I approach her side.

"No. Noah torments the chickens, and they hate being chased."

"I'll get him." Pressing a quick kiss to her cheek, I run after him. "Noah!"

He looks at me with a cheeky grin, his eyes wide with excitement.

"Seesaw!" He giggles, and I can't help but smile.

"Your ma said to stop chasing the chickens," I warn him as I get closer, but he just takes off at speed.

"Catch me!" he shouts through a giggle, the cheeky kid faster than he should be. I run after him across the field, chickens all around him, making a hell of a lot of noise.

"Gotchu!" Nearly out of breath, I scoop him into my arms. He lets out a giggly screech, his small arms wrapping around my neck, and I laugh with him, the two of us panting as I start walking us back up the small hill to where Annabelle waits. I look up at her, her wild hair blowing around her shoulders as she smiles. I'll never tire of how beautiful she is.

"You can't go chasing the chickens... They don't like that, buddy," I tell him before I feel a little prick in my ankle and look down, startled.

"The chickens play chase!" Noah says in glee as I start to walk faster.

"They chase?" I ask him, wondering what the fuck is going on, just as another one starts pecking my shoes, and then another and another.

"Run!" Noah screams. I hold him tight and run, making a beeline for the stunning woman who's now laughing at me and the fact that there is a flock of fucking psycho chickens chasing me, pecking at my shoes. Noah's giggling so much as he jiggles in my hold that I think he might wet himself. Meanwhile, my fucking shoes are getting torn to shreds, my laces loosening more every time one of those fuckers comes close.

"You think this is funny?" I call out to Annabelle, who has now almost doubled over with laughter.

"Yes!" she shouts back, and I speed up.

"Ahhhh!" I jump from foot to foot as more and more chickens come to my feet. It looks like they are spawning in numbers, each of them pecking before they finally tire out and I get away from them. "How about I chase you, Mama!" I yell to her, a smirk spreading across my face.

She looks up at me in surprise before she shrieks and turns to run.

"Ma chasies!" Noah yells, still giggling, loving this game. I'm quick and get to her with ease, reaching out with my spare arm and wrapping it around her waist, hoisting her into the air and onto my body.

"Sawyer!" She laughs, her hair wild, her smile wide, her eyes glistening with happiness.

"I got you!" I run with them as best I can over to where Kevin is watching this spectacle unfold.

"Kev!" Noah wriggles from my grasp and runs to him, the two of them jumping on the hay bales and starting to climb them. Noah's energy is never-ending.

"Did I save the day?" I ask Annabelle as I slowly lower her to her feet, the two of us out of breath from running and laughing so hard.

She hums, kissing my lips sweetly. "My real-life Superman."

"Only for you, Lois." I pull her into my side as we watch

the boys play, and never once do I think about New York or the deals I need to make, my work now no longer front and center in my mind. It feels better than I could have ever imagined.

"Can I test my monster spray, Seesaw?" Noah asks me, and I grin. He does this almost every night when I stay over, and I swear he just likes seeing glitter on my clothes. But I don't care, because tonight he asked me to tuck him in. Usually, he sprays me, my shirt turns into a glitter paradise, and I leave Annabelle to take care of the rest. But his instructions tonight were explicit. He wanted Seesaw, and I'm here to follow through.

"Sure, buddy, go for it." I step back from him and throw my arms wide, offering him my chest. He aims his spray bottle and shoots, the water and glitter liquid coating my t-shirt, the nightly glitter spray now seemingly our thing. So much so, I find glitter in my hair at work sometimes. And every time, it only makes me miss this place more.

"See, it works." I take the bottle from him and place it on his nightstand, tucking him in. My nights now look very fucking different. If anyone had told me that I would be tucking a toddler into bed instead of having a whiskey at the Polo Bar, I would have told them they were crazy.

Yet here I am.

"Night, buddy. See you in the morning." I ruffle his hair before walking out of the room. Stepping carefully down the hall, I see Kevin also in his room, lying in bed reading.

"What are you reading?" I lean on his doorway, hearing Annabelle clattering in the kitchen, putting away the leftovers from dinner.

"Just a book on baseball." He puts it down, looking at me.

"Why am I not surprised…" I grin at him. There's only been one other kid I know who loves baseball as much as Kevin, and that was me.

"Sawyer, can I ask you something?" He sits up, suddenly serious, so I tentatively take a few steps into his room.

"Sure, anything."

"Are you Ma's boyfriend?"

I bite the inside of my cheek so I don't chuckle. I want him to know I take his questions seriously.

"Would that be okay with you if I was?" I turn the question back to him. Annabelle and I haven't talked about exclusivity, but I sure as hell am not spending time with anyone else, and I know she isn't either.

"Yeah… I mean, you make her happy. She smiles more when you're here, and she's real pretty when she smiles."

I swallow roughly, nodding in understanding. It's a beautiful thing how much he loves his mom.

"Yeah, she sure is." We had a great weekend all together. This whole thing is so domesticated and should feel completely foreign to me, yet it doesn't. It feels right. "I miss her and you boys when I'm not here," I tell him honestly.

"She misses you too," he admits, and I nod again, knowing the connectedness we're all starting to feel is becoming very real.

I clear my throat. "Okay. Must be lights out soon. Don't stay up too late."

He gives me a small smile and goes back to his book, and I slowly retreat, walking down the hall to the kitchen, where I find his mom just finished cleaning up.

"You need some help?"

She turns, looking at me with her wide smile, the one that temporarily disarms me every time.

"No, all done. Thanks for checking on the boys. Do you want to go sit on the porch? It's a nice night." As she steps closer, I don't hesitate to grab her hand.

"Lead the way, Mama." We walk out to the front, keeping the door ajar, and sit on her patio swing. We relax in silence for a little bit. This swing is starting to feel like our own private time once the boys go to bed. We've sat out here almost every night whenever I'm here. My balcony at my penthouse in the city doesn't have the same peaceful effect. I know. I've tried it.

"Kevin asked me if I was your boyfriend."

She looks up at me in horror, and I laugh. "What did you say?"

"I asked if he would be okay with that, and he said he would be."

Her lips turn into a small smile, her head resting on my shoulder.

Pressing a kiss to her head, I tell her, "Give me your feet."

She leans over and shuffles a little, bringing her feet to my lap, and I squeeze the arches.

"That feels so good..." she moans, her head falling back, and I grin as I look up to the night sky.

"I know we haven't talked too much about what we are or what we're doing..." I look back at her and find her watching me. It's so quiet out here, I can hear her breathing. The only other noises are the nearby crickets.

"Well, if you're offering free foot massages, then I'll be anything that you want me to be."

That makes me chuckle. "That all it takes, huh? A foot massage?" I tease her.

"And the amazing orgasms you deliver... Can't forget about those."

I bark out a laugh. She's softened around me. When I first met her, joking like this wouldn't have happened. I was too wired and hustling with work, and she was too focused on what needed to happen for her and the boys to be safe and happy. We both still have those things in our lives, but out here, in the peace of the night, with no one and nothing around us, all of that feels less and less important.

"I like this. I like being here." I rub along her feet, one by one, releasing the tension. While I was at my desk for most of the morning, I know she's been on her feet all day. This woman is a workhorse, there's no doubt about it.

"I like having you here."

"I mean, I could pass on the chickens with the foot fetish…"

"Sorry about that. Should've warned you." She giggles, the sound hitting me straight in the chest. I take a deep breath, the cool, fresh air filling my lungs as my shoulders lower, my body fully relaxed, and my mind only on her.

"I never thought I would feel so at peace here in Whispers, here with you," I say seriously.

"I never thought a city boy would turn up to my farm and feel like he was always meant to be here."

We look at each other as my hand trails up her shins and back down.

"I guess it's a surprise for both of us." I lean my head back, getting more comfortable, wondering if this could be my life, if I could be the man she needs, the man I know I need to be.

My inbox is still overflowing, my cell continues to ring, but I'm no longer jumping at every call or rushing to every meeting. Subconsciously, being in Whispers has made me step back from the grind, from the daily rush of corporate life, but I look at her and know, while the town is amazing, I've worked from different places before and never felt like this. Like it's okay to let go a bit, and it's because of her.

24

ANNABELLE

My eyes are peeled to the game. We're in the top of the sixth inning, and the score is close at 4-3. We're just one run behind and have runners on first and second base with two outs.

"We just need one good hit here," Sawyer says as he, along with Hudson and Lacy, watch one of our own team members step up to the plate.

"That's Harry, he's usually pretty good," Hudson murmurs. I look at my son on first base, having just hit a ground ball and sprinting to secure his spot. Harvey is on second base, and if we win this, we are two for two.

"God, even though it's a kids' game, it's still so stressful," Lacy says with a nervous little shimmy, sealed to Hudson's side, watching their son with pride on their faces, not dissimilar to the expression I have, I'm sure.

"You've got this, Harry!" I hear his father yell from somewhere nearby. God, I swear if I knew kids' baseball was going to be this nail-biting and anxiety-inducing, then I may have reconsidered my choice to allow Kevin to play. But as I look at my son on first base, steely determination on his face, I know it was the right move.

"Look at Kevin…" Sawyer says to me.

"I know." My eyes stay on my son. He's concentrating hard, taking a step away from the base in preparation to run.

"It's almost like he knows what's going to happen before it actually does," he says, as Noah sits comfortably on his broad shoulders, looking over everything and pulling at Sawyer's hair every five minutes. The city lawyer now appears more casual than ever. He's been in Whispers more often than not for a few weeks now and comes to every game he can.

But it isn't his looks or his money that have me feeling things I haven't in a very long time. It's the way he's here, with my son on his shoulders, watching my other son play baseball on a Saturday. It's the way he talks to me like I'm his equal, not looking at me with pity, but looking at me like he admires me, desires me, and can't get enough of me. And his actions only prove his admiration to be true.

While we're getting closer, I still see so much of the city in him, and weekends in Whispers aren't exactly vibrant. But I'd be lying if I didn't do a happy dance inside, knowing he wants to spend more time with us. Should I put my solid walls back up and expect heartbreak? Maybe. But just like everything else in my life, if it happens, I'll get through it.

"Here he goes," Hudson says, and I hold my breath just as the pitch is thrown. Harry hits it well, and Kevin sprints. I had no idea he was that fast, probably from all the running around he does on the farm. He makes it to second and keeps going as the parents start to cheer.

"Go, boys!" Hudson shouts, and I squeeze my hands together as I watch. The ball is being thrown back, but the kids in the field can't throw too far, one stumbling a bit and dropping the ball, giving us more time.

"Keep going!" Sawyer calls out, and I watch both Harvey and Kevin reach home base, little Harry following behind them and the cohort of us parents cheering and clapping loudly, our kids winning their match, albeit much closer than their last.

"Wow, what a game." Sawyer looks down at me, grinning from ear to ear.

"Can we go to the playground now?" Noah moans, and I chuckle.

"Sure, honey. Let's just grab Kevin, and we can all go."

Sawyer lowers Noah to the ground, and I grab his hand as we make our way over to the team.

"I've just got to talk to Bob about something. I'll be right back." Sawyer kisses my head, then takes off to the side. As we approach the players, I smile wide at Kevin, who gives me a sheepish grin.

"Good job, honey! You were amazing." I give him a side hug as we start to say goodbye to all the parents. Looking over to where Sawyer is, I see him still talking to Bob.

"Thanks, Ma." Kevin's excitement is palpable at having another good game.

"Good job, Kevin. Brilliant running," Sawyer says, coming back over to us.

"Thanks," my son murmurs as he grabs his things. I look down at the small bag he carries, containing his glove and ball, and my heart clenches as I notice all the other kids with bigger bags, all with more equipment, extra clothes, and fancy looking drink bottles. "I'll just go say bye to my friends," he says before turning and jogging over to the kids, and I watch as they all give each other high fives.

"You alright?" Sawyer asks with a pinched brow. Obviously, my emotions are written all over my face.

"Um, yeah, just... he doesn't seem to have all the equipment." I look through Kevin's bag he left with me, still eyeing the others.

"Still one of the best kids on the team, if you ask me. Probably doesn't need all the fancy stuff. He has the skill to back it up."

"You're right." I take in a breath, trying to push the feelings of not being good enough out of my body. But it's always present, my need to provide for my family running strong. I never want my kids to go without.

"Ma... playground..." Noah says impatiently.

"Okay, kiddo, let's go." I ruffle his hair, just as Sawyer's phone rings.

"I'll just take this. Meet you over there." He frowns, and I lead my little one over to the swings. About ten minutes pass, and Kevin's still talking with his friends, and Sawyer's in the distance, looking increasingly concerned on his phone call.

I think about his job then. What he does, what it entails. Why would a man like Sawyer, who doesn't even really like being in Whispers, even think about me as a long-term prospect? I have this daydream that maybe he'll stay here. That our quiet country nights might become something more permanent. It's silly, really. He's a rich, powerful lawyer. Maybe this is just a nice little side distraction, something to alleviate his stress from city life. That thought leaves my stomach feeling heavy as Kevin walks up to us, Sawyer now not far behind him.

"Kevin, swing your brother for a bit, and then we'll go," I tell him, noticing the tension in Sawyer's shoulders as he approaches. "You alright?" I ask, sensing something is off.

"Yeah. It's work. I need to get back to the city and sort out a few things that are pretty urgent, so I'll get you guys home, and then I have to organize a few things and head to the jet."

Sawyer kindly drove us today, and the kids were super excited to be in a new truck. Can't say I minded it either; it was a nice, smooth drive. But when he talks about catching his jet in a moment's notice to go back to the city, my uneasiness from moments ago creeps right back in. The clear difference in our two lives hits me right between the eyes.

"Would you like to stay for dinner before you go?" I'm hopeful, yet the look on his face tells me the answer before he does.

He shakes his head, his gaze seemingly just as disappointed. "I can't. I need to be in the city by tonight, and then I'll be there for the week."

My chest burns, but it's not reasonable. I have no claim on him at all. He doesn't live here. This isn't his life. The life of a high-profile lawyer, a billionaire at that, clearly has him not committing to anyone or anything other than his work.

"Of course." God, I sound almost needy.

"I have an issue. I need to see my team face-to-face to work it all out."

I wave him off. "You don't owe me an explanation."

Reaching over, he takes my hand. "I do. I planned to spend the weekend with you and the boys, and now I'm rushing around, needing to leave. I don't want to go. But I need to."

I nod again, swallowing roughly. "So, how big is your law firm?" I should already know this, but my mind is full of my own workload; I don't spend time thinking about anyone else's.

"My entire team is over two hundred people. They work across corporate and commercial, mainly. But this particular client is one of our criminal cases. I personally don't do criminal cases very often, since I don't really enjoy the long trials."

"Oh, okay." I'm a little surprised. Managing a business with over two hundred people is a massive responsibility. I mean, I struggle looking after just me and my two boys and the farm, so I can't imagine managing that many people or being responsible for putting food on the table for that many families. God, no wonder he needs to leave. I have to stop thinking about myself so much.

"Are they all in your New York office?"

"I have a small entertainment team in LA that mostly helps me manage my brother's business affairs and a few other actors and producers in the industry. I have about fifty staff over there," he adds, and I can't help it when my eyebrows shoot up. I'm now understanding why he's hesitant to move to Whispers full-time like Tanner's wanting. It makes no sense, really.

"And you now have your little office here..." I say, bringing it all together. Even just thinking about his workload is overwhelming. His work is important to him, and this small office in Whispers is never going to be enough for him. I'm never going to be enough for him.

"Yeah, one day, I'm trying to manage a high-profile criminal case, and the next, I'm working for Tanner here, and then the next, I'm meeting my new commitments of sponsoring kids' baseball in Whispers. Or on days like today, trying to manage all three at once." He releases a heavy breath, and I do the same, nodding my understanding.

"It's a lot." I lift my hand, touching my forehead, the gash from a few weeks ago now all healed, but the scar still there. A reminder of what my life is, and it isn't city trips in a jet, heading off to meetings before enjoying fancy dinners.

His thumb rubs my hand where he still holds it, bringing my gaze back to his. "I'm not sure what day I'll be back in Whispers…" As he looks at me, his brow crumples, like he can read my thoughts. I mentally try to find those steel walls that were around my heart, the ones I started lowering for him, feeling like I need them back.

"It's fine. I survived many nights without you before, and I'll survive many after," I say, more for my own benefit than for his, but he doesn't look impressed.

"Make no mistake, Mama…" Stepping closer and bringing us flush, he leans over me, his mouth right near my ear, his breath hot on my cheek. "I would rather be at your dinner table, eating your food, in your bed, eating your pussy, and falling asleep with you in my arms… than anywhere else… Don't you for one damn second think any different."

My heart skips a beat, my body instantly warm all over, as I soften for this man who says everything I didn't know I needed to hear. I look up at him, wide-eyed, to see a very serious expression. There's only honesty there in his unwavering stare, in the firm set of his jaw and the slight pinch to his brow. No one has ever said anything like that to me before, and it was hot as hell.

"Well then…" I clear my throat, looking around to ensure no one heard him. "Looks like I'll just have to take care of that myself until you return." With that, I turn around and walk to my boys, biting my lip so I don't release a full-blown grin as I hear a slight growl come from Sawyer.

He knows I'm independent. I wasn't lying; I can take care of myself, in every way. So I don't really need him. But wow, do I want him.

25

ANNABELLE

I get the boys ready, glancing up at the bright blue sky and feeling good. As I pull my hair back into a pony, my cell chimes, and I grab it immediately, knowing it's Sawyer.

You sleep alright last night, Mama?

I grin instantly before I reply.

Terrible, you?

Awful. I had a nightmare that those chickens ate my feet.

I burst out with laughter.

We probably need to get you some farm boots.

I send the message, unable to wipe the smile from my face.

Already ordered. Should be arriving at your
place later today.

Very efficient of you.

I bought you and the boys some too. So we
all have new pairs.

I read his message, and my breath gets caught in my
chest.

You didn't need to do that.

Even though, as I look down, seeing a hole in the toe of
mine, the need for new boots is evident. His kindness is one
of the things I like most about him. The thoughtful and
generous gifts, the sweet and meaningful comments... He
builds me up without really doing a thing.

I wanted to. Besides, if the chickens eat
your toes, I'm not sure I could cope with
that.

I swear, I'm permanently giddy around this man. Before
I can reply, another message comes through.

Miss you...

I feel it in my chest. The pull to him, the ache when I
know he's so far away and not sure when he'll be back.

I miss you too...

I miss the boys...

My breathing halts. My boys are my world, and for him

to admit he misses them, too, means more to me than anything.

They miss you too.

They don't need to say anything; I see it. It's like they deflate a little when he's gone.

It's hard being without you. I don't like it.

I don't like it either.

"Ma! Ready!" Noah screams, bringing me back to reality.

Sawyer left us yesterday, giving me a scorching kiss on our porch that I know Kevin and Noah didn't miss. I heard Noah giggle, and Kevin just rolled his eyes, so on our morning walk today, I thought I would talk to him about it. Even though Sawyer's been around a lot, we don't show much affection in front of them. Even after Kevin asked Sawyer if he was my boyfriend, I've been hesitant. Like I was waiting to see if he'd bring it up to me, too. But I think the time for waiting is over.

I quickly shoot off another text to tell him we'll talk later, then pocket my cell as the boys join me.

"Ready?" I look at them both, about to start our usual Sunday morning stroll around the back of the property to check the lavender. "It's a great morning."

"Ready!" they reply in unison, and we get to walking.

Noah runs to the side, not able to stick to a slow pace, grabbing a daisy and plucking it from the ground.

"Here, Ma." He passes it to me, and my smile is instant.

"Thank you, honey." I make a show of putting the daisy to my nose and smelling it, before placing it behind my ear, where it will, no doubt, get tangled in my hair at some point.

I turn to my older son as we wander over the hill, getting a full view of the farm. "How do you feel after your game yesterday, Kev?"

"Good. We're a great team." His expression brightens, and I smile at the sight.

"Well, we were all cheering."

"I heard, Ma." I don't miss the grin he tries to hide. He might be embarrassed by me cheering for him, but I also know he loves it.

"Did you hear Sawyer? He was cheering too." I hold my breath, and his smile falters a little.

"Yeah."

"Do you like having him around? Here at the farm and coming to your games?" I swallow, my nerves starting to fester.

"He's okay." Kevin shrugs. "Doesn't seem like he'll know what to do around here much, though."

I chuckle. "No. No, he doesn't. But he's smart, and he has lots of other great skills."

"Is he your boyfriend?"

I stop short. Here we go, the moment I was waiting for. And I thought I'd be more prepared with an answer.

"Oh, um, well, we're just getting to know each other." I'm not sure how in depth to go with this. It's new territory for us. "But if you don't like him, then he doesn't come around anymore. This is your home, Kevin, and I need to know if you don't like or don't want Sawyer to be in it." It would break me, but my sons have to come first.

"I like having him around," he admits, offering me a soft smile. "I like him coming to watch me play. I like that he makes you smile."

My eyes burn with tears. "He does make me smile. Are you okay with him being around more? Spending the nights, staying with us regularly?" I'm not really sure if Sawyer will be, but I want to make sure Kevin knows he has a say in what happens in his safe haven.

He nods, giving me a side hug that warms my heart. "Yeah, I'm okay with it, Ma."

Both of us smiling and walking side by side, we notice Noah's gotten into something up ahead.

"Uh-oooohhhhh." I wonder what trouble he's found.

"What's happened now?" I look at Noah from top to toe, seeing nothing amiss.

"Ma!" Kevin's voice has my body stiff. I look to where he's pointing in the direction of my fields, and I feel life slowly leave my body.

"What?" I barely squeak out as I step forward, then take another step, then another before I'm running, my boys right behind me.

"No... No... No!" I shout as I get closer, my limbs shaking.

The entire far field of lavender, my best producing field, is in disarray. The plants chopped, pulled out, and raked over. I search every plant, look up and around at every nearby field, wondering what the hell has happened. My chest tightens, my mouth going dry, my eyes watering as my heart pounds so hard and fast, I feel lightheaded.

"Ma... What happened?" Kevin asks tentatively, just as distraught.

As I gaze along the fence line, I see something. Walking over to get a better view, I suck in a sharp breath when I see the metal wires have been cut, which could only be done by using bolt cutters, making a hole in the fence big enough for a person or persons to fit through. Clearly, whoever it was came in via Bob's land, so the neighborly thing to do would be to call him, maybe see if he has seen or heard anything. Let him know that he might have had unwanted visitors on his property. This side of his land is left well alone, because he's so busy with the hardware store and managing the kids' baseball team and he doesn't run any cattle or crops over this way anymore. But there's no damage to his land at all, just the fence. I swallow down the bile that's rising and come to the mental conclusion that I can't tell him, because then he'll start asking questions, wondering why my land is ruined while his isn't and I don't have any answers.

"I don't know. Maybe horses," I tell Kevin, wishing that it was, but knowing there are no horses in this field, and there haven't been for a long time. And it doesn't matter if there were, since there's no way an animal could chew through a steel fence.

"Never knew horses could chew through a metal fence." He's a smart boy. He knows I'm lying.

I take a deep breath and look down at my son. The whole thing almost topples me over, and I take another deep breath, looking between him and Noah, knowing that even though I want to fall to my knees and scream, cry, and give up, instead I need to keep going. I'm all they've got, and I can't stop now.

"We've got a bit of a mess to clean up now. We best get to the shed and grab some tools," I tell them, shaking off any bad feelings and putting on a brave face. It works on Noah, but Kevin frowns.

"Ma, I'm scared."

"Nothing is going to happen, Kevin. It's just some wild horses, okay?" I try to alleviate his concerns even though mine are growing. I have no idea what's going on here on the farm lately, but I don't like it. I don't like it at all.

26

SAWYER

I sit at my desk, looking over the files for what feels like the hundredth time. The criminal case that my firm is currently working on is an absolute shit show. We've had early starts and late nights, and I've had to make two statements to the press. Our client had been hiding things from us, which put us in a terrible position, one I wasn't prepared to stay in for fear it would completely tarnish my firm. So I made the decision to end our representation, unfortunately leaving him scrambling to find new lawyers, which had the whole thing playing out in the press.

It's only been a few days, and I'm itching to get out of here. My bed in my penthouse is hard and cold and empty. My dinners have been late-night takeout, making me feel bloated and sick, and nothing like the home-cooked goodness that I've been enjoying. And Annabelle, I think of her every morning when I wake and every night when I go to sleep, and probably every hour in between.

Not sure how it happened, but it's true what I told her before I left. I would rather be with her and in Whispers than here dealing with work, and that scares me to death.

I've been hustling in high-profile business law for almost my entire adulthood. It's what drove me in my youth, the need to get a law degree so I could help my mom, not only with money from my job, but legal expertise, because of the constant roadblocks she came across as a struggling single parent. I wanted better for her, better for us.

Over the years, my career turned into my lifeline. I wanted the biggest and best business clients, I wanted to manage multimillion-dollar deals, and I've succeeded. I have everything I've always strived for. But every night, I sleep alone. For years, I loved it. The silence was golden after a stressful day at work. But now, after spending time with Annabelle and the boys, experiencing the craziness of their house and dinners at their table, the calm comforts of relaxing at the end of a long day with someone by my side, the appeal of a life outside of work is growing. As is my need to find out what's happening with her.

Just the thought of her being hurt is too much to bear. The scar from the gash on her forehead still makes my shoulders tense, knowing she isn't telling me everything. But I see it in her eyes, at times when she doesn't know I'm watching her.

My eyes flick over to the three bags on my desk. The one thing I've managed to do already is get to the Mets team store. After an owners meeting I had yesterday with the Mets business team, I grabbed gloves, mitts, tops, balls, jackets, caps—you name it, I bought it. I guessed on both the kids' sizes and Annabelle's, hoping it all fits. I even got a sports bag and drink bottle for Kevin for his games. Next week, he'll be the best dressed kid there.

I see a media alert come though on my screen, and I quickly read it. Sutton had a vehicle incident last night.

Photos of his car, a pedestrian, none of it looks good. Feeling uneasy, I grab my cell to call him.

It rings with no answer, so I shoot him a text.

> Just saw the news, what's going on? Are
> you okay?

>> I'm in a meeting so can't talk, but shit hit the
>> fan big-time last night.

My brow furrows, not liking this.

> What's going on? What do you need?

I ask, not just as his lawyer, but also as a brother. I'm ready to fire up the jet and go to him, if that's what's needed.

>> I had some fans push their way into a
>> restaurant where I was eating and one
>> jumped in front of my car as I left. He's okay,
>> but it's a fucking nightmare.

>> I just need a break. Bad things keep
>> happening, and fans are out of control.
>> Media follows me everywhere, even
>> camping outside my home.

I'm already two steps ahead of him.

> Come to Whispers for a while.

>> They'll find me; they'll track the jet.

I balk. What the actual fuck is wrong with people? I think about it, knowing I can't send him my jet, because they will likely track that too.

I'll send you Tanner's.

I offer it up quickly, knowing Tanner will help if I need it.

> It'll have to be at night because they'll follow
> me. The paps are vultures. They seem to
> know exactly where I am at all times. The
> media have blown up the story about the girl
> in my bed. Apparently she was underage
> and they're making up all sorts of lies.

"Fuck," I murmur, clicking on the story again, looking through image after image. Sutton in different outfits and at different places, the latest ones all with a full media pack swarming him as he tries to walk down the street.

> I'll have Tanner's jet at the airport for you
> this week and meet you in Whispers.

> Thanks, Sawyer. I knew you would know
> what to do.

I hold my cell in my hand, looking at my laptop screen and feeling protective. By the looks of things, my brother has completely taken over the internet. He's on the front page of every gossip site, every Hollywood forum and magazine. I blow out a breath. It'll be good to see him.

Scrolling through my contacts, I press Tanner's name, wanting to get this all sorted.

"Sawyer, where are you?" he asks, and I roll my eyes.

"New York," I tell him, even though he already knows.

"Why?"

"What do you mean, why? I have meetings with other clients. I had that shit show of a case to deal with."

"Yeah, how's that going for you?" Tanner's tone is sarcastic, already aware it was a fucking disaster.

"In our defense, when we took him on, all evidence indicated he was innocent."

"Innocent until proven guilty."

"Well, hopefully we got out of it soon enough. Although the media are having a field day with it." I look back at the newspapers on my desk, seeing the legal pages full of stories about us removing ourselves from the case and basically indicating that the client we were representing is guilty without doubt.

"You need to put down roots. Here in Whispers. Get out of all that criminal side of things. You're so much better at business law anyway," Tanner pushes, and I rub my eyes, feeling a headache coming on.

"You know I'm not a country boy, Tanner." My words have almost no meaning anymore. I don't believe them, and neither does he. But I'm scared to admit it out loud. My life for years has been this office, this business. Leaving it all for a small country town and a woman I barely know sounds crazy. But my feelings are hard to deny, and every minute I think of her, I fall a little more. The pull toward her takes me away from all I've ever known, from the security of what I've built.

"I don't know about that. I've noticed quite a change..."

"What do you mean?" I ask him.

"I mean, *you've* changed. For the better. You're no longer as rushed, you seem to enjoy life a little more, and while I know Whispers is special, I have a feeling it's because of Annabelle."

I inhale a deep breath. I'm not prepared to tell Tanner anything about my feelings before I tell Annabelle directly, so I stay the course.

"She's great. Whispers too. But I'm also needed in the city. You know that." The words taste bitter.

"Yeah, I know. Anyway, we have a situation."

I nearly groan. This seems to be the week that keeps on giving.

"What situation?"

"Bob wants to sell off some of his land. The fields closest to Annabelle. He needs legal advice on what to sell and the documentation drawn up." I go to say something, but he continues. "Peter is looking at expanding his taxi business from one car to two. He needs help with the legal paperwork on hiring staff, as well as the business registration information changes."

"Need I remind you, I'm a high-profile New York lawyer. I don't need to be looking into land titles and basic business expansion contracts." I eye the certificates on my walls, the ones I worked my ass off to get me where I am today.

"Yeah, but aren't you sick of it?"

I heave an exasperated sigh. "I grew up in the city, Tanner. I'm not built the same as you." It's the truth. I can't work the land or live in complete isolation. Shit, I still wear a suit every day. I look so out of place, not only in Whispers but with Annabelle. I wonder briefly if I should buy some shirts and jeans, maybe some more boots. I rub my face again, feeling like a moron, continually perplexed by my current situation.

"No truer words have been spoken," he mumbles, giving me no assurance whatsoever.

"Anyway, just be back by Thursday. We have the Van Cleef team coming. They're checking out the distillery and Connor is chatting with them about extended distribution."

I stretch my neck, willing the tightness to dissipate.

"You couldn't start with that?" I stand, needing to move. The past few weeks, I've been quietly working on trying to understand the Grant Holdings business. There's opportunity there, so if we can keep Van Cleef to domestic partnerships, we can build a global partnership with Grant Holdings. It's a juggle, as we don't want to piss anyone off, but legally it's doable. "Why isn't that meeting happening here in New York?"

Most of our dealings of this nature happen here, which is why working for Tanner all these years has been fine. My trips to Whispers haven't needed to be too regular.

"Because Valerie wanted to come to Whispers because she knows how amazing it is, so she and AJ are flying in and staying at Marie's Place for a few nights for a break after our meeting. Now make sure your ass is here so you're prepared. It's a big deal. Lots of dollars on the table."

I nod, not that he can see me. "I'm always prepared."

"True, that's why I hired you. I always said you're the best, and I mean it."

"On that note... I need a favor."

"What do you need?" he asks.

"Your jet," I tell him.

"You've got your own, why do you need mine?"

"Sutton needs a late-night jet to bring him to Whispers. Things are getting out of hand for him over in LA, so he's gotta lie low and hide out for a while. They will track his jet and mine."

"Hmmmm, okay. Victoria has to go over to LA with Griffin and quote a job. Maybe she can take the jet over and they can fly back with Sutton. She'll take some photos for her socials while she's there, giving the media no reason to suspect we're picking up Sutton for you." Tanner comes up with the plan, obviously thinking as he speaks.

With that, I breathe a little easier. "Sounds perfect. Thank you. See you later in the week."

"See you then."

We end the call, and I look at my watch, my headache now coming on stronger.

This is much harder than I originally thought. Each time I'm in the city, the phone calls bring me right back to Whispers. Each time I'm in Whispers, the work calls me right back to the city. But regardless of where I'm located, Annabelle is always on my mind. She's becoming my North Star, and where she is, is where I want to be.

I rub my eyes for what feels like the hundredth time today. I can't be in two places at once; it's already grinding my gears. The talk with Jerry comes back to me. How he gave up his firm in the city for life in Whispers, and I scoff at myself, not believing I'm even entertaining such a thing.

With my cell in my hand, I pull up our text exchange.

Coming back on Thursday. Can I see you
when I land?

I shoot the text off before I can think about how desperate I sound, yet smile when I see the bubbles dance immediately.

Thursday night is casserole night.

I miss you.

I miss you too.

I swallow, letting the warmth her words provide me to sink into my bones. She makes me feel that no matter what happens, everything is alright. I think about heading home early tonight to start packing, and I frown, realizing that I never unpacked.

My suitcases are all still full. I'm treating my penthouse more and more like a hotel that I'm visiting, rather than the home I've had for years.

I guess it's true what they say... Home is where the heart is.

27

SAWYER

My jet landed in Whispers about an hour ago, and I still haven't seen Annabelle. My first stop had to be the distillery, where I'm now sitting in the boardroom across from Valerie Van Cleef, her husband AJ, Tanner, and Connor, discussing the new distribution of a limited edition line of whiskey, only available through her hotels.

I look at my watch, knowing that being the middle of the day, Annabelle and the kids will still be in school, but my knee bounces under the table in anticipation regardless.

"So we'll have limited stock, but that just makes it all the more exclusive," Connor explains. He and I have known Valerie for a while now, seen her out and about in New York a bit. She and AJ now keep a quieter life, although her company is thriving, and the two of them make a great team. Their future may be clouded by the new hotelier family that's pushing into the country, the Grant brothers making major moves in property development for the past few years. But Valerie is smart; she knows what she's doing.

"Sounds great. I love having anything that's special or

exclusive." Valerie smiles wide, the contracts now all signed. I take in her words, and my mouth opens before I really think about what I'm doing.

"What about Gertie's?" I ask the table, and they look at me. Tanner's eyebrows rise before he nods, obviously not having thought about it himself.

"What's Gertie's?" Valerie asks curiously, while Tanner and Connor try to hide their shit-eating grins.

"Well, we're talking about Whiteman's single malts distributed through your bars. How about Gertie's Soaps distributed within your bathrooms? Amenities at your hotels? Gertie's is a locally made and owned brand of organic soaps, not sold anywhere else... yet."

Her eyebrows rise. "The timing is interesting..." Valerie looks at AJ, who doesn't give much away.

"Gertie's is Victoria's side hustle. She's in business with a local woman, Annabelle, whom Sawyer has been working with," Tanner says, giving me the nod to continue.

"Gertie's isn't currently available to everyone. It's sold here at the distillery and locally in town, some at the next town over, so it's exclusive and high quality, which is what you're looking for, for your hotels. Plus, it's all organic, made by hand right here in Whispers."

"We had to cancel our contract with our current amenities' supplier due to a conflict of interest, so your timing with this one, Sawyer, is impeccable. It's a cute idea. Want to run me some numbers and send them over?" she asks, and Tanner practically beams, but I decide to push.

"Can you offer exclusivity?" I know being exclusive in her business means a strong, steady income for Annabelle, something she desperately needs.

"I'm sure we can arrange something," she says easily.

I look at Tanner, who nods, looking at me appreciatively.

"Great." My grin is wide, not able to be tamped down.

"Well, let's eat. I'm starving." Connor jumps up, and we all walk to the restaurant for lunch.

"Good work, Sawyer. Good fucking work... This is why I hired you. Can't believe I didn't fucking think of that," Tanner says to me quietly, and I chuckle. "Thanks for keeping Victoria and Gertie's in mind."

"We need to get it over the line first," I tell him as we walk through the hallways. I've been here so many times, I could tell you the number of lines in the wood that's under my feet. "And... I was thinking of Annabelle, actually."

He gives me a knowing look. "Well, after lunch, before you go running over there to see her, I need you to stop by Bob's place. He wants to show you that parcel of land he wants to sell."

There's no point complaining. This is the work that needs to be done in a small town.

"Sure, no worries."

Tanner stops dead in his tracks and looks at me. "See, I told you, you're a changed man."

I wave him off, but I'm still smiling. The minute my jet wheels hit the tarmac on the Whispers airstrip this morning, the tension eased from my body, and I think that tells me all I need to know.

"Your brother is coming in tonight. Victoria has him meeting her in the jet on the tarmac later this evening. It sure must be serious if you need my jet at nighttime."

I blow out a breath. "Yeah, not sure exactly, but he's fleeing and doesn't want anyone to know where he is."

"I'll get the word out. The town will cover for him," Tanner says, and I still.

"What do you mean?" I'm clearly missing something.

"Whispers is small, everyone body knows everybody.

They're going to know pretty quickly that there's a new person in town and people talk. But if we tell them it's your brother and he needs to hide, the town will hide him. They'll call you when the media are in town so he can stay at home and lie low. Rochelle usually gets them first, since all new people go to the diner and start sniffing around. She's brilliant at steering them off course. But she'll call you the minute she sees anyone new, and Tony, the sheriff, is usually good too."

My jaw almost hits the floor. "Seriously?" I was thinking how I would need to keep him indoors, wondering how he was going to get around whenever I'm in the city, and this makes it so much easier.

"Yeah, well, he might still need to wear his cap low and not have photos taken and things, but once the town knows, he'll be able to roam around pretty freely." Tanner makes it out to be no big deal.

"Small towns talk, you even said it," I question him.

"To each other, not to outsiders, especially ones who may harass our own. That's what being part of a small town means. They look after their own. That's what you've become, their own. Now you just need to have their backs as well."

I'm nodding before he's even finished. "I've got them."

He smiles, patting me on the back. "Good, better celebrate it with a whiskey, then."

We follow the rest of the team into the back of the restaurant and take our seats. I have a new spring in my step, one that hasn't been in my working life for some time. The thrill of the chase, of making a difference to a business, to a brand, to a woman I can't stop thinking about.

If I can pull off this deal with Van Cleef, it would mean increased production for Annabelle, but it also means that she won't need to work so hard at two jobs. She could let go of the teaching and concentrate on Gertie's. Maybe with some convincing, she could also hire some help on the farm. I know she wants to manage quality, but now that she's in business, she needs to let go of a few things and embrace where her hard work has gotten her.

I'm used to getting deals like this over the line. I do them in my sleep. But none of them have given me this high I'm now feeling, none of them have meant this much until now.

"So you been in Whispers for a while?" I ask Bob as we walk out of his place and hop into his truck. He wants to show me his land, the parcel he's thinking of selling. Not that I need to see it in real life; I just need the plans, but I'm learning that this is how things go in a small town.

"All my life. Born and raised."

I nod, knowing that this is how most country land ownership works.

"If you are as good a lawyer as Tanner thinks you are, then finding me a buyer for my land should be child's play."

I look at my watch. There's another hour or so before school ends, so I have time to indulge him.

"You got a lot of land out here." Glancing out his truck window as he drives us over his fields, there are rolling green hills that seem never-ending. I have no idea about land quality, but it looks good to me. The grass is green, and the whole place looks vibrant.

"I have a few hundred acres here, close to the house, that I want to keep, but I'm getting older. The hardware store takes up a lot of my time, and I never use the fields over the back, so that's what I'm looking at offloading," he offers.

"How much do you want to get rid of?"

"I have two hundred acres I want to fence off and sell. But there's a catch."

I quirk my eyebrow. "What's the catch?"

"There's no access. The parcel of land I want to get rid of is landlocked between mine and Annabelle's farm." I squint through the windscreen to where we're going, and sure enough, while I can't see her house, I can make out the hills and the trees that surround her farm, the familiarity making me smile.

"You'll need to put in an access road if you want to sell it," I tell him.

"I know. It would be ideal if Annabelle could buy it. Then she could just extend her farm, but I know she can't." He sighs as we drive over the land.

"So is that fence the border?" I point in front of us.

"Just over here... What has she been doing? It didn't look like that last week when I came for a look," Bob murmurs, and I follow his gaze as his truck comes to a stop.

I frown as we both get out of the truck and look over to her land. I see rich brown dirt, right next to flourishing lavender bushes, with scraps of plants in between. There's a significant amount of space that's just raked dirt, something I haven't seen on the farm before, since every space has a purpose for Annabelle. "Maybe she's replanting..."

"Off time of year to be doing that. What the hell is that?" Bob's tone has me on guard, and I follow him quickly as he trudges to the fence line.

"What is it?" I'm not caring that my leather shoes are now covered in grass and dirt, that my suit pants are probably getting muddy as well.

"The fence is cut. I put this fence in years ago, but you can see it's sturdy and in good condition. No one comes out here. As I said, there's no access..." He looks up and around.

"Could this have been opened by an animal?" I have no idea what wild animals roam around here.

"It's heavy-duty steel. There's no animal on this earth that would chew through it. This was done by a man. And bolt cutters."

I swallow. Annabelle hasn't said anything, but by the looks of how well the soil is ploughed into rows, she knows.

"I'm headed over there now, so I can talk to Annabelle about the fence. She'll fix it, you know what she's like." I smile, just from thinking about her.

He shakes his head. "I can do it."

"You offer that?" I ask, wondering if fencing is a service he does in Whispers.

"Not as a service, but I would do it for Annabelle. Neighborly thing to do, especially since she's on her own," Bob admits, and I admire that. Their familiarity has me wondering...

"Did you know her husband?"

"No good son of a bitch, that one. Not many people mourned his death."

"What do you mean?" I press. Maybe he can give me more insight than the guys did.

"He grew up here. Was troublesome. Annabelle grew up here too, one of those good girl falls for the bad guy situations. He was always a bit shady. Drinking, gambling, you know the type."

"I'm starting to get the picture," I murmur, needing to talk to Tanner about it all.

"I don't care about fixing the fence, happy to do it. But I'm never out here; that's why I want to sell it. Preferably without the added cost of putting an access road in."

Annabelle can't afford to buy any more land, yet I do know that if the Van Cleef deal goes through, and with a few tweaks to her finances, she could afford it eventually.

But I can afford it now, and while I know she has a lot of pride, maybe I can strike a deal with her.

"How much do you want for it, Bob?" I ask, and he looks my way with wide eyes as we get into the truck. All the way back to his place, we talk about numbers, and I leave him with the promise I'll get the contracts drawn up and the money in his bank by Monday.

28

ANNABELLE

I miss Sawyer. It's a dangerous feeling for a woman like me. It's been a hell of a week, and there's nothing I want more than to fall into his embrace. My body is weary, my mind a mess. Anxiety is a friend I've had for a while, but what's been happening around here lately has taken it to a whole new level.

It's been days, and I still don't know what to do. It's clear someone was on my land. I've lost half my crops to what looks to be a deliberate act of sabotage. My lavender was cut haphazardly, trodden on, ripped up. Like a bunch of kids came through on bikes and had a field day. But I know it wasn't kids. There were no bike marks, and kids would not be all the way out here, at night, cutting fences and ruining farmland, just for the fun of it.

I probably should've called the sheriff, let him know, and started an investigation. But that'll just take time, scare my kids, bring people onto my land who'll ask me questions, which will have them worried about my mental state, because I can't connect anything about what's happening on the farm to anyone. I have no enemies. I have nothing of value. No one has any reason to want anything from me.

The kids and I have spent every night after school trying to clean up the mess. Burning the damaged bushes, raking the soil, and now the entire half of that field is barren. Thank God it's on the side of the farm no one sees. It can't be seen from the house or the road. Bob's the only one who would notice it, but he's barely on that side of his land, and since he hasn't said anything, I'm assuming he hasn't seen it. It's hard to miss now, with half a field just brown soil, the other half flourishing with lavender bushes.

Now my yield for this year will be much lower than we expected, unless I can plant more over the next few weeks and somehow get more bushes into the ground. As it is, I've run out of room. I would love more land to grow more and have different varieties. But with no money and no chance of a loan, I've had to squeeze in as much as I can into the footprint of land I've got.

I'm relieved the soil is resilient and still in excellent condition, but I'll need to spend the next few nights after work making cuttings from the healthier plants I have and replanting them, watering them well, and hoping and praying they take. And unless I get some growing soon, the lack of lavender will have a direct impact on how many soaps I can make for distribution next year, and therefore decrease the income that I could receive.

The whole thing leaves me feeling sick to my stomach, especially now that Saturdays are taken up with baseball, leaving me with only Sunday and late nights after school to get everything done.

I've never had a break or taken a vacation, and right now, I feel like I really need it.

My body is sore. I'm tired, having worked twenty-hour days since Sawyer left. My hands are a mess, digging in dirt and pulling bushes, leaving me with a few scratches and broken nails. Poor Kevin is just as exhausted, but every night after school, he's with me, as is Noah, the three of us a formidable team.

The sun is starting to set, and even though we have a lot more to do, I need to get the kids bathed and fed and put to bed. I set the casserole to cook while we were down in the lavender fields. I'm not sure what time Sawyer is coming, but I assume it'll be late.

But as we walk up to the house, I see him standing by his truck, looking at his phone.

"Seesaw!" Noah yells and starts to giggle, which makes me smile.

Sawyer looks up immediately, pocketing his cell, his grin as wide as mine. "Hey, buddy."

Noah runs to him, and he picks him up, giving him a bear hug that looks all too good. It's clear that my youngest boy is just as smitten as I am.

"Hey, Kevin." He puts Noah down, and my older son walks up to him.

"Hey," is all he gets, but this time, it's with a head nod, so we have some progress. The way Sawyer is grinning, I assume he's happy with that less-than-stellar greeting.

"Go clean up for dinner, boys. I'll be in after I put these in the shed." My arm aches from holding the gardening gear in my hands, along with a shovel, hoe, rake, and buckets. You name it, I seem to be holding it.

"Hey, Mama." Sawyer takes a step toward me, arms out and ready to hold me.

"No! I'm all dirty!" I take a step back, not wanting to ruin his suit. Because, as usual, he looks completely fresh and polished, and I have dirt covering me from top to toe.

"You couldn't look more beautiful if you tried. Come here." He grabs my hand, and I put down my tools and do as he asks.

I walk to him and his hand moves around my waist. I'm not sure if my boys are watching, but I let Sawyer pull me close, his lips touching mine, his kiss searing, making me feel like he might've missed me as much as I missed him.

"You alright?" His brow crumples a little as he looks down at me, and I offer him a small smile.

I sigh. "Just another day on the farm."

He hugs me close, and as my head hits his chest, I close my eyes to keep the tears at bay.

"You sure?" He clearly knows me too well, as his finger meets my chin and he lifts my head a little to look me in the eye.

"Just tired."

His lips thin, not convinced.

"Are you doing something on the other side of the farm? I was over at Bob's place before, and I saw the lavender was all pulled up."

I think my heart stalls.

"Oh... um... yeah, just replanting." My hand reaches up to twirl a lock of hair that's fallen from my ponytail.

"You know, if there's something going on here, you can tell me." His fingers brush across my forehead and I swallow, my heart now racing, wanting to tell him everything. But when I open my mouth, nothing comes out. Years of my husband telling me not to rely on outsiders, telling me that we shouldn't have people in our business, telling me that we need to do things alone. The history of mental abuse I suffered suffocates me, and I start to panic.

"Hey... just breathe, Annabelle."

I look up at him, my eyes watering, feeling like I can't gather a full breath. I have no idea what's happening.

"Just slow your breathing... Keep your eyes on mine, baby..." His voice is calming, and I take in a shaky, shallow breath.

"Okay. Try taking a deeper breath. I'm here. I'm right here..."

I breathe in again slowly, my chest hurting. His scent smells nice, welcoming, safe, his hands warm as they grip on to mine.

"You don't need to tell me anything you don't want to. But I know something's going on here, and I'm worried."

All I can do is nod, the words still not coming out. But my breathing settles, and my hands that were shaking start to relax.

Sawyer looks at me seriously, searching my face. "Are you in danger out here, Mama?"

I can't lie to him. I can lie to everyone else, but I can't lie to him.

"I don't know..." I whisper honestly, and I see his shoulders stiffen.

"I'll stay tonight. I just need to run out for about an hour or so after dinner. My brother is flying in to stay with me for a while, and then I will come right back." He doesn't seem happy about any of it, and I shake my head.

"I'm fine. We're fine."

"I know you are, but I'm not. I'd rather be here with you, just to be sure. Who knows, maybe tonight will be the night we break your bed..." He adds some humor, making me smile, and I'm grateful he's letting me off lightly.

I lift onto my toes and press my lips to his. "Thank you."

Giving me one more hug, he says, "I got you guys some things. Let's go inside."

It's then I notice a few bags at his feet.

"You've been shopping?" I quickly put my tools away and pull myself together.

"Just got the boys and you some things." He takes my hand again, and we walk inside.

"Seesaw!" Noah says immediately as I move to the kitchen to check on dinner. All the while, I take some deep breaths to settle my nerves, which are now almost completely shot after the week I've had.

"Boys, I brought gifts," Sawyer tells them as he sits on the sofa, and I lean against the kitchen counter, watching them in the living room.

"What is it?" Noah peeks in the bags inquisitively, and I grin. I look at Kevin then, who's sitting off to the side, obviously trying to act cool, but given we've never had anyone bring gifts like this before, I can see excitement in his eyes.

"Here." Sawyer puts a cap on Noah, the logo familiar, and I look back at Kevin quickly, his expression brightening.

"Kevin... this is for you." Sawyer pulls out a baseball jersey.

"Is that signed?" Kevin's eyes nearly bug out of his head.

"Yeah, well, they're your favorite team, right?" Sawyer asks him as he stands and walks over to where Kevin is.

"Yeah. But how?" Kevin asks in disbelief, staring at the jersey that's covered in signatures.

"Well..." Sawyer scratches the back of his head, looking a little sheepish. "There's probably something I should come clean about."

Kevin looks at him, and my brow crumples, having no idea what he's going to say.

"I own the Mets."

Sawyer's words have me snapping my eyes back to him in shock. This is news to me, and I'm just as flabbergasted as Kevin.

"What?" Kevin looks at me, unsure, like he does when he doesn't understand something at school. Sawyer glances at me for a moment, then brings his attention back to my son.

"Well, in a lot of sports, teams are owned by businessmen. I love the Mets, like you, and I grew up wanting to play for them. So when I had some success in my business, I put in an offer to buy and, well... here we are a few years later, and I'm part owner."

"You? Own the Mets?" Kevin is in complete disbelief, and my heart starts racing all over again, understanding washing over me at exactly how wealthy Sawyer is.

This is a lot. The difference between the haves and have nots is now something I can't ignore. I look around my very humble abode, not feeling good enough, not a good mother, not a good farmer, not a good girlfriend. But I try to take in the joy of seeing my son feeling overwhelmed in a good way, which is something I don't think has happened much before.

"So, I was thinking, if you want, maybe we can go to a game?" Sawyer adds, sounding tentative.

"Game?" Kevin questions.

"Yeah, go watch the Mets, in the city?"

"City?" Kevin's head is about to explode, as is my heart, I'm sure of it.

"Yeah, I was thinking that maybe the four of us can go to the city for the weekend soon, catch a game?" Sawyer looks at me, and I swallow, because I'm not sure that can happen. "I think your mom might need a break from the farm, and in the city, she doesn't have to get up early, cook, or clean, or anything you all usually do each day."

I can't even comprehend what he's offering.

Kevin's gaze is equal parts *is this real?* and *can we go?* I give him a small smile.

"Maybe?" I shrug my shoulders. I'm not sure I can make it work, but I don't want to burst his bubble just as it's starting to grow.

"Ma! He owns the Mets!" Kevin says, scrambling to put on the jersey, now clearly on team Sawyer.

"I heard," I say as Sawyer grins.

"I got your mom some things too. Here, take a look." Sawyer passes the kids all the bags before looking at me. I can tell he's trying to gauge how I'm feeling, but I remain in the kitchen, watching this unravel in front of me, not able to move.

"You didn't need to..." I shake my head, not sure how to handle all this. Words don't seem like enough. This is something I can never repay. Something I could never do for my boys, yet it brings them so much joy I can't say no.

"I know, I wanted to. No takebacks, remember." He gives me a wink, leaving the boys to dive into the other bags as he walks my way. Once he's in front of me, his hand cups my jaw, his thumb brushing my cheek.

I bite the inside of my lip, still struggling with what to say. "You're spoiling them..."

"Good, I want to spoil you too." He looks at me in wonder, and I give him a small smile.

"Do you have a jersey for me?" I ask in jest, not even thinking he did.

"I do. Got us all matching ones. But... I also have something better."

My stomach tightens in anticipation. "Oh?"

"I had a business meeting today. I pitched Gertie's to a

large hotel client, asking them to place Gertie's Soap in all their bathrooms countrywide."

That's certainly not what I was expecting.

"Say that again?" I hold my breath, not wanting to get too excited.

"I had a meeting at the distillery with Tanner today, talking to a hotel heiress who's putting some whiskey in all her hotel bars. I mentioned Gertie's to her, suggested it for her bathrooms. She wants me to run the numbers and send her a proposal," he says slowly, gently pushing my hair behind my ear.

"That sounds like it's a big deal…" My eyes glass over, my emotions now about to get the better of me. I still don't feel like this is real.

"It would make your side hustle a full-blown business. It would bring in more money than you know what to do with. It will mean that you can do Gertie's full-time, do all the things you've always wanted. Send the kids to college, live the life you always dreamed of."

Nerves and hopefulness fight for priority as my mind tries to take this in. "That's a big offer you're making to a girl like me, Sawyer."

"You're worth it." He leans forward, brushing his lips over mine. And I kiss him, giving my heart exactly what it wants. While my boys are preoccupied, I kiss him like he's my lifeline before I pull back and look into his eyes.

"I don't know what to say. I don't know how I will ever repay you…"

"No repayment needed. I want to do this. It's a good business decision. Tanner and Victoria are both excited about it, and I knew that this would be amazing for you."

I swallow, nodding in agreement.

"It's not over the line, but I'm going to be trying very

hard to get it done for you." He kisses my forehead, and the softness of the way he's holding me makes me ask the question that I haven't been able to let go of.

"What is all this?" I'm too scared to really think about what he's doing for us. I mean, it's just caps and mitts and jerseys. It's just work he's doing for Tanner, which will help Victoria and, by association, me. But it feels like more.

"This is me, still trying to sweep you off your feet... Is it working yet?" He grins, and I huff a small laugh as butterflies flap wildly in my belly.

"You don't have to spoil us. We're not expecting anything like that from you. I just like having you in our lives..." I'm honest, hoping he knows that I'm not with him for his money. For any of this.

"I can't believe it took me so long to find a woman like you."

I hold my breath, waiting for him to continue.

"I sure as hell miss you when I'm not with you, and I miss you when I'm right near you. You're all I'm fucking thinking about, and still flying between here and the city is already killing me, knowing I have to leave you again."

"I miss you too," I whisper, my boys still emptying the bags in the living room.

"I was thinking... Maybe I can take you out tomorrow night? Friday night dinner at the bar in town."

"I'd love to, but the boys... I can't leave them alone. They're too young."

"Yeah, well, my brother is arriving tonight, and he'll need something to do, so I thought he could watch them at my place. Maybe you all sleep over for the night? Have a break from the farm for a bit?"

I think about it. I have so much to do, so much to organize, but a night off sounds so perfect.

"My brother is an asshole most of the time, but I trust him with my life, and I trust him with the boys," Sawyer reassures me, and I nod.

"Okay... I'd love to go on a date with you, Sawyer." This will be my first official date. My late husband and I never really did any dates; he didn't like me leaving the house at all, really.

"You're perfect, you know that." He brushes his lips tenderly against mine again. I'm not used to the compliments he gives me, and my heart races at each and every one of them.

"I'm so far from perfect..." I shake my head, but the grin on my face is hard to remove.

"You're perfect for me. Oh, before I forget..." he says, stepping back a little, his smile widening.

"There's more?" I grip on to the new dining chair for fear I might topple.

"I bought a few hundred acres off Bob today. Enough for you to double your lavender yield."

My jaw drops open, heart stuttering, knees weakening. I'm glad I'm holding on to the chair. "You *what*?"

"I don't know anything about soaps, but if you get this deal with the Van Cleefs, then you'll need to double your raw materials to keep up with demand."

"But... what if the deal falls through?" My heart pounds in my ears, my head filled with so many questions.

"Then we'll just be ready for the next one." His smirk of arrogance is now in place, his belief in me and Gertie's almost too much to digest.

"Ma! Look! A new drink bottle!" Kevin hollers from the living room, and I look back around and see my small space now covered in Mets merchandise, my two boys dressed in caps and jerseys, throwing balls around. Sawyer walks back over to them, helping them take all the tags off everything, and I pinch myself to ensure this is all real. Looking out the window, darkness now falls, and as positive as I want to stay, I know that after the good, usually comes the bad.

And I'm not sure I'm ready for what's coming next.

29

SAWYER

I walk around my place, fluffing pillows and ensuring things are neat.

"What the hell are you doing?" My brother looks at me as I step back through the living area, where he's watching an action film.

"Just triple-checking." I make my way down the hallway to the bedroom I've prepared. Flicking on the light, the bunk beds are fully dressed, the bookcase filled with books, and a wardrobe stocked with clothes, in case they forgot something. Signed Mets jerseys are framed on the walls and games are stacked in the corner.

"Triple-checking what?" Sutton sits up from the sofa, watching me like I've lost my mind. Maybe I have. I've never put in this much effort before.

"I'm taking her out tonight. The kids will stay here with you." I know my brother well enough to know that if I need anything from him, I need to spring it on him at the last minute; otherwise, he loses interest in that task pretty quickly.

"Kids?" He stands and walks quickly down the hallway after me.

"Yeah, Noah and Kevin." I smile, thinking about the joy on their faces over a few caps and jerseys. They were all overwhelmed. It cost me next to nothing to do, and it'll be a core memory for all of us.

"She has kids? Is that what the fucking bunk beds are about?" He checked out the place today after his late-night arrival last night.

"Yes, she has kids. And I need you to watch them tonight while I take her out." I step into my room, the large space spotless, with clothes for her in the wardrobe, the bathroom sparkling. I wonder if I should fill the bath when we get home later, knowing that the small one she has at the farm wouldn't be big enough for her to fully relax in.

He's looking at me like I've grown two heads when I turn around. "Do I look like a fucking babysitter?"

"Where the fuck else have you got to go?" I push past him back to the front of the house. She should be here any minute, and my nerves about having everything perfect for her are thrashing through my body.

"Good point," Sutton relents, just like I knew he would. He's excellent with kids, because kids love his movies. While they're action films with some violence, kids tend to gravitate to them.

"What do I do with them?"

"Kevin loves baseball and movies, so maybe a movie night? I got popcorn and snacks, and the kitchen is stocked." I see car lights coming up the drive, and I run my hands through my hair. I smile then, thinking of the boys and how the minute I said I wanted to take their mom out so someone else could cook for her, they were on board.

"Fucking hell, they must have one hot mom. You look

like you're about to break through your skin with nerves." He eyes me suspiciously, holding back a laugh.

"She never leaves the farm. The fact that she's coming out tonight is a big deal."

"One look at me, and she'll realize she picked the wrong brother," he teases, and I roll my eyes at him. Just as the doorbell rings.

"Just behave." I sigh, knowing it's futile as he stands tall and proud, waiting to greet them all the minute they walk in the fucking door. "Idiot," I mumble, but I'm too excited to see them to care.

"Hey." I open the door and see three pairs of wide eyes looking back at me.

"Hey, sorry, we're a bit late. Noah wanted to grab his monster spray," Annabelle rushes out, and I grin, shaking my head.

"You're right on time. It's okay." I press a kiss to her forehead before picking up Noah. "No monsters here, buddy."

I turn and walk toward my brother. He's looking at me like I'm crazy all over again, as his eyes flick to Noah in my arms and back to me.

"Who are you and what the hell have you done with my brother?"

I ignore his comment.

"This is Sutton. Sutton, this is Annabelle, Kevin, and Noah," I say, putting Noah down.

"Hi, Sutton, great to meet you. Thanks for watching the boys for us." Annabelle smiles warmly.

"No problem. Anytime." Thank God he's on his best behavior now.

I look at Kevin, who's looking at Sutton, wide-eyed, like he's seeing a superhero.

"You're the guy with the monsters..." Kevin says in awe,

obviously aware of Sutton's movies, and I laugh, as does Annabelle, while Sutton puts his hands on his hips and puffs out his chest.

"That's me."

"Monsters! No monsters!" Noah shouts, and before I know what's happening, Noah has his monster spray in his hands and starts squirting Sutton.

"What the fu—" Sutton's pristine white t-shirt gets covered in blue and green glitter as his hands shield his face from the water spray that's now coating him.

"Oh, Noah. No!" Annabelle panics, trying to get him to stop.

"This is Gucci!" Sutton wails, and I step in.

"Here, Noah, let me have a go." I grab the spray bottle from his little hands.

"Take that, you monster maniac." I spray my brother all over, his white top now saturated, and he looks at me with revenge in his eyes.

"Oh my God…" I hear Annabelle start to laugh, the sound pure magic to my ears.

"Kevin, jump on him!" I yell, and pride swirls in my chest at seeing him spring into action, clearly on team Sawyer as he jumps on my brother, Sutton going down onto the floor, both the boys on top of him.

"I am a monster! I'm the tickle monster!" Sutton wiggles his fingers, and the two boys scream in laughter. Meanwhile, I continue to spray him in the face like only a brother can.

Annabelle is still laughing, her love for her boys shining in her eyes before her gaze comes to me and doesn't falter. But I do. I stop spraying, attention zoning in on her as the three kids on the floor continue wriggling around, her sons trying to hold Sutton down.

She smiles. "Who knew my monster spray would be so entertaining."

I take that moment to really look her over. Her hair is free, flowing down her back in natural waves. Her blue eyes sparkle, her light makeup perfect to highlight her features. Her short white dress skims over her curves, ending just above her knees, and her feet are covered in knee-high brown cowboy boots. She looks like every country boy's dream girl, yet she's all mine.

"Maybe a new product line for Gertie's..." I suggest, chuckling, and she gives my chest a playful smack. My business mind never really switches off.

Sutton gets to his feet as Kevin and Noah calm down. "Alright, you got the monsters out of me, little dudes. Let's get these two out the door and pick a movie, then go into the kitchen and eat all of Sawyer's food."

He'll hand me my ass at some point for this.

"Thanks, Sutton," I say as the kids kiss their mom goodbye and run into my kitchen, where I know they will find cupboards full of food I ordered just for them.

"You got the look of love on your face, Sawyer. Haven't seen that since Becca Langer... or Mandy..." he whispers.

My heart beats a little faster at that observation, knowing he's spotted the feeling I've been nervous to name. He eyes me, before his gaze flicks to Annabelle, then back to me.

"Go. Enjoy. I'll run the kids around, so they fall asleep and don't wake until morning. Oh, and Sawyer..." He starts to walk to the kitchen, Annabelle still telling the boys to mind their manners and do as Sutton asks.

"Yeah?" I ask.

"Looks like she has the same look on her face as you do." He nods to me, and I swallow roughly, hoping he's right.

30

ANNABELLE

As we step into Whiteman's Bar, nerves prickle my skin, and I pull at my dress.

I had no idea what to wear tonight. I haven't been here for years. The last time I was, I sat outside in my car, waiting for Steve, ready to drive his drunk ass home. I waited all night, just so he could trash-talk me the entire way home, before giving me a black eye for my trouble. I shiver at the memory.

"Are you cold?" Sawyer holds my hand tight, walking us through the crowd to a booth in the back.

I shake my head, smiling. "No, I'm okay."

He looks good tonight in his black jeans and a button-up shirt that's open at the collar. Casual, yet still better dressed than half the people here.

"I thought we could hide down here." Sawyer pulls up to a booth, and I grin at how thoughtful he is.

"You know me too well." With a happy sigh, I slide into the booth opposite him.

"Well, by the looks you were getting walking in, I'd say most of the town now wonders how they can run me out of

Whispers, just so they could have you themselves." He looks around, and I blush. I see people looking at me, whispering, slowly realizing who I am, and I hate the attention.

"I haven't been here in years."

"I know. You've been busy, raising the boys, being such an amazing mom and always putting them first. But don't worry about them tonight; they're having fun." He shows me an image on his phone. It's a photo of my boys and Sutton building a fort in his living room out of cushions and blankets.

"Your brother is amazing for watching them."

"He's a big kid himself sometimes."

"Hey, guys." Connor and Daisy approach our booth, both looking happy to see us. They're panting, with light sheens of sweat, obviously coming from the dance floor.

"You dance?" Sawyer looks at him like he's grown another head.

"He does..." Daisy says, smiling.

Sawyer shakes his head with a teasing grin. "Never would've thought it."

"We're over by the pool table. Come over when you finish dinner, so I can beat your ass." Connor laughs, and we do the same. This is nice. Sawyer has friends, and they're all lovely people, all of whom I know but don't know well.

"You can stick with me, Annabelle. Us girls will hit the dance floor without them," Daisy offers.

"Sounds fun?" I say hesitantly, because I love to dance, but I wonder if I still remember how.

"See you later," Connor says, before they both walk over to the pool tables, where I see Tanner and Victoria playing and another guy who looks like one of their friends.

"So, burgers? Steaks? What do you feel like?" Sawyer

looks over the menu, and we decide the burgers are what we feel like, the waitress taking our orders and leaving us to it.

"Are you feeling alright?" Sawyer grabs my hand over the table.

"I'm actually feeling pretty good." I feel light and free for the first time in what feels like forever. I'm not on the farm, scared out of my mind. The kids are safe and happy, having the time of their lives with a real-life movie star. We're staying at Sawyer's place tonight, giving us some space from our nightly terrors, and I'm on a date with a man I think I might be falling in love with. I chew my bottom lip, thinking about it all.

"You look pretty good too, Mama. You look beautiful tonight."

"This ol' thing?" I joke about my dress, although it isn't really a joke. I estimate this dress is probably about ten years old. I found it in my old dresser from when I used to wear it as a teen, thanking the gods that it still fits.

"You'd look good in anything." There's molten heat in his gaze that has my stomach doing a flip-flop. He lifts my hand, then brings it to his lips, kissing me on the inside of my wrist, and a delightful shiver ripples down my spine. I look him over then, seeing him a little more settled into himself. While changing from a suit is obvious, it's more than that. It's like he has evolved, the way he is around people now, more welcoming, more warmth. His shirtsleeves are rolled up, showcasing his strong arms, giving him a more relaxed, casual vibe. He may sit behind a desk all day, but his physique rivals any man who works on the land.

I clear my throat, my body feeling hot, and try and get us on to balanced ground. He's already got me turned on, and our date has barely started.

"So how long is your brother staying with you?" I ask,

just as our food appears, and we start to dig in.

"He's going to lie low for a while. The press are after him, so he needs seclusion until things calm down," Sawyer says cryptically, but I pick up what he's saying.

"It must be hard, living in the spotlight like that." My life is basically seclusion, but I'm not running from anything, so I wonder for the first time why I'm hiding away so much.

"What's the frown for?" Sawyer's always alert to my emotions.

"It's just..." My lips purse, trying to get a handle on my thoughts. "Well, it isn't until now, until tonight, that I realize I've been pretty secluded as well."

He watches me with interest, waiting for me to continue.

"I mean, I knew, kind of. I live way out of town, I'm busy, but now that we are out and about with baseball and being here tonight... I was nervous coming here, nervous what people would think or say, but..." I look around, seeing everyone back to their own conversations, and the few people who catch my eye give me warm smiles and a wave. It's nice. Welcoming.

"But what?" he asks.

"But maybe I'm not doing it right." I shake my head, taking a deep breath before sharing, "Steve always said not to let people in. Outsiders were never welcome into our business or onto our farm."

"He kept you small," Sawyer grits out.

"I was home all the time with Kevin when he was just a baby, and Steve barely let me leave for doctor appointments." I've never told anyone any of this before, the release of information feeling cathartic.

There's anger in Sawyer's gaze as he says, "It's a manipulation tactic."

I bite my lip, seeing the reality of that now. "I just didn't know any different. I didn't know that..." I look around again, the colors and noise in the bar so vibrant and loud, making me feel alive.

"He made you think that being out on that farm was what you needed to do," Sawyer adds for me, and I nod.

"It's my livelihood, and I love it, but..." I see Bob over in the corner, and he's both a farmer and owner of a business. Then I spot Tina and Tim having dinner, both of them farmers with a business and kids too. They're all out here, living life, not hiding away, hiding from everyone.

"Maybe I've been holding back. Maybe I've been holding the boys back. Maybe I..." I start to feel a little panicked that I've done my sons a disservice.

"You're an awesome mom. You're allowed to do life on your own terms, and you're allowed to change those terms any fucking time you want," Sawyer says with so much conviction, I feel it in my bones.

"I... I think I know that now..."

Sawyer releases a heavy breath, his thumb rubbing back and forth on my hand in a soothing motion. "I probably should take my own advice."

I tilt my head. "How so?"

"Well, we aren't that dissimilar, you and me. While you kept yourself on the farm, kept your circle small, I've been burying myself in work for years, living and breathing my business. Growing it, yes, but not stepping out of it much. I always thought my office was my kingdom. I didn't let anyone in unless they proved themselves, and I worked day and night, not really coming up for air."

He's right; we've been doing life on our terms, and practically solo for years, both of us. It's nice to know that I'm not alone, which makes me feel a little more normal.

He continues, his eyes looking deeply into mine. "Now

I'm starting to see a different picture, a different dream about how my life might be."

"What does that look like for you, Sawyer?" I'm nervous about what he will say.

"It looks like quiet country nights, like throwing the ball with kids after school. It looks like home-cooked meals at the table, and doing it all with a woman who's just as driven as I am, someone who I can rest my head with at night, someone who I want to cherish, give her everything she's ever dreamed of, because I already know she gives me everything I could ever want or need."

My heart thumps harder as I whisper, "That's pretty descriptive..." He didn't mention my name. He didn't need to. We both know he was talking about a life with me.

"I don't want to scare you, but I guess I just want to let you know that I'm really enjoying spending time with you, getting to know your boys, spending time in your family unit. I'm no farmer, so I'm not sure what I can offer you there, but I'm not seeing anyone else, Annabelle. You're all I can think about and, well... I want to be exclusive. We haven't put a label on anything, and I want to. I want to try to make a go of what we've started, see where it can go..."

I hold my breath at his vulnerability, needing a second to internally pinch myself.

"You're not scaring me... I want that. I would like to see what happens, where things go..." I smile as my heart races, having never had these kinds of conversations before.

"Yeah?" He smiles back just as brightly when I nod. "I'm not sure what the next few months will look like with work. I'll probably still be flying back and forth for a little while, but I hope we can figure it out like we have been."

"All we can do is try, right?"

As he lifts my hand to kiss again, I notice my palms are a

little sweaty. With my heart still beating like it's trying to escape my chest, I think I need to cool off, get some air, and calm myself. I don't want him to take my obvious overwhelm as me not being sure about us moving forward.

"I just need to use the restroom."

He releases my hand, and I slide out of the booth, smoothing out my dress.

"Take your time. I'll be here," he says, his words laced with double meaning. I walk on shaky legs to the bathroom, where I hide in a stall and really pinch my skin, wondering if I will wake up, wondering if I might get my happily ever after, after all. My grin is hard to remove as I wash my hands and fix my hair, which, for once, is actually sitting just how I want it to.

Looking at myself, I've changed. My eyes hold more life, and I smile more now than I have in forever. It's the first time I've been out of jeans like this in years, and I reach into my bag, grabbing the light-pink gloss to swipe it on my lips.

I feel good. I feel like a young woman should. I feel confident to take on this new stage with Sawyer, whatever that may look like.

I step out of the bathroom and turn the corner to walk back out to the bar, my smile wide, my head a whirl of happy thoughts.

"Thought that was you." I hear a man's growl, and I stop midstep, my smile leaving my face instantly.

"Stanley." My body turns rigid. I haven't seen Steve's father in years, but I'd never forget him. I can smell the alcohol on him. His eyes are a little bloodshot, his face bringing back images of his son. Steve was physically, emotionally, and financially abusive. Skills he learned from his father.

"What are you wearing? Steve wouldn't like you

parading around the bar like a little slut," he spits out, and I take a step away from him, my fear tensing every muscle in my body.

Ignoring his insult, I say, "Well, I should be going." I try to walk around him, but he's quick, stepping in front of me so I can't pass and bringing our bodies closer.

"I see you're here with that fancy new lawyer. Are you spreading your legs for him?"

I feel sick, my fear and anxiety mixing. My eyes flick around him to look at Sawyer, seeing him in deep conversation with Tanner at our table, and I take a breath and straighten my shoulders. I've worked hard at getting my boys and me out of the hole his son left me in. I've worked hard to bring happiness and light into my life, and now Sawyer is here with me. I know how good it could be. Looking back at Stanley, I narrow my eyes. Sawyer has instilled more confidence in me than my husband or his family ever did.

"What I do and who I do it with is none of your business," I hiss at him, and his gaze turns murderous.

"You were always a stuck-up little bitch. No wonder Steve was always out, finding other women to satisfy him. Although, now you are a little older, Belle, I sure as hell see the appeal." His eyes rake down my body and back up again, and I feel bile rising up my throat.

"Get the hell away from me," I bite out, really wishing I had my garden hoe in my hand right about now.

"Maybe I should just take a little taste, Belle, feel your cunt. Always dreamed about it." He takes another step toward me, and I take a step back, not wanting to be any closer to this man.

My legs shake, voice wavering as I speak louder this time. "I wouldn't let your dirty-ass hand touch me with a ten-foot pole. Now, get out of my way."

"Why, you little fucking bitch," he snarls as his hand lifts, and I stand taller. I'm not going to cower, not anymore. His hand moves, and I brace for impact.

"You lay one finger on her, and I'll *end* you." Sawyer's voice comes from the side, his hand now grasping Stanley's wrist so tight I can see the skin turning white. His presence instantly fills me with relief.

"Fuck off, you city suit." Stanley turns to throw a punch, but he isn't quick enough. Sawyer's hand flies past, hitting Stanley right in the chin, laying him out flat.

The bar is quiet, my gasp echoing as the music stops. Everyone's looking, and I can't slow my breathing as Sawyer steps in front of me.

"I think you need to leave," he demands, sneering Stanley's way.

"I agree." Tanner steps to Sawyer's side, both men blocking me from view.

"As do I." Connor stands on Sawyer's other side. I feel someone grab my hand, and I turn, seeing Victoria on one side of me, with Daisy on my other.

"Me too," another man says, standing next to Tanner, a man I don't even know.

"So do I." Bob stands next to Connor, crossing his arms over his chest.

"Us too." Tim joins them as Tina stands next to Victoria.

One by one, it feels like the entire bar full of people stand around me, shielding me from a man who taught my late husband everything he knows.

That's when I realize without any more doubt that this town isn't the enemy. They're family. A fact I had forgotten for far too long. And my new boyfriend is at the helm, proving to me that he has my back, whether I need it or not.

31

SAWYER

I watch Annabelle leave for the bathroom, hoping I didn't say too much, but the thoughts spilled out of me before I could stop them. It's the truth; I can see myself with her. We've known each other for such a short amount of time, yet I feel like every time I see her, I'm home. I can't explain it, not really. I take a sip of my whiskey, wondering if Tanner's been spiking my drinks with something. Maybe he has used one of Daisy's tonics.

But even with how happy I am to have made things official with Annabelle, my mind also buzzes with anger. Anger at her shit late husband, a man who I'm piecing together was an abuser, both physically and emotionally. A man who kept her small when she's so full of life. Keeping her stuck at home, when she should be wild and free. Keeping her thinking she was nothing when she's the most beautiful and awe-inspiring woman I've ever met.

"How's the date going?" Tanner slips into the booth opposite me.

"Tell me about Steve," I demand, and he takes a breath.

"A real piece of work. Bounced around from job to job,

couldn't really hold anything down. Turned to drinking, got mixed up in a bad crowd, thought the world owed him something. You know, a real class act." Tanner takes a sip of his whiskey. All this sounds similar to what Bob had to say, but I want to know more.

"I'm pretty sure he was violent at home," I tell him, thinking again about how Annabelle flinched the first time I met her.

"Yeah, well, no one really knew for sure, but the town talked. He kept her pretty hidden up at the farm, and whenever she was in town, the ladies would all talk to her and ask her questions, but never really found out much about anything from her."

My frown deepens.

"So what? This town you love so much, this town you tell me helps each other, looks out for each other, just left her up on that farm with an asshole husband who used her as he wanted?" My anger is high, my body almost vibrating. If that asshole wasn't already dead, I would kill him myself.

"It was a few years ago, and there's only so much people can do in a situation like that. The sheriff went up for a visit almost every week, using one excuse or another, but Annabelle never said anything, and we could never find any proof."

The legal part of my brain knows he's right. Knows that you need evidence, a victim statement, that you can't just go to someone's house and throw around accusations and arrest them with nothing.

If the sheriff used to go up and check on her regularly but never did anything, it doesn't surprise me that she now doesn't tell anyone anything. She probably thinks no one would believe her anyway.

That prompts me to share. "Something else is going on up at the farm."

"What do you mean?" Tanner's eyes narrow.

"Not sure exactly, but something isn't right. The night she hurt her head, we all felt it. Tell me I'm wrong?"

He shakes his head. "I got a feeling, but I couldn't really understand it, though."

"This week, the field where her lavender grows was ruined. Bob and I saw the fence, and it was cut with bolt cutters. The other week, she had a flat tire, but she was a bit skittish about it. She makes excuses, but I know she isn't telling me something."

"She needs to know she can trust you. She may have feelings for you, may like having you around, but I think trust with a woman like Annabelle is probably the hardest thing to get from her, and until you have it, you'll be kept out of the loop."

He's right, and my shoulders are tight, knowing I haven't yet earned it from her.

Flying into town on my private jet, throwing around my money, giving the boys and her gifts that have no real value to her life is probably having the opposite effect. My brother's photo, the help on the business, and hopefully getting Gertie's into Van Cleef Properties will all help financially, but I need to do something so she knows I'm a man who will protect her, with more than just my bank balance and connections. She needs a steady shoulder, and all this flying in and out is probably just reinforcing to her that I'm not dependable. Highlighting that I'm not someone she can rely on.

"Uhhh... guys, we have a problem," Victoria says, coming to our booth, pointing behind me. I turn around, seeing Annabelle's back plastered to the wall, looking equal parts as scared as a deer in headlights and ready to gut the large man who's towering over her.

"Oh... Fuck no." I'm out of the booth quickly and striding over, not needing to look to know Tanner is right behind me. As I step up to them, the man raises his hand in a move to hit her, and I see red.

"You lay one finger on her, and I'll *end* you." I grab his wrist midair, my grip strength feeling like I'll break it. He looks at me, startled, seemingly surprised that anyone would come to Annabelle's defense.

"Fuck off, you city suit." The guy who looks like he has had way too many whiskeys turns to throw a punch at me, but he's slow and uncoordinated. My fist is in his face in an instant, and he flies back, hitting the ground hard.

The bar goes quiet, and Annabelle gasps. With the music stopped, everyone's looking, but I step forward in front of Annabelle, protecting her like a shield, putting myself between her and the danger she faces. Even though my hand stings like a motherfucker, I want to hit him again. I want to make this man bleed for even thinking he could get up in her face like he did.

I take a deep breath, trying to settle my adrenaline. I haven't hit anyone in a long, long time. As a kid, I was always roughhousing. My brother and I got teased for wearing old clothes, not having a dad, and all sorts of other things when we were younger, so as the older brother, my fist connected with faces more times than not. That all stopped once I went to college and put my head down, knowing the only way out for me and my family was a law degree. But those same feelings build in me again, the protective ones, the fierce determination to fight for what's mine.

"I think you need to leave." I stand tall and proud. One by one, the men in the bar join me, standing by my side, and

I feel their support. Even Griffin, who's only in town for the night. Tanner's builder often flies in and is currently here working on the Whiteman's Whiskey Accommodation build. Like me, he's always in town, not yet a local.

If this wasn't so serious, I would smile. This is what Tanner was talking about, how the town comes together. As the guy slowly gets up from the floor, a few of his buddies scramble to help him, aware they are completely outnumbered.

"Fine. Whiskey here's shit anyway." He spits on the floor in front of me, just missing my new shoes, and I grind my teeth.

"I'll walk you out," Tanner says as he and Connor and Griffin follow behind the small group, ensuring they leave, and I turn to look at Annabelle behind me. The crowd starts to disperse, and the music comes back on. I nod to both Bob and the others, a silent gesture of appreciation for them having our back.

"I'll get you some water," Daisy says to Annabelle before running off to the bar.

"Let me get some ice for lover boy's hand here," Victoria says as she follows Daisy, and I notice Annabelle's hands shaking.

"Come, let's sit back down for a bit, then we'll go home." I take her shaking hand in mine and hold her tight.

"You cut your hand." She lifts my hand to her face, inspecting the damage, and I wince a little.

"He had a hard head." I sit her down at a nearby table, Daisy delivering water and Victoria passing me some ice before they both join Connor over at the bar. When she doesn't say anything, just looks at me quietly, tears shining in her eyes, any remaining adrenaline turns to a sick feeling in my stomach, not knowing how she feels about seeing me hit someone, after who knows what she's been through.

"Annabelle, I'm sorry. I shouldn't have hit him. I don't condone violence, and I would never typically do something like that, and I—" My words tumble out, but she cuts me off, pressing a soft finger to my lips.

"Sawyer. Stop. I'm fine. It's okay. I trust you. You were protecting me. I know that." I still feel like shit, although a little less so. I take a breath, and she does the same, then I press a kiss to that finger before she moves her hand to rest on my thigh.

I smile sadly. "I'm sorry our date is ruined."

"Well, that just means you need to take me on another one."

My eyes search her face, and she gives me a soft smile.

"Already planning it."

"Here, let me." Annabelle takes the ice and grabs my hand, resting it on the table between us. "Are you alright?" I ask her.

Her eyebrows pinch. "I should be asking you that question; you're the one with the injury."

"Annabelle."

She looks at my hand and the ice, pretending to be busy.

"Annabelle, please look at me," I nearly beg, hating how I can tell something is still gnawing at her emotions.

When her eyes flick up and meet mine, my chest almost splits wide open, seeing her eyes full of fear, defiance, those tears back and hanging on to her lashes.

"Are you alright?" Lifting my good hand, I cup her cheek, and she takes another deep breath. She leans back in her chair and grabs the glass of water, the glass shaking in her hands while she drinks. I watch her, remaining silent, waiting for her answer.

Placing the glass back down, she says, "That was Stanley. He's my former father-in-law."

My jaw clenches.

"I guess you could say he taught his son everything he knows."

If I wasn't sure about her past relationship, I am now.

I huff a breath, my blood heating all over again. "He's a real piece of work."

"I haven't seen him in a long time."

"Has he ever hurt you in the past?" My heart pounds harder as I wait for the answer.

Her eyes look into mine, and she pauses, swallowing audibly. "No."

"Do the kids see them? Their father's side of the family?" I hope to hell they don't.

"Never," she says fiercely. I know this mama bear would protect her cubs with everything she has.

Tanner approaches where we're sitting, putting our conversation on pause. "They've gone. I'll speak to the sheriff and get this on the record."

"No." Annabelle's response is panicked, and I look at her with concern.

"It's important to have these things reported. He won't necessarily be charged; hell, he may even charge me for punching him, but unless this is on the record, then it never happened. It's important to have everything noted, so that if it happens again, you have a record of behavior that you can use if needed in the future."

"The sheriff may go and talk with him, but he won't be back here. He isn't welcome in any of my establishments anymore," Tanner says, looking at Annabelle.

"I don't want to cause trouble." Her eyes look so dejected, like this is somehow her fault.

I wish I could go back in time and erase whatever happened in her past. But I can't.

"He caused trouble the minute he stepped into your space. You did nothing wrong. None of this is on you at all. You were just here having a meal with your very handsome boyfriend." I get the small smile I was hoping for. "Let's go home, see what trouble Sutton got into while we were away."

As I stand, she joins me. I shake Tanner's hand and say goodbye to the others and Victoria, Daisy, and a few other local women all come to hug Annabelle. She smiles softly, opening up to them a little, and I know although it was a horrible first date, it might just be the one that has her accepting this small town as her own. And maybe accepting me as the man who can stand by her side.

32

ANNABELLE

My nerves are shot, my hands still trembling as Sawyer drives up his long and very luxurious driveway. As we pull up, he cuts the engine and turns to look at me.

"You know you can tell me anything. I'm a great listener."

Tonight changed things for me. Seeing Sawyer come to my defense. Standing in front of me, protecting me without any hesitation. He doesn't know this town very well, and he doesn't know Stanley and what he's capable of. He doesn't know any of my history, yet he stood there, protecting me and being the man I needed.

So, with a steadying breath, I decide to trust him with my past.

"Steve was never close with his parents. They had a rocky household. His father, Stanley, is a drunk, and his mother eventually left them all when Steve was young, because she'd had enough of the beatings Stanley delivered to her. A situation I came to know too well myself over the years." I feel my heart beating against my ribs as I remember it all. "Stanley never hit me, but he always leered at me, so the threat of it was always there. I saw him hit his sons multiple times, yet my husband always went back to him. Always went drinking with him. He never left him, just like I never left Steve. In a way, we were both controlled by Stanley."

Sawyer reaches over and opens his hand for me to hold, and I thread my fingers through his as I continue. "I thought I knew it all. I thought I had it all." I huff and shake my head at my own naivety. "Steve always told me no one cared about me. Said I was nothing. Useless and I felt it. I felt every word." I take another breath, trying to keep the shakiness out of my voice. "For a long time, I thought Steve was just stressed, you know. Stressed about running the farm, keeping it going, bringing money in." I huff. "But there was no money. When he left the house, he wasn't running the farm. He was going to town, getting drunk with his dad, no doubt finding a woman for the night before coming home and repeating it all over again. When he was gone, I would strap Kevin to my body and go work on the land, plant vegetables, tend to the animals. But it was hard."

I look over to Sawyer, knowing he's a safe space for me now. Knowing that I can trust him. He protected me and has been protecting me in his own way for months now. Showing me kindness that my own husband never did. "I haven't told anyone any of this."

He lifts his hand, cupping my cheek. His thumb brushes the tears that fall from my face.

"Thank you for sharing it with me."

I roll my shoulders back as I meet his eyes.

"I bet this isn't what you had in mind when wanting to

look at doing life together. Are you going to be on your jet tonight, or first thing in the morning?" I give him an out. Offering him the opportunity to say he needs to run back to the city, anything to get away from me.

"I'm not going anywhere." His voice is soft but stern. He means what he says, but I just...

"I like you, Sawyer. I really like you. But I'm not well put together. I'm not elegant, nor sophisticated. I have no money, I have two kids, I have a farm that's barely turning a profit. I have nothing to offer a man like you. I haven't been able to stop thinking about that... why you want to be with me seriously," I tell him honestly, and his jaw clenches.

"Your late husband told you what he thought of you. So, let me tell you what I think of you," he says, his eyes never leaving mine as he leans in a little closer. "You are determined. You are resilient. You're an amazing mom to those boys. You're smart, hardworking, and resourceful. You're a businesswoman who's finding success after starting from nothing. You're a multitasker, an excellent cook, stunningly beautiful, funny, scary when you have a hoe in your hand, stubborn, prideful. You're not great with numbers, but that's okay, because I am. You're the first person I've ever broken a dining table with. I love your smile, your wild hair. I love the way you play with your hair when you lie and the way you sound when you come. You're all I fucking think about, Annabelle, and I meant every word I said to you tonight at dinner, and every other word before then too. I'd like to give us a go. Your past does not define who you are. You can change your story at any point, and I think what you've been doing since your husband died is exactly that. You've started rewriting your story, and from where I'm sitting, it looks like it's going to be a dream."

I think I forget to breathe. My vision blurs as I look into his eyes.

"No one has ever said anything like that to me before."

He wipes another tear that falls, and I lean over, meeting him halfway to kiss him.

"Thank you," I exhale against his lips. He's right. I'm not my past. I can define my present and recreate a new future. My head was so locked into what it was that I couldn't see what life is now.

With his hand still cupping my face, I look up at the house, seeing a few lights on, and I think of my boys, knowing that all the work I've been doing the past years has brought me to this moment. To this place. To meet a man like Sawyer.

"We should go inside," I say, and he nods.

"It's at this point I would just like to mention that I have no idea how much sugar Sutton has given the boys and am not entirely sure what we are about to walk into..."

That makes me laugh, and he grins, the two of us now feeling a little lighter for sharing.

As we step out of the car, he pulls me close, and we walk inside, eager to see my boys after being away from them.

The house is quiet, and we step into the living room to survey the damage.

"I promise Sutton is an adult... I think..." Sawyer murmurs as we look at the candy packets, glitter, rugs, and cushions sprawled everywhere.

"Looks like they had fun," I say as he takes my hand.

"Let's check on the kids."

I follow him down the hall to what I assume is a spare bedroom where the kids are. Sawyer opens the door, and I pull up short. The bedroom is huge. There are bunk beds, toys, books, games. There's a bathroom off to the side that's bigger than mine at home, and from where I'm standing, I can see bottles of bubble bath.

"Sawyer?" I'm confused, and he rubs the back of his head, the movement familiar, and I find myself smiling.

"I hope this is alright? I had it done knowing they were going to stay over."

My heart clenches. "You did this for the boys?"

He nods slowly, seemingly unsure of my reaction.

"They're never going to want to leave!" I tell him, squeezing his arm playfully. His generosity is out of this world.

I walk in and go to my boys. Noah's sound asleep, cuddling a new teddy bear, his monster spray nowhere in sight. I kiss his forehead before moving to Kevin, who's on the top bunk.

"Hey, Ma," he whispers, half-asleep.

"Did you have a good time tonight?" I pull his blankets up a little higher to cover him.

"The best. It was awesome."

I kiss his forehead. "I'll see you in the morning."

"Hmmmm..." is all I get back, and I couldn't be more content, knowing he's happy.

"Come on, Mama, let me show you our room." Sawyer grabs my hand again, and we leave the boys, closing the door and walking farther down the hall.

"Where's your brother?" I look around.

"There's another wing. He left to go there after we drove up," Sawyer confirms, and my eyebrows lift. The house looks massive from the driveway, one of those mansions that you can't see from the road due to the large pines and tall gates, but a whole other wing brings it all into perspective.

When he opens the door to his room, it's like I forget how to speak.

"What do you think?" he asks.

"I think... I think..." I look everywhere, trying to take it all in. The room is larger than my kitchen and living room combined. The bed, I've never seen anything like it. Expansive windows overlook the manicured gardens outside, with French doors opening onto a large patio. I take a few more steps inside and see a walk-in closet, half filled with men's clothes and half filled with women's clothes. Frowning, I turn around to face him with a question on the tip of my tongue.

"I... ahh... I just got some clothes in for you, in case you left anything at home that you might need," he rushes to explain, knowing exactly what I was thinking. But then what he says sinks in.

"These are for me?" I ask in disbelief. There are jeans, tops, sweaters, leggings, dresses, everything you could imagine.

"Victoria helped me pick things out. We also got some for the boys in their room."

I walk around a bit more and step into the bathroom, this room again bigger than my own at home and fully marble, with a large tub, dual sinks, and a double shower.

"Are you okay?" He approaches my side, and I look up at him.

"Why in the world are you sleeping at my place when you have all this?" I'm gobsmacked, and he chuckles.

"Because as good as this is, it doesn't have you."

My chest is fluttering even before he takes my lips in his and wraps his hands around my waist, pulling me tight.

After the night we've had and the emotions I've moved through, I lean into him and give myself over. This man has continually shown me that he's here for me and the boys, and as his tongue slides against mine, I feel the last steel fence around my heart disappear completely.

"You feel so good in my arms, Mama," he murmurs against my lips, deepening our kiss as his hands splay over my back and hips, touching me as much as he can.

"Sawyer?" I say breathily.

"Yeah?"

"Make me forget about tonight..." I'm tentative, still a little nervous at how I approach sex with a man, although Sawyer makes it easier and easier all the time.

"Tell me what you want, baby." His lips slide down my jaw, and I feel my nipples pebble, my senses heightened.

"I want you... I just want you..."

I shiver as his fingers run down to the hem of my dress, reaching mid-thigh before he lifts it up and straight off my body. When I kick off my boots, he peels off his shirt, leaving him bare-chested in jeans, a sight I'm still not used to. I swallow roughly as I look him over.

"Take your time, baby. We've got all night." A wicked grin comes to his face as my cheeks heat from ogling him.

"I don't want to wait a minute longer." I barely finish saying the words before he's on me. His lips smash into mine again, and his hands find my ass, lifting me and walking us to his bed.

"I lose all control around you..." With lips brandishing my neck, his hands unclip my bra, then he pulls the straps from my shoulders, finding my pebbled nipple with his kisses almost instantly.

"Oh God... I forgot how good your lips feel..." I moan, biting my bottom lip as I throw my bra across the room before my hands dive to his waist, and I open his jeans. As I push them over his hips, he sits up, kicking off his boots and jeans and underwear before coming back to me, the only thing between us now my basic cotton underpants.

"I forgot how good your body feels against mine." His mouth trails over my curves, leaving a trail from my nipples over my stomach and hips. His hands mold my breasts, and I see the redness from his injury today, completely contrasting with my pale skin, and my arousal increases even more.

"So fucking beautiful," he groans as he sits up to look me over, and I grab his hand, pulling him back to me so our naked bodies collide. He's warm on top of me, my legs spreading for him as he kisses me until I'm breathless.

"Yes... please..." I pant out when I feel his hand hovering over my center, wanting to feel his touch everywhere, needing more.

"So eager for me... so fucking eager," he grits out, and as his finger brushes my clit, my body jolts, my back arching. His lips find my nipple again as he starts to work my body like he knows every inch.

"Oh God... yesss..." My hips grind against his hand almost instantly, needy for him.

"Fuck, you're so wet... so perfect for me, baby..." he groans as he works me over, my body tingling from the precise way he's playing with me.

"Sawyer," I pant out in warning, feeling my orgasm already building as he rubs against that spot inside me that makes me tremble.

"That's it, fuck my fingers," he says gruffly, before his lips claim mine again, and I moan into his mouth.

"Please keep going, please..." My back arches, his hand not stopping, taking me all the way to the edge.

"Yes! Sawyer!" I start to cry out, before he covers my mouth with his, and I come powerfully. My body shudders, my moans and whimpers falling on his lips as his fingers slow.

He pulls his head back to look at me. "I'm not finished with you yet."

I smile, a wanton giggle leaving my chest. I was hoping he wasn't.

33

SAWYER

I think I'm fucked. Actually, no, I know I'm fucked. This woman lying naked underneath me, looking perfect, flushed and still eager for me, has me completely bewildered about what I saw in every other woman who came before her.

As she catches her breath, I reach over to my side table and grab a condom, sheathing myself quickly.

"I'm so fucking hard for you, it hurts," I admit. I'm so close to coming just from her little moans and the way she responded to my fingers.

"We can fix that," she teases, and I grin like a fool. God, I would do anything for this woman. I would buy her land, I would punch a guy at a bar, and I sure as hell am going to make her forget about it, just like she asked.

"Lift your hands above your head," I demand, and she complies immediately as she bites her bottom lip in antici-pation. When she moves, her body arches in that way that makes me nearly feral for her, her breasts full, her curves so sexy. "Spread your legs, baby. Let me in."

Again, she does as I ask, all with a coy smile. I lean over, settling in between her thighs as I grab on to her wrists above her head with one hand. As I slide into her slowly, her eyes roll back, enjoying the stretch of me as I grit my teeth, willing myself not to come straightaway.

"Fuck yeah…" I breathe out as I start to move. She feels amazing, she looks amazing. She is amazing, and she's with me. Here in my bed, doing what I ask of her, and me giving her what she needs.

"Oh God, I love when you go deep like that," she moans as I thrust inside of her, feeling her body clench around me, watching as her breasts jiggle with every thrust.

"You feel so goddamn good," I grit out, my other hand lowering to her leg and lifting her knee up, sinking into her deeper and making her gasp.

"Sawyer… yesssss. Right there," she pants, her eyes locking on mine, and my balls tighten.

"I want to fuck you like this every day. Every fucking day…" Letting go of her wrists, she keeps them in place, gripping on to the sheets above her, and I grab her other knee. Pushing her legs wide, I fuck her nice and hard, as deep as I can go, relishing her whimpers and pants as her body tenses beneath me.

I watch her second orgasm start to build as she bites her lip, trying to hold back her moans as her head pushes back, body arching. She's close, and so am I.

"I want to taste you every morning, finger-fuck you every lunchtime, and then make you squeeze my cock like this every night." I'm dizzy with desire for her. I can't get enough of her. I'm currently inside her and already wanting so much more.

"Every day. Oh, oh God." Her voice grows louder, but the kids are asleep, and there are a few rooms between us, so I let her cry out as she comes, my name on her lips, and I follow her instantly.

"Fuck, fuck, fuck. Annabelle!" I groan, the sound rumbling from deep in my chest as her body clenches on to mine, before she lies back, spent, a light sheen to her forehead. Leaning over, exhausted, I trail small kisses all over her, everywhere I can reach without moving.

She giggles, her arms wrapping around me. "That tickles." Her body jolts a little as I kiss her side.

"Where? Here?" I ask her, doing it again, enjoying hearing her laugh after what has been an emotional night.

"Sawyer!" she squeals and bats lightly at my shoulders, balling up. I grab her then, carrying her to the bathroom, and we hit the shower, washing the day away together. And because I can't help myself, I fall to my knees, wanting another taste of her before bed.

WE LIE next to each other, the house quiet, the faint glow of the moon slithering into the room. We fell asleep as soon as we got back into bed after the shower, but it's now just after three in the morning, and we're both awake. The two of us were hungry for each other after a few hours of rest, and now, after having her come on my tongue again, we're relaxed and cozy.

"Do you see your mom much anymore?" she asks as her fingers trail along my abs.

"Holidays and a few trips each year. She has a lot of friends, keeps pretty busy. She's busier than Sutton and me sometimes." I huff a laugh, thinking about it. My mom and retirement go well together.

"That's nice. I miss my mom. She used to make the best cornbread."

I smile, knowing she doesn't get to talk like this with anyone, and I like being the person she shares things with.

"You're the best cook I know."

"Hmm, no matter how hard I try, I just can't get my cornbread the same as hers."

I press a kiss into her hair, where she lays with her head on my chest, my hand caressing up and down her arm, keeping her close.

"I don't even cook, so you've beaten me there."

"Tell me your favorite food," she says, and I'm surprised we haven't talked about this before.

"Yours," I say immediately.

"Sawyer!" she scolds me, laughing. "Really, tell me." I feel her grinning against my skin.

"It's the truth. I mean, the pasta at Mario's in Manhattan is pretty good, but I've loved everything you've cooked for me so far."

"Did none of your other girlfriends cook for you?"

We haven't delved into our pasts too much, although I know more about hers than she does about mine.

"Haven't really had many girlfriends. You're the first one in a while."

"Mm-hmm. Okay. Now I know you're lying."

"It's the truth. I date, sure, but I haven't committed myself to someone, been exclusive with someone for a long time."

"Who was your last girlfriend?"

I take a deep breath. "My last serious girlfriend was actually my fiancée."

"Oh? What happened?" She looks up at me, and I pull her tighter, not wanting her to feel any different about all this, but needing to share, especially since she's been so open about her late husband.

"We were together for a few years, engaged for about one." I clear my throat, and she remains silent, so I continue. "It was when I was young, late twenties, about your age." At a decade older than her, I'm more her senior, but it's an issue we don't seem to have.

"What was her name?"

"Mandy. We met at college, and she was a nice girl. But I had to work long days and nights to prove myself at the law firm where I was working. They make all new graduates do grunt work, but I enjoyed it. I always had a vision of owning my own firm, you know."

Her brow furrows, her eyes curious. "Why didn't you get married?"

I lift my hand, running my fingers through her hair, pushing it from her face so I can see her clearly.

"I had an issue with work. Lost an important case. The client, he was a bad guy. Made our lives difficult, scared Mandy, the pressure of it all was too much. For both of us. So she walked away, and I let her."

"Walked away?"

I nod, knowing that a woman like Annabelle wouldn't walk away from anything, no matter how hard things got. It's one of the reasons I've completely fallen for her. I know that if we continue what we're doing, that she'll always have my back and, I, hers.

Pursing her lips in thought, she asks, "How did he make your lives difficult? What happened?"

I blow out a breath. "He went to jail for murder. Still there, got twenty years. So he hated me, a young lawyer who lost his case and didn't prevent him from serving jail time."

"But he was the bad guy. He can't blame you."

"Well, he did. Had his men follow and threaten Mandy a bit. It never got physical, but she was scared to leave the house and just didn't want that life. I mean, the life of a lawyer is hard. Sure, there's money, fancy dinners and events, lots of good sides, but in criminal law, especially, there can be serious ramifications."

"But you still do criminal law after that?"

"A little, but nothing major. I prefer business law, so while I have a small criminal team, I think now that I'm here in Whispers, I might focus solely on commercial and contract law," I say what I've been thinking about out loud. It's been a long time coming. I should've closed that division years ago really.

"Sounds safer..." Her voice is unsure, and I understand her worries.

"Not really. Business law can be tough. I have this one client; she makes soaps and, you know, she's just really bad at accepting any help. Drives me crazy," I tell her, grinning playfully.

"Really? She sounds delightful. Tell me more about her?" she teases, making me laugh as I pull her close and kiss her like she deserves. Because this woman in my arms deserves the world, and I want to be the man who gives it to her.

34

SAWYER

I flip the pancake perfectly, my grin instant as Noah giggles.

"And then we watched another movie and ate all the popcorn." Kevin is now more talkative than ever, and if I thought getting Annabelle and these kids off the farm was going to be this successful, I would've done it a lot earlier.

"So let me get this straight. You had candy for dinner and then popcorn, followed by...?" I ask them both, the amusement on my face hard to remove as I see both boys sitting up at the kitchen breakfast bar, eating the pancakes quicker than I can make them.

"Ice cream." Noah giggles, and I swear, these kids are amazing.

"It was so cool," Kevin says, and I slide another pancake onto his plate. I left Annabelle to sleep. God knows, she needs it. After what happened last night, and the fact that I heard both boys awake early, I left her bundled in the blankets and got them up and in the kitchen so we didn't wake her.

"Your mom is going to freak out when she hears that." I'm only half joking.

"Hears what, exactly?" Her voice reaches me from the doorway, and I look up. My breath gets caught in my throat, just looking at her. Her beautiful hair is a complete mess in a top knot on her head. Her sleep shorts and top are all wrinkled, her face stunningly fresh, and as she pads closer on bare feet, she looks like all my favorite things rolled into one. She looks like she *belongs*.

"We had candy for dinner," Noah admits immediately, his reply so quick, I mentally note not to tell him any of my secrets.

"Oh, really?" Annabelle's eyes are full of knowing as she walks to her boys and kisses them both before walking up to me.

"You didn't wake me."

"You looked too perfect in my sheets. I didn't want to." My arm wraps around her middle, and she smiles as I lean down and kiss her good morning. Not the kind of kiss I want, given we have an audience, but one that leaves promises for more later.

"So candy for dinner, huh?" She turns to look at her boys.

"Gummy bears, to be exact," I tell her, showing her the empty packet I picked up from the living room floor this morning.

"Hmmm, better brush your teeth extra well this morning." As she takes a seat, I slide a coffee across the counter to her. She looks up in surprise.

"Pancake?" I ask.

It strikes me then that she probably hasn't had anyone make her breakfast since she was a kid. She's been the one making food for everyone else ever since.

"That would be nice." Adoration softens her eyes, the look warming me all over as I get to work on the pan immediately. I'm not a chef, by any means. Pancakes are the extent of what I can do, but I do them well.

"Sutton up?" She looks around for evidence of my brother.

"Not yet." I look at the clock. It's early, but these kids still probably have so much sugar in their system that I'm surprised they slept at all.

"What do you want to do today? Want to hang out here and go for a swim?"

All three look at me like I have three heads.

"What?" I shrug, plating Annabelle's pancakes and placing them in front of her.

"Swim!" Noah's smile takes up his whole face.

"You have a pool?" Kevin asks in disbelief.

"We don't have any swimsuits..." Annabelle says to me, head tilted.

"Well, the weather is nice and, yes, Kevin, there's a pool out back. And as far as swimsuits go, there are some in the clothes I got you all."

"Can we, Ma? Please?" Kevin asks immediately, and I look at Annabelle, loving how she says yes without hesitation and digs right into her pancakes. I know she'll probably need to get back to the farm and that I'm just delaying the inevitable. But I don't want them to leave. Not yet. Or ever.

As the kids start excitedly talking to her and over each other, my cell rings, and I grab it, seeing it's one of my managers from the New York office. My stomach sinks.

"Oh, this might not be good." I kiss her on the top of her head and walk out to take the call.

It's brief, another emergency that I need to go to the city to handle, the type of jobs we're doing seemingly not going as well as they usually do. But I know this is the game I play. I've just never noticed before, because I've never had anything else occupying my time.

I end the call, knowing I need to pack and get on my jet. Walking back into the kitchen to the kids still excited about swimming, I release a heavy sigh.

"Everything alright?" Annabelle asks. She sees it in my eyes. She knows I need to go.

"Sorry, I can't swim today. I need to fly out," I tell them, and Kevin immediately sinks back into his chair.

"But I want to swim?" Noah says sadly, and I feel like shit. God, leaving their mom even for a day kills me, but that look in his eyes. The one full of disappointment, and knowing I put it there, it kills me even more.

"We can swim another day. Sawyer has to fly back to the city now for work, and we all need to get back to the farm and do the same. But it's almost summer, so there will be lots of other days we can swim. Why don't you both go and clean up your room and grab your things so we are ready," Annabelle tells them, while I hang my head in shame for letting them all down.

"I'm sorry." I don't want to deal with the bullshit. I want to stay here. I scrub my hand down my face. I need to make some decisions, and I need to make them quickly.

"Don't be sorry. We know you need to go. You're busy; you have important things to do."

"*You* are important. *The boys* are important."

She offers me a small smile, and I wonder how in the world I can ever beat this and what I can do to make this more permanent.

"Sawyer, work is important to you. I know you have an office here now, but I also know you'll need to travel. We've already said we'll just have to figure it out. It's okay."

While I appreciate her understanding, it still does very little to erase the disappointment I just saw in all their eyes.

"Connor flies into New York once a month for a week and then spends three weeks here. Maybe I can do something like that."

"One week or one day, I'll miss you all the same." She looks up at me sweetly, and I smile, slipping my arms around her, never wanting to let her go.

"Why don't you stay here while I'm gone? Just go and check on the farm briefly each day, but sleep here?" I suggest, but she's already shaking her head.

"We'll be fine, Sawyer. You have to go back to the city, and we have to go back to the farm."

I hate that our little bubble has burst already.

"I'd feel better if you stayed here…"

"The farm is our home, and I have too much to do."

Nodding, I hold her tight to my chest as I take a deep breath. As much as I want this, I have no idea how I can keep leaving her when it already hurts this much. Something's gotta give.

35

ANNABELLE

This morning has flown by, which is unexpected for a Monday. After a great night at Sawyer's, the kids and I felt rested. The little break has done wonders for all of us.

We were a little melancholy when Sawyer left, so I let the kids relax once we got home yesterday, and I went to work on the vegetable garden, picking some new produce for dinner last night. I was disappointed to see that the tomatoes I planted recently haven't taken like I thought they would. In fact, they looked a bit sad and droopy, so clearly, they need more water.

After a night full of sugar, Noah refused to eat any vegetable put in front of him, so Kevin and I ate, and then the three of us fell into bed, exhausted. But while they slept, I woke numerous times to triple-check the locks on the doors and windows, putting a baseball bat near my bed.

The luxury of a fearless sleep at Sawyer's is now a distant memory as I grab a mug and fill it with coffee in the school staff room. I look at the other teachers around me, all talking and eating their amazing lunches, yet the thought of food makes me feel a little nauseous. Maybe because I didn't have time to eat breakfast this morning and I'm running off fumes.

"So what do you think of things so far?" Victoria's voice hits me from the phone.

"I love what you've done with the new label design. Looks very cool."

"Sawyer said all our contracts are now done and the new structure is all ready."

At just the mere mention of his name, I'm grinning like a fool.

"He's very efficient."

"Is he now?" she teases, and I roll my lips to hold back a laugh.

"I hear that he's spending a lot of time up at the farm with you and the boys. And after he hit that guy at the bar over the weekend, I think I saw all the women there swooning."

I cough out my giggle. I haven't had a lot of friends in the past few years. All my school friends moved away for college or went their own way, my life with Steve one where I was segregated to just be with him. This girl talk is new, but it feels nice.

"I love having him around. And he's great with the boys."

"I'm glad things are working out. It's nice to see you so happy."

"I am happy. Things are good." I still miss Sawyer, but I'm enjoying our time together, however much I can get.

But I guess I spoke too soon about things being good, as I see Kevin staggering into the staff room, looking for me.

"Ahh, Victoria, I need to run. I'll give you a call tomorrow," I tell her before we say a quick goodbye and I rush to Kevin.

"Honey? What's wrong?" I ask him, noticing he looks less himself.

"Ma, I don't feel well…"

"Oh no, what happened?" He did look a little pale this morning, but I put that down to a sugar hangover. I thought he would be over that by now.

"I feel sick…" is all he says, and as I touch his forehead and cheek, he's hot and clammy.

"Kevin, you don't look so good. Not feeling well?" the school principal asks as he steps up next to me, watching. Kevin remains silent but shakes his head.

"I'm so sorry, but I think I need to take him home." I look at my boss, who nods at me with empathy.

"Might be a good idea. We don't want anyone to catch a stomach bug or anything. Leave now, and I'll take over your afternoon classes."

"Thank you so much." I'm grateful to have a fantastic boss, who, as a father himself, knows the parenting issues we all deal with. I grab my things and walk Kevin back to his class to grab his bag and let his teacher know, before I bundle him in the car.

"Let me just stop by the drugstore to get some medicine, and then we'll pick up Noah and head home for a rest." I give him a soft smile.

I leave Kevin in the car while I dash into the drugstore, grabbing what I think I need, and thank God, I have the cash for it. At the checkout, I start feeling a little queasy myself. But I've been feeling off all day. And again, I just put it down to our weekend at Sawyer's, a different place, different foods, different bed.

Lost in my thoughts, I slip back into the car and momentarily freeze, seeing Kevin talking on my cell phone.

"Who are you talking to?" I frown. Kevin never uses my

phone. Not that I would mind, if he ever needed to call his friends or something; it's just that he never does.

"Sawyer," he croaks, his voice breaking like he's dying. My eyebrows rise in surprise at what he says but also dread that he's feeling so sick. "Here, he wants you." Kevin thrusts the phone toward me.

"Hey," I say as I put the keys in the ignition and grab my seat belt, multitasking my main job.

"Is he alright? He said he doesn't feel well."

My chest warms at the caring nature this man has for my boys.

"Yes, just running a little temp and a bit lethargic." My eyes sweep over my boy, who now looks paler, a light sheen of sweat coming over his face.

"I called Hudson. He's going to meet you at home."

I jolt at that, shaking my head, not that he can see me. "Oh, I'm sure we're all okay. Some rest and soup will help him." I'm thankful for the suggestion, although my stomach curdles at the thought of food.

"Too late, I've already told him. He said he'll meet you at home in an hour. He's out that way anyway."

"Sawyer...." He doesn't have to do this. He's in the city, and he should be concentrating on his work. Me and the kids don't want to be a burden.

"Acts of service," he says quickly.

"What?" I ask, confused.

"It's my love language. Get used to it. I'm getting on the jet. I'll be there tonight," he tells me before the call goes dead, and I sit, staring at my phone in shock for a second before Kevin rips me back into reality when he grabs his stomach and moans before vomiting all over me and the entire interior of my car.

This is going to be a long night.

36

———

SAWYER

Panic. That's what I felt when I heard Kevin's voice on the other end of the phone. He sounded weak and frail, and when he asked me to come home because he wasn't feeling good, I grabbed my things and was out of my office and in my waiting town car before Annabelle even got on the phone. I left my most senior manager in charge of our issue, something I've never done, but I didn't even think twice about it. The trip in my jet was quick. I instructed my pilot to fly like the wind, and I landed in Whispers just in time to witness what looks like the end of the world.

"God, I need water," Annabelle moans from where she's lying on her bed, her temperature soaring, her hair damp, clutching her stomach like she's in acute pain. My heart rate escalates.

"Bucket!" Kevin yells from down the hall, and I make a mad dash, passing him a clean bucket before I run to the kitchen, filling the water jug and taking it back to Annabelle. All the while, Noah is sitting on the sofa, happily watching cartoons, eating a bag of chips I had in the car like he's won the lottery. And from the looks of his family members, I'd say he has.

"Thank you," Annabelle whimpers. As I sit next to her, I reach out, pushing her damp hair from her forehead.

"Mmmmm... ready to run back to the city yet?" she quips. Her eyes are half-closed as she's barely lucid, and while I've experienced stomach bugs before, it's never been anything that looks remotely like this.

"Nowhere else I'd rather be." I watch her carefully. Kevin has pretty much vomited as much as he can, although I can still hear him dry retching. He's bedridden, weak, and barely keeping down water. Annabelle is deathly pale, her skin almost a gray color, the love and light that I usually see in her sparkling blue eyes absent.

"Liar. Let me get up, so I can get dinner for Noah. You don't need to stay." She starts to sit up, grimacing, and I frown at her stubbornness.

"I'm not going anywhere, and neither are you." I grab her shoulders and assist her to lie back down.

"What did you guys eat in the last twenty-four hours?" I ask her, keen to understand how this could happen.

Her eyebrows pinch. "You think it's food poisoning?"

"Has to be. This isn't just a stomach bug."

"When we got home yesterday, Noah didn't eat. He wasn't hungry after your place, but Kevin and I had some vegetables from the garden like we always do and some pasta." Pasta would've been fine. So should the vegetables.

"What about this morning?"

"I haven't eaten anything today other than coffee at work. Kevin and Noah both had Pop-tarts." She rolls over and groans, clenching her stomach. "Can we stop talking about food..."

My cell rings, has been all day. I had meetings planned, conference calls, but I left it all and came back here as soon as Kevin asked me. I was gone for less than a day, and I shouldn't have left in the first place.

"Sawyer, you don't have to be here. I know you have a million things to do. I'll be fine," she says after hearing my cell ring for the hundredth time, just before she sits forward, her eyes widening, and she dashes to the bathroom, the door slamming behind her, but not before I hear the now familiar retching that she's been doing all night.

Hudson has given me strict instructions to give them both plenty of water and keep them hydrated, but they can't seem to keep anything down.

In sickness and in health. I understand what those words mean now. I've never really thought about it before. I've never really nursed anyone like this. I threw my suit jacket off the minute I walked in the door earlier; my tie is lying around here somewhere too—probably with Noah since he seems almost obsessed with them. With my shirt-sleeves rolled up, I've been running to get water and buckets and checking temperatures nonstop, and I wouldn't change it for the world. Although I prefer them all to be healthy, being here and looking after them is where I know I need to be, so my calls and messages can wait.

With the sound of her vomiting on the other side of the paper-thin door, Kevin dry retching down the hall, and the faint sounds of the TV cartoons floating down to me from where Noah sits in the living room, it's in this moment that I know I'm completely and utterly in love with her. I still as the realization hits me.

I'm in love with her.

I'm in love with a woman whose head is stuck in the toilet bowl, who could decapitate me with one flick of her garden hoe, and who has two boys who could probably take me down in a monster spray fight.

I, Sawyer Silvers, billionaire lawyer to the country's most wealthy, am in love with a country girl. I take a deep breath and look around the room with renewed vigor.

When she opens the door and steps out of the bathroom, even sick as a dog, she's the most beautiful woman I've ever seen.

But now's not the time for romance.

"I think I need to take you both to the hospital," I tell her wearily. "You're pale. Clammy. You can't even keep water down. I should've taken you both hours ago." Grabbing my cell, I text Hudson so he can meet us there.

"We'll be fine," she says but then starts to sway. I jump up to catch her as she loses strength in her legs, almost fainting.

"Nope. We are going. Right now." Picking her up bridal style, I walk her outside, straight to my vehicle before I do the same with Kevin, putting them both in my truck with buckets and tucking Noah safely in his car seat.

I don't have a good feeling about this. And my gut is rarely wrong.

"WELL, YOU WERE RIGHT," Hudson murmurs.

"Usually am," I quip back. It's late. Noah's asleep in my arms, dribbling on my shirt as we sit in Hudson's office at the hospital. Annabelle and Kevin are in a shared room down the hall, now both sleeping with IVs in their arms, administering both liquids and medication.

"Got the test results back already. It wasn't just a stomach bug." Hudson looks at me in a way that has my senses on high alert.

"And?" I run my hand up and down Noah's back smoothly, as he's completely dead weight in my arms. Poor kid should be in bed, but he didn't want to leave his mom and wouldn't lie down anywhere else but in my arms.

"It's come back that they have both ingested glyphosate."

My head rears back. "What the hell is that?"

"It is a toxin commonly found in weed killer."

"What?" I'm confused, already shaking my head. "How?"

"Well, both Annabelle and Kevin have been pretty happy and active lately, giving me no indication that this is related to self-harm..." Hudson trails off, and my jaw twitches.

"Of course it's fucking not," I spit out, and he shakes his head.

"As a doctor, I need to eliminate all possibilities. With that eliminated, there's only one other option."

I bite my back molars so hard I'm surprised they don't crack.

"They unknowingly ingested it," he confirms. "What did Annabelle last eat again?"

"She said that Noah didn't eat dinner last night, but she and Kevin did. Just some pasta and vegetables from her garden."

"Well, it's most likely that they've eaten something that was from her garden that she had sprayed."

"That makes sense, but she doesn't spray. Her farm is completely spray free. She doesn't put any pesticides or other things on her crops. She runs a completely organic farm. I haven't even seen a bottle of weed killer around her place. Plus, I've eaten her vegetables before and never been sick. Hell, she and the boys have vegetables from their garden every night, and nothing like this happens."

While I haven't spent much time in her shed, I know she treats those flowers of hers with the utmost care and attention. I also know Gertie's business plan outlines the organic nature of the flowers, meaning weed killer would be a big no-no for them.

"Maybe she did a produce swap with a neighbor? Maybe she got some vegetables from someone else?"

"She didn't mention it. And she was with me all weekend, up until last night. She said she just had dinner at home and went to bed, mentioned nothing about seeing anyone or doing a produce swap, whatever the fuck that is." I rub my head, having no idea what these farmers do.

"Okay, so we should test her garden. See if it's that?"

I frown. "I'm telling you, she doesn't spray. She's adamant about quality control; that's one of the reasons she does everything herself."

"Maybe someone else did." Hudson looks at me seriously from under his brow, and my stomach churns.

"But who would do that? Who would spray her property deliberately?" I try to think, my anger at the possibility swirling.

"Well, you did mention that things have been happening out on the farm. Maybe more has been happening than she's telling you?" Hudson suggests, and the whole thing leaves me feeling unsettled.

"I need to speak with the sheriff," I tell him seriously.

"I'll call him now." Hudson grabs his phone.

"I'll call Sutton to come and get Noah. He's here at my place, might as well put him to good use." I kiss the top of Noah's head, wrapping him up in my arms, wanting to ensure he knows he's safe, regardless of what's happening.

Because something is, and it's about time I got to the bottom of it.

37

ANNABELLE

My hands wring the white sheets as I sit in the cold hospital bed, feeling like I'm being interrogated.

"I have sent a unit out to the farm to test your soil," Tony, our local sheriff, says, and while I've known him for years, I feel exposed, raw, and nervous about having people on my land, especially when I'm not there.

"Okay." I swallow and nod. Kevin sits on my bed next to me. We're both finally able to keep water down after having the worst stomach cramps I've ever had.

"But I don't use any weed killer on my land…" I reiterate, looking at the three men standing before me. They all walked into my room this morning to inform me that Kevin and I ingested weed killer. It's the most insane theory I could think of, given we've never had it on the farm in the whole time I've managed it. The sheriff looks at Hudson, who looks at Sawyer, and I know there's something they're not telling me.

"I know you don't," Sawyer says, and I've never seen him like this. He's in full professional mode. Still in his suit from yesterday, he hasn't had any sleep. The man just saw me vomiting for twelve hours straight, and the fact that he's still here is a miracle.

"So why do you need to test?" I'm confused about all of this.

"Annabelle..." Sawyer starts briefly, looking at Kevin before looking back at me. "You mentioned some weird things have been happening out at the farm."

I look at my son, swallowing my fear.

"Tell 'em, Ma," Kevin encourages me with scared eyes.

"You're safe now. I'm here, and I'm not going anywhere." Sawyer steps forward and grabs my hand, giving me a squeeze. I feel his protection, his support. Kevin's almost pleading with me with his gaze, and I close my eyes and I take a deep breath before I tell them everything.

I tell them about the cut locks and ropes, I tell them about the slashed tire. I tell them about the ruined crops, the fear I live in daily, and I feel Sawyer's anger radiating off him with every mention I make. Hudson looks deeply concerned, and the sheriff writes down all the details with a deep furrow in his brow.

"You've been dealing with all that on your own?" Hudson asks, sounding in disbelief.

"Wasn't anyone around to help... until now."

Sawyer lifts my hand to his mouth, kissing my knuckles, his hold on me tight.

"It all feels a little random to me. When all these incidents took place, was there anything going on that may have set them off?" the sheriff asks, and I shake my head, not thinking of anything.

"They all happened after Sawyer came," Kevin speaks up, and I take in a sharp breath of realization as Sawyer's head snaps up, looking at Kevin.

"What do you mean?" Sawyer asks, and Kevin looks at me for permission. I nod, giving it to him to continue.

"Well... Sawyer turned up with the paperwork for Ma the first time, and the next day, the ropes on the shed were cut."

I nod. He's right, they were.

"Then he came back after my first baseball game and had dinner. After that was when the tire got slashed." I hold my breath. I didn't see any of it.

"When you came for dinner the second time, that was when I hit my head in the shed," I say, putting some pieces together now.

"After you stayed over the field was all shredded," Kevin adds, and I look at my boy, wondering how he got so smart.

"Then you stayed at my place on the weekend, and you were poisoned," Sawyer grits out. The room tenses, the motivation for all this unknown, but new dots connecting.

"This has all happened because of me." Sawyer looks at the sheriff, who nods. His jaw is tight, and he won't look at me as a mix of guilt and deep remorse settles in his expression.

"No..." I shake my head. It's my farm, it's my problem. He can't take this on as his issue. He drops my hand quickly, like it now burns him, and I curl my hands together, clutching the sheets, my palms now sweating.

"No, that's not it. It's just a coincidence." I'm panicking. It isn't his fault, and he can't take this on. But I see that he is. The warm, caring man I've come to know now feels a little distant as he takes this all on his shoulders, bearing all responsibility.

"There's a connection, that much is obvious. Sawyer, why don't you come down to the station, and we can talk in more detail. If this is a connection to you, I'll need to investigate all possible leads, see if there's anything here trying to harm Annabelle and the kids because of your history or past," the sheriff says, and I see the murderous look on Sawyer's face, all aimed at himself.

"Sawyer…" I go to grab his hand.

"It's fine. I'll go." Sawyer still doesn't look at me. My heart breaks.

"This isn't your fault." I implore him to understand.

"Can you think of anyone in your life, Annabelle, who would be keen to bring harm to you and your boys?" the sheriff asks, and I stutter. I think, I really do.

"What about Stanley? I heard he was an issue at the bar the other night?" Hudson says, and all I can do is shrug.

"I've got no idea, but maybe…?" I look at the sheriff, wondering what his thoughts are. I haven't seen Stanley in years until the other night, and we've lived in the same town without him doing anything like this.

"I'll interview him as well. See if he has an alibi," he says, writing down another note.

"He would have weed killer," I add quickly.

"Most people around here do," the sheriff mentions, and I deflate, knowing there's no evidence to link anyone to this at all.

"I'll meet you out front," the sheriff says to Sawyer before he leaves, Hudson following him.

"Sawyer?" I'm desperate for him to look at me, and he finally does.

"I don't think I have any enemies who would hate me enough to follow me to Whispers and bring harm to you and the boys, but if I do, I will never forgive myself." There's indescribable pain in his eyes, and mine start to water.

He leans forward, kissing my forehead before scuffing Kevin's hair.

"You did good, Kev. Real good. Now look after your ma for me, okay? I might be a while."

Kevin nods, and we both watch the man we love walk out the door, wondering if we'll see him again soon, having no idea what can of worms we just opened.

38

SAWYER

I knew this would happen. The minute I let my guard down, the minute I found someone who makes me a very happy man, he would return.

"So you're saying this guy you locked away over a decade ago could be responsible?" the sheriff asks me as we sit in his office, cold coffee in my mug.

I've been awake for what feels like days, and I'm running on pure adrenaline at this point. But my gut is churning that I put Annabelle and the kids in danger. I did that. Again. I should've stayed away, I should've never moved here.

"It's a possibility. A strong possibility." I hate myself. I've hated myself for a long time now. When I proposed to my former girlfriend, Mandy, I thought it was love. We were both young, carefree, I was building my career. The engagement ended up being longer than she wanted, but I was on my first real criminal case at a new firm a few years after I graduated. They were my prime years. Those years are what make or break you in the legal world. They are the ones where you work twenty-hour days, take on any and every client, proving your worth to the partners and owners of the firm who sit in the fancy corner offices and drink coffee all day.

"I was engaged previously, when I was much younger, to a girl named Mandy. At the same time, I was leading my first criminal case, almost fresh out of college." I huff a laugh at the memory. "I was a kid. Had no idea what I was getting myself into." I shake my head at my naivety back then.

"Long story short, I lost the case. I was working with a firm that had a name for defending the undefendable. The characters we helped were dark, dangerous, and not the kind you want to have on speed dial, if you catch my meaning."

The sheriff and I haven't really formed a relationship yet, but I guess this is what they call a baptism by fire in that regard.

"Go on," he prods, giving me a head lift to continue.

"Well, I lost the case, and he went to jail for murder. He got twenty-five years, and I lost my job. My skills didn't really serve the firm's tagline. Plus, I wanted out. I didn't want to run criminal cases. I wanted business law, so that's what I went into. But the thing about these kinds of men, they never forget and they never forgive. Mandy was followed, threatened." The remorse I feel churns my gut. The same feeling I had this morning when Kevin brought up the connection with what's happening out on the farm now.

"He made her life hell in order to get back at you?" Tony says, and I nod.

"He was in jail, but he had people on the outside, and he wanted revenge. Classic, really. Probably should've expected it."

"But you didn't." It's not a question.

"I was young, between jobs, and had no support from the law firm. We had little money, and I was busy trying to network to get my foot in the door at a big firm, one that ran big corporate deals that I wanted to be a part of. But Mandy was frightened, never wanting to leave the house. It suffocated us."

"Did you report it?" he asks.

"Yeah, but it didn't go anywhere. The guy was in jail, so he wasn't a threat, and we had no evidence of anything tied to him."

"Is Mandy still…" he trails off.

"Alive?" I ask him, and he nods.

"Yeah. We broke up. She needed space from it all, and I don't blame her. She's now happily married to a bank manager, with three kids in Connecticut. After we went our separate ways, things all stopped. I got the job I wanted and threw myself into work, which is where I've been all these years later."

"No other wives or girlfriends since then?"

"No, nothing serious. Until now," I say honestly.

"That's why you think it could have something to do with this guy again?"

I grit my teeth. "I've never let myself get close to anyone else since. I never wanted to put anyone through that. I put him away for years. He had to leave his wife and family, so he tried to do the same to me. I've drowned myself in work just to keep my head low." *And my heart guarded.*

"Where's he serving?" He grabs his pen to take more notes.

"He's at Five Point Corrections Facility in Romulus."

"Heard from him since you and Mandy separated?"

"No. Nothing."

"I'll call a few people I know down there, get an update on him, his visitors, and see if there's anything we can find."

"It has to be him. For all this to happen the minute I

show up? The minute I've found someone new. What other leads are there?"

The sheriff sighs, leaning back in his chair. "Nothing. The boys went out to look around Annabelle's this morning and found nothing that looked suspicious or out of place. We sent some dirt samples from her garden to get tested, but we're pretty confident that's what the source of the poison was. They also looked around her property and the outhouses. Found no weed killer, no pesticides; it was all organic compost, just like she said."

"What about Stanley?"

"Has an alibi. He was over in Williamstown for the last week, working on some building site. He goes where the money is if he can be bothered. Apparently, this week, he can be bothered. He's probably our most obvious person of interest, so we're keeping an eye on him, looking for any unusual behaviors, but he's airtight, and just because we don't like him doesn't mean he's guilty. So we can't focus on him entirely; we need to cast our net wider than that."

"It's attempted murder." This is no accident, and whoever did this has clearly attempted to take Annabelle's and Kevin's lives. Deliberately or not.

"That's what I'll be pushing. Given the lead-up of events, someone is obviously trying to spook her. Taking it right to the edge with the poisoning last night."

I rub my eyes; they feel raw.

"Anyone else from your past or present you think might be a suspect?"

I shake my head, stomach rolling with nausea once again. "No... I don't think so."

"Why don't you go get her and take her home. Both of you probably need showers, a good sleep, and to talk. I will call you with any updates, keep you in the loop on things."

"If I think of anything else, I'll let you know," I tell him as I stand.

"Oh, and Sawyer? Probably a good thing that you don't leave town."

"Am I a person of interest in this?" My eyes narrow.

"Until we get some leads, everyone is."

While it grates me that he thinks I have something to do with this, the guilt of bringing my past monster to Annabelle's doorstep almost cripples me. My chest tightens, my stomach clenching every time I think about it.

"Good. Cover all bases."

I want no stone unturned. I give him a nod before I walk out of the station, feeling like the world is crashing down on me. The sun is bright, and I lift my eyes to my truck and balk. Because there, in the parking lot, are Connor and Tanner, waiting for me. Being the support to me that this town now provides, and I've never been more grateful for it.

39

ANNABELLE

This has been the longest week of my life. After Sawyer finally came back to the hospital and we were both discharged, we picked up Noah and came home. Not without a heated discussion. Sawyer wanted us all to stay with him, and I fought for us all to come back to the farm. He thought we would be safer with him, but I didn't want anyone to run me from my home. So he relented, packed a bag, and he's been staying with us all week.

The house, of course, was a mess, evidence of our sickness spread throughout, and as Sawyer attempted to return calls and catch up on emails at my new dining room table, I tried to soothe the boys' fears and get us all back to normal. Or our new normal. Which now consists of looking over my shoulder every five minutes.

And while Sawyer hasn't left physically, he hasn't really been here mentally. He's drowned himself in work, bent over backward for me and the boys, but it's all done with a very firm armor of self-loathing. We've talked a little, so I know he thinks this is all connected to his past fiancée,

Mandy. But that was years ago, and I fail to see how it would be his fault. I don't know what this means for us, and the thought that this might derail what we started festers inside me. The soft touches we've shared, the passing kisses and affection, they've all stopped, and my heart aches, knowing he's putting emotional distance between us because of fear of him being responsible for our issues. Fear of me leaving him because he brings danger to my door. Just like Mandy did.

Now, as I dig in the dirt, trying to get my lavender cuttings in the soil so that my harvest for the next year isn't a total loss, I look up for the hundredth time, watching Kevin and Noah finish the milking, my eyes on them both now more than ever before. The new rules at the farm are that everyone has to stay within sight. No one can run around, play hide and seek, or be anywhere without anyone else. Much to Noah's sulking.

As the boys lock up the shed, I watch them run down the hill to where I am, and I smile. I haven't smiled much this week, but I need to show them we are okay, even though I don't believe it.

"All done, Ma," Kevin says, slightly out of breath.

"All done, Maaaa." Noah's also breathless, his little legs taking him a touch longer to get to me.

"Good. Thanks, boys. I'm nearly finished here."

Kevin starts to help, and Noah digs in the dirt. The wind is calm, the sun is high, and it feels nice, being on my land, with my boys, albeit still lingering with nerves.

I look up and around again and spot Sawyer. Stressed? Yes. Had little sleep? Also, yes. But he's still suited up, looking well out of place like he always has. Even though he stays every night, he's ridiculously underprepared for farm life. But I know he's still working on the deal for Gertie's, having emailed the final proposal to Van Cleef only yester-day. So while my hands are in the dirt, he's taking care of the business side of things, and our fingers are crossed that we'll get some good news soon.

"You know, you look so beautiful when you dig around in the dirt," he says as he approaches, and I pause, looking up at him.

"You really need to get out more, if that's the case." I laugh lightly, and he smiles. It's small, but it's there.

"I really wish you would come to my place. Stay with Sutton and me until this all blows over." He says the same words he says to me every day.

"I'm not letting whatever is going on push me from my home. I've lived here all my life, and if I ever leave it, it will be my choice, not one I've made under duress."

He nods, having heard it all before.

"Stubborn. Sexy, but stubborn." I smile at that. Liking that he's acting a little more like himself. My heart stutters, hoping he's coming back around, hoping that I haven't lost him.

"How's it going? Do you think it will take?" He comes to where we're digging, looking over the replanting I've done.

"Looks hopeful. But if I had more space, I would do another crop just in case. Worst case, they both don't grow. Best case, they both grow, and I have a lot of product." I stand, wiping my dirty hands on my jeans. The kids wander in front of us, packing up and sorting things for me. My hair flies in my face as the breeze picks up, and his hand lifts, pushing it from my cheek and behind my ear. He hasn't touched me like this all week, and it makes my stomach flutter.

"Well, you've got two hundred acres waiting for you. Bob

has signed it all over today. That land is now ours." He offers me a small smile, which doesn't reach his eyes.

My lips purse, unsure what he means. "That's your investment, though."

"I bought it for you."

I think my heart stops. "I can't accept two hundred acres! That's ridiculous, Sawyer," I tell him, huffing a breath. He's truly something else.

"Of course you can. Acts of service, remember?" His smile widens, and I could melt from the sight.

But I shrug that off and shake my head. "I'm not taking your land, Sawyer." That's way too much. This man does so much for me; I can't just take a large parcel of land like it's a simple gift or something.

"Fine, pay me a lease and do with the land what you want." He shrugs. My breathing escalates at the prospect. I could do a lot with that land.

"You know I don't have the money." I'm disappointed by that fact, but it's the truth.

"Well, that's not exactly true…" he says cryptically with a smirk.

"What?" I pause, eyes widening, knowing something has happened.

"Just had a call with Valerie Van Cleef. She accepted our proposal. Congratulations, Annabelle, your business has just had a multimillion-dollar investment, with your rose-scented soaps now going to be found in over one hundred hotels around the country."

The world around me stops, and I think I almost faint.

"What?" I whisper, completely shocked, happily so.

His tone centers me as he takes another step closer. "We got it, baby. We got the deal."

My hands start to shake and my eyes water. I search his

eyes for any sign that this isn't true, and when all I find is sincerity, I throw myself at him. He barely has time to catch me before I jump up into his arms, my legs circling his waist as I hold him tight.

"You got it, Sawyer. Oh my God, you've changed my life. Oh my God... Oh my God!" Tears fall, good tears today as I grip on to him. He wraps me up in his arms firmly, never letting me go, and I squeeze my eyes shut, feeling like he's back.

"You will have money for the kids' college. You can let go of the teaching job and focus on the farm and Gertie's. You can get the repairs done to this place like you want to," he tells me close to my ear, listing all my dreams. I bite the inside of my cheek to hold back a sob of joy, feeling the sting of new tears, my cheeks wet, my heart still thudding harder than ever.

"I can't believe this is happening..." Pulling back to look at him, my mind goes back to the other good news. "So I'll need to lease your land, after all."

"It's yours for a dollar a month."

I balk, but I can't help laughing, even as more tears fall. "Sawyer! That's ridiculous!"

Chuckling, he slowly lowers me to the ground. "For the first six months. Once Van Cleef kicks in, we can renegotiate with Gertie's paying the lease if that makes you feel better."

I think about it. It's still not remotely equal, but I know that's the best he's going to offer.

"Deal." I hold out my hand for him to shake, and he grabs it and pulls me to his chest.

"Thank you, Sawyer. Thank you," I say against him, genuinely thankful for everything this man has done for me and my boys.

"I'm sorry I've been distant this week," he whispers into

my hair as his hold on me tightens, his head ducking into my neck, like he's scared I will disappear.

"It's okay..." My hand rubs up and down his back.

"It's not. I just can't be responsible for danger coming to you. I can't be the one who hurts you."

I pull back and look at him, reaching up to cup his face. "You never would hurt us, and regardless of whether or not what's happening around here is connected to you, that's not on you at all."

He looks unconvinced.

"What is a crime is the fact that you haven't touched me all week. You haven't fulfilled your promise of breaking my bed." A small grin comes to both our mouths.

"How about we rectify that tonight? Once the boys get to sleep?" He leans in to kiss me.

"I think that's a great idea." I smile against his lips, before he kisses me thoroughly, like he hasn't seen me for months.

"Ew. Please!" Kevin says, and we pull apart, seeing Kevin holding his hand over his eyes and his other hand over Noah's, my two boys standing right there next to us.

"Ahhh... Wait till you fall in love, Kevin. You'll want to kiss your girl every chance you get," Sawyer says easily, and I still. *Love? Did he just say love?*

40

SAWYER

"**I**can't believe Van Cleef came through." Her voice is awed as she repeats the same thing she has all night. It makes me smile.

The paperwork is now all signed, and she and Victoria now have some serious planning to do. When this is all over, I'll take them out to celebrate properly.

"I knew it would." I'm grinning as we move around her room. The boys are fast asleep, the locks and windows checked and cross-checked three times over.

"Thank you, Sawyer. My life has changed so much since you walked into it." She steps toward me slowly, in nothing but the cute tank and shorts sleep set she wears that gives me just a little hint of the cheek of her ass, which teases me to no end.

"Not for the better, really." My thoughts go right to who's out there in the dead of night, probably watching, most certainly waiting.

She shakes her head as she looks at me with soft eyes. "If it wasn't for you, my boys would have a very limited future, and now they have a choice. Focus on the positives and what we know for certain."

"If it wasn't for you, I would still be working day and night just to scrape up enough money to put dinner on the table," she continues, and I grind my teeth.

"If it wasn't for you…"

I cut her off. "You wouldn't have a psycho murderer canvassing your home."

"If it wasn't for you…" She steps into me, my hands automatically wrapping around her waist as her chest brushes against mine. She raises her hands, placing one on either side of my face, eyes looking into mine.

"I wouldn't know what true love feels like," she says sweetly, making my breath catch in my chest.

I look down at her in awe. After everything that's coming at us, me in two places, her working her ass off, me bringing danger to her life, she loves me?

"You love me?" I frown, wondering how, and she grins like she knows a secret I don't.

"I think I fell in love with you when I saw you sitting in that cow manure the first time I met you." She giggles, the sound soothing and whirling around my body rapidly.

I huff a laugh, rubbing my hand up and down her back. "Not my finest hour…"

"But your rawest one." The look she's giving is one a man like me has wished for time after time and started to believe would never happen.

"I fell in love with you the moment I saw you standing there with your garden hoe, ready to use it." I grin, the memory in full color in my mind.

"Hmmm, I thought about it. Wasn't sure who you were or what you wanted."

"Well, I can tell you that I'm a man who was lost for years, and when I saw you, I felt like I was found. I was a man who worked long, hard days, was married to my work, who after Mandy, never thought that I deserved a woman, especially not one like you. But I'm now a man who's found the one thing I've been missing, the one thing that's going to make me whole. That's you. You're the most amazing woman I've ever met, and I don't care if I need to leave the city and live on this farm for eternity. I'll do it, just so I can be with you."

"Make love to me, Sawyer..." Her eyes search mine, waiting for any hesitation, and there isn't any. I lean over, rubbing my nose on hers before my mouth claims her lips, and I'm lost in the woman who I know will become my wife.

As I peel her sleepwear from her frame, I take my time, wanting to show her what she means to me and wanting to ingrain it in my mind.

Her hands land on my chest as she slowly undoes my shirt buttons, and I open my jeans, then kick off my shoes as she puts her hands behind her to release her bra.

"No, let me..." I stand before her in nothing but my underwear. I'm hard already, and her eyes lower, taking in my bulge. When she swallows, my smirk is instant, and I glide my hands around her back to open her bra delicately. Slowly pulling the straps down her arms, our breathing grows heavy, the only noise in the room.

She grabs the waistband of my tight white boxers and pushes them down as I finger her underwear, doing the same until we stand in front of each other completely naked.

"My God, you are beautiful." My chest tightens as her cheeks flush. I notice she seems to take in my compliments now, like they hit her differently, my words building her up instead of ricocheting off like they used to. I run my hands over her soft body, before I smooth them down her back and cup her under her thighs, lifting her to me.

"Show me how beautiful..." she whispers.

My lips collide with hers in a savoring kiss, and I walk us to her bed, the one I promised her we would break. But tonight is not that night as I lay her down gently before crawling over her, our lips never parting.

Heart hammering, I kiss down her neck and across her shoulders before lowering to her breast, wanting to kiss every inch of her. I palm her breast while kissing the other, and her back arches slightly. I can almost hear her heart pounding just as hard as mine, reminding me that she's real, that this is real.

My hand reaches lower, trailing over her fantastic curves, and my lips follow, kissing over her stomach, across her hip, and she replaces my hand on her breast with her own, pulling her nipple, playing with her own body, which is such a fucking turn-on.

"I could drown in you and die happy," I murmur against her skin as I lower farther, my kisses hitting her sweet center, causing her hand to fall to the back of my head. With long, languishing kisses, my tongue caresses across her clit, and she begins panting, her legs spreading even wider for me, letting me in, opening herself up. Her taste on my tongue is one I now crave.

"Oh... yes..." she moans, and I bring her right to the edge with my tongue, not letting her topple over just yet.

"You're so wet, baby." I kiss her thighs, leaving her whimpering and a little frustrated.

"You're a tease," she complains, and I look up, seeing her grinning.

"Oh, don't worry, Mama. I'm going to make you come. I

just want to watch you when I do it." I feel in control as I make my way back up her body.

She lowers her hand then, running her fingers down my side, feeling my torso muscles, making them twitch before her hand grips my length. I hiss with relief as she pumps me, my cock hot and heavy and so ready for her.

"Two can play that game..." She strokes me nice and slow, feeling all of me, and I throb in her grip. A trail of pre-cum hits her fingers, and I feel her body almost vibrating in need.

She moans, and I push into her grip, my eyes almost rolling in the back of my head. My fingers pinch her nipple and her hips thrust up, looking for friction. Not able to wait any longer, I kiss her briefly before I lean over, grabbing a condom from the bedside table, the movement quick.

"Are you my girl? Are you all mine?" I position myself at her entrance and look into her eyes.

"All yours," she whispers as I slide in, gasping, her back arching and taking me in all the way.

"I'm yours." I give myself to her completely as I start to move. Her legs fall wider, core clenching around me with every swipe of her clit I make on every thrust. "Every fucking inch of me, you now own."

"Sawyer," she pants in that needy tone she gets, making my skin prickle with heat. The emotions of the past week run through me, the feeling of being here with her, in her bed, her feeling loved and safe and full of ecstasy. It's like I'm having an out-of-body experience.

"That's it, Mama." I watch her, my eyes never leaving her face, seeing every little movement that shows me her plea-sure, feeling her hands on me as my movements increase, thrusting into her, showing her how much she means to me.

"Yesss. Oh my God," she moans again, her legs starting to shake a little around my waist as she nears her release.

"Come for me," I tell her, and she does. She bites her bottom lip hard, and I watch in awe as her body convulses beautifully as she lets go. "Look at me."

Her eyes shoot open, and I smash my lips to hers, just as she starts to scream my name. With only a few more thrusts, I'm coming with her with a guttural moan.

"Fuckkkk." I grind into her, my lips not leaving hers, kissing her thoroughly, our bodies now spent.

"Mmmmmm... you're so good at that."

I grin as I continue to kiss her across her bare shoulders.

"We're good at that." I lift off her and take care of the condom before turning off the lights. She's smiling dazedly when I come back to bed.

Grabbing her, I slide her body across the bed to me, and I pull her in tight, spooning her, ensuring she feels safe and loved.

Yet as her breathing slows, my eyes are wide open, looking at the window. Waiting.

41

SAWYER

The sheriff still hasn't found anything. The only news he brought this week was that the soil in Annabelle's vegetable patch had been found to be contaminated with glyphosate, which is what we were all expecting, not alleviating our fears at all.

He also spoke to his contacts at the jail, where my former client resides, confirming that he's had no visitors for months, made no phone calls, and now lives a somewhat quiet life, reading and playing cards in a three-by-three that he calls home. There's no indication that he would've orchestrated this recent spate of stalking behavior. None of it makes any sense to me, and it keeps me up at night.

I've hardly slept, wanting Annabelle to sleep while I jump at every fucking noise I hear. But this week since I've been here, nothing has happened. Which doesn't sit well at all. Because it reaffirms what we all think. Nothing will happen while I'm here, but something certainly will happen the moment I leave. I can feel it, and so can she, and the guilt that eats at me is ever present. It's connected to me, and I rack my brain, trying to think who it would be.

I also live in fear that she'll want me gone. I've brought danger to her and the boys, and I'll never forgive myself if anything happens to them. But I put up a wall of protection around me, in the hope that when she leaves me, just like Mandy did, it won't hurt as much.

I ignored everyone and everything and dove headfirst into work. It's always been my saving grace in these kinds of situations, and I've had a lot to catch up on. But I'm turning the wheels a little differently than before. My meeting with Benjamin Rothschild was one filled with mixed emotions, and one that has been brewing for some time, if I'm honest. It was a great chat, though, and the outcomes are going to be just what I need.

But all the work and all the emotional distance has been pointless, because as I've watched her all week, working the land after a long day at the school, then looking after the boys at night, I know she'd never leave me because of something like this. She isn't the kind of woman who would give up on us because of some outside force. It isn't in her nature. She would meet it all head-on, which is exactly what she's doing by staying out here on the farm, giving whomever it is a big *fuck you*, and damn, if that doesn't make me love her more.

While I've been trying to create distance, she's been the calm, steady force at my side, waiting for me to come back around, and today, when I saw her digging in the dirt after getting confirmation of the Van Cleef deal, I realized what an ass I've been and how I now need to step up and be the man I know she thinks I can be.

It's early morning now, just after two a.m., and after a few hours of sleep, I woke to find her lips wrapped around me. Every dream I had since I was a teenager literally came to life right then and there. As did I, right down her beautiful throat.

Now, sated for the moment, I run my hand up and down her bare back as she curls her naked body into mine, together listening to every movement, every noise.

"Tell me more about Steve." Maybe I'm a glutton for punishment, wanting to know about a man who treated her so badly and one I can't even go after to put behind bars for her. But Steve is the boys' father, and I want to know as much as I can.

"Not much else to him, really. He was nice to start with. It wasn't until we both moved in together here with my parents and got pregnant with Kevin that things started to change."

I frown. "Pregnancy and early parenthood can be times of heightened risk for domestic violence. Research shows that women are at an increased risk of experiencing violence from an intimate partner during pregnancy. If violence already exists in the relationship, it often escalates during this period." Unfortunately, I know these statistics too well, having had clients who've dealt with similar pain.

"Yeah, it sounds about right. It started so gradually. It wasn't until my parents died that violence became my nightly routine."

I grip her tighter, trying to protect her from her memories.

"Was he close with your parents?" I know grief can have different effects on different people.

"No, not really. My parents worked hard. Were out on the farm from sunup until sundown. Steve was around, pitched in a little, but his work ethic wasn't the same. I remember my dad had a chat with him about it not long before he and my mom died. Telling him that he needed to step up to help out. The farm back then was busy, full of cows and goats and an array of animals. But Steve didn't really like my dad telling him what to do. Never really liked anyone telling him what to do." She takes a deep breath.

"Sounds like a real peach." Hating the dead isn't something I've ever done, but I hope like hell he took the lift down instead of up for his sins against this woman. "How did the car accident happen?"

"He was never home, always out drinking. Came home drunk almost every night. He'd been at his dad's that night and was driving home. The sheriff said that due to the impact marks, it was obvious they were speeding, and he crashed into a tree not far from here."

"The car was beyond recognition. A mangled wreck. It caught on fire. The sheriff told me that he would've died on impact before his body burned." I feel her body get heavy in my hold. Regardless of what he did to her, he was a massive part of her past, so the effect on her would be significant.

"I'm sorry you had to go through all that." Kissing her head, I wonder how in the world this woman is so strong and resilient.

"We buried him on his dad's land. I haven't been to see him since."

"Did Kevin ever see or suffer his wrath?" I grit my teeth, wondering if this asshole would hurt a child.

"Kevin was a toddler, so if he was quiet, he was fine. I think Steve forgot about him most of the time. But just before Steve died, Kevin started coming out of his room, and he saw me fixing my face, wiping the blood. Too much for a little boy to see."

My chest tightens at the thought of her suffering. "When he died, I imagine it was pretty tough?"

She huffs. "Understatement of the year. So many things

to navigate. He left me in a mess." Her fingers scrawl patterns on my bare chest, leaving trails of sparks in her wake. I'm glad she's opening up. I don't think she really talks to too many people, and here, lying naked, there's nothing between us, and she's giving me her trust, her history, her emotions. And I'll never get tired of her hands on my body. I'll never take it for granted either.

"He had a gambling habit. He took everything my parents built, all the money from our accounts, the money I thought he was paying bills with, all went to his hobby. He sold our tractors, some cows. I had to ensure I ran the farm in a way that allowed Kevin and me to eat, but in a way he wouldn't notice. So when I was pregnant with Noah, I got a milking cow from Bob. An old one he offered to us, and it was a lifesaver. It wasn't worth any money to anyone, so Steve let me keep it, but I needed that milk for my boys and was so grateful to Bob for that."

It's then I feel my chest growing wet, tears falling from her eyes.

"Did he have a life insurance policy?" But I already know he didn't; otherwise, she wouldn't be living in so much financial distress.

"No. Couldn't even pay the electricity bill sometimes." My stomach rolls, thinking of her and Kevin going without the basic needs.

"You will never go without again, Annabelle. You have Gertie's now, and you have me. You and the boys will get everything and anything you want, anytime you want it. I love you, and I love those two boys. I would do anything for them. I want to chase after Noah and play ball with Kevin and give you all everything I can and more."

She looks up at me, before looking down, her fingers scratching at my chest a little as a smirk curls her lips.

"What are you doing, baby?"

"Looking for the *S*."

My brow furrow deepens, having no idea what the hell she's talking about. "*S*?"

"Yeah, Superman has an *S* on his chest; I'm just looking for yours."

I bark out a laugh. "Tough as nuts, stubborn as a mule, and sexy as sin. How did I get so lucky, Lois?"

"You just had to move to Whispers and come find me." She leans her chin on my chest, looking up at me like I gave her the world. It's at this moment I know I owe Tanner a large debt, because without him, there wouldn't be an us.

And she's right. I had to move to Whispers to find her. I just didn't realize that I would find myself in the process too.

WITH ANNABELLE and the kids at school, I walk into the sheriff's office, needing to talk. I've been mulling over Annabelle's words all night, talking about her ex and their life, and my gut is still churning over what she had to endure.

"Sawyer. Coffee?" Tony shuffles into the small kitchen at the station, a few other officers tending to paperwork and taking calls around us.

"Sure. Black, please." I run my hands through my hair, the heaviness still sitting on my chest. "Find anything?" I need an update, even though I asked him yesterday and the day before that. My visits here to the station are now a daily occurrence.

"Nothing new." He passes me a cup, the black liquid steaming.

"Mind if I chat with you in private?"

He stops mid-sip.

"Let's go to my office." He leads the way through the admin area to a large office at the end, where I take a seat, and he closes the door, looking at me seriously. "What's on your mind?" As he sits behind his desk, the array of paperwork and files on it makes me almost shiver with anxiety. Do people around here never do their paperwork properly?

"I wanted to talk to you about Annabelle's late husband."

His eyebrows shoot up.

"Steve?" he asks, like there's another option.

"Yeah, heard he was a bit of trouble?" I push, not knowing what he'll tell me and what is confidential.

"Well, I'm not sure what Annabelle has told you…"

"She's told me he was violent. Told me he drank, gambled. Tanner and Bob have also said he wasn't a great guy."

He nods slowly.

"Well, we never found any traces of violence. I went to see Annabelle almost every week. She never said anything, never asked for help. Our hands were a little tied in helping her in that regard."

I grind my teeth. I know he couldn't do anything without proof or request from Annabelle, but the fact they let it go on for so long without intervention of some kind still frustrates me.

"What about his death?" I question, which gets his interest.

"Motor vehicle collision. Died on impact."

"Do you have the file?" I ask, and he frowns.

"Why are you interested?" He's immediately suspicious.

"Annabelle said the car caught on fire. I've been thinking about it all night, wondering how you identified the bodies."

I see the moment the penny drops, and he laughs at me.

"He's dead. It isn't him, Sawyer." I haven't worked my ass off in law for years to be laughed at by a small-town sheriff, regardless of if his wife makes the best coffee in town.

"So I can take a look at it, then?" He sighs.

"Suit yourself. But we investigated that accident well. A team came in from Williamstown, and they did the forensics." He stands, moving to a wall of file cabinets. He opens the drawer, pulls out the file, and hands it to me.

I open it, look over photos of what was left of a burned car, the flames obviously big, given the size of the charred marks on the ground and up the tree.

"Full tank of fuel in the car?" I ask him immediately, my eyes still glued to the file.

"Looks like it."

"And... time of impact was predicted to be about an hour before emergency services arrived?" I ask, knowing that an accident out there would probably go unnoticed for a while. Until someone smelled smoke or saw flames or drove past.

"That's the estimate." He nods, looking at me expectantly. "What exactly are you looking for here, Sawyer?"

I take a deep breath, about to open the biggest can of worms for this small town and for Annabelle with no evidence and just a gut feeling.

"There's something going on here, Sherriff, that doesn't feel right. It feels personal." I give him a look that tells him exactly what I'm thinking.

"Are you suggesting that Steve didn't die that night? Because if you are, you're out of your goddamn mind," he grits out.

"Maybe. But tell me that's not a possibility. Tell me that bone fragments were found?" I press him.

I close the file, placing it on his desk, waiting for him to refute my claim. But he doesn't.

"I know men who hurt their women do so because of power, because they want to control them. Annabelle has been controlled for a long time, and the moment she steps out of character with me, things start happening."

"That's a very long string you have attached there, Sawyer, but I'll humor you, if for no other reason to ensure Annabelle knows he's gone for good. I suggest you leave it with me, for at least a few days. I'll speak to the team in Williamstown, get them to go over things on their end to ensure no stone was left unturned."

I breathe out the breath I've been holding.

"Can I make a suggestion?" he asks, just as I start to stand.

"Sure." I wait.

"If you think things only happen when you're gone, then maybe you should go."

I look at him like he's crazy, because he is. "I'm not leaving her," I tell him adamantly.

"I don't think anything is going to happen while you're there. If we have any chance of catching who it is, then we need you gone, and we need her alone." He looks at me, unwavering, and I think I need to vomit.

"You're asking me for the one thing I just can't give you."

"I know. But maybe we can come up with a plan?" he says in a way that makes me think he already has one, and so I lower back down and take a seat.

42

SAWYER

Looking at the jet, I grit my teeth.

I left Annabelle. Not only have I left her, but I had to lie to her. She can't know what we're up to. We need her to act as she normally would, which killed me, because I saw the fear in her eyes when I walked out her door. She was quick to mask it, acting tough and stoic, as is her nature, but I saw it. I saw it in Kevin's eyes as well. Their gazes pierced me straight through the heart, enough to have me almost pulling the pin on the entire thing. They both understand what happens after I leave, but the sheriff is right; if we want to encourage the perpetrator out of hiding, then this is the only way we can do it.

Now, as I stand on the tarmac at the small Whispers airport, night having fallen, I take a deep breath and force myself to walk up the metal stairs to my jet slowly. My legs feel like lead, my body begging me to turn around, my mind a mess. It's true, I have work to do, a lot of it. But jumping in my jet and leaving her is the last thing I want.

"All ready, sir?" my pilot asks, and I nod as I look at him from under my brow. *No,* I feel like telling him. How can I be ready to leave the woman who I know is my forever in a situation where she could come to harm? How can I leave those boys? I swallow hard, giving him approval to leave, unable to speak the words.

I look out the window, the dark sky making me feel more trepidation than normal. As the jet door closes, I pray that the sheriff is in place with his men and can handle it. Tanner knows something is up. Both he and Connor, along with my brother, Sutton, have been calling every day, and when I said I needed to go to the city, I was surprised they didn't turn up and give me a black eye themselves. They weren't happy, offering their place for Annabelle. Sutton told me how disappointed he was when I said I was needed in my New York office, putting this plan the sheriff had into place. While I don't love it, it does make sense. Me leaving Whispers and jumping on my jet will bring out the perpetrator and the sheriff and his team can then catch him before I fly straight back here to be with my family.

Doing circles in the air nearby is not my idea of a good time, though. That, and the fact that the sheriff is severely understaffed, yet quietly confident he knows what he's doing. It leaves me feeling unsettled. But I don't have much of a choice.

The whole thing makes my muscles constrict and my stomach churn. I left her at the very last moment, after dinner, right before the boys went to bed, not wanting her to be alone all night, yet having to trust the law enforcement that they actually know what they are doing.

"We'll be at altitude in about fifteen minutes," the pilot says over the speaker, and I close my eyes as I feel the wheels leave the tarmac, my heart lurching now that I'm no longer on the ground. As we ascend, we cut through the clouds, and my knee bounces as I grab my cell.

I hit the number and wait.

"Anything?" I ask, like I didn't just call the sheriff ten minutes ago.

"Not yet. You left?"

"I'm in the air," I tell him.

"I'll call the minute we have something. I have a feeling it won't be long," he says, ending the call just like last time, and I grip on to my cell a little harder.

As soon as the seat belt sign is switched off, I'm up, walking to the back of the cabin and pushing open the bathroom door, emptying my stomach. Retching for my penance.

Wiping my mouth, I look at my reflection in the mirror as I turn on the tap, filling my mouth with cold water and splashing it on my face. I feel like a failure, like I've let her down. I hold on to the small basin as I move farther and farther away from her.

The sheriff asked me to trust him. Asked me to leave it to them. I have no idea how many men he has or where they're watching from, but I need to try to take solace in the fact that their eyes are on Annabelle.

I walk back to my seat, my knee jumping, adrenaline pumping, and I pull at my shirt collar. Still wearing a fucking suit, the whole thing feels restrictive for the first time in my entire working life. I rip off my tie and pull the jacket from my frame, throwing them on the seat next to me, undoing the top few buttons of my shirt, needing air.

I grab a bottle of water, drinking the entire thing, then I look at my watch. We're circling at about an hour out of Whispers, still close, but too far away for my liking. It's almost been an hour and a half since I left Annabelle's place. I roll my neck, releasing a groan from how uneasy I am.

Looking down at my lap, I take in another deep breath before my eyes spot something. I look closer, the sparkle on my leg flashing me in the light, before I see another and another. Noah's glitter spray remnants shimmer on my suit pants brightly, and my jaw twitches with emotion.

I can't do it. I can't do it anymore. I jump up from my seat and stalk through the jet, straight to the cockpit.

"Sir?" the copilot asks, looking up, surprised to see me. I never disrupt them when they fly.

"Turn back around," I grit out, and his brow furrows.

"Sorry? What?" he clarifies. We're meant to circle for another hour, but I can't wait that long.

"Back to Whispers. Now!" I bark, adrenaline rushing through me, panic now building, wanting to get back there right away.

"Yes, sir," he says, nodding quickly. "Everything alright, sir?"

"No, everything is not fucking alright," I seethe. I shouldn't. It isn't their fault, and I mutter an apology before I walk back to my seat.

It was a stupid idea. I can't leave her. It's like leaving a lamb at the slaughter. She needs me, she relies on me, she trusts me. I can't let her down.

I sit in my seat, and the jet makes a sharp turn around, cutting through the night sky, nothing but black as far as the eye can see, and I pray I'm not too late.

43

ANNABELLE

Kevin sits on the sofa, baseball on, but he's no longer watching it.

"There, all done." I try to be upbeat, even though I just added yet another lock to the door, taking the tally to three. There's no way that Sawyer won't notice when he comes home, but while I put up a strong front for him when he left, I'd be lying if I say that I'm not completely scared out of my mind.

With Noah already asleep in my bed, I walk around the house, checking if the baseball bat is beside the front door and there's a knife now under my mattress. As I do, I grab the small pocketknife usually reserved for trimming the lavender and put it down my bra. Call me crazy, but I want to be prepared, because even though Sawyer didn't say anything, I know exactly what's going on.

He's trying to draw them out. Whomever is behind this only comes when Sawyer isn't here, and there's no way Sawyer would leave me for work, not now. Also, I saw it in his eyes, the extreme hesitation he had, the poor excuse of a business client, the way he didn't pack anything like he normally does. I may not have gone to college, but I know things. I know he loves me and my sons, and I know this is the only way we are ever going to get them. I roll my shoulders, my stomach feeling raw. I've got it. I can do this.

"Can't we call Sawyer? Or Sutton? Or Tanner?" Kevin asks, the panic in his voice evident. I should've sent him to have a sleepover. But Sawyer didn't tell me he was leaving until the last minute, and it was too late to organize anything.

"We'll be fine, honey. No one's getting in here with all these locks. But if you would feel better, you can have a sleepover with Sutton tomorrow night, if Sawyer isn't back." I walk over to sit with him, brushing his hair back off his face.

"I'm not leaving you, Ma," he says firmly.

"I'll be fine. Besides, I'm sure Sutton has some of that candy you boys like so much."

"I'm not leaving you," Kevin says again, with so much determination it breaks my heart.

"We'll be okay. We always are," I tell him softly.

While I was scared before, now that we know these things happen once Sawyer leaves, the fear has escalated. We're expecting it. But this is my home, and I'm not leaving it.

Walking toward the front window, I peel back the curtain an inch and look out. I can't see any cars. I can't see anything. It's as black as it usually is, but I know Sawyer wouldn't have just left me here. There's someone watching, maybe the sheriff, maybe Tanner. I don't know who, but I know someone is out there, and that eases my worries slightly.

I let the curtain drop and look over my home. With Sawyer gone, I decide to focus on the soaps and plan to make a big batch that will get our stocks replenished. It's much needed, as I've ignored the soapmaking this past week, so my usual production schedule has been interrupted. I know I won't sleep anyway, so I might as well make use of the time.

"You should go to bed, Kev. I'm staying up for a while, making some soaps. I'll come get you if I need you," I tell my son, and he frowns.

"Better one of us gets some sleep. You get up early, and then I can sleep for a few hours before morning?" I offer, knowing I won't wake him, but this is how I can get him to go rest.

"Fine," he grumbles, turning off the TV, giving me a hug, and heading to his room. He leaves his door ajar, and I hear him get into bed as I grab my ingredients and start preparing my things, sinking my thoughts into the rose oil goat milk soap that I'm about to make.

I RUB MY EYES. They're sore and dry after getting lost in my soapmaking for the past hour. I have all my molds full, and I'm clearing up the last bowl when I hear a noise. I pause immediately, the sound so faint, I'm not sure if it's the wind or something else.

As I place the bowl down softly, I hear it again. It's coming from outside, and I look out the kitchen window, not able to see a thing, the blackness surrounding the house so thick that I feel like I'm on an island.

I creep out of the kitchen and down the hall to check on the boys. Noah's snoring in my bed, and Kevin's sound asleep, and I feel more settled that they are safe.

Stepping back out to the living room, I'm convinced I'm

hearing things when I hear it again. Louder this time, and I still. Fear wraps its familiar fist around my throat, and I swallow roughly, trying to create moisture in my dry mouth.

But when I hear the noise again, the sound of the shed door banging in the breeze, fear gives way to anger. Anger at how someone who's faceless is making me scared in my own home. Someone who's trying to ruin my livelihood when I worked so hard for it. Someone who wants to see me suffer when I've suffered enough.

"Not anymore," I grit out, my shoulders tight, my teeth clenched. I spot the old baseball bat near the door and grab it before unlocking all three locks. Opening the door tentatively, I look out. My eyes adjust to the darkness, my heart thumping in my ears, but if someone's out there, this ends tonight.

I step out onto the porch and hear another thump and what sounds like people talking. Men's voices carry to me in the wind, and I look toward the shed, the door now open, even though I know I locked it earlier. Something I checked three times over before I locked us all in the house.

Fear completely leaves me now, although my body still shakes with nerves. I lift the bat over my shoulder, ready to swing, and step quietly toward the shed.

The gravel crunches underfoot, but I'm so focused on getting to the shed door, I pay it little attention. I should have paid more, though, because I also don't hear the footsteps that come from behind until it's too late.

"Hey, honey, I'm home..." the familiar voice singsongs like a death rattle, skirting up my spine before I feel a sharp thud to my head, the pain instant before I fall to the ground.

I scream, dropping the bat, my hands clutching my head, feeling blood on my hands instantly. The hit was so fierce, it shakes my brain.

"Look at you, thinking you're fucking captain courageous with your little bat," he mocks me, and I look up slowly, my vision a little blurry, but even in the dark of night, that voice is one I'll never forget.

Any bravado I had earlier completely dissipates as I stare up at my late husband. Memories take over, and I feel like that lost young woman I was when he was here.

"How? What? Why?" The words tumble out. I'm shocked to my core.

"Oh what, where, how, why? God, you're still a nagging fucking bore," he spits out as I hear footsteps nearby. My eyes flick in that direction, spotting his father Stanley, and my breath catches.

"But you're dead!" I shout at Steve, head pounding. I'm having a nightmare. This can't be happening.

"Clearly, he's not," his father huffs, looking at me like I'm worthless.

"I don't understand!"

"I was so sick of your nagging, your fucking farm this and farm that. You had no more money for me. You stupid women can't run farms. Look what you've done; you've turned it into a fucking florist! You're an embarrassment." He swings his arms around, a large piece of timber in one hand, one end coated in my blood. At least now I know why my head hurts so much.

"But the car caught on fire...?" I question. None of this makes sense.

"I bet you were really happy about that too, weren't ya," he seethes, and I don't bother answering him, because we both know what my answer will be. "I didn't want you or the debt of this fucking farm. So we faked it." He's so nonchalant, I'm starting to understand he's completely deranged.

My anger returns with a vengeance. "You're the one who

put us in debt. Your gambling, you wasting money on liquor!" I scream, smacking my hand on the ground.

"Yeah, well, I took out a life insurance on myself." He has a smart-ass smirk on his face, making my stomach churn.

"What?" How did he manage that when he's one of the dumbest people I know?

"Got a pretty penny too. Three hundred thousand..."

My breath gets caught in my chest.

"Had a pretty good lifestyle, haven't I, Dad? Living in Vegas for a while, road tripping to the coast and back." He grins at his father, who just huffs a laugh and nods. I look at his dad again, remembering the clothes he was wearing the other night at the bar, the nice appearance now making more sense. He's got money now. From his son faking his own death.

While I've been counting every penny for years, looking after the kids, working late on the soaps, this asshole has been living on hundreds of thousands of dollars.

"So if you're so rich, what are you doing back here, then?" I bite out.

"Well, money only goes so far... Besides, I heard pretty quickly about your new rich boyfriend. And well... you know I've never liked sharing... You're mine, Annabelle. Always was, always will be." He looks me over, and I think I vomit a little in my mouth. "You don't belong to anyone else but me, you hear that?"

It's always like this with him. He may not want me, but he sure as hell doesn't want anyone else to. It all starts to make sense now. What Kevin was saying. Every time Sawyer was here, something would happen. My eyes flick to Stanley. He was obviously Steve's eyes and ears for years. Only now that Sawyer has turned up in my life has Steven bothered to come back. Not to see his sons, not to spend time with them or get to know them. No, he's back because he wants to own me.

Too bad I'm not for fucking sale.

"You're dead!"

"Yeah, on paper I am, but in life, you're still mine, and no other man is going to be sleeping with my wife and fathering my kids," he shouts back at me, and my insides coil.

"You were never a father and sure as hell were never a lover," I spit at him, and he takes a step toward me. I flinch a little, but his slap never comes. He looks at me like he's just thought of something.

"You were always worthless and still are... Maybe I need to take some sort of payment from him to ensure I stay away from you, then..." Ah, his real intentions. Blackmail.

"Payment?" I question. "What, now that I've finally found happiness, now that I'm finally making things work, you want to come back here and take it all again?" I huff out a sarcastic laugh, which just pisses him off even more.

"You always got everything. Me, nothing but stress, bills..."

The audacity of this asshole.

"Bills you created yourself, putting bets on horse racing and giving your money away to slot machines over in Williamstown."

I don't see his fist as it flies from his side and straight into my jaw. I fall backward, my head hitting the gravel. My head now thumps even harder, and I wiggle my jaw, wondering if he broke it.

"You always acted better than me." Stepping back, he looks around before bringing his attention back to me.

"That's because I am," I say to him as I sit forward, readying to stand. If this son of a bitch is going to kill me, he's going to do it when I'm standing on my own two feet, on the land my parents and grandparents owned.

"No, you're not. You're fucking stupid."

As I stand up, my head feels like a bowling ball, making my top half almost too heavy for my legs to hold up. My feet stagger a little, knees wobbling.

"Why?" I ask, trying to give myself time for my vision to clear.

"Because, when I hit you, you should've stayed down, you fucking bitch." His fist comes back around, landing on my cheek with such force, it lifts me from my feet, but not before I reach out, scraping my nails across his cheek, clawing at him with every bit of strength I have left.

I lie on the gravel, his father watching like he's bored already. But I see his eyes flicking around. Watching. Waiting.

"We need to go, son..." his father says, but my husband is too far gone. He wants power over me, and I'm not letting him have it.

"Go? Oh, so soon... we were just getting started..." I moan as I grip my head, not showing any weakness. I think of my two boys inside, praying they're still asleep, praying they don't find me here in the morning.

"Shut the fuck up!" Steve yells as his foot lands in my side, the impact making me vomit. I curl onto my side, heaving and trying to breathe through the pain. Opening my eyes, I spot the baseball bat on the ground near the shed, so I moan some more, rolling over to it and grabbing it underneath my body.

"Steve, we need to go," his father says, looking antsy.

"You can't leave!" I say in a high-pitched voice before I sit up with all my might and heave the bat into the side of Steve's knee.

He screams, cursing as he falls, and I roll away before trying to stand again. He jumps up, limping slightly, pure venom in his eyes. I've never fought back. This is a new side of me he hasn't seen. We stand, facing each other, both seething for different reasons.

A light in the house comes on, taking my attention, and I run, trying to bolt past him to get inside, wanting to protect my babies. But then I feel his hand wrap around my ankle, and he pulls me back, my body falling face-first to the ground before he drags me back to him.

Groaning, I kick him with my other leg, trying to hurt his already injured knee, and he lets me go momentarily. Breathless, I jump up and dash. I'm halfway to the house when someone grabs me from behind.

"Not so fast," his father hisses in my ear, his breath stinking of old liquor.

"Let me go!" I scream, wriggling in his tight hold. He's bigger and much stronger than me, but I then remember the small pocketknife I slipped into my bra strap, and I lift my hand, just able to reach it. Pulling it out, I flick it open in one motion and slice it across his arms.

He screams, releasing me immediately, just as I see lights, a lot of lights, reds and blues, coming up the driveway.

"Fucking bitch!" Steve yells, and instead of running away, he runs toward me. He never liked losing, and I'm not a quitter either, but I still run toward my kids, my hair flying, blood dripping down my face and getting into my eyes. The harsh pull of my hair brings me back to him with a pained gasp.

"Steve! We need to go!" his father yells at him, and I wriggle free.

"Not yet!" He's not finished with me, and I take a few steps away from him as cars pull up and shouting starts.

There's pure evil as he looks at me. "If I go, you're coming with me."

I take in a deep breath and brace for impact as he runs straight into me, his chest hitting mine, but I still have my blade in my hand, and it goes directly into his gut.

44

———

SAWYER

I jump out of the car and run straight to her. Police car after police car follow me, because I drove right through their roadblock, interrupting what I'm sure was their carefully laid-out plans of catching these assholes. Yet seeing Annabelle right now, I know if I didn't come back, they wouldn't have rescued her. It's too dark; they weren't in the right positions, and trying to look at what's happening hundreds of yards away was never going to work.

"Annabelle!" I scream, still in my suit pants and shirt, my work shoes slipping on the gravel, no weapon on me. This is probably the stupidest thing I've ever done. But I don't stop. I can't. I see one man on the ground, and she's standing there, looking like she's in shock, so she doesn't see the other man. Stanley, the same man I hit at the bar the other week, creeps up behind her with a block of wood in his hand.

"Annabelle!" This time, she looks up, almost in a daze. I almost falter. She has blood running down her face. She's beaten, battered, and I push myself to run faster. Somewhere in the distance, I hear yelling, the sheriff and his team now surrounding the place, guns raised. But I can hear next to nothing, my eyes solely focused on her.

"Drop!" I tell her, imploring her to understand me as I see the shock on her face at seeing me here. But my words register, and she falls to the ground, almost in defeat, not having the strength to stand much longer.

As I finally reach her, I put myself between her and the timber as it comes down hard to hit her on the head in what would no doubt be the final blow to end her. As I fall, I land on her, covering her body with my own before I hear a gunshot. I squeeze her body underneath mine, protecting every inch of her.

Looking back the way I came, I see the sheriff standing, his gun in hand, having shot his weapon. Police cars skid in behind him. Stanley screams from above us, dropping the timber in his hand, which hits my head, grazing my cheek. But I don't even feel it before I grab Annabelle fully in my arms, picking her up bridal style, and running back behind the police line. Uniformed men run toward us, securing the scene, one I have yet to really take in because my eyes are still only on one thing. Her.

"No... the boys... Sawyer, the boys are inside..." she shouts at me. Panic-filled eyes gut me completely.

"I'll get them," I tell her, putting her in the safe arms of the paramedics who are already on the scene, coming to her immediately. I look back up toward the house, seeing a light on, the door ajar, and I don't hesitate to run back to the scene of the crime. I wipe the liquid from my face, the graze on my head bleeding and running down my cheek, but I care little for it as I watch the police surround the two guys who are here, both looking a little beaten up. Stanley with a slash to his arm and a gunshot wound in his shoulder, the other one limping slightly and holding his gut that's currently bleeding. He looks at me like he's the devil himself as I run inside the house to get the boys, proud of my woman for inflicting so much pain on him.

Opening the door, I stall immediately because Kevin is standing there, Noah behind him, and he has a baseball bat in his hand.

"Kev?" I swallow, catching my breath.

"You came back?" he asks me as he lowers the bat.

"I did. I came as quickly as I could. Don't worry, the police are here. We caught the bad guys."

"You caught 'em?" he asks again, almost like he doesn't believe me.

"I did. Your mom's fine. She's outside with the paramedics and really wants to see you," I tell him as the bat hits the floor, and he looks at me, tears filling his eyes.

"Are you going to leave us again?" he asks, and I take another deep breath as my heart thuds.

"I'm never leaving you again. I want to stay with you forever, if you'll have me?" I ask, hoping with everything inside me that these boys want me here just as much.

"Seesaw!" Noah yells and starts running toward me.

"Hey, buddy." I pick him up, holding him tight and sealing him to my chest. I look over to Kevin, who hasn't moved.

"How about it, Kev?" I ask Annabelle's oldest child, the one boy who has no doubt seen and heard too much for his years.

"I'd like that," he whispers, before running to me, and my heart bursts open as I catch him and lift him up, a boy on each hip.

"Let's go out to your mom and make sure she's getting looked after. Hold on tight and just keep your heads on my shoulders. Don't look around." I'm not sure what they'll see and what will upset them. They listen, curling into me, burying their heads on my shoulders, and I open the door, looking out. Red and blue lights streak across the sky, and I see Tanner and Connor looking disheveled as they jump out of a truck. Word around here obviously gets around fast. I look back to the criminals who attacked my family, seeing both the men now down on their knees, handcuffed behind their backs, getting read their rights, and paramedics are all over Annabelle.

"Okay, let's go." I stride out the door, my boys in my arms, holding them tight, and walk straight to Annabelle.

"Boys!" she yells, relief overtaking her expression as I get to her. They both lunge for their mom so violently, I almost drop them midair before I put them down and they both hug her.

"How is she?" I ask the paramedic.

"She needs to go to the hospital but won't go," he says, exasperated, and I frown as I look at her. This is the kind of woman I'm dealing with. Stubborn, stoic, but also soft, precious, and all mine.

"Lois, you're going to the hospital," I tell her, and she looks at me over the top of her boys, her smile small at the use of her nickname.

"You really were my Superman tonight, Sawyer. Thank you for coming back."

"I should've never left in the first place," I grit out, not needing her thanks. I feel like I failed her tonight.

"I knew what you were doing. I knew you didn't want to leave, so I put two and two together. You were trying to draw them out, and it needed to be done." She nods, and I look at her in awe, wondering if she could get any more perfect.

"Ma'am, we're ready to take you now." The paramedic comes over again with the gurney to put her on.

"But I don't want to leave the boys..."

Sweeping the hair from her face, I see her cheek turning black, the blood drying in her hair, and it feels hard to breathe.

"We'll take them. Look after them over at your place with Sutton," Tanner pipes up as he steps forward from around the corner.

"You got here quick." I look at him, raising my eyebrows.

"It's hard not to hear the sirens around this place. Bob called me, and we got here as soon as we could." Tanner slaps me on the shoulder before pulling me in for a hug.

"Is this what you had in mind when I asked you to move to a sleepy small town called Whispers?" he murmurs to me, and I pull back to give him a deadpan look.

"Firstly, you never asked, you demanded. And second, I'm never leaving. I'm officially a Whispers resident," I tell him as Annabelle gets settled on the gurney and the boys step toward me.

"Boys. Tanner and Connor are taking you over to my place. Sutton will get you into bed and you all can have a sleepover tonight. I'll come get you in the morning, okay?"

"Tannnneeerrrr," Noah says, and Tanner grins, picking up the boy, the two of them looking almost comical due to his size.

"Okay. Take care of Ma." Kevin looks at me, before glancing back at Annabelle.

"I'll be fine, honey," Annabelle reassures him, and as the boys leave, I see a lone tear fall down her cheek. I don't hesitate to wipe it gently.

"I'm okay..." she whispers, the sound barely hitting my ears before I lean over and kiss her forehead.

"I know. I'll be right behind you."

Tilting her head up, she kisses my lips lightly, and I

notice her pretty top lip is split. "Okay," she says against my mouth, and I frown as the paramedics take her away. I watch until she's safely inside the ambulance, and it slowly drives down the road.

"Well, looks like you got back just in time," the sheriff says, and I turn to look at him, murder in my gaze.

"Why weren't you all over this? You told me you were watching. Had I not come back, she..." I don't finish that sentence, because I can't say the words. I feel sick all over again.

"The team from Williamstown were watching the back of the property. Not sure how they got through, but they did." At least he looks remorseful. I rub my eyes, thankful it didn't all go completely wrong, yet feeling angry that it almost did.

"So it was Stanley? Who was with him? Who has been stalking her and making an attempt on her life?" I grit out. Fisting my hands, my anger has now fully bloomed, knowing Annabelle is in safe hands and the boys are not here.

"Turns out, you were right," he says, a little sheepish, and my eyebrows rise.

"Her ex?" I almost choke, not believing that my far-fetched thoughts were actually accurate.

"Yeah. We're taking them in for questioning, and they'll remain in lockup until their court date. You go be with your family, Sawyer. I'll speak to you tomorrow. I'll have more details then."

I look over my shoulder and get eyes on the two men. Stanley looks at the ground, and Steve looks right at me, and I know for sure that's her former husband. I meet his gaze, knowing that I will ensure he's behind bars for a very, very long time.

45

ANNABELLE

"My headache is gone," I tell Hudson and Sawyer, who have both been here all night, Sawyer never leaving my side.

"Good," Hudson says as he scribbles something down on my chart. "I'll organize some breakfast for you now. I think you should be fine to eat a little something. I'd like you to stay here again tonight, just to keep an eye on you, but Sawyer can take you home tomorrow."

I nod. I'm not ready to go home just yet anyway. My body feels like I went through the washing machine. Bruises all over, my head heavy, my face with abrasions and cuts. I haven't looked in the mirror, but I'm sure I look terrible.

"Thanks, Hudson."

He grins. "Anytime. I'll leave you guys to it." Slapping Sawyer's shoulder, he walks out the door, and I look at Sawyer.

"You look like a mess," I tell him honestly. He obviously hasn't slept. He also has a gash on his head, a white bandage now taking up the side of his head above his ear.

"You look beautiful."

Shaking my head, I smile. "You should go home, take a shower, get some sleep."

He shrugs, narrowing his eyes at me playfully. "Superman doesn't sleep."

I huff a small laugh before I grimace a little at the pulling in my head.

"So it was Steve," I say tentatively. I'm sure he knows, but we haven't spoken about it yet.

"It was." He nods, watching me. I see his jaw clench a little, and I take a deep breath.

"Never in a million years did I ever think that was a possibility." I still don't understand it. "Before you came, he told me that he took a life insurance policy against himself and faked it all. Not sure how. That car was a wreck." Thinking about it all makes my head hurt.

"I had an inkling it could be him," he says, and I frown.

"What? What do you mean?"

"I spoke to the sheriff a few days ago. I asked to see the police reports of his crash. There were no remains. So I questioned it."

When I don't respond, only look at him with a pinched brow, totally confused, he continues.

"When a car with a full tank of fuel crashes and bursts into flames, the heat can cause a lot of damage. Soft tissues burn away quickly, but bones are tough, so they don't usually disintegrate completely unless the fire burns superhot for a really long time. Teeth are even tougher because of their enamel, which is why they're usually still around and can be used to identify people. But larger bones, like parts of the skull or pelvis, also tend to survive. So, if there are no bones left at all, it's unusual. It just made me think that it could be possible. The sheriff was going to investigate it some more, but in the meantime, he offered this solution of me leaving town so they could catch whomever it was."

Wow. I knew Sawyer was smart, of course, but his knowledge on these things is extensive. Thank God.

"Well, it worked."

"It worked because I came back. God, if I hadn't come back..." He looks to the ceiling, his expression pained.

"But you did. And we're all fine." I know the emotions that he must be feeling are leaving him riddled with guilt over nothing.

"I love you, Annabelle." He looks right at me, his eyes glassy, and my breath halts in my chest. "I never want to leave you or the boys again. I'd really like to stick around more permanently, if you want that?"

"I want that. I want that more than anything," I whisper, almost too scared to say what I want out loud, but he grins before lifting my hand to his lips and kissing it.

"But..." I start, and he looks at me with worry. "But what about your work? You have your firm in the city, Sawyer. I can't ask you to leave that. I mean..."

His answer is simple. "I sold it."

I lose my breath for the second time in a matter of minutes.

"You... You what?" I ask, trying to understand. Wondering if the bump on my head left me with cognitive issues.

"I sold eighty percent of it to the Rothschild Law Firm. They're a firm in Baltimore, but they've wanted a presence in New York for a while, so I called them and made them an offer. They'll take all my criminal law business and some of the commercial and contract business, and I'll keep Tanner and Whiteman's, my LA office and clients, and a few other business clients from New York that I've worked with for years. I'll still need to fly back there a little bit, at least initially, to do a handover, and then perhaps once every few months or so, but I'll base myself out of Whispers now, just like Tanner wanted after all." He huffs a laugh at himself.

He's really done this... for me. "So you're staying in Whispers?"

"Yeah, well, I met someone... She's the most beautiful, amazing, stubborn, prideful, most perfect woman..." He looks at me with pure admiration, his voice trailing off and his mouth turning into a grin.

"She sounds like a real catch," I tease, grinning, finally feeling like my life can now start.

"She is. She thinks I'm Superman." His smile widens even more.

"Maybe she needed a Superman?"

"Nah, she doesn't need rescuing. She can rescue herself. But I sure like trying to keep up with her." He kisses each of my knuckles, and I try to breathe slowly.

"I love you, Sawyer. I never wanted anyone or anything, but I'm sure glad you found me."

"Good, because now you're stuck with me. I'm not leaving you again, Annabelle. You and the boys mean the world to me."

"I miss my boys..." I really want to hug them right now.

He squeezes my hand. "They're on their way."

My happiness level rises even more, and I smile whole-heartedly.

"Just tell me one thing?" he asks me tentatively.

"Anything," I say firmly.

"Are there any other skeletons in your closet?" he asks jokingly, and I decide to tease him some more.

"Well... there is Gladis."

He looks at me with wide eyes. "Who is Gladis?" he asks,

and I can't stop the snort of laughter that comes from my mouth. But I'm quickly reminded of exactly why I'm in this hospital as my head thumps.

"The baby goat Victoria gave Kevin last week that we've adopted…" I tell him, and he rolls his eyes.

"With you, me, the boys, and now Gladis, I know life is going to be amazing. Nothing is going to ever stand in our way again," he says, just as the door opens, and my boys run in, jumping up onto the bed, the pain in my head worth it as the four of us snuggle together.

I finally got my happy ending.

EPILOGUE - SAWYER

"What the hell are you wearing?" Sutton looks at me like I've grown a second head from where he sits in the theater room, watching yet another movie.

"What? I think I fit in," I say, fixing the cuffs of my new shirt, walking toward him.

"Well, news flash. You don't." He jumps up from the sofa to get a good look at me. It's true, I feel like a fish out of water in these clothes, but now that I'm a Whispers local, I thought I should at least try to look the part.

"You don't like the jeans or...?" I look down at the blue denim adorning my legs, wondering what I've done wrong. The bright-blue shirt is a little loud, the jeans a little tight, but this is what the local shop had in stock, so I just had to go with it.

"You look like a rich rancher who has never ranched before in his life." Sutton grins at me, holding back a laugh.

"Tanner said jeans and these more casual shirts are what I need to be wearing."

"Yeah, well, Tanner should probably stick to making

whiskey and less on fashion advice. You can't wear dress shoes. You need boots at least and a Stetson," Sutton says, and it's my turn to look at him like he's crazy.

"A Stetson? Tanner doesn't even wear one of those."

When his smirk widens, I realize he's deliberately trying to encourage me to go all out.

"I'm home…" Annabelle singsongs from the front door, the sound fast becoming one of my favorites of the day. It's been a few months now since the incident and she and the kids are doing great. Their resilience has really shown through, as has the town's heart, all coming together to offer support in one way or another. I think I've put on at least ten pounds due to the cooking the local ladies have done for us.

"In here!" I call out to her as I wiggle the buckle of my new belt, wondering how cowboys wear these large metal things around their waist all day long.

"Speaking of home, what the fuck are you doing still hiding out here? When are you going to leave?" I ask my brother. He's been lying low for months now, only doing small trips into the diner and the bar a few days of the week, and while I love having him here, now that Annabelle and the boys live here with me, I wouldn't mind some space.

"Bobby has been contacting me flat out, so I want to lie low for a while longer. But then he said he has a Hallmark movie for me."

"Hallmark?" I frown, knowing that's the complete opposite of what his brand is.

"Yeah, apparently I need to show a good side. All those fighting monster movies are making me too siloed. After being away from LA, he thinks I need to do something totally left field to get people really talking." He doesn't look convinced and neither am I.

"Sounds like shit advice, if you ask me," I tell him honestly.

He sighs. "Doesn't matter. This is the game if I want to play it."

"And do you?"

"What?"

"Want to play it?"

"What are you two talking about?" Annabelle breezes in, looking like the other half of my heart that she is. My grin is instant. But then she stops short when she sees me. "Oh, what are you wearing?"

"That's what I said." Sutton stands by her side, the two of them ganging up on me, and I roll my eyes.

"I'm wearing Whispers fashion. Besides, we're talking about when he's moving out." I nod to Sutton.

"Oh, you going back to LA?" Annabelle asks him.

"I kinda like it here. Bought a plot of land just next door, actually," he says, so nonchalant.

My eyes nearly bug out of my head. "What?" I ask, totally blindsided.

"Thought you would like me around some more. Plus, I love the boys, and I'm still hoping Connor will give me a new whiskey to promote. I put the paperwork on your desk for you to look over and settle for me." I rub my eyes but smile, loving that he's going to stick around.

"Kevin and Noah will love having you here permanently." Annabelle smiles brightly, and if she's happy, I'm happy.

"Great. Okay, I'm going to the diner." He's already walking away, slipping on his baseball cap.

"You're going there a lot lately. Sure it's safe?" I ask him, knowing that as soon as the paparazzi finds him, he'll be eaten alive since he has been gone so long.

"Yeah, Rochelle puts me in the back. I keep my hat on,

and the locals are the perfect bodyguards. They shield me and lie if anyone comes sniffing." He grins, and I know what he's talking about, because I've seen it in action. I love Whispers; it's like one big family.

"You can take my truck. It's out front," Annabelle offers and passes him the keys, another safety privacy method for him. Always in different cars so no one ever knows it's him. Good thing I purchased her a new truck.

"Thanks. Later." He swings the keys in his hands as he walks out the door.

"He seems to love the diner. He goes there all the time?" Annabelle says once he leaves.

"Yeah..." I frown thinking about it, knowing my brother. He doesn't just go there for the coffee, even though it's the best.

"How did you do today?" I ask her, smiling. She and Victoria were packing all the soaps for the Van Cleef project. The deal in progress, adding millions to her bank account, and her life has completely changed.

"It was so good. Victoria took a lot of footage for socials, and I think we must have packed over a hundred large boxes." She's never one to shy away from hard work.

After everything that happened up at the farm, we decided it was best for her and the boys to live with me, closer to town, where they can hang out with their friends, Kevin can get to baseball quickly, and Noah spends many an afternoon baking with Debbie. We have a nice little routine going where I drop them to school in the morning on my way to the office and pick them up at the end of the day. Except for days like today, when I come home and work from my home office, knowing Annabelle was going to be home earlier.

"The new distribution shed going okay?" I step up to her,

my hands finding her waist with ease. We had the farm completely renovated, thanks to Victoria and her brilliant design expertise and Griffin's amazing team. The old farmhouse has been remodeled, and Gertie's Soaps now runs from the farm, right on the doorstep of the beautiful lavender and roses that make up the product itself. Each room has turned into an office for each of the girls; plus, they have a large meeting room and kept the kitchen for their lunch requirements.

She hums. "It's beautiful."

"So what do you think?" I ask her about my outfit.

"I hate it," she says without hesitation, then rolls her lips.

"Seriously? I was trying to fit in." I chuckle, knowing that I do look ridiculous.

"You don't need to fit in, Sawyer. I love you for exactly who you are. Fancy suits and all." She steps into me, and I wrap my hands around her, loving nothing better than having her close. Her hands loop around my neck as she looks up into my eyes.

"You sure? I mean, the lady in the store said that I look exactly how country men do around here?" I ask her, and she laughs.

"Don't change, Sawyer. I think you're perfect." She leans into me, her lips brushing mine.

"Hmmm, I think you're perfect," I say, taking her lips slowly, wanting to savor her, since the house is normally not this empty and quiet.

"You know... we have a few minutes before..." I start to say when the front door whips open.

"We're home!" Kevin yells from the front door.

"Fuck," I curse under my breath, having missed the opportunity to take her to bed.

"In here!" she calls out, grinning, looking even more beautiful, if that's remotely possible.

"What are you wearing?" Kevin balks from where he is at the door, looking at me, wide-eyed, like I rolled in shit.

"New clothes, like them?" I ask him, and he huffs a laugh.

"Ahhh, no," he responds quickly and honestly, just like his mother.

"Can I use your phone, Ma? I got to call Harvey about baseball," he asks her.

"Sure, honey." She passes him the phone.

"What do you think, Noah?" I ask and watch him look me over with a frown, and I sigh.

"Okay, back to suits it is," I say, just as I hear Kevin on the phone.

"Oh my God, you should see my dad, he's wearing the stupidest clothes..." Kevin giggles as he walks off to his bedroom, and I freeze, my eyes darting to look at Annabelle. The shock on her face is obvious.

"Did he just call me..." I ask her, my heart about to crack wide open.

Her eyes shine with tears as she nods. "He did."

I cough, clearing my throat.

He just called me Dad.

To find out where Sawyer and Annabelle are now, grab their bonus epilogue HERE

ALSO BY SAMANTHA SKYE

SUTTON

Small towns aren't meant for **billionaire Movie Stars**, but somehow, Sutton Silvers fits right in. I know I should ignore him, the diner regular with his easy charm and quiet intensity. He belongs to another world, one of flashing cameras, billion-dollar contracts, and fake Hollywood smiles. I belong here, in the safety of routine. In the safety of Whispers.

But Sutton sees through the walls I've built, through the **secret past** I keep hidden. He should walk away, just like I should guard my heart. But there's something about him, the way he looks at me like I'm worth the risk, that has me wanting more.

I know better than to dream of a future with a man like him. And yet, when danger starts creeping closer, he's the one stepping in, refusing to let me face it alone. He has a choice to **leave Hollywood behind** and risk it all for the chance that I'm his forever.

And me? I have a choice too.

Run again. Or finally let someone catch me.

GRAB SUTTON HERE

ALSO BY SAMANTHA SKYE

The Billionaires of Whispers

Tanner

Hudson

Connor

Sawyer

Sutton

Griffin

SCROOGE: A Billionaire Christmas Story

The Baltimore Boys

The Charming Billionaire

The Arrogant Billionaire

The Damaged Billionaire

The Secret Billionaire

The Bossy Billionaire

The Billionaire Babe

Men Of New York

My Legacy

My Destiny

My Fight

My Chance

Boston Billionaires

Coming Home

Finding Home

Leaving Home

Building Home

ABOUT THE AUTHOR

Samantha Skye is an international bestselling author. A country kid turned city slicker, she writes spicy and suspenseful contemporary romance novels that leave you hot under the collar and on the edge of your seat.

Samantha lives in Melbourne, Australia and when she's not plotting her next novel, she can be found travelling, drinking margaritas and enjoying a sunset or a stargaze somewhere.

To join in the conversation join Skye's The Limit Facebook group here;
https://www.facebook.com/groups/skyesthelimitbooks